VOICE
OF THE
GODDESS

VOICE
OF THE
GODDESS

JUDITH HAND

Pacific Rim Press
Cardiff, California

Published by
Pacific Rim Press
A Division of California Health Publications
Cardiff, California

Copyright © 1999 by Judith Hand
First Edition Printing 2001

More information concerning this title is available at:
http://www.questpub.com

Jacket illustration by Mark Clements
Jacket painting by Peggy Lang

Permission to use the photograph of the Phaestos Disk on the dust jacket kindly
granted by TAP Archaeological Service, 57 Panepistimiou Street, Athens, Greece.

Library of Congress Cataloging-in-Publication Data

Hand, Judith, 1940-
  Voice of the goddess / Judith Hand.
  p. cm.
Includes bibliographical references.
  ISBN 0-930926-26-9 (alk. paper)
  1. Crete (Greece)—History—To 67 B.C.—Fiction. 2. Goddess religion—
Fiction. 3. Minoans—Fiction. I. Title.
  PS3558.A46196 V65 2000
  813'.54—dc21

00-008734
CIP

Printed in the United States of America
10 9 8 7 6 5 4 3 2 1

This book is dedicated to

My mother, who loved me,
The brothers Menendez, who
taught me the meaning of tragedy,
My husband, who shared with me
my life's greatest joys.

Preface

The people of ancient Crete created a society of unequaled Bronze-age magnificence. Many scholars even believe their sophisticated Mediterranean culture was the origin of the myth of Atlantis. And unlike **all other high cultures known to me, the inhabitants of Crete appear to have reached this pinnacle without engaging in war** (defense of their island perhaps, but not internal warfare or wars of aggression).

They lived roughly 1600 years BC and their fleet was reputed to have dominated the eastern Mediterranean for centuries. A number of remarkable features distinguish them, but perhaps most especially, their art shows an astonishing deference to women. Other known facts:

- None of their cities, towns, or villages had fortifications.
- Weapons or depictions of them are uncommon and usually ornamental, suggesting only ceremonial or hunting uses.
- Their elegant art often depicts scenes of nature and notably lacks scenes of violence, conquest, or subjugation.
- There are no cramped buildings around their cities that, in other cultures, indicate slave quarters.
- Their vast temple complex at Knossos stands, in places, six stories high.
- They enjoyed luxurious three-story townhomes and invented flush toilets.
- They constructed the first known paved roads in Europe.
- When groups of men and women are depicted in frescoes, the most prominent figure is virtually always female.
- In their famous Bull Leapers fresco—which depicts what must have been an important public event—two of the three human figures are female.
- Their chief deity, Potnia ("The Lady"), is female.
- The ceremonial gown of women exposes and projects their breasts in a manner suggesting not just nurturing but possibly a celebration of sex.
- There are no great tombs or burial chambers containing vast gravegoods, such as one would expect for a king or queen.
- Although bulls were in some manner central to their religion, there is no evidence (except from possibly very late periods) that they practiced animal sacrifice.
- There is no evidence that they slept with locked doors.

Their Egyptian contemporaries referred to the people of ancient Crete as "Keftians." The familiar modern term, "Minoans," did not come into use until applied by British archeologist Arthur Evans when he discovered and began to excavate Knossos in 1900 AD.

Regrettably their writing remains undeciphered, which leaves vast blank spaces in our understanding of how they lived. Although *Voice of the Goddess* is a work of fiction, I've taken great care to remain faithful to the silent artifacts the Keftians left behind.

In his *Life of Greece* (p. 8), before he presented his own interpretations of the physical and mythological remains that have been left to us, Will Durant said:

> "If now we try to restore this buried culture from the relics that remain—playing Cuvier to the scattered bones of Crete—let us remember that we are engaging upon a hazardous kind of historical television, in which imagination must supply the living continuity in the gaps of static and fragmentary material artificially moving but long since dead. Crete will remain inwardly unknown until its secretive tablets find their Champollion."

I've used what I know of subsequent Greek history and mythology, of natural history, and of cultural anthropology to supplement what the artifacts tell us. And then, like Durant, I've relied on imagination to fill in the gaps.

My research began over eight years ago with the volumes by the Minoans's discoverer, Sir Arthur Evans, and works by R. Castleden, J. Chadwick, C. Doumas, S. Hood, N. Marinatos, C. Pellegrino, and R. Willets (see a selected bibliography at the book's end). I relied heavily on the book by Marinatos (*Art and Religion in Thera*) for my interpretation of the meaning of several frescoes. The excellent non-fiction account by Pellegrino (*Unearthing Atlantis*) was an invaluable resource, one I highly recommend both for scholarship and readability. I considered also works on the Mycenaean culture that replaced the Keftians and, given the importance of the Keftians's female deity, recent studies of so-called "goddess cultures." Heated debates can occur over the existence of or nature of such cultures (e.g., the collection of articles edited by Goodison and Morris, *Ancient Goddesses*). UCLA archeologist Maria Gimbutas (*The Gods and Goddesses of Old Europe* and *Language of the Goddess*) influenced my thinking, and whether or not one agrees with her interpretations, her books and work are indispensable for anyone interested in goddess worship in the western world. Several feminist scholars on this subject (e.g., Riane Eisler, *The*

Chalice and the Blade, and Elinor Gadon, *The Once And Future Goddess)* were also thought-provoking.

Readers of historical fiction centered in the Mediterranean will enjoy the works of the late Mary Renault, a meticulous student of archaeology and a superb story weaver. I wonder in what direction her stories might have been spun if written with the benefit of more recent research and insights by investigators such as Gimbutas, Nanno Marinatos, and the authors in *Ancient Goddesses*. Clearly the Greek myths, the basis of many of her tales, express the point of view of a people who entered the historical scene long after the Keftians themselves had disappeared into the mist of time.

I went to Crete in 1992 when I attended the First International Minoan Celebration of Partnership sponsored by Riane Eisler (attorney and author) and Margarita Papandreou (author and peace activist). I visited the museum in Knossos and the ruins at Knossos, Phaestos, and Gournia. In Athens, at the archeological museum, I interviewed Dr. Christos Doumas, the principal investigator of the excavations on Santorini (Thera). In Turkey, I visited Ankara's archeological museum and numerous sites where ancient goddesses have been worshipped. I also trekked to the seventh millenium BC site of Çatal Hüyük, thought by its discoverer, James Mellart, to be one of the earliest known sites of goddess worship, a view now the center of controversy.

One often hears the assertion that humans have never lived and cannot live in complex societies without war. Unfortunately, when we read about ancient high cultures, Keftians (Minoans) are usually given brief treatment, and little attention is paid to their apparent peacefulness and possible reasons for it. By studying many different societies we learn what is possible for humans. Keftian society clearly deserves more and significant attention because of the uncommon—and all evidence suggests, positive—example of social organization within high culture that it illustrates.

Readers with a whetted appetite for more background on *Voice of the Goddess* are invited to review the Author's Commentary at the end of the book.

Acknowledgements

For help in the creation of *Voice of the Goddess*, my gratitude to many people runs wide and deep. My weekly writing buddies, the friends and professionals who were always brutally honest because they cared are a long list: Drusilla Campbell, Shirley Allen, Barry Friedman, Phyllis Humphrey, Pete Johnson, Suzanne Middleton, Mark Clements, Chet Cunningham, Bev Miller, Cyndy Mobley, Toni Noel, Ellen Perkins, Ken Schafer, Tom Tucker, Tom Utts. I thank friends in the San Diego chapter of Romance Writers of America, my earliest writing support group. One of their founders, Marian Jones, was my first, generous writing mentor. Terry Blain let me know she believed I had talent long before I felt any of that kind of confidence. Christie Ridgway kept me from making fatal plot errors. Others who offered critical ingredients were Maureen Caudill, Lynn Kerstan, Judythe London, Deanna Padilla, Miriam Raftery, Marsha Stone, and Honey Shellman. John Lewis (and others) told me the story had to be cut; he was right. Patricia Finaley helped when help was needed. Curt Humphrey, Marlo Miller, and Bob Holt helped me understand the arcana of getting published. Book editor Sophia Shafquat was the first person outside my writing circle to read the manuscript. Her spontaneous, enthusiastic praise lifted my confidence like nothing before or since. Christos Doumas, head of excavations on Santorini, granted me an interview that added enormously to the story's plot and authenticity. Photographic and artistic skills of Charles Pinkney, Joyce Musial, Mark Clements, and Peggy Lang give the cover its special look. My dear husband granted me the love, support, faith, and time spent away from him mentally that made this dream possible. And finally, I thank two friends whose brilliant minds, caring spirits, and long hours of work on my behalf enabled me to give the book life by being published: writer and artist, Peggy Lang, and editor, Diana Gale Matthiesen.

Judith Hand (February, 2001)

There occurred violent earthquakes ... and a night
of rain, and the island of Atlantis ... disappeared,
and was sunk beneath the sea.

Plato (from Timaeus)

... there formerly dwelt in your land the fairest and
noblest race of men which ever lived, and you
and your city (Athens) are descended from the seed
of the remnant of them which survived. (Egyptian priests
speaking to the Greek philosopher Solon about 590 BC. The
priests claimed not to know the location of the lost world.)

Plato (from Timaeus)

Be careful whom you let drive your cart
or you never know what
miserable ditch you'll end up in.

Zuliya of Memphis

List of Characters

Alektrion — Kallistan-born son of an Achean woman and Keftian man.

Aliya — daughter of Talos.

Anchices — Keftian marine, friend of Alektrion.

Aristala — Mistress of Dance at the Bull Academy.

Atistaeus of Pylos ("The Red King") — Achean mainland king.

Belamena Sonaria — a courtesan and Alektrion's lover on Samos.

Bemis — farmer on Lemnos.

Blauthea — a Wise One, supporter of Galatea.

Blauthophon — one of Leesandra's Memories.

Brisus — young aide to Alektrion.

Cleos — inn owner on Lemnos.

Damion — Keftiu's diplomat to Kalliste and father of Leesandra.

Damkina — the high priestesses of Knossos, the Voice of the Goddess.

Danae — a temple seer and mother of Leesandra.

Demos — a marine on *Sea Eagle*.

Dolius — Achean marine on *Sea Eagle* who trains Alektrion and Laius.

Dolmanthes — an Achean guest in Leesandra's home on Kalliste and a man in the court at Pylos.

Drydenax — piper on *Sea Eagle*.

Eumos — Thracian marine from Lemnos who trades places on *Sea Eagle* with Alektrion.

Full Moon, New Moon — brothers and marines serving on *Sea Eagle*.

Galatea — friend of Leesandra at the Bull Academy and daughter of the Achean collaborator Minyas.

Glaucon — chief of the guards at the temple of Knossos.

Gleantha, Kronos, Dromalis, Renon — along with Galatea, the members of Leesandra's *compathos*.

Grimaldius — captain of *Sea Eagle*.

Heebe — nursemaid and friend of Leesandra.

Hopthea — lead dance instructor at the Bull Academy.

Hylas — Achean prince, Galatea's lover.

Kampenthes —navigator/steersman and second officer of *Sea Eagle*.

Kishar — Wise Woman and Leesandra's chief mentor.

Kladia — prostitute on Samos.

Kleos — squad leader on *Sea Eagle*.

Klemonair — oldest mercenary on *Sea Eagle* when Alektrion signed on; becomes second in command.

List of Characters — Cont'd

Kryson — Speaker of the Council of Knossos
Laius — Alektrion's best friend on *Sea Eagle*.
Leesandra — Keftian girl thrust into the heart of Keftiu's conflict with mainland Achean Poseidonists.
Lynceus — physically malformed poet and brother of Galatea.
Meidra — childhood best friend of Leesandra.
Menalopolox — Thracian mercenary aboard *Sea Eagle*.
Menapthus ("Hot Sauce") — cook on *Sea Eagle*.
Mestra —chief Temple attendant of Leesandra.
Metis — mother of Galatea.
Minyas — Keftian merchant and father of Galatea
Ninarin — ship's priestess aboard the passenger vessel *Asphodel*.
Ninsuna — chief scribe for Leesandra.
Nonia — most senior of the seven Wise Women.
Nothos ("The Badger") — vizier of the temple at Knossos.
Oenopion — Achean Poseidonist priest in Knossos.
Philoxea — ex-hetaira mistress of Alektrion on Lemnos.
Prion — Lydian mercenary on *Sea Eagle*.
Sarpedon — Keftian admiral and mentor to Alektrion.
Semlena — a councilwoman loyal to Sarpedon.
Serena — ship's priestess on *Sea Eagle*.
Sinon — Leesandra's male cousin, living within her household on Kalliste.
Sestrae — Wise Woman and supporter of Galatea.
Talos — one-eyed Keftian marine and friend of Alektrion.
Trusis — Kallistan youth on *Sea Eagle* with Laius and Alektrion.
Xenia — Leesandra's initiation teacher.
Zuliya — Nubian teacher, mentor, and friend of Leesandra.

Deities

Cybele — the Great Mother's name on Samos.
Isis — the Great Mother's name in Egypt.
Kokor — one of the Great Mother's demon children, her disobedient, oldest son.
Poseidon — Achean god, *The Earth Shaker*.
Velchanos — the annual god, ceremonially married to the high priestess of Knossos.

Map — Eastern Mediterranean ca. 1628 BC

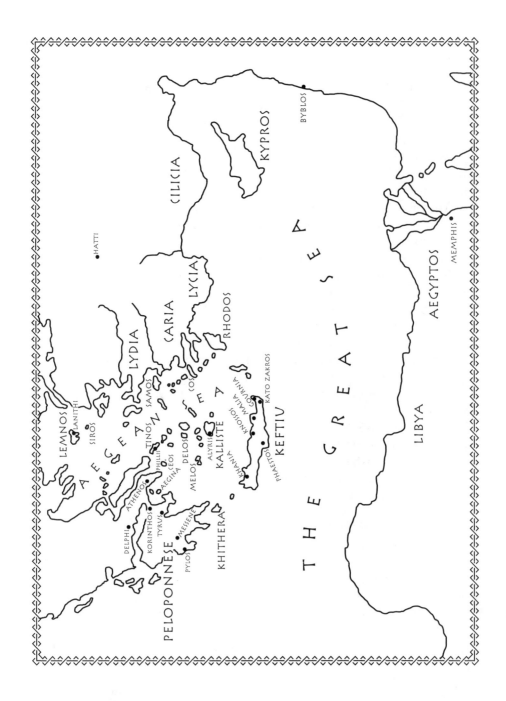

Prologue
February, 2000

The Goddess speaks through me.

I first read these words two years ago, translating them haltingly—but with great excitement—from the pages of a 3500-year-old manuscript recovered in 1960 in Egypt.

They are the opening words of the autobiography of Leesandra, a young Minoan woman, and they are accompanied by another set of scrolls, the biography of a warrior, Alektrion of Kalliste, Leesandra's contemporary. The writings can be dated precisely because both Leesandra and Alektrion describe, first hand, the 1628 BC explosion of the Mediterranean island of Kalliste, which we now call Santorini. This eruption, a stupendous geological event, is considered by many scholars the likely origin of the myth of Atlantis.

In 1900, on the island of Crete, Sir Arthur Evans discovered the fabulous "palace" at Knossos. Since then, many experts have puzzled over the Minoan language, and these ancient Mediterranean people have been known almost exclusively from their architectural ruins and graceful art. Their language remained undeciphered, their voices silent. Two years ago I broke the code. One result of that breakthrough is the book you now hold, in which I intertwine Alektrion's biography with Leesandra's words.

What we learn about that long ago world is valuable if only because it gives voice to a fascinating past that was lost until now, but the story of Leesandra and Alektrion also has special relevance for us. Crete's goddess culture was remarkably egalitarian and peaceful. The People of the Goddess, as the Minoans called themselves, were besieged. Then, as now, civilized people struggled to prevail.

Here is the way Leesandra described her dilemma [note that ancient Crete was called Keftiu]:

The Goddess speaks through me.

I am Leesandra ...

I write this in my twenty-fifth year, and because I swear to record only the truth, I bear witness that I no longer hear the Great Mother's sweet voice.

I make this record because my beloved Keftiu is imperiled, and it is my duty to ensure that those who come after us know the truth. Bloodlusting Acheans from the mainland threaten us. Even as I write, these death-worshipping Poseidonists ready ships to attack the Mother's Heart this coming spring.

It is said, truly, that Keftians have no stomach for war. Nevertheless, within days ... the People must prepare a defense ... or make a bitter and defiling compromise with their supporters in Knossos. If the People fight, I fear we cannot win. The Memory Keepers say they can give no guidance from the past because never before has there been any possibility mainland forces might threaten Keftiu. Through fasting and prayer and poppy dreams, I've listened for the Goddess to speak. I hear only echoes of my dread.

The People come daily to the Temple's west court: mothers with babes in arms who ask their children's fate, lovers with clasped hands who want to know if they can trust the future, the elderly who can't believe the world they thought would last forever may be swept away. The fears and hopes of the people press on my heart with the weight of the great stone pillar of the Law itself. In the dark of my nights I tremble. But there will be no escape ... and as I no longer hear the Great Mother's voice, the choice I make will be mine alone. An unholy compromise with heretics—or war?

I begin this record with the day my feet took the first step on this path of confrontation with the Acheans. If the Lady chooses, I will live until spring, long enough to reach the end of this telling.

I translated Leesandra's ominous words about her death in the first three months of my work on the documents. Another two years passed before I learned her fate. Though I could reveal it to you now, I think it better to let you experience the unfolding of Leesandra and Alektrion's story as it emerges from the ancient texts.

J. Rosebrook Evans
Department of Antiquities, Brightmore University
Brightmore, England

1

Violent and bloody death stripped the innocence of youth from me when I was twelve. Years later I learned that on that same day the Poseidonist Atistaeus of Pylos murdered the oracle of the Great Goddess at Delphi. The Red King then fled to his home city of Pylos and soon launched his brutal campaigns of conquest, while I began a journey that led to this room and painful time of decision.

For me that evil, long-ago day began as one of beauty. A weeklong storm had passed, leaving the sky an unblemished blue and the ocean tranquil. The sea-scented winter air crackled with the promise of delightful discoveries. I fidgeted in the classroom, scarcely listening after having been confined almost a week. My usual habit after morning school was to explore the beaches or foothills of the volcano that gave our island its name, but today I couldn't wait to hike higher up Mount Kalliste to my hot pool. There, while I was alone, the Goddess came closest to me. I'd let my spirit go to Her, and She'd replace my restlessness with harmony.

The teacher finally said the magical words, "Cover your tablets," and I bolted into the courtyard. At the gate shrine I did wrestle my eagerness into submission to do reverence to our Lady: the People are not free to let their own will run unchecked, and I fought a constant battle to keep what my nursemaid and parents called a willful spirit in control.

Two boys also knelt, but were up again too quickly. They couldn't have said the full prayer. How could they be so careless! I heard my nursemaid's voice: "By their obedience to the Laws, the People keep the world in harmony." Alarmed and then angry, I called out, "Come back! Finish the prayer."

A girl at my side lanced me a startled look. I bit my lip. My angry words had only made things worse.

Flushed now with regret, I did the best I could to restore balance: three times more I repeated the thanks for calm seas. At the end, for good measure, I added, "Dear Mother, help me to always be obedient."

I leaped up and set off, heading north, threading Alyris's narrow lanes. At the public shrines the smell of the morning's baking of barley bread mingled with the musky scent of sacramental wine. A maker of giant water storage pithoi gave me a ride in his rattling donkey cart almost to the village of Dallia. On foot again, I climbed a steep trail until one of the Temple meadows stretched before me. A breeze rippled across whispering yellowed grasses. On the other side, a flock of the Lady's breeding ewes was grazing—so far away they looked like white toys. Beyond Kalliste's coast, the Aegean spread like a deep blue bed-cover that, where it was tucked under the island's chin, was trimmed lighter blue and green. Two large rocks, the guardians of my spring's privacy, stood on the meadow's right edge. The pathway I sought was little more than a goat-run behind the two boulders.

At the bottom of a ravine, under an ancient plane tree, I wriggled out of my tunic and waded into steaming water. Using my toes, I felt my way to a submerged stone where I could sit with my shoulders covered. Releasing myself to the heat, I let my mind drift. I thought of my mother's naming day party and my own duty to play my lyre. I wanted to play flawlessly. To see my mother smile, to have my father approve of my progress—that would make the party perfect.

When my skin cried, "Enough!" I climbed out and lay on a rock to dry. For a time I tossed pebbles into the water and pretended I could, like my mother, read the future in the water's disturbed face. Then I dressed and went to my special place, a shallow depression under the plane tree shaped on one side by an exposed root and on the other by a flat boulder.

This hidden place embraced my spirit. Here I communed with the Mother in a way I shared with no one. Indeed, I suspected my behavior, if known, would cause strong disapproval. To be different among people who prize the ability to blend in creates alarm and invites criticism. Often my nursemaid, Heebe, told me, "When a person stands out she breaks harmony." Yet I felt so close to the Goddess here, so much at peace.

I lay down and felt the cool, humid soil, the body of the Great Mother of All. My scalp, shaved of all hair except queue and forelock, prickled. I had once asked Heebe if there was any Law forbidding long periods of solitude.

"No," she said, but added, "Why would anyone other than a holy person want to do such a thing?"

I didn't tell her about my pool.

With open palms I felt the earth. I listened to the rustling leaves as the passing wind tickled them. Here I could become anything. Perhaps a cloud so I could hover over Alyris. No. Today I'd travel with birds' wings to Keftiu. Perhaps even far off Agyptos.

My spirit lifted to take flight, but something warm touched my hand. A boy's voice said, "Are you all right?"

I jerked upright, my heart a knot in my throat. He jerked back.

I recognized Alektrion, a boy three years older than I. He had remarkably fair skin and light brown hair. The forelock and queue he'd worn at school had grown in and become a cap of wild curls. My people are a dark race: olive skin, dark hair, dark eyes. Alektrion's skin and hair had always held attraction for me.

"You nearly scared the spirit out of me," I said.

He grinned. "I'm glad you're not dead. What are you doing?" The sun caught his eyes at a sharp angle, flecking them in an astonishing fashion with gold.

"Resting. Isn't that obvious?" Not for anything would I tell him the truth of my solitary doings here. I suddenly wondered if he'd followed me. Had he been spying on me?

"Sorry if I frightened you. I'm Alektrion. You're Leesandra, Danae's daughter. I've seen you at school. Are you going to be a priestess, too?"

What a dreadful thought! I shook my head. "Never. I love being outdoors. I'm going to raise bees." I didn't add that I intended to make the best honey in the world. It would be boastful. "And of course my mother is a seer, not a priestess."

"Bees?" He laughed. "Pretty odd. Aren't you afraid of getting stung?"

"If you know how to treat them, they don't sting you."

"Perhaps." He stood and, walking toward the pool, said, "I think this place is Goddess touched." He turned and gave me a puzzled look. "I've never seen anyone else here before."

I rose and scrambled after him. "Neither have I, and I come often."

"You do?" He sat by the pool on my flat rock, his tunic hitched halfway up his thighs, his eyes wide with surprise. I sat on the ground, wondering if I should tell him he was sitting on my favorite rock. "That's hard to believe."

"Why?"

He fingered some pebbles. "You come alone?"

Painfully aware of betraying my secret, I hesitated.

He tossed a pebble into my pool. "It's a long way for someone your age to come alone."

"I come alone to commune with the Lady," I said, then sucked in a sharp breath. I'd exposed a part of my secret. I was feeling and speaking quite unlike my usual self.

He said, "I like to swim in the hot water."

"I made the pool."

He grinned, leaned to me and shoved my shoulder. "That's a silly thing to say."

"But I did. I gathered all of those rocks,"—I pointed to the dam—"and put them here."

"You want me to believe a little girl like you made this pool?"

"I don't care if you believe it or not."

He studied me, clearly surprised by so much bite in the speech of a seer's daughter who should know better manners.

Whatever was the matter with me?

"Have you ever talked to a jumping spider?"

I shook my head. Such an odd question.

"Come. I'll show you."

I stood and followed him, intent on the swing of his hips, the easy movement of his shoulders. His curls reminded me that Alektrion observed our customs, not those of the outlanders who didn't shave their children's heads. Though his mother wasn't one of the People, she clearly was among the many outlanders who worshipped the Goddess. I suddenly recalled that my mother would expect me to take leave of this "half-breed" as soon as possible. It didn't matter that Alektrion's father was Keftian. His father, a Bird clan metallist, had married outside the People. Without a Keftian mother there could be no clan membership.

I'd once told my mother, Danae, I thought Alektrion was interesting. She'd said, "All of Kalliste's children must attend school, Leesandra, and though you are to treat all persons graciously, it's not wise for you to associate too closely with outlanders. Or with a half-breed. Make other friends."

We crossed under the aqueduct that carried hot and cold water to Alyris. At the wooden fence beside the Temple meadow, he began searching the posts and rocks. I gazed a moment at the Great Sea and the strangest feeling struck. The sea was calling to me. The sea wanted something.

"Here!" Alektrion shouted.

I couldn't shake off the odd feeling, and for a brief moment a stunning white light blocked my vision. Alarmed, I stretched my hand out to force the light away.

"Don't you want to see it?"

The light disappeared. The spell broke, and I released the moment of fear. I turned. He was on hands and knees, peering intently at nothing. I crouched beside him.

He said softly, "See her?"

I saw nothing.

"See her? Pretty black with white stripes. On the rock. About the size of a periwinkle shell."

Now I saw the tiny spider. White stripes crossed the shiny black body and startling white rings circled a row of four enormous black eyes.

"See how she's moving her front legs."

The spider turned sideways, wiggling several short, leg-like structures beneath the large head.

I said, "She's very elegant."

"They talk to each other with those legs. I've even watched them have leg-waving duels. And they'll come if you call. Watch!"

He leaned closer so his head stopped five hand-spans from the spider. To my astonishment, she turned to face him, and she did seem to peer most earnestly at him with her four white-ringed eyes. Alektrion suddenly made his eyes large and round, and holding his hands below his nose and using his first two fingers, he imitated the spider.

She hopped onto the dirt and dashed toward him. She stopped. I held my breath, thinking it impossible to be more amazed, when the spider made a last dash and, with an astounding leap, landed on Alektrion's nose!

I doubled over giggling.

He held quite still and crossed his eyes trying to see her. I leaned closer. She turned on his nose and gave every appearance of studying me.

Finally he touched his finger to the side of his nose. The spider leapt off and skittered away to hide under a blade of grass.

"Wonderful!" I was enchanted.

Alektrion's face glowed. "I can show you even more astonishing things. An Achean ship-of-war was caught in the storm and nearly capsized. She came into the harbor last night. This afternoon they'll offer gratitude to Poseidon. We can watch their ceremonies in secret."

A chill of excitement ran through me.

Then I imagined my mother's face, her forehead creased, her eyes saddened. I should leave Alektrion, shouldn't I? I bit my lip. "I couldn't be out past sunset. My mother expects me home for omas prayers."

He shrugged. "The ceremony begins around the time of manis. How long can it last?" He stooped and scratched his ankle. "Besides, you can leave whenever you want."

"Maybe we can't get there in time?"

He straightened and caught my gaze as tightly as the weasel catches the mouse's, testing my spirit. "Can you run well? It's downhill almost all the way."

I wanted so to stay with this boy. He had offered to share an adventure with me. I'd certainly never have a chance to do something this exciting again. Pulse racing, I nodded. He turned and loped downhill.

Never had I dashed down Kalliste at such speed. I was determined to keep up. My chest heaved, my lungs burned, and the closer we drew to town, the hotter my curiosity burned. I was afraid now we'd be too late and miss everything interesting.

The Lady's Temple, glowing pinkish white in the afternoon sun, sat overlooking the harbor, its inner world of countless rooms and corridors still a place of mystery to me. The city lay below it. The temple of Poseidon stood near the center of an outlander district. Single-story and somber, of rough-hewn black stone, it sat with its back against a hill.

Instead of heading for the entry, Alektrion circled around and ran halfway up the shoulder of the hill. Beside a boulder he stopped and glanced behind us at the open field, I supposed to see if anyone was watching. I was panting. He was scarcely breathing hard. He dropped to his hands and knees and crawled between the boulder and a great bushy clump of sweet bay laurel.

I followed him into a low leafy tunnel. We rose and, bent at the waist, wound our way uphill along a fine red-dirt path. My empty stomach growled. "How many times have you done this?" I whispered.

"Twice."

"Where does it lead?"

"To the temple's north wall. High up on one side. There's a place we can see in without anyone seeing us."

A thorn caught my tunic's hem. I tugged it free, and as I looked for damage, realized my heart was beating not only from running hard, but because what Alektrion and I were doing was …

Was what? I knew of no Law against spying on outlander temples. But I was suddenly very sure if my parents learned of my spying, I'd suffer at least a day's shunning. I shouldn't really be with this boy. My mouth felt as if it were suddenly coated with the same red dust that clung to my legs and tunic. I'd once suffered a shunning. I'd taken another girl's hoop without asking, lost control of it so that a cart wheel crushed it, and then I lied to my nurse and mother, insisting that I'd never touched it. But I'd been seen by one of my nurse's grown sons. For five days no one spoke to me. Not at home. Not at school. The prospect of enduring the draining aloneness of another such punishment made my knees weak.

I looked up. Alektrion had twisted around to watch me. "Want to go back?"

I remembered the golden glow of his eyes. This most interesting boy would think me a scared little girl. I shook my head, waved him forward. "How did you find this place?"

He continued up the narrow tunnel. I began to think even my brown tunic would show traces of this much dirt.

"There's a no-good thief who steals from people's pockets whenever crowds gather. One day I was practicing bull dancing with friends in the field behind here, and he poked his head out of the spot beside the boulder."

I stopped. Alektrion and his friends had dared to play at bull dancing! To dance with the bull is a sacred test of discipline, strength, and courage. Bull Dancing is restricted to the elite of the Snake Clan, who might be chosen priestesses or priests, or of the Butterfly Clan, who might aspire to high political office. Alektrion's friends were all mainlanders or other outlanders. None would ever be allowed to so much as apply to the Dance Academy in Knossos.

"You shouldn't …" I had another thought. What I was doing this very moment was itself questionable. I really shouldn't even be with Alektrion. I bit back my words and followed in silence.

He explained that he hadn't told his friends about the thief but returned later to discover the man's secret. "I think he sells information to a woman from Tyrns who claims to be a seer. My guess is she uses what she knows about the secrets of Achean worship to trick her clients."

A seer tricking people! Surely not. My mother was a seer, with a wonderful gift. Alektrion's dry accounting of a seer deceiving people seemed almost more shocking than that he'd played at bull dancing. I began to feel I'd never had a more shocking day in my twelve-year life.

We stopped three arm-spans below the roof. He squatted and tugged the edge of a loose brick back and forth. The scraping sounded so loud to me that tiny alarm shivers ran along my arms. I heard chanting in Achean, a language I barely understood. He removed four more bricks, then we sat, side-by-side in our dim, leafy tunnel, and peered through a jagged-edged hole.

A rectangular altar of light gray stone, not round like the Lady's, lay below us at a distance of ten oxcarts. I could see perhaps a third of the chamber. People packed the room elbow-to-elbow, and overhead lamps strung in a line led from the altar toward the entry door, beyond my view. The lamps spread so much light that the swaying people and sparse furnishings cast no shadows. Mixed with the balsamy smell of frankincense was the odor of cooking lamb. The smell drifted through our viewing hole, encircled my head, grew stronger. I found the combination unpleasant, but still my mouth watered.

Maybe a hundred people stood in rows facing the altar. A wide path in the middle of them cut down the room's center. A patch of something glistened darkly red on the altar's surface. A chill crossed my shoulders and I hugged my arms.

An undulating, chanting row of priests with shaved heads and floor-length black robes stood in front of the altar swinging silver incense burners. The priest presiding was sashed at the waist in scarlet. Of course male priests conducted Poseidon's worship. I knew that. But seeing so many men and no women was a marvel, exactly the exotic wonder I'd hoped to see. And deep in my bones what I saw felt … unbalanced. As if all the people in a small boat had rushed to sit on the same side.

Behind the chanting priests, dressed in light armor and carrying red-plumed boar-tusk helmets, the warship's marines stood stiffly, fiercely at attention. Just looking at these Acheans tickled the hair at the back of my neck. Each held a collared dove. Behind them, arms and chests bulging from the work of rowing, stood the ship's oarsmen. Local residents came next, a few of whom I recognized.

I leaned closer to Alektrion and whispered. "Why do you think the warriors have birds?" His left arm was so close his warmth heated my skin. Strangely, I felt both comforted and alarmed.

"Offerings of thanks, perhaps. Maybe they release them at the end of the ceremony."

My gaze was drawn to the glistening red-topped altar.

Awe warmed Alektrion's voice. "Do you know they have to cut and polish forty whole pairs of boar's tusks to make the flat pieces for just one of their helmets?"

He continued, saying that his father made weapons for the Keftian navy. He began comparing Achean, Keftian, and Kallistan swords. I barely listened, but when he said those of the Acheans were superior to ours, I felt another prickling shock. I couldn't imagine anything Acheans might make that could be superior to something the Lady had given the People.

Alektrion's stomach rumbled. I said, "I smell roasting lamb."

He nodded. "Maybe it's meat for an afterfeast." He shifted a bit, and his arm brushed mine. "See that priest there. The one with the red sash. He came with the ship. They barely made it to the harbor's mouth. That's why the port master let them in." Alektrion continued, his talk now of the ferocity of the Achean warriors, and once again the awe in his voice surprised me. "This ceremony is to thank Poseidon for sparing their lives. They also had victory against the Carians." The tone of his voice shifted to disgust. "The ship carries over twenty Carian slaves for the market at Korinthos."

Well, at least Alektrion didn't admire the loathsome Achean practice of slavery.

The chanting stopped. The worshippers turned to look backward toward the entrance. A new chant began, faster and louder. Down the central aisle two priests approached the altar with solemn stride. Between them, held by his hands, walked a boy of about eight dressed in a short white tunic. Angry-looking red marks circled his ankles. His head turned right and left as, with a sleepy look, he scanned the faces in the crowd. Twice he stumbled.

All eyes fastened on him, as if the people were hungry to see him. How could he feel so tired in the midst of such a big crowd? He was quite pretty, with large dark eyes, a sweet mouth, and a fine complexion.

I asked, "Do you understand what the people are chanting?"

"The priests call out the illustrious deeds of Poseidon, and the people answer with one of his several names."

Row after row that the boy and priests passed turned forward until, at last, the trio stopped at the altar and the crowd faced forward. The chanting had become a roar and in perfect rhythm each person stamped the floor with one foot. The scarlet-sashed priest moved slightly to the side. The noise was so loud my thighs felt vibrations coming through the stone and earth.

The two priests clasped the boy's arms tightly to his sides. Two other priests stepped forward, grasped his legs, and the four men lifted him and laid him lengthwise on his back on the altar. The presiding priest strode forward, pulled a dagger from beneath his robe, and before my mind could accept what my eyes were seeing, slashed it across the boy's throat.

I gasped, then clapped my hand over my mouth. Blood gushed from his neck; his body quivered and lurched beneath the restraining hands. Hundreds of sandaled feet stomped the temple floor. The name Poseidon rang out three times more, and then the crowd fell silent.

Alektrion swore. The smell of the lamb sickened me, my stomach twisted and bile rushed upward, burning the back of my throat.

I turned from the spy hole and vomited. I'd eaten little, but my heaving continued as if the convulsions of my stomach could purge the assault to my eyes. I felt Alektrion grip my shoulder.

He whispered, "Are you going to be all right?"

My heart pounded so hard my head felt as though it would burst from the pressure. I clung to the wall retching violently until at last it stopped. I sucked in two deep breaths, then pushed away from the wall and fled down the dim tunnel through the laurel toward the open field—away from this horror. The sounds of Alektrion's foot-steps followed me, loud and close behind.

2.

I burst into the open. I didn't look back. I bolted from the field onto a wide path leading to the Keftian Snake Clan district. A red sun hung low over the Aegean. Blood red. My stomach lurched again.

I ran, not caring if I drew stares. I stumbled on an uneven cobble and crashed into a shopkeeper's display. Sun hats rolled across the street in every direction, but I scarcely noticed the shopkeeper's yelps.

At the stone-paved street fronting our townhouse door, I finally stopped. I was terrified. What I'd witnessed might show on my face. I must compose myself before my mother's seeing eye.

When I could breathe without gasping, I entered the front door praying I could slip unnoticed to my sleeping room. I removed my sandals, washed my feet in the door basin, and climbed the stairs to the living quarters.

At the refectory door, Heebe, my nursemaid, spotted me. She held a mending basket and several of mother's ceremonial kilts. The hair at the side of her face had worked loose from her snood, and gray-streaked brown curls bounced as she smiled and clucked. "You look a fright, Little Bird. Wash your face and change, then go to the library. Your father wants to see you about your mother's naming party."

In my room I threw myself face down on my bed. Why had I acted so rashly and followed Alektrion? I longed to blot out the sight of the shuddering boy, of the blood streaming from his severed neck.

Before this day, what was the worst thing I'd ever seen? The Law forbids the People to strike another person, even in great anger. And I had witnessed murder. Butchery.

Icy tentacles slithered around and squeezed my flighty stomach.

I washed in haste and threw on a clean tunic. The door to the study creaked on its hinges. My father, Damion, was the Keftian ambassador to Kalliste. He sat behind his writing desk, a massive piece of Keftian cedar. Seeing me, he shifted the shoulder fold of his tunic and waved me in. I forced my bare feet across the rug and dropped onto a cushioned footstool.

When he was displeased, the long scar on the edge of my father's right jaw turned white and made his face fearsome. He'd earned the scar as a young man during a bull dance. I searched his eyes. A fearsome look now and I'd confess everything.

He smiled. "Tomorrow your mother will be thirty-one." His after-noon cup of honeyed wine stood on the desk. He took a sip. "Is your music ready?"

I couldn't think. Part of me wanted to get away. I had been wrong to spy. I had been wrong to be with Alektrion. If anyone found out, my punishment would be severe. Days of shunning. Perhaps even weeks.

And yet, at that exact moment I yearned to confess. I needed to ask how such an evil could occur. And in a temple!

A shocking thought stopped my breath. Did my father know that Poseidon worshippers did such evil things within their temples? Did my mother know?

Damion allowed outlanders into our home, as far as I knew with-out regard to their religion. He had spent more years in foreign lands than on Keftiu and Kalliste put together, and somehow these experi-ences had produced a man I respected, but his thinking sometimes lay outside rules I understood.

A riot of questions exploded in my head. At least four Acheans and their wives would be at my mother's party. Surely all outlanders weren't bloodthirsty. Maybe only Poseidonists? I recalled that the spice merchant and the importer of Keftian bronzeware were not only Achean, I had seen them going into the very same temple. Tomorrow they would be here, in my home. Could I keep from screaming at them that they were murderers?

"I'm feeling ill, father. I still don't play the piece well." My voice shook. "I think I'm not ready for guests. I won't honor the Lady or mother."

His smile vanished. "It's your mother's naming day." He set the cup down with a sharp clack, and a drop of wine rolled over the rim and slid down the side. "It's not a hard piece and you've had plenty of time to practice. What were you doing today if you thought you still weren't ready? Where have you been?"

"I went up by Dallia."

"If you can cavort around the mountain all afternoon, then you can play for your mother's party. If you're not ready, I suggest you go immediately upstairs and practice."

I nodded and fled, my knees shaking. In my room I plucked harshly at the lyre, angry and confused. How often did the Acheans do such vile things? What kind of ritual, and how many of them, must the holy ones perform to mend the disharmony caused by the boy's death? Why, why had Alektrion taken me to such an evil place? If I didn't tell a priestess and accept my punishment, what horrible thing would happen to me? And … and how could the Goddess permit such evil?

I stopped playing. That was the most awesome question of all. How could She allow such evil? She should have protected the boy.

In the room's stillness I listened. I heard only the loud beating of my heart. She knew me. She knew what I was thinking. What would She do to me?

∾ ∾ ∾ ∾

At the party I played perfectly. My skin shrank against my bones every time an Achean came near, but I insulted no one. At evening's end, I fell exhausted into sleep.

In the days that followed, Alektrion was seldom absent from my thoughts. I ached to find him, desperate to ask what he felt about what we'd seen, but I also feared I would encounter him and be forced to speak of the unspeakable, the unthinkable: a child killed in the name of a god. Night terrors tormented me. I would awaken and lie listening, trembling, in the darkness. With a careless slip of my tongue I might reveal my anger that the Great Mother permitted such a death. That was my deepest pain—my anger at the Mother of All. How could I bear to live cut off from Her love?

Several weeks before Silvanos, the mid-winter festival, I was adding dried thyme to the stuffing of my pillow—my mother claimed it a preventative for melancholy—when the beaded curtain at my room's door rustled and Heebe swept in.

"Your mother needs a new hooded cloak for Festival. I need to buy the material and have the cloak made at once so I'll have time to embroider it myself." She ran a finger affectionately down my back. "Want to come shopping?"

Heebe was the only servant my mother had brought from Keftiu to Kalliste. She'd been indentured to my mother's family when she was eleven and was mother's childhood companion and later my nurse. She became her own woman when I turned three. That was the seven times seven seasons plus one year—the Great Jubilee. By the Law, all major debts are canceled and all indentureds are freed, and Heebe chose to remain in mother's paid service.

"Perhaps we'll find cloth for a new festival tunic for you."

Eager for any diversion from my gloom, I agreed. Perhaps at the market I might also see Alektrion. If only I could talk to him!

The cloth bazaar lay in the Spider District—the best Keftian weavers have always been Spider clan. In Copper Alley, Abramanthus, son of the wine maker, ran up from behind and passed us, his arms flapping like a bird. Twenty now and still incapable of useful work, he had been possessed as long as I could remember. His demon wasn't dangerous; Abramanthus just wandered the streets talking to it. Heebe, as was the custom, called to his demon to "leave this child of the Lady in peace."

Just before Weaving Lane, I felt a light shaking of the earth. Our volcano was sometimes restless. I scarcely noticed it, but Heebe turned and stared, her brow deeply creased.

I asked, "What is it?"

"For some reason …" She shook her head. "It's probably nothing."

Her frown faded, she took my hand, and we walked on to the cloth bazaar as she continued a stream of gossip. We meandered, fingering materials, comparing prices. The vendors on the lane's opposite side sold birds. I watched for a crowd of rowdy boys. Perhaps I'd see Alektrion.

I was having the most pleasant moments in days, thinking that it would indeed be nice to have a new tunic, when a child's angry shout slashed through the twitter of birds. We whirled around.

The shriek of a green and yellow parrot nearly split my head. The bird clung to the bars of a wicker cage. In front of the cage stood a foreign woman in Achean dress—a mainlander—and two very young boys —her sons or her charges. The boys were pressed close to the parrot. Next to the three Acheans stood a woman whose hem embroidery indicated she was of Keftian Butterfly Clan. Her eyes were round with amazement. Beside her stood another boy of the same age, also pressed close to the cage. He appeared to be her son. His gaze was locked onto the stone pavement.

One of the Achean boys yelled a foreign word and, in the selfish way children have, shoved the Butterfly Clan boy hard to push him away from the cage. I guessed it was the second time he'd done it.

I felt my face flush. My fists tightened. I longed for my Keftian brother to return the barbarian Achean's shove, though I knew he'd never do so.

The Keftian mother smiled at the foreign woman and moved her son by his shoulders to the other side of the cage. The Achean woman smiled and shook her head and said something that sounded polite, but she didn't correct her boy's shocking behavior.

"I hate the Acheans," I said softly.

Heebe turned on me. "Your words break harmony. Take them back."

"I won't."

Her frown deepened. "Take your words back."

"The Achean is at fault. It's wrong to push."

"Yes, pushing is wrong. But your additional wrong will only cause further imbalance. I say again, take your words back."

I stared at the cracks in a paving stone as Heebe's gaze burned the top of my head. She took my hand and whispered, "The shopkeeper's watching."

She drew me outside, and we sat on one of the stone benches of a nearby fountain. She was right, of course. We shouldn't publicly shame my father by arguing, a serious break in harmony, unacceptable for any Keftian. But it was hard to always put on a proper face. I sulked, staring at the sea view, a white sand beach dotted with idle fishing dories. The onshore breeze brought the smell of fresh fish from the bazaar.

Heebe patted my hand. "Why are you troubled?"

"I'm not troubled."

"But you are, my Little Bird. You're having bad dreams. Bad dreams come when we're troubled."

How could Heebe know of my terrible dreams? To my knowledge she had no ability as a seer.

Recalling the shame of my shunning, I bit my lip, summoned will. "I'm not having bad dreams."

"Little one, something's wrong. I hear you toss and call out in your sleep. I've never heard you speak with such bitterness before. What do you mean you hate the Acheans?"

Starting to panic, I shifted ground. "If they don't obey the Law, then why shouldn't we push back?"

"Is that what's bothering you? That the Acheans don't follow the Law?"

"Why doesn't the Lady punish them and insist they behave in harmony?"

She slipped her arm around my waist and hugged me. Then she sighed. "We're the Lady's People. We are the envy of all outlanders, and do you know why? Because we live in peace. The Lady's People have always lived in peace. And by our obedience to Her Laws we keep the world in balance. The others fight. They kill. They live with great unhappiness, but not the Lady's People. And were we to fail in our duties and in that way fail to balance the outlanders' evil, all harmony would cease. The world itself would come undone. You'll learn all this during your initiation. It's too hard to explain simply."

That was no answer at all.

"Listen, Little Bird. Both your mother and I believe you've been touched. There must be no place in your heart for hate. I want you to ask the Mother to take such feelings away."

These were strange words. What could she mean? I said, "I suppose the Law says we mustn't hate. But ..."

I just couldn't change my feelings, not even for Heebe. We finished shopping, but she made clear that a girl who wasn't certain what the Law demanded and who was unwilling to change bad feelings didn't deserve a new tunic. In my heart, I agreed.

I hadn't caught even a glimpse of Alektrion. I tried to remember how often in the past I had chanced to see him. It seemed I should have seen him at least once by now. My spirit was in turmoil, my life turned upside down, and all because of him.

Within the week, my feelings about Acheans boiled over again. My father and my cousin Sinon went to the graduation ceremony for the latest class of navy recruits, and I tagged along. The largest naval academy had always been at Knossos, but the Keftian fleet's real backbone lay in Kalliste. Keftiu was so vast and bountiful it supplied all of the People's needs there, and so Keftians were landlubbers compared to the shipbuilders and navigators of tiny Kalliste who had to bring back so much of what their island needed. It was the sons of Alyris, not Knossos, who provided knowledge born of generations of seafarers, so the naval alliance between Knossos and Alyris was the most important in Keftiu's world of influence. The graduation here was a major annual event.

As custom dictated, my cousin Sinon, son of my mother's brother, was living with us during the three years leading to his initiation. He and I disagreed about everything, so I saw little of him except at meals and prayers. We passed the mainlander family of a Dinian recruit, and one of the girls dropped her sidebag into a puddle of water. Her mother struck the girl's arm.

"Outlanders are mean people!" I said to my father, anger sharpening every syllable of every word.

We'd barely returned home when he summoned me to his study. His scar stood sharply white against his face. He skewered me with accusing eyes. My knees grew unsteady.

He launched into a lecture on the importance of his work as a diplomat, then said, "I've noticed the poor grace you are displaying toward foreign guests in your mother's home. We represent Keftiu to the outlanders and, therefore, the Lady Herself. I expect you to be gracious. Furthermore, as a mere child, you're in no position to make judgments about other people's ways. Do you understand?"

I nodded, though in truth I did not understand. My father was angry with me. The Lady was too. And I knew that to be separated from the Mother is to starve the part of us that lives forever. For the first time in my life I felt the gnawing emptiness that comes from such separation—because I was angry at Her.

3

Why hadn't I seen Alektrion? Was he avoiding me, thinking me childish for throwing up? Maybe I'd misjudged him; maybe he'd taken me to the sacrifice to be cruel. To keep that thought away, I threw myself into plans for the Silvanos festival, and when the day arrived at last, even my gloom lifted enough that I awakened early.

At mid-day our household of ten, which included the servants, joined throngs of families on lanes leading to the Temple. For me, Silvanos was the year's best festival because, after the sun set, the People would march to the mountain shrine. Kalliste disgorged new earth continuously, but it flowed away from Alyris into the sea. From the mountain shrine at night, though, a person could watch the lava burn its way down the mountain, and only during Silvanos did the People go to the shrine at night.

Our servants carried food baskets. Tomorrow morning the household would break the Great Fast together. The Fast had begun yesterday, and my empty stomach rumbled.

I studied mother. She was so very beautiful. High cheekbones. Lustrous dark eyes, set well apart. Skin like the smoothest cream. Snake Clan emblems, in intricate patterns of blues with gold, emblazoned the hem of her yellow ankle-length woolen robe. Lapis lazuli set into her headband, arm bands, and earrings matched her long blue cape.

Smiling, she bent and whispered, "This is your last year as a child. Next year you too can dance. I know how you're feeling. I've always loved the dance. My blood runs hot, and so does yours."

She gave me a warm hug. The warmth only reminded me of my terrible secret. She wouldn't hug me so if she knew what I'd done.

We turned into the central avenue leading uphill. During early winter the Lady's consort, Velchanos, sleeps in the underworld. Seven days ago priestesses and priests had begun preparations to waken him. Today, the People would do their part. We would pray to the Mother as Maiden—the Virgin who is the earth unawakened—and we'd ask Her to find Her lover, a sleeping babe, and to rouse Him. During their long journey back to us, the Maiden would care for the rapidly maturing God, and, by spring, He would again be in the full strength of young manhood. At Belamnos, the spring festival, the es-

sences of the world—female and male—would become perfectly
joined at the Sacred Wedding and the earth would burst into life.

Silvanos, though, is a most dangerous time. The energy of life burns
low. It was hard to fast each morning until after mid-day prayers, but
I knew how necessary it was. Two years ago, fishing had failed in the
entire west of the Great Sea as far away as the Pelloponesis, and the
Temple said it was the carelessness of too many of Her children during Silvanos. To do what I could to make up for the boy's death, I had
kept the fast each day until evening meal.

Several thousand worshippers already filled the Temple's west
park. My father took Sinon to stand with the Butterfly Clan. My mother
joined the seers. I was too young to be unattended, so I followed Heebe
to where the Earth Clan gathered. She fell to chatting with her sons
and daughters-in-law, and I heard her say, "Does the mountain seem
especially troubled? Something feels different."

I frowned. What could be so different? Kalliste had provided the
island with water and heat for as long as there had been Rememberers.
The volcano was our island's steady, warm heart.

I caught sight of Meidra, my best friend, who was with her mother
and two brothers. "Heebe says you can come with us," I told her. "We
can go up the mountain together."

She turned pleading eyes to her mother.

I hadn't decided yet whether to tell Meidra about Alektrion and
playing with the spider. We kept few secrets. But I would never tell
her what I had seen at the barbarian temple, so I had to be careful.

Meidra's mother, only too aware of my parents' status, gave me a
smile so sweet Heebe would say it would sicken a fly, then nodded.

With a great boom, the four great temple drums announced the
procession's beginning. Heebe had, as usual, found a place with an
excellent view. Later she and her cronies would gossip, and Heebe
took pride in gossiping with authority.

The drums sounded again, and silence spread over the crowd. Behind me, a mother cut short her baby's cry with a tit. I knew the energy
of all worshippers should be directed only to the Virgin, so I strained to
concentrate. Perhaps in this great moment of worship, I would feel at
peace again. But my mind wandered. To the mountain. To the Achean
temple and the hideous barbarian ceremony. To Alektrion.

I squeezed my eyes shut, tried to see the weary Maiden, exhausted
and injured during her search through the perilous underworld.

My stubborn mind saw only Alektrion's mysterious eyes.

Parading up the freshly swept pathways, newly lined with boughs
of cypress and myrtle, priests in dappled sheepskin robes headed the
procession accompanied by the rattling of sistrums and the clanging

of cymbals. Then the incense bearers—youths and maidens in green and yellow—walked down the two paths that converge near the center of all West Courts. The balsamy scent of frankincense reached us. Priestesses followed, wearing open-breasted blouses and the girdles that narrowed their waists and lifted their naked breasts in adoration of the life-giving Great Mother of All. Their ankle-length kilts were a frenzy of color and pattern: red and black, white and brown, checks and swirls and spirals—symbols of the Goddess and her power: life, birth, growth, fertility, harmony, health, wisdom, death, rebirth.

The afternoon sun dropped low. "Expect me shortly before sunset," mother had said. The drums' rhythm changed. Two snake priestesses appeared, one at the head of each path. I could just discern that on each arm they carried a living *charis*, the striped brown snake that embodies the Lady's spirit.

Finally, mother appeared amidst her fellow seers. Everyone said that Danae of Phaestos was beautiful, and I compared her to those who stood near her. What was said of her outer beauty was certainly true—and she was beautiful inside as well.

Too much pride breaks harmony, I reminded myself. But I loved her so much.

The chanters faced west, women in front, the men behind. Meidra squeezed my hand. Now we could participate. Even uninitiates were permitted to sing in answer to the chanters' ancient questions.

The music stopped. I waited with a breathless throng of thousands as the sun dipped lower. Finally the earth bit a chunk from the sun, and the chantesses began: "Who is Mother of us all?"

"The Lady: Maiden, Mother, Ancient," the crowd sang in fervent, reverent response.

Then the chanters, their male voices booming: "Who wakens Velchanos and returns him to the People in spring?"

"The Lady in Her youth, our Virgin Maiden," we chorused.

"Who bears and suckles all life?" the chantesses asked.

"The Lady, our Mother, in the fullness of Her days."

"Who brings the final sleep, renewal in Elysium, and life again?" the chanters called.

"The Lady, the Ancient, who waits at the end of our path."

The music and singing rolled sweetly into the darkening evening. For the first time in weeks, even my agonized spirit felt the Mother's peace.

Again the temple drums sounded. It hurt to have to let go of that wonderful moment. On the other hand, the mountain with its glowing streams of molten rock was waiting! Meidra tugged me. "Hurry. Let's get torches."

At the Temple wall, a group of boys initiated last season were light-
ing and handing out the long poles. They were about Alektrion's age.
Sadness touched my heart. Alektrion wasn't of the People. He had no
clan. He could never attend the great festivals. I burned for a moment
with anger. It wasn't fair. Then I thought, It's the Law. *It's not my place
to question the Law.*

We raced back to Heebe, and, as dusk closed in, a great crowd left
the heart of Alyris and streamed onto the wide trail up Kalliste's broad
slope.

Night slipped quickly onto the mountain. Before and behind us, a
trail of weaving torchlight extended, and to either side pinpricks of
light marked shepherds' campfires. I wanted to run ahead, to hurry,
but all of life must follow ordered ritual, so I reined in my impatience
and tried to calm my heart.

Two hours' walk from the summit, I saw the first glowing boulders. The noise of the crowd covered the volcano's grumbling at this
distance, but boulders the size of houses shot into the black sky amidst
fountains of fire. They arched red-hot from the volcano's mouth, shattered into incandescent white and red splinters, then tumbled
downslope and disintegrated into red and yellow froth.

The bursts seemed closer together and larger than those I'd seen
before. The red streaks of running lava were wider. My pulse quickened. Tonight's show would be many times more wonderful than last
year.

Heebe shook her head and clucked. "The mountain feels troubled."

"What do you mean, troubled?"

"I can't put it into words, Little Bird."

Something about her tone made my heart thump an extra beat.
Was there something truly wrong with the volcano? Surely that
couldn't be.

I should tell the Goddess I was sorry I'd spied on the Acheans.
And I wanted to pray my own disharmony wouldn't be damaging to
the People or to the Mother's body. But then, in my mind's eye, I saw
the boy's shuddering form and his spewing blood. Repentant words
wouldn't come to my heart, let alone to my tongue.

Dressed gypsum walls enclosed the holy grounds. Burning rushes
set in cressets flanked the many wooden bull horns that line the
tops of all sacred Keftian walls. The light from the rushes cast quivering shadows over the uneven ground. Outside the entrance stood
a massive set of horns, shoulder high to a man, cut from stone. For
good luck, Meidra and I rubbed the tip of the eastern horn, worn
smooth from the touch of countless others. I went back and rubbed
it again.

I didn't feel any better.

Only the priestesses, clan elders, shamans, and notables, such as my father, would be so fortunate as to spend the night within the walls of the shrine. Below the shrine, the meadow hosted clan bonfires twice the height of a man. Households staked out ground near their clan's fire. I helped Heebe spread a blanket, then rushed to meet Meidra. We found places to sit atop a cart-sized boulder, and then, while watching Kalliste spew glowing rocks, I listened to the Earth Clan Rememberer retell the story of the Virgin and Velchanos. A sharp, hollow boom announced a particularly forceful belch from Kalliste. I jumped, and my heart raced with excitement. *It would be such a splendid night if only ...* if only the frightening disharmony gnawing at me would go away.

After the retelling, Meidra said, "I want to watch the Spider clan first."

So did I.

We ran to their bonfire, and I eased between people, aiming for the center. Meidra stuck close. We found a place on the front row and sat. The dancing women moved with bows and great leaps, and for this first piece, the men played only the big drums. The ground beneath my thighs quivered. I swayed, aching to lose myself in motion. When the final ritual performance ended, freeform dancing began, but I was too restless to sit any longer. I left Meidra and roamed from one cluster of music and movement to another. By accident, Heebe and I met at the Butterfly Clan circle. We linked arms and swayed, and then on the far side of the fire I saw Alektrion. I blinked several times. He was staring directly at me. How dare he come to a festival!

He nodded, and continued to watch me. He had to be wondering if I'd tell Heebe. What would happen if I did? Such a flagrant offense might earn him a shunning. Perhaps the Temple would include his whole family! He signaled with a nod that I should come away and join him.

My anger put fire to my pulse. Sometimes I had dreaded seeing him. Sometimes I had thought I would die if I didn't. I looked away, thinking, Ignore him. *He shouldn't be here.*

But my heart defied me. I hugged Heebe's waist and let her go. I backed away, hoping she wouldn't miss me.

In the darkness Alektrion took my hand—I hoped he didn't think I was a child who needed reassurance—and I ran with him to a pile of rocks on the outskirts of the Boar clan's bonfire.

He let me go and, in three leaps, hopped onto the tallest rock and sat. His face lay mostly in shadow, but what light there was emphasized deep lines on his forehead. "I'm very sorry about what happened," he said the moment he sat.

My heart had jammed itself in my throat. I still felt the warmth of his hand. From my palm it had spread to my heart. I felt honored he trusted me not to tell others he was here.

"I've been thinking you'd never speak to me again." His voice was changing, taking on a man's deeper tones.

I finally found my tongue. "I have bad dreams."

"I'm sorry," he said softly. "I was afraid you might avoid me." His eyes searched mine. "And you'd be right to be angry. But I speak true. I expected nothing worse than maybe an animal sacrifice." He stared at his feet. "I've since decided even showing you an animal sacrifice would have been wrong. I was stupid."

So, it was only by accident that we had not met. I felt a surge of relief. He hadn't been avoiding me . "I'm not angry with you." I climbed onto a rock slightly below him and found a place where I could lean back. "I went of my own will. But I loathe this false god Poseidon. I would think the people who worship him would die of shame."

He remained quiet a moment, his eyes glancing at me only briefly before he looked down again. "Did you tell anyone?"

"No. How could I? My mother would be unspeakably angry."

"I didn't either. But I told my mother I'd heard that Poseidon demands the death of humans. She said it happens only on special occasions."

I made a derisive snort. "It's disgusting. It's a breaking of harmony so sickening—well, so sickening I can't imagine anything worse. What a horrible thing they believe."

"You know, the Poseidonists see the Lady's worshipers as weak."

I shook my head. "You worship the Lady. Do you feel weak?" Alektrion was fifteen years old, and to me he seemed strong in every way.

"That's not the point. Poseidon is a powerful god, and his worshipers believe that to keep things in balance, like when their lives were saved at sea, they have to pay him back in kind, with life. They know we make no blood sacrifices, and they think those who serve the Great Mother are gutless. That's the word I heard a Lydian mercenary use."

I sensed no disdain from him, only interest, and my spirit winced. "If you're such an admirer of the Acheans and their horrible god, why have you come to Silvanos?"

He straightened his back. "I come to Silvanos because I don't like being told what I can and cannot do." After a short pause he added more calmly, "And because I worship the Lady."

We sat quietly, then he said, "I do admire the Achean warriors. Their marines and infantry are the best in the world. I don't admire everything about them, but surely your father has told you we can learn useful things from other people."

"Poseidon worshippers have nothing of value to teach us."

"This sea-season I'm going to join the Lady's navy. I want to learn how to be the finest warrior possible. I think it's important, even while in the Lady's service, to be strong and fierce. And if I have to learn from Acheans, I will."

Only Keftian initiates could enter the naval academy, and hired outlanders had to be seventeen to join the lower ranks. "Aren't you too young?" It occurred to me that, if he entered the navy, he would be away every summer. Perhaps he meant to leave Kalliste altogether.

"I'll be sixteen. At sixteen I can ship out as a cook's mate."

"Why not stay on Kalliste? Won't you miss your friends?" I was thinking the last thing I would ever do was to leave Kalliste.

"I don't always feel I fit here."

A familiar form caught my eye. Heebe. She spotted me, turned, and strolled our way.

Alektrion saw her and shot to his feet. "I hope to see you again," he said, then bounded into the night.

"Well, he's certainly a skittish one," Heebe said with a big grin. "Who is he?"

"A boy I know from school. Son of Meela." Still vexed at Alektrion's defense of Acheans, I was in no mood to lie for or about him.

Heebe's smile faded. "I know the marriage. I know his mother. A fine woman, but not of the People. His father is famous as a maker of weapons. You do know the youth shouldn't be here?"

Already sick that I'd told, I reluctantly nodded. What would she do? Heebe was meticulous in her obedience to the Law, but she also had a bountifully kind heart.

She gestured for me to join her. I slipped under her arm and put my hand around her waist. She said, "It's no business of mine. Or of yours."

A heavy weight floated off my chest. Dear Heebe. We strolled side by side together back toward our blanket. Sunrise wasn't long off.

At dawn, I stood with Meidra and my family in the position of reverence in prayer, left arm tight to my side, the back of my right fist pressed to my brow. Drums and conchs heralded the rising sun. The beauty of a darkly pink sun rising behind low-lying, gold-rimmed clouds filled all of me. The soft glow lightened, grew brighter. Shafts of faint pink broke through and shot upward. My throat tightened.

My heart so longed to again be in harmony, and tears slipped down my cheeks.

The ground gave a sudden lurch, shoving me to the left. A stunning roar emerged from Kalliste. Heebe fell, a shrill "Aiee!" on her lips.

The terrible roar continued. Panic clawed at my throat. The sound was unlike anything I'd ever heard: sharp, deep, rapidly expanding, it engulfed the mountain. My father and mother were dashed to the ground. Meidra and I clung together struggling to stay on our feet. A stench, like rotten eggs, fouled the air as stones clattered downhill toward us.

4

Terrifying thoughts smashed through my fear. *The Lady is going to punish me.* For refusing to confess. For refusing to accept my punishment. For being angry with Her.

A rock struck Meidra on the back. She screamed. Torn from my grip, she crumpled to her knees and began weeping. I quivered from head to toe.

Then a light flashed in front of me, round and fist-sized and incredibly white—so close, a few steps and I might touch it. The groaning of the earth, the thunderous clacking of colliding rocks, the cries of the people: all receded. A dense cloud of pure white, the light exploded, expanded, engulfed me. The stench of Kalliste's breath faded and a soothing scent, like bunch-flowered narcissus, caressed me. *Dearest Mother!* Surely she was going to strike me dead. Or take my sight. *I will never never again disobey, in even the smallest way.*

But no. Time flowed by. I felt no pain. A calm spirit settled over me. I was all right and there was no need to fear. Inside the light, all was in harmony.

From somewhere close I heard a murmuring, a gentle sound. Was that someone speaking? Was the sound coming closer? The gentle murmuring was the last thing I remembered.

ॐ ॐ ॐ ॐ

I recognized mother's face, then with surprise I realized that, though my body was upright, I was on my knees.

"Don't rush her, Danae." My father's voice. "She's not able to rise."

I sank slowly down onto my heels. The splendid light was gone, so too the calming smell and the murmur. I felt peaceful, and happy, and confident.

Heebe patted my hand. Mother stroked my cheek.

"The shaking?" I asked.

"It's over, Sweet," mother said. "What happened to you? A stone perhaps?"

I shook my head. "It was the light."

She frowned. "The sunrise?"

"No, no. A white light. So bright. Everywhere. Surely you saw it. And then there was such a gentle smell. And then the voice."

She grasped my chin. "Of what voice do you speak?"

Father knelt next to her, put his arm around her shoulder. "I don't think Leesandra should be pressed now."

I started to rise, but father bent and swept me into his arms. "I'll carry you."

I was nearly thirteen, and I thought I was much too big for him to carry. But he began walking, and I curled against his warmth. At Dallia he sat me on a low wall. I was amazed he'd carried me so far. To mother he said, "Perhaps I can find a litter."

I insisted I could walk, and we set off again, slowly. Everyone was talking about the shaking. What did it mean? Would fishing fail this year? Would the crops come in stunted? Danae said that all such events were a lesson and that the temple would surely call for a High Seeing to determine what the Goddess wished the People to hear.

No one else had seen the white light. Why had I? When the earth moved, I had been sure beyond sure of the Lady's wrath. But oh, the wonderful calm of the light. More than an hour since the shaking, and still the beautiful calm lingered.

By the time we reached home I sensed the wonderful feeling would soon be only an astonishing, sweet memory. Mother put her hand on my arm. "When you've washed and changed, come to my bed chamber. We must talk."

My heart leaped from my chest to lodge in my throat. This was it. My spying, my failure to confess. All was going to be exposed.

I changed clothes as slowly as I could, then, on leaden feet, walked to her door. She had put on a chamber robe of light-brown wool and loosened her waist-length hair. She put down her comb and pointed to the cushioned stool beside her dressing table. "Leesandra, to be in the favor of the Goddess, we must be willing to hear Her."

I nodded, staring at the floor and tracing the pattern in the floor tile with my toe, my stomach churning.

"It's important that you be in Her favor."

I took the stool, but concentrated all the more intently on the flowered tiles at my feet—trying to suppress tears I felt welling up inside. *Oh, please, let me go.*

"I want you to tell me again about the voice this morning."

This wasn't what I expected. "I don't remember exactly," I said, raising my gaze to meet hers.

"Then tell me what you do remember."

My stomach's turning eased. There was such compassion in her eyes, so I told her how the light had throbbed and how calm I'd felt. She nodded. "What else?"

"I remember, just before I heard the murmuring, I felt dizzy."

She took my hand. "What do you mean by murmuring?"

I struggled to remember the words. But I couldn't. "It was like someone talking, very softly."

She released my hand and folded hers in her lap. "What did the voice say?"

I realized I was chewing my lower lip in the effort to recall.

"It's all right. Don't worry at trying to remember. You'll know the words when you're ready."

The comforting warmth I had begun to feel gave way to a sudden chill. "Must I understand?"

"Don't worry. When the Goddess speaks, we don't always know her meaning, not at once. But what happened is important. It's time at last for me to tell you about your birth." She stood. "Come. Sit with me on the couch."

Did she truly think the Goddess had spoken personally to me? She threw open the shutters in the small alcove, and cool air drifted in. She draped a soft wool throw around us, drawing me close as we sat and looked out at steam rising from the mountain.

"Why would the Great Mother speak to me?"

"The voice you heard can only be the Lady. You smelled her perfume, sweet and soothing. And you felt calm. When her demon children whisper to us, they leave us with fear."

I decided in that moment that what the Lady must have said was that to make up for the spying, I must observe each and every ritual in careful detail. In that moment of fear, hadn't I said I would always obey?

I was making my resolve and missed something mother said. Then I realized she was talking about my birth.

"... exactly at sunrise. An owl called. And then the earth shook, Leesandra. Like today. I heard the owl and felt the shaking. So did Heebe and the midwife. On your naming day, the highest-ranking priestess of Phaestos came to your party. She lifted you for all to see and said, 'This daughter of the Snake Clan is destined to lead.'"

A shiver swept over my arms and neck—and not from the winter air. What had Heebe said not too many weeks ago? "Your mother and I believe you are touched."

I didn't want any such special attention. No, not at all.

Mother moved back so she could watch my face. "What happened to you this morning—the light, the voice—was another touching by the Goddess. Perhaps in a dream the meaning will come clear. It's only necessary that you be ready to listen. Do you understand?"

I nodded.

"You enter initiation soon. You'll learn what it is to be a woman." She sighed. "So many secrets, so many things to learn. But promise me to listen carefully at all times, now and even after you leave Kalliste, to hear when the Lady speaks again."

I craned forward. "Leave Kalliste?"

"Yes, of course."

My blood ran as chilled as winter rain. I pulled away. "I don't want to leave Kalliste. Not ever."

"But of course you must, Sweet. Haven't I just said that the Lady has chosen you? Your destiny isn't here. It's at the Bull Dance Academy."

"I won't go."

A crease of vexation appeared between her eyes. "Your words are too strong."

"But I can't leave you and father." I thought of Meidra. And then of Alektrion. "And my friends are here."

"I appreciate you can't imagine leaving now. You're too young. But when the time comes, you'll be ready for a great adventure. I've foreseen that you'll serve the Lady at Knossos."

I couldn't believe what I was hearing. The Bull Academy. Knossos. And most incredibly, my mother expected me to follow her into religious service. Had she never listened the many times I'd told her how I would someday become the maker of fine, sweet honey? The very idea of being confined to the Temple every day! Now those welling tears could not be stopped. "I want to work under the sky, mother. I can't imagine the Lady would have me be a Temple seer. I'm not fit for it."

She brushed at a tear. "You're still too young to know how you might love service in the Temple."

"But I love the mountain. And the sea. I'm sure I'm meant to work out of house."

"How did you plan to do this out-of-house work here in Kalliste? Our family property is all on Keftiu. To work the land you'd have to leave Kalliste in any event."

"I've always thought to work on Meidra's family property. She and I have plans. Surely you ... I'm sure I've said ..." Another fat tear escaped and ran down my cheek.

"Dear one." She hugged me. She spoke soothing words, but then, though perhaps she thought to console me, added more searing pain. "You never know. After you've completed your training for the priesteshood, maybe you'll serve on one of the temple farms."

A blaze of rebellion shot through me. I drew away. The priestesshood! She didn't expect me to be a seer, like herself, who might marry and live in the community. No! She saw for me a life lived almost entirely within Temple walls.

Nothing could ever make me be a seer. And never, ever would I be a priestess. I opened my mouth to tell her how impossible her idea was, but I saw in her eyes the conviction that comes when a seer believes she's had a vision. Words would get me nowhere.

I said I would be careful to listen for the Mother's voice, then rose and left.

I would talk no more about leaving Kalliste, but I would launch a determined campaign to show how unsuited I was for religious life. A priestess could never marry, never have children or a house of her own. Terrible thoughts. She wouldn't send me to Keftiu until I was fifteen. Time was my ally. I would wear her down.

∾ ∾ ∾ ∾

Meidra and I attended classes for spring initiation in the same community house, the one set aside for women of Snake, Earth, and Water clans. Classes would confine me inside nearly every afternoon, but at least I would learn the secrets of womanhood. In truth, I eagerly looked forward to the classes, but I was also resolutely determined to use them to change mother's mind. I'd pretend to be uninterested in them. Now and then I'd express some small rebellion about what I was learning. Danae would see how mistaken she was.

On the first day, I met Meidra after school on our favorite grassy space, between the chandlery and the tallow house. We ate mid-day meal and watched dockhands loading three merchant vessels.

She grinned and said, "I hear we'll learn how to please a man in bed." She studied the fig she was about to eat as if it were a potential lover. "My sister took many lovers in the year before she began Temple service. I'm going to do the same." She kissed and then bit into the fig.

Her mention of our required year of Temple service set me to worrying again about my fate. Mother had served as a Temple cook. Her sister had served as a hetaira, one of the Temple's sacred lovers. Because of their beauty and special training, the hetaira were renowned lovers, and my mother had once hinted she wished she'd taken their training. I, unfortunately, faced the prospect of being shipped off to the Bull Academy.

I thought of Alektrion and his spider. "I want to find a lover who makes me laugh. My father makes mother laugh and she is so happy with him. Of course, I will want many lovers. Every woman does. But only if they know how to have fun."

We finished eating, then scrambled up, looped the straps of our sidebags across our chests and hurried toward the community house. The priestess gathered our little flock of twenty in a comfortable room. Cushions for two were arranged in three semi-circles. Dressed in a pale-blue, bee-decorated blouse and dark-blue sari, the priestess sat on a larger cushion. She had a beautifully wrinkled face and gray-streaked black hair caught at the back of her neck in a net.

She told us her name was Xenia, offered us words intended to put our anxious minds at ease, then said, "Today you begin a great journey together. Much of the journey will be fun. All of it is important. And at the end, you'll be strong enough to complete the difficult part of the trip alone." She didn't explain what she meant by difficult.

Her voice was so pleasing that some time passed before I remembered I needed to find something to use with mother. I must think!

Xenia's face suddenly lost its glow of good humor. Her tone turned solemn. "One of the most important of the Mother's gifts is the ability to bear children, the greatest of mysteries. You'll learn how to prevent the beginning of new life. How to know when life has taken hold. How to stop a life that comes too soon. But today's lesson, the foremost of all, is that you must ensure your children come no closer than three years apart. Children born too closely together can't be properly cared for."

If the bringing of children is such a great gift, and if the Mother wants them to be well cared for, why does She not protect them from evil people? I pushed the painful thought away.

She told stories showing how balance is upset if children arrive too close together or, much less common, too far apart. I couldn't remember a time when I didn't know that having children too quickly was an offense against the Law, but now Xenia explained why. The Law made sense, but this was the part of the lesson I would use.

At home, I went straight to my room intending to bathe and go quickly to mother. Since Silvanos, my hair had been growing in making my head itch constantly. I scratched the base of my quque and forelock, then, wrapped in a linen drying cloth, I padded down the hall to the bathing room. When the clay tub held enough scalding water, I turned off the hot spigot and turned on the cold. I heard water going down the drain of the water closet, and then Heebe came in. She wore her favorite house robe, embroidered front and back with emerald-green flying fish.

"Ah, Little Bird. Does it feel good to have your feet on the path to being a woman? And see! Your breast buds are growing rapidly. All in all, you're becoming quite alluring."

Heat rushed across my shoulders and up my neck—my ears felt like they must be glowing.

"I ... I'll never be the beauty mother is."

The tub reached comfortable warmth. I closed the spigot, stepped in, my feet landing on the backs of two painted dolphins. I folded myself into the hot water.

Heebe sat on a stool. "I've known your mother since she first suckled. You'll outshine her many times over. But that's another matter. How do you like your teacher?"

Maybe I could get Heebe to side with me against mother. "Oh, she's all right, I suppose."

"And what did you learn?"

"She said we shouldn't bear children closer together than three years." A rapid pulse beat in my throat. I added, in a stubborn tone, "I don't think I agree."

Heebe's smile faded. "Do you say that to distress me?"

Oh, such a stab of regret I felt. It was terrible to trouble Heebe.

"Who are you, Leesandra, to agree or disagree with one of the Mother's chosen? You're a child. If you were older, your questioning the Law would show you lack wisdom."

I forced my tongue into further protest. "I don't see why, if a woman feels she can care for two little ones, that she shouldn't be allowed to."

Her shoulders slumped still more. "We can never know all the reasons for each of the Laws," she said softly but firmly. "We only know for certain that to disobey is to create disharmony. You mustn't even think such rebellious nonsense. It'll bring you trouble, sweetheart."

I lowered my head and squeezed the waterlogged hot sponge against my closed eyes. I couldn't force myself to say more. She rose, knelt beside the tub, pulled the sponge away and kissed my cheek. She offered to wash my back. I nodded.

The months that followed drained me. Perhaps I might have found harmony again if I'd been able to go to my pool, but there was no time. I thought often of Alektrion, how it had felt when he held my hand, how I'd laughed when we played with the spider, how serious he had been when he apologized. Then I would remember that he planned to leave Kalliste. It was just as well, I would say to myself, that I had no chance to see him.

Despite much inner turmoil, I found the classes were interesting, sometimes even fun. Xenia once let us practice boiling down the sugary paste used to remove body hair. Another day, Meidra and I were amazed to learn that soon we would bleed regularly, once every cycle of the moon. Some of the other girls already did so.

"Blood is power and blood the source of life," Xenia said in hushed tones.

We learned how to collect the blood in pads of linen and thistle down and how to burn it as an offering. Nothing in this lesson could be used in my campaign. These were matters far too serious.

The lessons moved to the subject of sexual pleasures. Xenia assured us that during their initiations, boys would be given similar instructions. We learned the "passion points" of our bodies, the most powerful being a tiny bud between our legs. It was even more astonishing to learn of the passion points on a man's body, like his nipples and a firm spot deep between his legs at the base of his male organ.

"Learn well and you can make any lover moan with pleasure. And any man you wish to keep will never leave you."

I had never seen even hints of the private pleasure from my father and mother. Any such display would have been scandalous. Now, I couldn't stop myself from imagining them sharing such acts. When my mind created images of myself with some youth, I found myself imagining not Parmenos, who had once been a close friend, or Sinon, whom I saw every day, but Alektrion. My cheeks would warm, and I'd force the image away.

One day Xenia said, "You must never marry outside the People. If you're wise, you'll not even take a non-Keftian lover, because one of the demon children might tempt you to take him as spouse—an unacceptable disaster for all concerned."

Alektrion! My back stiffened. I'd found no boy, ever, that I liked half as much as Alektrion. Why should caring for Alektrion be a disaster simply because his mother wasn't Keftian?

She folded her hands in her lap, leaned forward and announced that the next day we would be given a demonstration of sexual pleasure. She didn't tell us the names of the hetaira and hetairon. "Identity isn't important. The experience transcends individuals."

We entered the classroom the next day to find its mood mysteriously altered. Fewer lamps. Jasmine incense. Where Xenia's cushion usually sat, a small table of offerings — cakes and wine — stood on the carpeted floor. Behind the offerings, on a low couch, were the man and woman, his arm around her shoulder, both washed by subtle, golden-hued lamplight.

They wore only the brief ceremonial kilt. Their curled hair was bound up off their shoulders, his with a laurel wreath and hers with a crocus garland. Their bodies gleamed with oil. He was no longer young, but his hips were narrow, his skin smooth. She was too small of breast and eye to be beautiful, but when she put her arm around his waist, her hands and neck moved with grace.

Excitement warmed my skin. Xenia stood and faced the table of offerings in the position of reverence. "Great Mother," she intoned joyfully, "for the gift of physical uniting in pleasure we adore You. For the harmony of spirit such joining brings to the People, we thank you. Make ready the hearts of those here to learn."

The music of two flutes floated over us as the man turned to the woman. He slid one arm around her waist, drew her to him, and placed his lips to hers. My breath died.

Of course, I knew what a kiss was. After weeks of imagining, we all did. I had even thought of Alektrion perhaps kissing me. But goose bumps along my arms raised to actually see such an act. With the speed of lightning across the sky of a summer squall, my mood shifted. My heart pulsed in my throat.

The kiss lasted forever. Then she removed the binding on his hair and tossed it to the floor, and his hair fell to his shoulders.

He touched her face, then kissed her where he'd touched. She returned his kisses, and all the while her hands caressed his skin in just the ways Xenia had described: his shoulders, the back of his neck, his arms, his face, his chest.

Their caresses continued until finally he freed the crocus garland from her hair and let the dark curls fall to her waist. I heard him whisper, "You're beautiful."

From her I heard a sigh.

He kissed her throat and as he did, he used one hand to pull away her kilt. My pulse thumped insistently. *That will never happen to me!* I couldn't imagine myself letting any man—any person—so intimately near my body.

His lips went to one of her nipples. Yes, we all knew the breast is a "passion point," but the woman gasped, and so did I, and so did girls all around me.

I was taking tiny gulps of air. The flutes' wavering, hypnotic melody increased in intensity. The hetairon's arousal was clear beneath his kilt, and when the hetaira removed the kilt, his organ stood tall. It was surely too enormous to go within her! I could focus on nothing but its livid color.

He laid her on the couch on her back then lay facing us on her far side, supported by one elbow. I held my breath. The skin of my chest and belly tingled. The caresses he began to press to her body moved lower and lower. The hetaira curled her fingers in his hair. Her moans became intense. He spread her legs and his kisses continued. Her gasps and sighs crawled under my skin. The tingling spread under my arms and down the insides of my legs.

His organ seemed so enormous. To be told such a thing happens during coupling had simply not prepared me for this astonishing transformation. The sight of it—red and stiff and so huge—whisked away thought. Fire burned between my legs, fire licked my skin. Inside my belly, fear and fascination boiled together.

He took his head from between her legs and once again took her breast in his mouth and sucked on it like a babe. She put her hand on his organ and began to massage it in rhythm with the music. The hetairon groaned, and the sound of his voice—deep, so different from hers—sent shivers across my back.

They lay for a long time that seemed no time at all, their bodies moving slowly as they touched and kissed and licked.

Then he put his hand between her legs, massaged her as she began to writhe in what seemed to be pain, and soon she said softly, though in the hushed room it seemed loud, "Now I want you. Now."

He rose over her, with one knee spread her legs, and they coupled, face to face.

My flesh tightened. I couldn't draw air. Faster and faster he moved; he strained with the effort. Faster and louder pulsed the flutes.

The hetaira arched her back and gave a cry I was sure must come from terrible pain, but Xenia had assured us was from great pleasure, and as his body stiffened he seemed to roar. They sank back together onto the couch. The music stopped.

In this moment I knew that, in a small part, they'd become one. He'd given her his seed. Her body would take his seed and make it part of her flesh. I sat breathless. I'd witnessed a great mystery.

The next day when Meidra and I compared all aspects of the performance, Meidra was full of giggles. "I can hardly wait until initiation is over. I'll have many lovers."

Not me. Even contemplation of such intimacy seemed to steal my breath. My body had experienced a frightening power, and I was certain I could never perform as I should. And certainly not with the one boy I constantly thought about. Alektrion.

5

On the day before the festival of Somnos, our teachers excused us from school and initiation classes. I expected Meidra to come to the beach with me, but her mother said she was needed. I started helping Heebe, but she soon said, "Away with you. Run off some of that restlessness."

I tossed some fruit and bread into my sidebag and headed for my favorite beach, a walk of half an hour. This beach was seldom used and was a favorite flying place of gulls. The late winter sky had the look of dull gray tin, but there was no smell of rain and a vigorous breeze guaranteed the gulls would be up.

On the edge of a bluff overlooking the sand strip, I found a place where a lone twisted sea juniper had sunk its roots to hang on to life. I propped my back against the tree and dug a pear from my bag. The beach gave way at one end to a jumble of boulders against which a restless sea beat its irregular rhythm. I listened to the sea and the cries of the swooping gulls. I could see no reason for their daring, no purpose for their play with the wind. Their goal seemed the same as mine—pure pleasure.

After I finished the pear, I lay on my stomach, chin propped on my hands, and studied the sea. Sometimes monk seals landed on the rocks, but not today. If I was patient, I would almost certainly be rewarded with a family of dolphin. If lucky, I might see one of the mysterious black-and-white whales.

Below me, a bit too far for a man to jump to it, a wide ledge blocked a part of my view of the beach. On the sand lay a lone boat. Though its fishing net was torn and twisted around its bow, it looked in remarkably good shape to be left this way. Then I remembered hearing Heebe talk of an accident only days ago. A man had been killed. Perhaps his family had not yet come to fetch the boat.

Something dark and accompanied by the whir of wind in bird wings flashed in front of me. I jerked away. The bird landed on the ledge below at about the distance I could throw a rock: a male falcon, with an elegant slate-blue back, white throat, and dark mustache. He let out his harsh, chattering call and, from a recess in the bluff behind him, his drab brown mate emerged. This wasn't breeding season, but this must be where they laid their eggs. I lay still, my heart hammering against the ground. How wonderful to know their place! I would come here in season, maybe bring Meidra, and we could watch them with their young.

Suddenly, I felt a lightness in my head. I knew this feeling. It came almost immediately before I would see the white light. And being excited often seemed to come just before the light-headedness. Alarmed, I sat up. I was alone. I must move away from the edge. Then a male voice said from behind me, quite clearly, "You do like to be alone."

I spun around to see who had spoken, but too late. The white light flashed, at first small but rapidly exploding. I felt dizzy, smelled the narcissus, felt myself falling.

I awakened, as I always did, quickly and feeling warm and at peace. But where was I? A solid wall of dirt and roots and rocks draped with what looked like fishing net stood in front of me. Someone was holding my head and shoulders tenderly in their lap.

"Meidra?" I sat up and twisted to see.

"Not Meidra," Alektrion said. "It's Alektrion."

My breath caught. How extraordinary! His face was somber. He was clearly worried. His short tunic showed the muscles of his shoulders and arms and his sun-darkened skin. His light-brown hair was sun streaked.

I said, "I'm all right. In fact, I always feel wonderful when this happens."

"You wouldn't have felt fine if this ledge hadn't been here."

I looked around. He was quite right. I apparently had been stopped from my fall only by the ledge. I crawled to the rim and peered down. Jagged boulders. I grinned at Alektrion, a silly, nervous grin.

"I might have …"

"I know you like to be alone, but isn't it too dangerous? Because you … because when the Lady speaks to you, you could fall almost anywhere?"

I wasn't really surprised that he'd heard of my hearings. I imagined everyone knew of this strangeness because not long after the beginning of the initiation classes the Goddess had spoken to me again, in school. But unlike the first time, just before I heard the murmuring, nausea sickened me. Afterward, to my embarrassment, I learned that before fainting, I'd vomited.

My mother explained what she called "hearings" to the teacher, and the teacher told the other students. "Leesandra has a very special gift."

They bombarded me with questions, including, "What does the Mother say?" I would squirm inside because, for the most part, I couldn't answer any of the questions. A few, who had been friends, avoided me.

Once or twice each moon cycle, I had been touched like this; and despite the feeling afterward of bliss, I couldn't feel this was a wonderful gift. I still did not feel in harmony. I was doing everything I could to avoid being sent to Knossos. Why would the Goddess bless me?

What Alektrion had just said about being alone was true. My parents and Heebe had said almost the same, and I realized none of them would have thought I'd come to this bluff alone. "How is it you're here?"

"You're sure you're all right?"

"Oh yes. Quite. But how did you find me?"

"Don't you remember? I spoke to you. I saw you fall."

I remembered the male voice.

He bent his head and gave me a small, embarrassed grin. "I followed you."

I had a sudden vision of Alektrion's lips pressed to mine in a kiss and grew hot from crown to toe.

"Maybe I should apologize for following you. Did I scare you? Did I cause you to fall?"

What a ridiculous feeling, all this heat. "No. I saw a falcon. I became excited. I felt the dizziness coming before I heard you."

"What does the Goddess say?"

"I don't understand the words."

"Never?"

"Not so far. My mother says I'm not to fret, that when the time is right, I will."

He looked disappointed. Well, so was I.

He became serious. "I've been wanting to see you. I knew today was holiday for you, so I waited near your house hoping you might go to your mountain pool."

"So you followed me here?"

"Yes."

He must have watched me a long time. Why hadn't he spoken sooner? And why did I feel reluctant to ask him why he hadn't?

"I used a fishing net to climb down here. It's tied to the juniper. Are you able to climb up?"

"I think so." I stood and so did he.

I tugged at the net's hemp loops.

He said, "I doubled it to make it even stronger. Put your hands and feet in at least two loops. It will easily hold us both. I'll climb just behind you, in case you start to fall."

I nodded, grabbed a handful of netting, anchored my left foot firmly into it and started climbing. The distance to the top wasn't a stretch much taller than the height of two men. Halfway up, though, I stopped and started to look down. He put his hand low on my back. "Don't look," he said. He didn't take his hand away. I hung there, oddly unwilling to move from his touch.

"Can't you go on?"

"Yes." I started climbing again and made it quickly to the top with Alektrion right behind me. We sat side by side, looking at the sea— and in a suddenly awkward silence. I remembered my sidebag. "Are you hungry? I have some fruit and hard bread."

"Fine."

I retrieved the bag and sat again next to him, just not so close. He took the bread, broke off a piece and bit into it. My gaze went to his tunic, to where his male organ would be. I yanked my attention back to his chest, but my stubborn mind recalled the demonstration by the hetaira and hetairon. I was alone with Alektrion. He had followed me. Could he possibly care for me as something other than a peculiar little girl? I knew what Meidra would do. I wondered what Alektrion might do next.

"Are you angry that I followed you?"

"No. But why did you?"

"You're not like other girls. You're especially not like other Keftian girls."

He'd pressed a sore spot. "Yes I am."

"No you aren't. You talk to me. Even though I'm a 'breed.'"

He frowned when he said, "breed." So he, too, had a sore spot. "Well." I thought a moment. "You're not like other boys."

He laughed. The sound of it made the hair raise on my skin with pleasure.

"And when I said you didn't make the pool, you got really mad. You're proud of the pool, aren't you? Of making it. Come on. Admit it!"

"I like my pool."

He grinned. "Very un-Keftian, that pride."

He wasn't going to get away with teasing me this way. I thought of something sharp to reply, but he stopped me. "Why did you come out here?"

"I like to watch the gulls."

He'd finished the bread. I offered him the bag again, and this time he picked a pear. I took some dried figs.

"I don't know any other girls that spend time watching gulls."

I liked the sound of how he said it. He thought me special, and to him it was in a good way.

"You told me you intended to sign on as a ship's cook. Will you still? When would you do it?"

He started talking about how difficult it sometimes was on Kalliste to be half-Keftian, half-Achean. He talked lightly, sometimes laughed, but underneath I felt bitterness. He was eager to get away from the island. The thought of his leaving ... just thinking it made me unhappy.

He asked about my family, and I told him about father's work, how important it was to Keftiu, and how mother was a seer. To my amazement, I suddenly said, "They plan to send me to Keftiu. To study." I didn't mention the Bull Academy or their plans for me to be a priestess. It would be too much like bragging to this boy who would lead a very different life.

He straightened and leaned back on his palms. "What a great adventure! What wonders there must be there, at the Mother's heart."

"But I don't want to leave Kalliste."

"Don't you want to see what else there is in the world?"

"I like to read about it, or hear stories—my father tells wonderful ones—but that's good enough."

"Well, I want to travel as far as I can."

I told him one of my father's stories about Kyprus and Byblos and, while talking, decided Alektrion showed no signs of feeling for me the kind of strange undertow I felt pulling me to him.

The afternoon grew late. If we didn't leave soon we'd both miss prayers. What an agony I was in! I simply could not miss prayers, but I didn't want to leave him.

He settled the matter. He handed me my bag and stood up. "It's time to go back."

I moved to put the bag across my shoulder, and he stepped close and helped me. And then he took my hand. I looked up into his remarkable eyes, my heart racing. We were in a world just our own. No one else. His hand tightened on mine. I had never looked at anyone this way before. I thought I saw my confused feelings reflected in his gaze.

"Don't ever change," he said softly.

He let go of my hand and waited for me to start walking. For the first few steps, my legs felt heavy as anchors. "Are you afraid about your initiation?"

"No." But, in truth, all of us were. What had me aching at this moment, though, was the sense that something that should have happened had not.

At the outskirts of town we fell silent. A good silence, like that between close friends. The road where we had to part came all too soon, and he grinned and said, "Don't go to dangerous places alone anymore."

The thought of him kissing me rose in my mind again. With every morsel of my being, I wanted that kiss. Instead, he turned and ran down his lane.

For days I floated, with exquisite joy at some times and painful grief at others. He hadn't kissed me, but something almost as special had happened. School, classes, housework, lyre practice, gymnasium. Everything I did was happy. If only he had kissed me.

One of Xenia's final lessons was to tell us that, if we took a lover, we should drink an extract from the giant fennel to guard against new life, especially before we took husbands. I certainly wouldn't need Xenia's fennel potion any time soon. Even if I could master this shyness about my ability to perform, I knew I would have no man but Alektrion, and he'd made it very clear he thought of me as a girl, not a woman to kiss.

On our last day, Xenia told us that the final ceremony was a testing. It involved pain. A clamoring of questions: "A testing for what?" "What kind of pain?"

"I've told you all I can."

Fear flamed again. If the initiation included a testing by the Goddess, could I keep silent? Would my spying with Alektrion be found out? I began to suffer panics, at odd times breaking into sweat and feeling dizzy. Despite my sufferings, the earth stayed on its course and winter turned to spring."

The corn poppies, anemones, and crown daisies that announce the change of season appeared early, and on the first day of Belamnos, mother and Heebe were to walk me to the Temple to begin seclusion.

"A good day to begin your journey," Heebe said when she awakened me.

I was at the street door when father rushed down the stairs, grabbed and hugged me. "Did you think I'd let you go without a good-bye?" He held me at arms length. "You leave me a girl and will come back a woman." His deep voice seemed oddly gruff. "I will always be proud of you. Wherever you are, my daughter, on Kalliste or Keftiu, wherever your path goes, you have my love."

Most initiates went to the women's house in their district, but because of their high status, Snake and Butterfly clan families could choose to send their daughters to the Temple. Naturally, mother had chosen the Temple for me, even though it meant I'd not be with Meidra. At the west entry, mother laid her hand on my shoulder. "You mustn't be afraid. You'll do fine." She squeezed my hand and held on just a bit too long to be reassuring.

Several priestesses waited. Heebe handed me a basket stuffed with things I'd need, and one of the priestesses led me through the Temple gate. For the first time in my life, my feet touched sacred grounds.

I wasn't at all as confident of my bravery as my mother, but I was jaw-clinchingly determined, no matter what, not to cry. Or tell.

∾ ∾ ∾ ∾

I awakened to seamless, silent, unfamiliar darkness. Panic. A feeling of being lost. My heartbeats stumbling.

Then I remembered.

During four days of prayers and cleansing rituals, I'd slept each night deep in the Temple, where religious rites were performed and the dedicated lived and worked. I listened to the soft breathing of the other girls. Today we reached the end of childhood. Within hours, I'd be made to suffer—to remind me that the Goddess suffers on Her journey to find the God and that She suffers when She gives birth, and that when I bore children I'd share in Her suffering. And a very real possibility existed that this child of the Goddess was going to be revealed at last as dangerous, disobedient, and rebellious.

The walls pressed in on me. I took a deep breath. My father and mother expected so much. Why, oh why, had I ever gotten myself into this box of lying? I would never be sorry for meeting Alektrion. Never. But why had we gone to that horrible sacrifice? I thought of Meidra. I missed her terribly. On the second day of Belamnos, priests had bled the sacred bulls; and to insure a rich harvest, priestesses had mixed the energizing bull blood with wine and gone to the fields and anointed the ground. Today was the fifth of the seven days. To insure my fertility, I would soon drink wine mixed with more blood from those same sacred bulls.

And like the Maiden, I would suffer.

Sweat rose on my palms. I rubbed them on my nightshirt. Whatever was done to me, I'd be brave. *I'll be a good servant, Dear Mother. But I just can't tell anyone about the boy. I've kept the secret too long to tell. Please don't make me.*

Did She hear me? Did She understand? Except for my fear, did I care whether She listened to me anymore?

A shimmering sound of wake-up bells reached into the room. Attendants followed. Novices for the priestesshood brought bathing tubs and hot water. If mother had her way, someday I'd do similar duty.

Never! Never! I could never be cooped up in such a place.

The initiatress told us to dress. I knew one of the twenty other girls—Klemna. She waved, smiled, and called, "Come sit by me."

I brought my cosmetics palette and sat on a stool beside her before a large polished brass mirror. I complimented her on the clever design of the stone palette that held her make-up.

She beamed. "My grandmother's."

I understood her warmth. Today I'd wear crescent moon earrings of worked gold that had been my great-grandmother's, sent to me from Phaestos. Also two Snake Clan armlets from grandmother Ninkasi. The armlets, two sacred snakes, were my favorite pieces of jewelry. The body of each charis was of gold, its head of lapis lazuli, its eyes of a blood-red stone from a land said to lie so far away my family didn't know its name.

We helped each other apply kohl to our eyelids. The excitement of, at last, being able to make up my eyes, to rouge my cheeks and lips, to wear the jewelry of a woman, compensated at least a little bit for the dread.

Klemna laced me into my first corset. I wriggled into my blouse, then I lifted the calf-length kilt—my first ceremonial kilt. Every flounce, every stitch, every shiny brass disklet, designed and placed there by my mother, the work of years.

As I dropped it over my head, I felt tears of love welling. Yes, I thought, straightening my back as I observed my image and smoothed a turned-up edge, I am Danae's daughter, granddaughter of Ninkasi, great-granddaughter of Deianira, Snake clan. Today, no one shall be able to fault my behavior.

Barefoot and in single file, we followed the initiatress. In places where no rug lay, cool stone triggered more shivers. The priestess led us through brightly lit and tapestry-covered passages. We entered the Central Court, passed the Tree of Life—the stone pillar upon which were incised the Lady's laws—and reached the entry to the antechamber of the most holy part of the Temple: the Mother's Womb.

My palms grew damp again. I clutched the pink crystal necklace in my left hand, my gift to the Goddess. In my right, I carried my folded veil. Of transparent Coan silk, the blue veil was embroidered with gold stars. One by one the initiates in front of me disappeared into the dark rooms. The time between the disappearance of each stretched forever.

Then, I was the one standing before the entry. A priestess nodded. I stepped inside. Only faint light from the outside court touched the space. A pungent, unfamiliar scent heightened my feeling of disorientation.

Two priestesses waited, one seated behind a stone cleansing basin. The standing priestess had me open my mouth. She placed a ball of something bitter on my tongue saying, "Tuck it up tightly next to your cheek and don't swallow it, no matter what." My mouth puckered from its bite. Her sister washed and dried my feet. When she finished, the first priestess took the neatly folded veil from my hand, flung it open, and draped it over my head. Front and back, it hung to my ankles. "Stand before the door and, when the chanting stops, enter."

I moved deeper into the antechamber's shadows. The bitter taste flooded my mouth, and I again felt a rush of light-headedness. Blood pulsed in my ears like the sound of a stream.

I suddenly became terrified that I'd experience a Hearing. I'd see the white light and fall. I might vomit.

Not now! Please, Dear Mother, not now!

The priestess tapped me on the shoulder. I hadn't noticed the chanting had stopped. Knees shaking, I stumbled through the door and into the Mother's womb.

6

The room was smaller than our refectory. Three tiny floor lamps cast only enough illumination to heighten its mystery. The same smell hung heavy in the air and, without thinking, I inhaled deeply.

The presiding priestess sat stiffly against one wall in a gypsum chair, eyes closed. She bore high rank: she wore a dragonfly necklace. Robed in a kilt-covered skirt and a free-breasted blouse, her nipples glowed red with rouge. A pair of birdsphinx, symbols of the Goddess's unlimited dominion over land and air, were painted on the wall, one on either side of and facing her chair of high honor. Three other priestesses also waited.

I won't tell and I won't cry.

Opposite the seated priestess, a partition with three sections shielded what I thought was another room, for I saw flickering lamp light behind them. To the left of the partition, five stone steps led downward, ended on a small landing, then turned right and disappeared behind the partitions. I knew, just knew, I'd walk down those steps.

A priestess led me toward them.

Suddenly, as if their sound sprang from the air, I heard rattling sistrums, yet there were no musicians in the room. I gulped several times, as if I could swallow away the fear rising within me. The leftmost section of partition folded back.

Depicted on a wall painting before me stood a brightly-lit female figure. By her dress and her hair, she was clearly a maiden, initiated but never married. In her extended left hand she carried a necklace, very like the gift I'd chosen. I squeezed my necklace tightly. From a thousand stories I knew this was Monlea, the Maiden's friend. The rattling sistrums ceased. Silence. Then once again, the sistrums sounded.

The center partition opened. Behind it, the figure on the wall was the Maiden herself. She sat on the rock where She rested to gather Her strength after nearly falling into eternal sleep from the scratch of a poisoned thorn. Her hand stretched down toward blood dripping from Her injured foot.

The priestess spoke in gentle words. "You, too, bear gifts for the Goddess. The gift in your left hand and the gift of your life."

The right-most partition opened at the sistrums' insistent rattle, and on the wall I saw an initiate, dressed like me. "Like this girl, you come to honor the Mother. You will see and feel as this girl does. Go down now into the earth, the body of our life-giving Mother."

She nodded toward the steps. The gauzy cloud of scent wrapped my head. My feet felt light. I blinked several times. The flickering of the light slowed. The painted figures grew in size.

I don't remember my first step, but I reached the landing and turned right. At the bottom of four final steps, in a tiny stone chamber, stood a white-haired priestess dressed in a blood-red sari. It was the fresco above her, though, that captured my gaze. I shuddered.

An altar dominated the painting. The altar was decorated with lilies, signifying the renewal of life, and running spirals, symbolic of water from which life comes. Atop the painted altar was a painted pair of sacred horns. Streaks of life-giving blood drenched them and ran down the lilies and the spirals. They led my gaze to a small table on the floor below the fresco on which sat a pair of wooden horns darkened with great age. On the horns were smudges of red.

The priestess beckoned. I descended the final steps. She took my necklace, placed it in a basket holding other gifts. "The Mother accepts this token of your devotion." She turned to her left where a cedar chair sat against the crowded chamber's wall. The chair resembled the stools in which women give birth, with supports to lift and spread a woman's legs, but this one stood taller and had two wooden stairsteps alongside.

"Sit! Raise your veil and skirt, so I'll be able to see you."

My knees began to buckle. My feet refused to move.

I am Leesandra. The words rose from some deep well of my spirit. I forced my reluctant legs to move and, grasping one of the stool's arms for support, mounted the steps, turned, lifted my clothing, and sat.

"Raise your legs into the supports."

A small round table beside her held a lamp, a golden bowl filled with twisted strips of white linen, a golden cup, a bowl containing brown liquid, and something covered by a gold and purple cloth. She reached under the cloth and withdrew a small, crystal-bladed knife. She continued speaking but my mind emptied. I saw only the knife. Not until she put her hand over mine and squeezed did I hear her again.

"As the Mother of All suffers and sheds blood when she gives life ..." she leaned in toward me, and her knife-bearing hand disappeared behind the folds of my skirt. I felt her fingers on me, then a brief, searing pain in the most private part of my body, and I knew she must have cut me with the knife "… you will suffer and shed blood when you give life. But your joy, too, shall be great. By rending the Veil of Hymen, she has taken from you the sign of childhood."

With another stroke of the crystal-bladed knife, she cut into my foot, at exactly the spot where the Maiden bled, deep enough that blood welled and trickled down my skin. I clenched my teeth to keep from crying out.

The woundings hurt, but not enough to force me to release the tears that watered my vision.

I will not cry.

My vision blurred, and inside my head, all was swirling.

The priestess exchanged the knife for a linen strip, which she pressed to the private area she'd cut. She turned and smeared my blood onto the wooden horns before discarding the linen into a basket. Then she dabbed another strip into the liquid in the shallow bowl and, when she touched my private area again, it burned so sharply, I gave an uncontrollable flinch—yet managed not to cry out.

She squeezed my hand. "You may lower your legs and garments." Her voice was the gentlest cooing of a mother to her babe. "Your spirit has been brave. Your courage has been tested. You will live well as one of the Lady's People, and well you will serve Her all of your life."

She lifted the golden cup. "Drink of this cup, the fruit of the vine and the blood of the bull, so you will continue to grow straight and strong and bear children straight and strong."

She lifted the edge of my veil and raised the cup to my lips. Until now I'd drunk only very watered wine. This drink was strong. I couldn't taste the bull's blood, but I tried to imagine I did.

Again she took my hand, and we remained poised in silence. I became sharply aware again of the bitter taste of the wad in my mouth. Her eyes grew enormous. Dark pools they were, pulling me inward.

"You are one with the Mother," she said in the singing tone of blessing. A voice so sweet—the distilled essence of sea and air, flowers and light. Hot tears of release flooded my eyes and rolled down my cheeks. "Obey Her laws and keep faithfully Her rituals, for then you will be fruitful, your own children well, the People protected, and the world in balance. Go, Leesandra, daughter of Danae, with the Mother's blessing."

She stepped to my side and, supporting me under one arm, helped me to my feet and down the two short steps removing me at last from the grip of the chair. She hugged me, then aimed me toward the stone stairs.

I felt a strange joy so profound, so intense, that the pain of walking streamed way from my body, and I floated up the steps, incandescent happiness my wings. In the main chamber, two priestesses lifted my veil. The older said, "You are reborn as Maiden, giver of life. Heed your duties and obey the Law, for it's the work of the People to keep the world in harmony."

They refolded the veil, placed it over my arm, and stood me before the seated priestess. They took the position of reverence, and I followed their example. I could have stood there for days, transfixed with wonder, and beauty, and the peace of the Mother's presence. The kind Lady had forgiven me for keeping my spying secret. And as sure as I had ever been of anything, I knew I would always obey the Law and I would love Her with all of my heart for all of my life.

∾ ∾ ∾ ∾

At the end of Belamnos, mother and Heebe fetched me home. They called me Maiden Leesandra. I was so happy I refused to let myself think there was any possibility they would ever send me away from Kalliste.

Within the week, the winter weather broke, and the Temple sent word that sea-season could begin. I attended school and sometimes gymnasium, but I always looked for Alektrion on the dock or when I'd go to my pool. If I were ever to take a lover—a long time away, of course—but if I were to take a lover, I still could think only of Alektrion, half-breed or not. I reminded myself sometimes that he was unsuitable. But still I looked for him.

When I thought about the slave boy's death now, instead of anger for permitting it, I burned to understand why. All of my life I'd been told the Mysteries were great and Wisdom came only with age. I decided it was true, as Heebe often said, that I was still too young to understand all the "whys." I let my heart accept the peace the Goddess had returned to me. What she required of me was patience. Someday I would understand.

Early one morning, our youngest serving girl appeared in my doorway. "Your father asks to see you," she announced. "He's on the roof garden."

I found him stepping out of the cookroom-sized cage that held his birds, a flock of singers called canaries, yellow on their bellies and greenish-yellow on their backs. Their true home, he'd once told me, lay far to the south even of the fabled Agyptos. A Nubian trader had given two pair to my father's mother when he was five and she was the ambassador to Byblos. She had bred them, and now so did my father.

He fastened the door and waved me to join him. From a basket he selected several barley cakes and handed some to me. "I've received good news," he said, checking the sky. We tore the cakes into bite-sized pieces and lined them up in a row on top of the terrace wall. "Tomorrow a ship brings an old acquaintance. Dolmanthes of Messenia. He's highly placed at the Achean court of Pylos, and he's on his way there after spending a year at the court of Thutmoses."

The man was Achean. I stiffened at the thought.

Ten rooks from a nearby roof descended like a whirring black cloud and began bolting down the bread.

"He'll bring fresh news. And most importantly, I can probe him about his king, Atistaeus."

My heart gave a little shudder. "I know that name. The dockworkers call him the Red King. They say he wears a giant's sheepskin cape smeared with blood of his enemies. Do you think he would really do such a horrid thing?"

My father's lips twisted, as if he'd tasted soured wine. "It wouldn't surprise me. Atistaeus is a dangerous man."

Just like an Achean, I thought. *There is probably no evil thing they don't do.*

"I've heard rumors of piracy among the northern islands for months. The Red King's name always comes up. As you're no longer a child, I want you to go to the ship with me as part of the greeting delegation. While his ship resupplies, Dolmanthes will lodge with us."

Distracted by watching the birds, I failed to hide my displeasure.

"What's the meaning of those pursed lips?"

I'd heard about the ship. It carried slaves for the slave market on Delos. And I cringed at the thought that we'd have this Achean as a sleeping guest.

My father stepped back and folded his arms. His scar had gone distressingly pale. "I've about lost all patience with you. You should be eager to meet Dolmanthes. A brilliant man. A shrewd one. What is the source of this dislike for foreigners?"

"I've watched the outlanders. They don't honor the Laws. And they're so ... so aggressive. Especially the Poseidonists. I know for your work you must endure them, but I can't see why I need to."

"By the Goddess, Leesandra. You're in no position to judge. Your contact with outlanders has been nothing but superficial."

The rooks, having snapped up the last barley-cake morsel, flashed with a fanning of dark wings into the air and headed toward the harbor.

My father leaned towards me and skewered me with hot eyes. "I want you to listen carefully. The world is large, and there are as many ways of living as there are numbers of birds in the sky. You criticize the followers of Poseidon as aggressive. Compared to us, you're right. But aggressiveness isn't all bad, just as I hope you'll learn that to be conciliatory isn't always good. Their assertiveness produces great adventurers. Men able to prevail in spite of great adversity." He stepped back and crossed his arms again. "We Keftians could learn a lesson or two in assertiveness."

I stared at him open-mouthed. I remembered the disapproval in a teacher's voice, so many years ago, when she'd spoken about how *different* my father was. My gaze flashed to his scar. A scar is a flaw, something that would grieve most Keftians, but my father was actually proud of his.

He continued speaking about his friend, Dolmanthes, and the terrible realization worked through me that my father was more different than I'd ever suspected. He had qualities hidden, not only from me, but perhaps from mother, too. Being different, thinking different, these were dangerous things. I wrapped my arms around myself to ward off a chill. Harmony does not flow from dissonance.

"You'll begin formal training to serve the Lady when you leave for Knossos. But I want you to begin now by promising me you'll keep an open mind when you meet new people."

Anger struck fire in my chest. *They are still determined to exile me!*

The next afternoon he forestalled any excuse I might offer to escape, and so I went with him to meet the man from Pylos—a burly, simply dressed person with a gray-streaked reddish beard and a hearty laugh. Dolmanthes stayed with us a month, and within the first day, I learned he worshipped Poseidon. I wanted to dislike him. I needed to dislike him. But he told the most spellbinding tales of curious creatures and lands whose people did such strange things. Agyptos, Mittani, Hattusis. When he confirmed that his king did indeed have a blood-soaked cloak, I shivered with fascinated horror.

When Dolmanthes left, I embraced him and told him I'd never forget him. Yet, as he boarded his ship, I felt somehow a traitor. My emotions seemed continually in conflict and utterly beyond my control. I loathed the Acheans and their false god, yet Dolmanthes had won my heart.

That same day, while father and Sinon and I waited on the quay for Dolmanthes's ship to sail, I saw three of Alektrion's companions throwing stinky fish guts to a flock of raucous black-headed gulls. I excused myself and ran toward the boys. I quickly realized I shouldn't let them see me running as if I were an eager child, so I slowed to a dignified walk.

"Have you seen Alektrion, Meela's son?" I asked.

"Why do you want to know?" said the tallest boy, grinning.

I felt myself warming, feared they could sense my embarrassment. But I hadn't seen Alektrion in so very long. I pressed on. "He said he would show me a place where I can see a pair of falcons."

"Well, he's gone," said the tall boy.

A boy with a gentle face who looked too well fed said kindly, "He left four days ago. On the warship *Sea Eagle*. He's their cook's helper."

I could scarcely believe the boy's words. Alektrion had left, and he had not even found me to say good-bye!

"My thanks," I stammered. I turned and walked back to my father and Sinon, my heart bitterly empty.

I lived alone now with my secret, something for which I should have been glad. But I remembered the exuberant look in his gold-flecked eyes. Alektrion and I would never again talk together to a spider.

Tears welled, spilled onto my cheeks. I turned aside, brushed hard at them to stop their coming.

~ ~ Author's Note ~ ~

What little is known about Atistaeus of Pylos comes to us from brief mention in the works of three writers from much later periods: Homer (~ 850 BC), Hesiod (~ 750 BC), and Thucydides (401 BC). Though each author gives a different reason for the killing, all agree that this Poseidonist king killed the snake oracle of the Mother Goddess at Delphi, the only known example of the killing of a delphic oracle.

After the murder of the oracle, Atistaeus returned to Pylos only to find that his Goddess-worshipping brother had assumed their father's throne. After a struggle for power, Atistaeus prevailed and, having killed his brother, wiped his brother's blood onto a sheepskin cloak— the first blood of many fallen enemies that would stain the cloak and win for Atistaeus the epithet, "The Red King."

Through conquest and alliance, Atistaeus enlarged his kingdom. His major resistance came from the followers of the Mother Goddess, whom he ruthlessly subjugated: destroying their temples, killing their holy ones, and forbidding their ancient practices. Once his hold on the Peloponnesus was secure, Atistaeus looked with greed to the islands of the Mediterranean.

JRE

7

I belong at sea.

Alektrion sat on *Sea Eagle's* starboard side, beneath the overhang of the raised aft deck, elbows propped on his knees. In front of him on the main deck, forty tanned backs strained as the rowers pulled to the piper's slow cadence. Thirty marines packed the deck's mid-section, their shoulders still wet from a passing summer squall that now rushed east-northeast toward Kalliste.

Alektrion sucked in warm damp air, licked his lips, and smiled at the taste of salt. Merit, not birth, counted in this world, at least in most things. He was non-Keftian and could never attain high rank, let alone a captaincy, but if he learned well, had good luck on drawing rich booty assignments, and, during winters ashore, saved like a wood mouse storing seeds for winter, nothing would stop him from someday owning his own merchant vessel. He must serve midday meal soon, and as he planned to be the best cook's helper *Sea Eagle* had ever had, he would make sure the warriors had no complaints.

Serena, the ship's priestess, stepped from her small cabin on the raised foredeck. With a feminine movement that put a kick in his pulse, she threw a sheepskin wrap over her yellow woolen robe, then circled around toward the prow and disappeared from view as she settled down behind the cabin. She was perhaps thirty and was as good as any sailor at repairing lines. For exercise she regularly took a turn rowing in place of one of the young recruits. His erotic dreams of her were to be expected. There wasn't likely a man aboard who didn't think about coupling with Serena.

A gust from the south licked his skin, and he shivered. Since mid-morning prayers, they'd been rowing into this strong, southern wind. Seven weeks at sea and, so far, the only exciting thing that had happened was one evening, long after dark, when they nearly ran onto the rocks putting *Sea Eagle* into shore. Rumors ran wild about brigandry near Khithera, an island that lay in their patrolling sector, but so far *Sea Eagle* had encountered nothing unusual, let alone exciting.

His body rocked with each thrust and ebb of the rowers' strokes, and his thoughts returned to the ship that would someday be his. The snapping of the two pennants atop the mast intruded. The topmost pennant—a field of white with the butterfly-winged symbol of rebirth sprouting from golden horns—identified *Sea Eagle* as Keftian navy. The lower pennant—a depiction of the Goddess standing on the crater rim of Kalliste—identified the ship's home port. His ship's pennant would be a golden spider.

He remembered teaching Leesandra to talk to a spider. Perhaps some day he would take her sailing on his ship. If she remembered him. And if she would still talk to him. He was a "breed," and, as she got older, she'd probably become like all the other Keftian women—pleasant, but unwilling to get too close. Her family, for certain, would reject him. That's why he hadn't said good-bye. Why complicate her life? Now he thought himself a fool. He would always regret not seeing her one last time. She was different. She hadn't shunned him.

Thumping steps on the overhead deck broke his thoughts: Grimaldius, pacing like a caged fox in front of his cabin. In addition to the crack of the pennants and the captain's pacing, other sounds had grown familiar: the creaking of the deck, the moan of forty oars turning in their hemp locks, and when *Sea Eagle* had sail up and the rowers were at ease, the sound of men's voices, rough and irreverent.

Laius, seated in the line of port rowers, caught Alektrion's attention. He grinned and mouthed the words, "I'm starving."

"You'll live," Alektrion mouthed back.

Laius and four other Keftian youths from Kalliste had boarded *Sea Eagle* with Alektrion. All of them were beginning their obligatory two years of service. Weeks had passed before the other four dropped the haughtiness so many Keftians carried, which at sea, and among men from many nations, became irrelevant. Or nearly so. But from the beginning, Laius lacked it. Nor had Laius's warmth cooled when Alektrion subtly, but defiantly, made his own half-breed status clear.

The pacing stopped. "Ship oars!" Grimaldius barked. Dripping oars rotated skyward and downward. Alektrion felt the familiar letdown as *Sea Eagle* lost way. He lifted the hatch cover to the aft hold, dropped inside the cramped space, grabbed one of the food baskets and shoved it out the hatch.

The ship's cook appeared above him—Menapthus by name, but affectionately dubbed "Hot Sauce" because he always overspiced the food. The marine's dark hair was shot with gray, but his muscles were as hard as Alektrion's. "I put grapes into that square hamper," Hot Sauce said, pointing.

The square hamper joined the other basket.

They passed forward food prepared while still on shore: red snapper wrapped in seaweed, olives, goat cheese, bread-sticks, raisins.

Alektrion dropped back into the hold. From the man-sized storage pithos lashed to the central beam, he filled two amphorae with wine-laced water.

By the time he resurfaced and he and Hot Sauce began to pour into the cup each man kept ready, their second in command, the navigator-steersman, was riddling. "What expands as fast as a mushroom and gives birth to ten where there was only one?" he called out.

Between bites of food the men hazarded guesses:

"A widow's desire for a good fuck."

"A slaver's claims for the beauty of his women's privates."

Much laughter. The piper, the steersman's partner in the riddling game, sang out the answer. "Prian's imagination when he's counting conquests."

More and louder laughter. Prian, a Lydian mercenary and one of the most respected marines, was known for tall tales when it came to women.

"What grows bigger every day but yields its owner less and less?"

"Klemenair's pride," said two men at once.

The steersman popped an olive in his mouth and shook his head. More guesses.

Finally the piper stopped the guessing. "All wrong you are. It's Laius's weakness for playing skull and bones."

The laughter was accompanied by the stomping of boot-shod feet. The men already thought Laius a clever-tongued clown, and now he was developing a reputation for gambling—and losing.

"What rises in bed every morning but has never yet been inside the house?" the steersman called out.

Serena came to sit on the stern side of her cabin to eat with them and listen. Finally the piper sang out: "Alek's cock."

Even louder laughter.

Alektrion felt himself warming. Somehow everyone had figured out he'd never had a lover; was, in fact, the only unproven on the ship.

"What's that?" Hot Sauce called out. He pointed south.

Alektrion's gaze followed the line of the cook's finger and settled on a twisting curl of smoke. He tensed. Smoke rising from the sea meant only one thing: a ship on fire.

Pirates? His pulse accelerated. Maybe at last he'd see some action from these warriors whom he'd begun to think had no purpose other than to drink, eat, joke, and practice fighting maneuvers—in that order of importance. From behind, Grimaldius's gravelly voice boomed, "Secure the deck. Distribute arms." Once again the oars came out, and soon *Sea Eagle* raced south. From the main hold, marines fetched and distributed helmets, shields, lances, swords. Alektrion helped Hot Sauce stow what food hadn't been tossed overboard.

He thought of his own sword, his father's parting gift, a superb blade that rested in his stash in the main hold. The night before he'd come aboard, his father had embraced him and said, "I pray you never need it." His voice was gruff and choked. "That you use it during a long life for nothing more than a wall decoration. But if fate decrees otherwise, wield it only in defense." Alektrion had shown the sword privately to Laius, who'd ribbed, "You're a sixteen-year old cook's helper. What did your father think you'd be doing with that? Slicing bread?"

The rising smoke billowed from a large merchant vessel. Flames ate at her bow and stern. Hot Sauce went forward. Alektrion stood and moved to the cook's assigned resting post on the port side. Here he could see better. The trader lay dangerously low.

"Increase!" the captain's voice bellowed. "Two-fold."

The piper's tune shifted. The rowers' backs knotted. Veins on their arms bulged. The moaning of the oar locks shifted to a leathery shriek, and he heard the sucking of the oar tips into and out of the water, the boom of waves against the hull, and the sea hissing as the warship cut through it.

Grimaldius snapped out orders that would bring them alongside and downwind. Alektrion smelled smoke, and then a sweet-sick smell. He stood on tiptoe and craned over the rail looking for signs of life.

"Ship port oars!"

Even in this choppy sea, the captain's orders maneuvered *Sea Eagle* so she glided neatly, with the navigator-steersman working the steering oar hard, on a course parallel to the merchant ship. The wind brought the sound of a wailing shriek. Shivers of horror washed over his shoulders. "Kokor's breath!" he whispered. The shriek seemed neither animal nor human. Perhaps demon children had taken possession of the ship. Maybe the demon Kokor himself.

Sea Eagle drew alongside. The men struggled with grappling hooks, poles, and lines to keep the two tossing ships together yet prevent them from colliding. The merchant vessel stood tall relative to the warship. Boarding was dangerous. From atop *Sea Eagle's* aft deck, Grimaldius issued more orders. Ten men scrambled onto the taller vessel. Alektrion ached to climb up next to the captain, the better to see.

The mercenary Prian shouted, "There's a survivor. Badly wounded."

Alektrion wondered if the eerie keening could be made by a wounded man—it seemed unlikely such sounds could be human.

Footsteps thumped overhead. The captain's legs appeared on the short stairs. Skipping the steps, Grimaldius leaped onto the main deck, strode up the center, then swung across on a line to the trader.

I have to see! Alektrion scrambled up onto the aft deck and then onto the top of the deckhouse.

An image burned into his mind, its outlines, colors, and textures unerasable. Five bodies lay on the merchant vessel's deck—five women in colorful Keftian dresses. Blood covered their faces and chests. Their throats gaped, slit from side to side.

The hair on his skin rose. Stomach juices burned their way up the back of his throat. Gagging, he swallowed repeatedly.

The women lay in dark red pools of blood, their skirts pushed up their thighs. Alektrion gulped in breaths through his mouth. Fists clenched, he fought to keep his thoughts clear. What purpose—what honor—could there possibly be in killing women?

Other bloodied bodies lay strewn on the ship's deck, most dressed in the simple loincloths of rowers. Amazement stunned him. The crew hadn't been taken captive. Like animals of no worth, they'd been slaughtered. And they would have been unarmed. Madness!

Because of the recent increase in piracy, a few merchants had hired mercenaries for defenses, but most owners, like this one, still relied on the Keftian navy. Sold into slavery, the dead would at least have brought a profit.

His stomach, which had taken weeks to settle into *Sea Eagle's* motion, turned over from the horrid, sweet-sick smell and the sight of gruesome death. The unholy screaming trembled on, clawed its way into his brain.

He realized he was shaking. *Take hold of yourself!*

A cracking sound split the air. On the merchant vessel's deck, a young boy of about eleven, sopping wet and dressed in the kilt of a city child, crouched on all fours in a pool of water at the feet of one of the marines. Strewn around him were fragments of a giant pithos. The marine held a mallet, doubtless used to bash the container open. The boy had hidden, or someone had hidden him, in the huge clay storage pot.

Another shriek raked the air. Prian and three marines circled a well-dressed man in a knee-length tunic who lay on his back on the foredeck. The trembling scream came from the man's mouth. His hands clutched at his bloodied stomach.

Grimaldius reached the man, knelt, leaned over him. He clutched the man's hands, pulled them away from the belly wound, then let them go. He rose, looked at Prian, and gave a curt nod.

Prian, who stood with sword in hand, stepped to the screaming man, placed the tip of his sword slightly below the ribs, then made a mighty diagonal thrust upward into the heart. The agonized warbling ceased.

Alektrion ran to the starboard side, where no one would likely see, and threw up so thoroughly his guts felt like they were turning inside out. When he stopped shaking, curiosity drove him back. Most of the marines had reboarded *Sea Eagle*. On the merchant vessel, Serena, with Grimaldius at her side, moved quickly from one dead body to the next. She touched each over the heart to offer them good journey and anointed with honey the lips of those clearly dressed as Keftians.

She'd not yet finished when the merchant ship pitched forward. Serena fell to her knees. Grimaldius grabbed her around the waist, carried her like a sack of barley to the gunwale amidships, and stood her on it. They walked on one taut boarding line and pulled hand-over-hand on another, hurrying back onto *Sea Eagle*.

The rowers scrambled to free the lines. Alektrion rushed down from the cabin roof to his post. The captain stood at the bow, hands on hips, and shouted orders that took them a safe distance from the sinking ship.

Alektrion squatted, wrapped his arms around his legs to stop quivers that kept sweeping through him. At the bow, Grimaldius and Kampenthes, the navigator and ship's second officer, hovered around the confused, frightened boy, now wrapped in Serena's comforting cloak.

Alektrion's mind raced. Rumors blowing across the islands said these new pirates weren't rogues but Achean soldiers. But surely no Achean warrior would kill women and non-combatants. For years on Alyris's docks he'd listened to the exploits of Achean marines with pride for his ancestry. Tales of honorable combat. There'd been no combat here, only senseless slaughter.

Moments later Grimaldius stood and ordered *Sea Eagle* to turn north.

Kampenthes took charge and directed the oarsmen. The captain bent to the boy again. *Sea Eagle* came round, and the wind blew at their backs. Kampenthes directed the raising of the sail, which snapped once as the sea's breath filled it. The mast and central beam groaned, the warship ran with the wind, and the rowers put their backs into rowing.

Alektrion stared at the men gathered around the boy, but more powerful images gripped his mind. Dead women, their skirts raised and their blood congealing around them. Huge, gaping throats. In his head echoed the inhuman keening of the gut-wounded man.

What was the captain learning from the boy? Hot Sauce loitered on the edges of the circle. In addition to the captain and priestess, three men always had the run of a ship, even during an alert: the navigator, the piper, and the cook with his water jug.

Marines secured the bulwarks that protected the oarsmen during battle. Grimaldius must expect the worst. Word filtered back that the trader had carried pottery. No notable booty. Someone passed one of the rectangular shields to him. It felt good to have his fist wrapped around its grip—but he couldn't imagine himself actually using it.

Hot Sauce, shield and sword in hand, worked his way sternward through the mass of marines, pausing to answer questions. When he reached Alektrion, he laid his gear down and squatted. "The boy says his father saved him. Grabbed him up and shoved him in the pithos."

"Who did this?"

"The boy speaks Lycian, Prian's mother tongue. He says he couldn't understand their speech, but once they gave a shout together and one of the words shouted was 'Pylos.' That's the name of the town where he and his father were headed."

Alektrion repeated with heat, "But who did this?"

"Atistaeus rules Pylos. Those two names keep bobbing up all over the Great Sea. These stinking seal dung are either Pylian freebooters or the Red King himself is behind the raiding. We're probably going to get a chance pretty quickly to find out."

"Why? How?"

"The merchant vessel had a sister ship. She had time to turn and run. Grimaldius thinks two raiders worked together to strip this ship and then went after the second trader. We're going after all three."

"Two raiders?"

"That's what the boy says."

Would *Sea Eagle* dare challenge two ships at once? Alektrion started to ask, but caught himself before he implied insult. Hot Sauce puckered his lips, twitched them to catch saliva, and spit with practiced skill over the port rail. "We'll teach 'em a lesson they can take home to Pylos."

They all fell into silence. The muscles of Alektrion's shoulders bunched painfully. The marines' tension showed in their straight backs and intent study of the horizon. Suddenly, Alektrion spotted the flash of white from sails, and the excited lookout shouted, "On the port, a quarter off the bow."

The wind and rowers swept them ever closer to the enemy. One raider, the smaller one, stood upwind of the two other ships. At a greater distance, now off *Sea Eagle's* starboard bow, the second, larger pirate ship rode alongside the trader. Even at this distance, Alektrion could see the pirates using lines and slings to transfer baskets and pithoi to their ship.

Hot Sauce let loose another bolt of spit. "Maybe we're still in time to save the crew. And passengers, if she has 'em."

Altogether, how many marines did the raiders have? Alektrion was still too far away to count. *Sea Eagle* carried thirty, a mix of Keftians and mercenaries. Her forty rowers were battle proven, but their fighting experience was minimal. And besides, they were rowers. They were non-combatants.

"Hard to port," Grimaldius yelled.

Sea Eagle aimed for the smaller, closer vessel. "Shouldn't we attack the larger ship?" Alektrion blurted.

Hot Sauce ignored him.

The smaller raider lay dead in the water broadside to *Sea Eagle*, her sail up but slack. Men swarmed over her deck. Her sail began dropping even as Grimaldius called out, "Prepare to lower sail."

"Watch closely, boy," Hot Sauce said tightly. "We're gonna try and catch her 'afore she can get any speed comin' at us. First she's gotta turn. And then they'll be rowing into the wind. With a little luck, at the speed we've got now, Grimaldius'll get us lined up, drop sail quick, and we'll shear her port oars off as we run past."

"But ... but what about the people on the trader?"

"Use your eyes boy! The surf scum see us comin'. Can't you see they're already hauling in line? They'll come to aid their little sister, but first they gotta run off with the wind and then turn and row back. Grimaldius will have us finish off this little water bug before the bigger one can get back here."

Neither privateer showed a pennant; whoever they were, they weren't shouting for all the world to know. The smaller raider was roughly *Sea Eagle's* size. Pulling hard, her port rowers had brought her to a quarter off the wind, but she still lumbered in the rough sea. Men crammed her main deck, dressed in battle gear.

Alektrion's heart was pounding wildly in his chest. Maybe it would explode right out of him. *Sea Eagle* bore down so fast, he feared they'd crash into the pirate's bow. He clenched the rail in front of him, braced.

"Drop sail," Grimaldius shouted. "Ship port oars. Steersman, hard to starboard."

The sail was down and secured even as the port oarsmen groaned, the oarlocks moaned, and *Sea Eagle* slowed forward thrust and turned parallel with the pirate vessel's port side.

No more than four ship-lengths separated them now. He could see details. Shields and boar-tusk helmets identified the crew as soldiers, not pirates.

Soldiers!

The rogue captain realized his danger. His roar, "Ship port oars," carried even to Alektrion.

Their helmet plumes showed blue in the center, surrounded by gold. The pattern meant nothing to him, but *Sea Eagle's* experienced marines would recognize it. What was certain was that they were mainlanders. And as much as he didn't want to believe it, their double circle shields indicated they were Achean.

Hot Sauce crouched behind his shield. Alektrion followed his example. In a hail of whirring lances and a screeching, cracking, and splintering of wood that made Alektrion's every nerve jump, *Sea Eagle* glided past the rogue vessel, shearing off her bank of port oars. A shaft of splintered wood arrowed past his left side.

Two ship-lengths beyond the pirate vessel, Grimaldius shouted, "Circle to port." The starboard rowers bent to it.

Hot Sauce said matter-of-factly, "Looks like some piece of seal shit made a lucky hit on The Squid."

Alektrion glanced to the post of the long-armed marine. Blood oozed from the man's shoulder onto his stomach. Serena knelt beside him. With a cloth from her basket of potions she swabbed at the blood. Alektrion scanned the rest of the crew. So far only The Squid. Soon there would be other wounds. Maybe some much worse.

"The sea's calmer now," Hot Sauce said. "We can board her." He added, his voice gruffly commanding, "You stay here, boy, and you won't get hurt." He smiled, flashing the gold replacements of his two front teeth. "A cook's helper is no good to me hurt."

Hot Sauce stood, and Alektrion followed the sound of the cook's steps ascending to the deck above. He counted the number of armed men aboard the pirate ship: thirty-five that he could see.

Grimaldius roared, "Make this quick, men. The other demon is already coming around." He commanded them to raise the oars. They glided alongside. Marines from both ships put out grappling hooks.

Alektrion clutched his shield's grip. Squatting here on the aft deck, he was defenseless. He longed to have his sword in his hand, even though he hadn't the simplest knowledge of how to use it.

A swell lifted *Sea Eagle*. Her crew now had the advantage of elevation. Lances flashed between the ships. Two thudded against Alektrion's shield and clattered to the deck. Cries of pain rang out. A marine fell back from the railing, his cut thigh spurting blood.

The sea rolled. *Sea Eagle* dropped, but the enemy refused the chance to board. They would force the Keftians to make the first move; time was on their side. Reinforcements were on the way.

Again the sea lifted *Sea Eagle*. "Attack," Grimaldius shouted.

Leaping and swinging from lines, half of *Sea Eagle's* marines thundered onto the pirate vessel's decks, Grimaldius in the lead. The air trembled with grunting and shouting, the clang of metal upon metal. Alektrion gripped the shield so tightly it felt fused to his hand. His arms and thighs shook.

The sea lowered them again. Ten of the enemy hurtled onto *Sea Eagle's* foredeck. Prian and a handful of men, the rear guard, met the attack. Prian hacked off a man's hand, sliced through the belly section of the corselet of another. The action became a blur of flashing swords and twisting flesh. Two men Alektrion knew well fell, how seriously wounded he couldn't guess. In the main deck's packed center, combatants slashed and jabbed, twisted and lunged. An Achean, who faced the line of *Sea Eagle's* port rowers, lowered his sword and with an odd thrust, up and back, severed the arm of the Kallistan rower crouched closest on his right.

Alektrion gasped. Laius? He shot to his feet. No. The youth sat in the row in front of Laius. But Alektrion remained shaken. The mainlander had used an unusual backhand stroke, but his thrust hadn't seemed an accident. Had he purposely attacked a non-combatant?

Again, his helplessness set him reeling. His mind flashed a vision of the slaughtered women. When this battle was over, and if the Keftians lost, who would be left?

Still clutching the shield, he stood and scanned the Achean ship. Grimaldius and a score of men continued to thrust and parry, hack and slash. *Sea Eagle's* crew was winning. Alektrion noticed for the first time, high on the shoulder of each of the Achean ship's rowers, the mark of the slave.

The slave rowers watched impassively as, one by one, the mainlanders fell to *Sea Eagle's* marines. Suddenly, Grimaldius pointed in the direction behind Alektrion and bellowed, "Regroup. Regroup."

Alektrion spun around. The larger Achean vessel was bearing down hard. She carried at least forty armed men.

She came up at grappling speed on *Sea Eagle's* exposed starboard side. His cowhide shield suddenly seemed as useless as a leaf. Yes, he was a non-combatant. Yes, he was unarmed. By the rules of war, he wouldn't be killed. But the cries of pain, the grunts of anger, and the smell of blood and urine mixed in sea air blurred his mind.

Grimaldius waved frantically, yelled for the men remaining on the raider to return to defend *Sea Eagle.*

Alektrion swung his gaze back to the deck in front of him. Prian raised his sword hilt and bashed a man across the face. The man shrieked, fell into Prian's arms. Prian dropped the man to the deck, then ran to the starboard railing, shouting for *Sea Eagle's* men to regroup there. Those who could disengage tried to obey. Others formed a shaky line, protecting their comrades' backs.

The bigger vessel pulled alongside *Sea Eagle*. Out came the grappling hooks. One warrior, a huge man, poised along the rail, straining in eagerness to charge onto *Sea Eagle's* deck.

This time the sea favored the mainlanders, and as a swell lifted their vessel, the warriors swung or leapt downward and crashed into the men lining *Sea Eagle's* starboard rail. The giant landed with sure footing next to Prian, bellowed a thunderous roar, and with one lightning stroke, ran Prian through.

Even as Prian sank to the deck, the giant turned to the line of rowers crouched behind their shields and, before Alektrion could draw a breath, the brute grabbed first one rower and then another by the hair and, like a butcher slaughtering lambs, cut their throats.

A bolt of pure terror shot through Alektrion. By the Goddess, he had to have protection. Death was coming.

8

If he could reach the weapons cache in the main hold, Alektrion could have his pick of the surplus weapons, but writhing, scuffling bodies blocked his path to the hatch cover.

He dropped the shield and, kneeling, snatched the cover off the aft hold and dove into the darkness below. Two bulkheads lay between him and the weapons bin. He unlatched the first bulkhead cover and pulled it free. Wood scraped his back as he wriggled through the narrow passage.

The plate-sized portholes were covered for sea-going, so in near darkness, surrounded by the smell of damp clay and wet reed matting, he bumped his head, his hands, his knees on first one box or storage pithos after another. At the next bulkhead, he ran panicky fingers over the wood at the height where the cover should be. The decking above creaked. Each thump, bang, and thud sent another jolt of fear through his guts. Hurry, hurry! was all he could think.

His hands raced blindly over the bulkhead's uneven surface. He jammed his forefinger against one of the latches; searing pain shot to his wrist. He twisted the latches, then wrestled the cover open and climbed through into a black void.

Must have light! He inched at what felt a worm's pace to the starboard side of the hull, found a porthole, opened it. In rushed a damp gust and a thin shaft of gray light. To his right lay the weapons bin. But even closer was the basket holding his father's gift.

Two steps. He flung the basket open, threw his extra kilt, tunic and sandals on the deck and jerked the sword from its sheath. The din from above became even louder. He clambered up the ladder rungs to the hatch and pushed. Nothing. Of course. It was secured from above. The raiders would be keeping anyone from going below deck for extra weapons. "Fool!"

He backed down the ladder, turned and retraced his path.

From the aft hatch, immediately above his head, came sounds of rolling. When he came out, whom would he find? Who was winning? Maybe he should hide.

Am I to wait, trembling like a frightened hare? Better to die!

He thrust the sword through the belt of his kilt. Using both hands, he pulled and then shoved himself upward and out. He sat on the edge of the hole—and stared into dead eyes. In front of him, Hot Sauce lay stretched and still.

The clang of metal, the grunts, the shouts faded, and a strange quiet engulfed him, as though he'd stepped out of the world. He was some other place. The detachment seemed forever. Suddenly sounds rushed back. Then rage. So powerful it choked him. It tinged everything red. He leapt to his feet, sucked in air.

He turned, and behind him two men fought on the deck, washed reddish by his bloody mental haze. The man on top wore a mainlander's helmet. Alektrion pulled his sword, gripped it tip down and two-fisted, like a woman might hold a dagger, and plunged it into the man's spine, just below his corselet.

The man arched, screamed, collapsed.

Alektrion jammed his foot onto the man's back, as he'd seen others do, and yanked. The sword came free. Heat blazed across his skin. His ears rang. The sword, which had felt heavy, now seemed nearly weightless.

The Keftian marine, who lay on his back on the deck yelled, "Behind you!"

Alektrion whirled. A dagger sliced into his left arm. He felt the warmth of blood flowing over his skin. His own sword hand was coming round. Alektrion threw his back into his swing. Bellowing, he brought the sword up. The razor-sharp blade cut into the mainlander's exposed armpit. The man shrieked.

Again, with both fists, Alektrion grasped his sword. He swung toward the man's head. The blade hit the helmet cheek-plate, slid down, sliced into the man's neck. The warrior half twisted; his hot, spurting blood gushed onto Alektrion's chest. The man went to his knees; his blood sprayed Alektrion's thighs.

His enemy fell facedown. Over his body Alektrion glimpsed the milling, straining forms of men bound in death struggle. *Sea Eagle's* crew was doomed; the warriors still on their feet were mostly mainlanders. Many of *Sea Eagle's* unarmed oarsmen had snatched weapons from the hands of the dead or wounded and flailed awkwardly to defend themselves. One was Laius. A defiant elation surged through Alektrion.

In front of him, two men exchanged sword blows. The mainlander's back was to him, protected by a bronze-reinforced corselet, but huge ... inviting.

Honor dictated he yell and wait until the man faced him, but his body was hungry for the feeling of metal cutting flesh. He plunged the sword at the man's back.

The mainlander's corselet held; Alektrion's blade slid off. He tightened his fists on the grip. He drew the weapon back but, from behind, the weight of a bull dropped onto him.

He crashed facedown to the deck, air whooshed out of his mouth, the sword spun away. With sick terror he imagined his back, bare and exposed. He imagined a sword in his attacker's hand. Again rage exploded inside him. Grunting, he lurched to his knees, twisted left, and grappled his attacker's weapon arm.

They rolled face to face, the enemy above him, a double-edged dagger in the man's hand. Alektrion strained to keep hold on the man's wrist and stared in fascination at the dagger's slow descent. The warrior was a man in his prime, Alektrion but sixteen. His arm was burning. His muscles quivered. This was no match; in a few moments Death, the Ancient Crone, would take him.

The man stank of garlic, of sweat and excitement. Suddenly Alektrion became oddly aware that the dagger was beautiful, its blade ornamented and finely detailed with a cat stalking waterfowl. Gold and silver inlay. From nowhere came the thought, my father would have been proud to have created this weapon by which I die.

The tip pressed against the skin of his bare chest, dug in. Alektrion's arm shook wildly now, muscles at the point of failure.

Something moved in a blur. A sickening crack. His attacker jolted sideways and sprawled on his back, his forehead bloody.

The blur snapped into focus. Grimaldius stepped over Alektrion, raised a good-sized mallet and smashed it with an even louder and deeper crack onto the mainlander's head.

"Find a weapon," his captain commanded in a rush, then charged into another soldier. The two men struggled over a sword.

Alektrion's mind faltered. Limp from his brush with the Ancient, he shook himself and looked around. The battle's course had changed. Slaves from the pirate vessel attacked their former owners with cooking pots and forging tools. Someone must have unlocked their chains. The merchant vessel stood alongside, and even her crew was attacking with whatever came to hand.

Alektrion scrambled on hands and knees to his sword, clutched it, lunged to his feet. He needed an opponent. His body ached to feel again the cutting of flesh.

But the battle was over.

He reeled with exhaustion and spent emotion. He searched for Laius, but his weakness grew. He sat on an overturned crate. Blood streaked his thighs and covered his hands. The deck was slick with blood and feces and urine. The spine-chilling screaming of a man in pain stopped abruptly. Serena wouldn't treat that wound. Nausea struck.

He rose and staggered to the windward rail, inhaled gulps of clean air. Through jumbled thoughts, clear ones surfaced. What had happened to him? He'd wanted to kill and not stop killing. He'd ... he'd gone mad. He searched again for Laius among the stooped, kneeling, and sprawled bodies—the exhausted living, the wounded, and the dead. He needed to see a friend's face.

Laius was ladling water from the storage pithos into buckets. Their eyes met. Laius sent him a shaky, crooked grin. His lips stiff, Alektrion grinned back.

He was alive. Laius was alive. But—

He turned and hurried back to Hot Sauce.

The cook's eyes were still open, but forever sightless. Grimacing, Alektrion closed them. Kampenthes was also dead, and Prian. How many others? He rose and went to Laius.

Wordlessly, they embraced. Laius held Alektrion at arm's length. "I thought for certain I was for the sharks," Laius said. "But I knew you'd make it. Unlike me, my good friend, you were born with a lucky wind blowing."

They searched deeply into each other's eyes. A bond formed, forged by the joy of life and the fear of death, unbreakable.

Grimaldius gave them little time to consider their good fortune. Following orders, Alektrion painfully gathered his remaining strength and threw himself into securing the mainlanders who'd survived and who would now become slaves. Other men cleaned the ship and bound the many bodies into linen shrouds for burial at sea. Alektrion worked feverishly despite the greatest fatigue he had ever known. He didn't want to think. His thoughts were terrible.

How could he have been so eager to kill?

The pirate vessels had been searched, someone said. The search turned up two messages in clay addressed to one of the captains. The messages implicated Atistaeus, The Red King of Pylos, in the raiding.

Once all four ships were again underway, headed for Khithera and manned by lean crews, Alektrion stopped long enough to have his wounded arm bound. "You've not lost much blood," Serena said, "but I'm afraid you'll have a bad scar."

A scar. What was a scar? He'd seen his death and survived. He'd killed.

The men debated about the slaughter of non-combatants and the rape and killing of the women. A few argued that the vessels, though clearly Pylian, must be rogues. Klemonair, a hardened, taciturn mercenary whom Alektrion admired and who was now the oldest man aboard, shared Alektrion's revulsion that Achean soldiers might be responsible. No Achean warrior acting under orders would commit such a dishonorable breach in the rules of combat, Klemonair said. But most of the men believed otherwise and were quick to say so.

"The Pylian king is a barbarian!" said one.

Drydenax, the piper, snorted and then said, "The brave Achean warrior, cloaked in honor, is a barbarian myth."

Heads nodded in agreement. Deep inside, Alektrion felt a crack split wide in the foundation of his world.

ɶ ɶ ɶ ɶ

Well before the sun touched the sea, they put into Khithera. The trader's captain tied up at the wharf. *Sea Eagle's* crew anchored the three warships.

Today he'd earned his first booty: his share of the sale of the two Achean vessels including their remaining crews and whatever the ships carried. He would trade all of it and countless times more to see Hot Sauce spit again.

"The vessel lies secure," the second in command finally called out. Alektrion stripped and dived into the sea. The Aegean embraced him. Warm. Clean. He scrubbed. He'd rinsed off soon after they'd begun the sail to Khithera, but now he scrubbed every crease and crevice of his skin. Blood seemed to cling to him.

He'd just changed into a fresh tunic when Grimaldius found him. "Place a table for offerings in front of Serena's cabin," he said, "and two lighted lamps on either side of her door. Before we leave the ship for the night, *Sea Eagle* must be cleansed."

With Laius's help, Alektrion did as ordered. Grimaldius directed the entire crew to assemble. Alektrion wasn't sure how many of the non-Keftian mercenaries actually worshipped the Goddess. Probably not most, but all participated daily in the ceremonies Serena led, and all would participate in the cleansing.

Alektrion stood, Laius at his side, and watched a painfully exquisite pink western sky shade into purple. He kept seeing the five dead women, lying in the gore from their slit throats. The hair-raising screams of the merchant vessel's mortally wounded passenger rose and fell in every corner of his mind. His former—and, he now thought, childish—notions of the glory of honorable combat lay in shreds. Perhaps worst of all, though his stomach turned each time the horrors rose to consciousness, his right hand tingled with an ardent memory of the death blows he'd dealt.

Serena stepped from her cabin, appearing for the first time in the blue and green sari worn only on official occasions. The lamplight shimmered on her gown like moon-glow on purling water. She held a melon-sized, spherical incense vessel. The evening's breath came from behind her and carried the resinous scent of myrrh across the ship.

He dropped his eyes to the deck. A terrible pain throbbed in his chest: guilt and anger and shame. His hands were soiled, his spirit defiled.

Serena sang a hymn of purification. His gaze shifted back to her, drawn by the clear beauty of her voice. The song's melody snaked its way to his heart. The words implored that the ship be cleansed from the vile force of rage. His throat tightened. He tasted the salt of tears he fought to swallow. Why didn't he feel relief?

In a low voice she offered words of comfort, reminding them that their comrades had fought for the Goddess and that She would soon welcome them to rest and feast in Elysium, until their spirits were ready for rebirth. Serena assured them that their own efforts were valiant.

He waited, still tensed. Would she say anything forgiving about the satisfaction that had raced through him like liquid fire when he drew his sword from the enemy's back? About the eagerness with which he'd searched for yet one more man to kill?

She addressed the new recruits. She said the Lady would give them the peace to counteract the pain of seeing friends die. She said nothing about frenzied blood-lust.

She turned to the west and stood in the position of reverence. With the other men, Alektrion followed her example. He wanted to believe what he'd done was necessary and honorable and that he should go to bed in peace. He let himself search his feelings again. He saw the women. Heard the screams of the dying and wounded. Saw the exquisite knife. Saw the fountain of blood from the Achean's neck. His gut twisted and he pressed his fist hard against his forehead.

All pain and waste! And there could be no doubt: Acheans were responsible. With wrenching effort, he forced his mind to the beauty of the setting sun. He wanted to leave his body.

∾ ∾ ∾ ∾

Khithera was a small harbor, and her biggest tavern, the Two Dolphins, would never have held *Sea Eagle's* full crew. Now the remnant of her crew sat gloomily at backless wooden benches around the room's two long tables. The bar's owner had hung the white-plastered walls with fishing nets, bidents, dried red starfish, and conch shells. The man's double jowls shook as he hurried to and from the serving area.

Oarsmen and marines tended to separate on leave, so Alektrion was surprised when the old mercenary Klemonair grabbed him by the arm at the door. Now he and Laius sat between Klemonair and the piper, Drydenax. He was certainly out of place amidst the warriors, but it was flattering that Klemonair, the man he most admired, wanted his company.

He drank one tumbler of ale. Another followed, as if a demon inside him demanded it.

After the second ale, Klemonair pushed a platter of lamb and a basket of bread under Alektrion's nose. "Better eat something, Alek. You're not gonna be able to walk outta here."

The sight of the meat rolled his stomach over. He shoved the platter down the table. To placate Klemonair, he tore off a chunk of bread and forced it down.

Storytelling had started. It continued, but Kampenthes, master riddler and chief storyteller, slept now in the Great Sea. The absence of his voice left an aching void.

The evening progressed, the talk grew louder, the jokes more bawdy. Klemonair clapped Alektrion on the shoulder and shouted, loud above the din of shuffling platters and conversation, "You all have little to brag about compared to Alek. Our cook's helper, barely free from his mother's skirts, killed two men."

He felt his face burning. He wanted to clamp his hand over Klemenair's mouth. The old marine told how he himself had been fighting, pinned to the deck with an Achean poised above him, and how Alektrion drove a sword through the man's back.

"Not much finesse, but it did the job. Next thing I see is a man behind Alek. I yelled, 'Watch out,' and the boy turned and cut off the barbarian's head!"

Alektrion cringed. Not only was it not true that he'd severed the man's head, he hated what he had done. No. He hated that he'd taken pleasure in it. "I didn't actually—"

Laius shouted, "So, my friend Alek kills as good as he cooks."

Laughter and "well done's" erupted. Everyone knew now what he was supposed to have done. He wished he could vanish.

Then Drydenax made the horrible situation worse. "Does everyone agree, it's way past time that a man who can cook and kill should bed a woman?"

"Aye, aye," voices thundered, men eager to be diverted from grim visions.

Klemonair clapped Alektrion affectionately on the shoulder. "To-night will be the night, then."

An oarsman at the far end of the table shouted for more meat, and a marine began a story describing the barbaric Achean custom of buying wives. Alektrion knew for a fact this myth wasn't true. Mercifully, the focus of attention shifted.

In one long gulp he finished his half-consumed ale, then ordered another.

And another.

The night became a blur.

The following day he also spent in the Two Dolphins, drinking with Laius and whoever happened by. The drink kept his thoughts unfocused and his emotions free. If he slept, he didn't remember when or where.

Days later Klemonair and Drydenax found him there, still with Laius. "Enough of this drunkenness," Klemonair muttered.

Someone grabbed the back of Alektrion's tunic. He was yanked to his feet.

The room spun. His stomach rolled several times, and he retched. He sensed—barely—that Klemonair and Drydenax were carrying him out, toward the water. Yelling so loud that Alektrion thought his head would split, they tossed him into the sea. Moments later Laius splashed in beside him.

The water treatment worked. At least he was able to walk—with help. So could Laius. At the nearest public bath, Klemonair alternately doused Alektrion with hot and cold water and then beat the muscles of his back, arms, legs and chest. Drydenax treated Laius to the same punishment. Eventually, Alektrion could speak a straight sentence or two. Klemonair grinned. "So how do you feel now that your sword has felt the pleasure of the silken sheath?"

Alektrion gasped, wondered in a panic if, during his drunkenness, he'd described the wild, sick, heady pleasure he'd felt during the battle?

But, no. Klemonair was grinning. This wasn't talk of killing. But if not of killing ...

"I don't know what you mean." An embarrassing suspicion was shaping up in his head.

"Laius says you and he bedded two women who live in the street of the Two Dolphins."

In his mind flashed a brief image of a smooth brown curve of waist and a dark patch between brown thighs. No other image surfaced. Warmth flushed to the roots of his hair. Was it possible to lie with a woman for the very first time and remember nothing?

Astounded, he started to ask Laius—still stretched flat on his stomach on the neighboring table—but checked himself. He hardly wanted to admit he hadn't known what he was doing and remembered nothing. The jokes at his expense would never stop. To Laius he said, "So how would you describe what happened?"

Laius embroidered a description of himself and Alektrion going with two women to eat a home-cooked meal. "Alek was so eager to experience his first taste of the salt of the sea, he skipped the food altogether."

Klemonair and Drydenax chuckled. Alektrion prayed he could return to *Sea Eagle* quickly, lest he encounter the woman again.

The woman. He didn't even remember her name. Had he asked? Had he been able to pleasure her? What if their paths crossed and she teased him in front of someone? Great Mother, what if he'd been unable to perform!

They returned to the ship in the late afternoon—Alektrion avoiding the eyes of every woman he passed—and Grimaldius ordered *Sea Eagle* out of Khithera. They rowed north for an hour, then camped on a white sandy beach. After dinner he took the empty cooking cauldron to the surf and squatted to scrub it with sand. He heard footsteps and looked up to see Grimaldius.

"I've heard of your bravery, Alek," he said as he handed Alektrion a dagger. It was the very weapon that had been in the hand of the man with whom Alektrion fought. "The dagger is yours. Your first booty. And if you're going to grow strong, your muscles have to be put to harder work than stirring stew. You're uncommonly well-developed for sixteen. Though you're still a bit young, I think you can row. Would you accept promotion to rower?"

Alektrion shot to his feet and accepted the dagger. As a rower his share of all booty would be much larger! His dream of owning his own ship that much closer. "I would be honored, Captain. And I thank you for the weapon."

"Consider it done then. Within the week we'll put into Melos." The sun-baked creases in Grimaldius's face deepened, his eyes darkened with sadness. "We'll be taking on new crew, a new cook. I'll see to it that among them is a new cook's helper."

After Grimaldius left, Alektrion forced his hands to finish scrubbing the pot, but then rushed to tell Laius. Laius threw his arms around Alektrion. "Great good news! I swear you're the luckiest man alive. And let me see that blade."

The hearty embrace warmed his spirit. He hugged back with a full heart. But during the night he dreamed. Five beautiful women danced in a circle, hands upon each other's shoulders. They danced on a white beach. Their dresses melted away. They were naked and dancing on the deck of a sleek black ship.

He was on the ship too, seated cross-legged below the deckhouse. One by one the women approached him. Joy possessed them, and each smiled at him differently. Their large eyes were bright, their ringlets of dark hair jiggled with life. They whirled, full of the Maiden.

Suddenly, the wind brought to his ears the sound of unendurable pain. Ripple after ripple of terror rushed across his skin. Sweat drenched him. He knew the scream, the voice of the man on the merchant vessel before Prian's blade silenced it forever. The fair sky above the ship darkened as if the most horrendous summer squall were racing toward the ship. The enemy was coming.

Get up and take the women below, he told himself, his heart hammering. Get up. Make them safe. But his legs wouldn't work. "Run and hide," he tried to yell, but he couldn't move his lips.

The dark sky reddened, as if a bloody cape had been cast across the heaven. A scarlet demon, four-armed and five times the size of the ship, formed from the stuff of the sky. One scaly hand snatched a dancer, laid her on the deck. A finger of another hand, pushed up her skirt. A double-edged knife formed in a third hand.

Alektrion screamed. He knew what would come next.

"Merciful Lady, Alek! Wake up, man."

He woke sitting upright. Laius was shaking him so hard he bit his tongue. "You've roused the whole beach." Sweat stood in beads on his skin and the night breeze gave him a sudden chill. He blinked repeatedly, clenched his fists.

"Sorry," he said. "Bad dream."

"Must have been. You were … well, it sounded like someone was gutting a live goat."

Laius lay down again. Still shaking, Alektrion did the same. He stared at the stars, listened to the lap of water on the shore. Sleep refused to return. The night passed while he listened to snores and grunts.

In the next months the terrifying, oppressive dream came often. Laius took on the job of waking him. The men joked about how his first experience with a woman must have been remarkably bad, but they knew it was the battle with the Acheans and not lovemaking that left him screaming in his sleep.

9

In less than five days, he would be home. Having been laid up in harbor at Ceos for over a week, *Sea Eagle* headed now through still rough water to winter port in Alyris. Alektrion dug his oar into the sea and pulled. Two moon cycles had passed since Grimaldius rewarded his wild killing of Pylian raiders by elevating him to rower. He gave no thought to his movements. His mind wrestled with the vision of seeing his mother, having to talk to his father. Tonight he would endure another evening around the fire listening to the eager talk of men preparing to see family and friends and lovers for the first time in months. But blood stained his hands. What if the rage in his heart showed in his face? He would bring his parents grief, not happiness.

Laius sat in front of him and, in front of Laius, sat another of the new Keftian recruits, a skinny youth named Trusis. Trusis's mother was from Dallia and a maker of fine seal rings. She had great hopes that her first son would rise to high rank.

A shout from their lookout shattered his thoughts. "Two ships off the port beam. One of 'ems flying no pennant."

Alektrion tensed. Twice since the battle with the Pylian ship, *Sea Eagle* had come upon pirate ships flying no identity, and both times, though Grimaldius had pursued, the raiders had warning and favorable winds. They escaped. And both times, just as now, Alektrion's heart had clenched in dread at the thought of engagement. He tightened his grip on the oars as if he wanted to squeeze the life out of some demon. Did Laius feel this revolting weakness?

"Hard to port," came the command from Grimaldius.

Alektrion dug his feet in and bent hard to the oar. The ship began to turn. He could feel her every move now, as if she were part of his body. And his body had grown so muscled he wondered if his mother would recognize him.

They were moving south along the coast of Tenos, a stadia or two to sea, keeping the land in view. The sighted vessels must be close to the island. From the bow the word was passed back. "One's a coastal ferry. The other's a pirate. Probably Pylian."

Grimaldius ordered maximum speed. Sweat trickled down Alektrion's sides. More word from the bow: "Pirate's seen us. She's starting to flee, and this time we're close enough to catch 'em. But the ferry's gone onto rocks!"

Let's go after the sons of Kokor! Alektrion willed his words to touch Grimaldius. The Red King wouldn't be stopped if his ships always got away. But if they caught up to the ship, there would be another battle. Good! *That's our job.*

Despite himself, despite his earlier dread, the growing excitement around him now had him eager to engage the raiding vermin.

The command to turn again to pursue should come soon. Instead the next command was to slow to half speed. Then to boarding speed. He heard screams coming from a great distance, the voices of women. The urge to stand up and look made his eyes itch. As if he sensing Alektrion's thoughts, Klemonair shouted, "Tend to your oars!" then added, "but when we put up on the beach, prepare to give aid."

The screaming grew closer, and now Alektrion heard the sound of breakers.

A huge surge lifted *Sea Eagle*. They were in the surf line. Any spot they chose to beach on would not be protected here. Grimaldius must fear the worst for the ferry's passengers to risk such a beaching.

Another huge surge. Alektion tensed.

"Up oars! Secure!"

Another surge, then a lancing thrust and a bone-jarring jolt as they hit the sand. The men were thrown forward, *Sea Eagle* groaned, then settled. Grimaldius ran down the center of the ship between the marines. "Starboard rowers secure the vessel. All others, follow me. We've got a sinking ship and people in the water."

Alektrion leapt to his feet and looked toward the cries. Sitting at three times the distance he could throw a stone, a large ferry with gaily painted canopy and hull wallowed next to rocks. Already half full of water, she was sinking fast.

With Laius and Trusis and the other port rowers, he stepped onto the side rail and jumped into the sea. The surf battered him as he and the others found footing and struggled onto the beach. They ran toward the stricken vessel. Floating debris littered the water: cushions, pots, bags of clothing. A screaming woman caught his attention. She held a child with one arm and with the other waved frantically and then stopped to grab at a woven basket floating beside her. Alektrion ran into the surf, dived into an oncoming breaker, surfaced, and swam for her.

Still screaming, she grabbed onto his bare, water-slickened shoulder. Her hand slipped. She panicked and grabbed for him again. Her nails raked his skin. Her child, a boy of five or so, slipped from her grip and went under. She shrieked his name and splashed frantically where he had been. Then she went under, as if pulled from below. Alektrion guessed she must be exhausted and her sodden dress would surely kill her.

He dived, aiming at where the boy had been. The water was dark, but clear, and he saw the child immediately. He grabbed him by the back of his tunic, kicked hard, and the two of them broke the surface. He held the boy's face free of the water as he tried to think what to do about the woman. Suddenly her face appeared, three strokes away, but her forehead, nose and mouth just barely cleared the water. She gasped for air and started under again.

Tugging the child by his tunic, Alektrion kicked to where she had disappeared, swept his hand under the water, touched her hair. He grabbed it, yanked her up and tilted her face upward. She gasped again for breath.

"I have you safe," he said. He didn't know if she spoke his language, but maybe the words would calm her.

This time she didn't fight.

He clutched her across her chest with one of his arms and the boy with his other. Kicking furiously, he searched for possible aid, but there was no one who wasn't already struggling with his own human burden.

He rolled onto his back and started kicking for shore. A huge swell, and then they were into the breakers. The water folded him, slammed him onto the ocean floor. He gripped the woman and boy fiercely in anticipation of the receding surf. The water rushed back, eager to tear them from him. His grip held. Another wave scraped him along the sand, burning his back, and then strong arms reached down and took the boy.

The arms belonged to Laius. Alektrion strained to his feet, lifting the woman to hers as he did. The four of them splashed through the water and up onto the beach. Laius ran back toward the water to help others. The woman threw herself against Alektrion. "My daughter," she said in Akkadian, "my husband." She waved toward the ferry and the water. "Please."

"Yes," he answered in her tongue, one he knew, but not well. "I'll help them. But first your boy."

The woman threw herself next to her son, scooped him into her arms and began to rock him. He didn't seem to be breathing. Alektrion turned the boy onto his stomach and compressed his chest. He did this twice and the boy expelled some water, sucked air, and began to cough. The woman again began to rock him, tears streaming down her cheeks.

Alektrion pulled two more women from the water before it became evident that all who were going to be saved had been. Bodies began to wash ashore. Dead men. Stabbed or throat-slashed. The Pylians had boarded the ferry and begun killing before they saw *Sea Eagle*. And not only dead men. Alektrion was staring at the drowned body of a beautiful girl of perhaps ten, long black tendrils of what had been curls lying across her face, when the first woman he had rescued rushed up and threw herself onto the child. The woman's wailing seared his heart as if it were the screaming he still heard in his nightmare. In the space of perhaps an hour, this woman had been robbed of her husband and a beautiful child. Her pitiful crying fed boiling rage.

They had rescued thirty-one women and children. Grimaldius ordered that the marines would spend this night and the next on the beach. *Sea Eagle* would take the survivors into the nearby town of Phillis, spend the night and another day there, and then return for the marines. In Phillis, the ship's carpenter would ensure that the beaching had not harmed the ship's structure before they undertook the longer voyage to Alyris.

They put into Phillis late in the day, so the thirty-two men of *Sea Eagle* found only rude lodgings in a run-down inn at the end of a dark, foul-smelling alley. They had to bed down in a common room. Laius, Alektrion and Trusis picked places in one corner, left their markers to hold the spots for them, and headed three abreast for the nearest alehouse. Alektrion wanted a drink as fiercely as a man denied water for a week.

He could see the light from the alehouse's entry when he passed a doorway with the symbol of the eye on its lintel. Suddenly there was something he wanted, needed, even more than ale. He grabbed Laius's arm. "I want to talk to this seer before I eat and drink. You and Trusis go on. I'll catch up."

Laius grinned. "We'll come too."

"No." He gave his friend a shove. "I won't be long. It's private."

Laius grinned again. "What can it be that I don't know?" He held up his hand. "No. No. I understand. Just don't be long."

The two men strode off, and Alektrion turned to the door. He knocked, waited, received no response. Maybe this was a sign he should keep his thoughts to himself.

The door opened. A girl of initiation age stood before him. She said, "You wish to see my mother?"

"Yes."

"Follow me, then."

She turned and hobbled down a short hall. Her left leg was at least a hand shorter than the right. He noted that the farther away *Sea Eagle* ventured from Keftiu and Kalliste, the more often he encountered people with deformities. The seer was not Keftian, otherwise the nurse-maid attending the girl's birth would have taken the baby before her mother had a chance to hold her and returned her to the Goddess by leaving her on one of the hilltops consecrated for that purpose.

The room smelled of incense. A pale woman sat in a corner in a deeply cushioned chair. She waved Alektrion to the chair opposite. He hesitated. "Do you worship the Mother? I want to talk, but I prefer one of the Mother's seers."

"The Great Goddess is the Maker of the world," she said gravely. "All others are pretenders."

Somewhat reassured, Alektrion took the chair.

"Do you pay in Keftian pistatas or otherwise?"

He asked what she charged and gave the money, in pistatas, to the girl, who then left them.

"What do you seek?"

He drew a deep breath. "Something is happening to me I don't understand."

"Yes."

"I'm serving on a warship."

"Yes."

"There was a battle. My first. A terrible battle. And I killed. And while it was happening and immediately after ..."

She peered deeply into his eyes. She wasn't pretty. Nose big, eyes small. But her look was kind.

"I became crazed. I found pleasure in the killing. I don't understand how I could feel this way."

She didn't seem surprised. "You seem much too young to be fighting on a warship. What else do you want to tell me?"

Encouraged, he told her about the nightmare: the dancing women, the blood red sky, the demon, the unearthly screaming of the gut-wounded man.

"There's more you want to tell me."

"No. I just want to be free of the dreams. And I can't get out of my mind how I felt. It was a kind of killing lust. I fear it. I want to be clean of it. But every time I see again what the pirates are doing, this rage captures me. It dominates me. I know such a rage isn't right for one of the Mother's children."

She rang a bell, and her daughter reappeared. Without directions, the girl brought a table and sat it in front of the seer. She brought a shallow dish fashioned of pale yellow crystal and sat it on the table and then left them. The seer straightened and lifted a silver pitcher from the table at her side. She poured water into the crystal dish. Then she looked at Alektrion. "Give me your left hand."

He held it out. From her table she took a silver pin the length of his little finger and pricked his thumb. A drop of red welled into a small ball on his skin. She touched the blood to the water.

They sat in silence watching his blood spread from a single drop into several tendrils of red against the yellow of the bowl. The seer studied the spreading of his blood in the water. The drop became diffuse and disappeared. She closed her eyes and continued the silence.

He began to think he'd made a mistake. Her silence was unnerving, and he didn't like the smell of the incense. And how could he think there would be any way to get rid of the effects of the terrible thing he'd done? As his punishment, the Lady would probably let the dream torment him his whole life.

The woman opened her eyes and once again probed deeply into his. "Sometimes you think of something else. What is that?"

He started to protest.

"No," she said quickly. "Don't say there's nothing. The water says there is something that troubles you even more."

The pounding of his heart he felt in his throat. He still wanted to say no, but she had forbidden it.

"Would you like a chance to fight again?"

He looked down, and thought of the Red King and of his hatred for what the man was doing. "Yes."

"Will you be glad when you have your next chance to fight? Think carefully."

This very day he had thought they might engage once more. And he'd told himself it was their job. And that he wanted Grimaldius to pursue. And he'd told her how he'd taken pleasure in killing. He ought to have been eager to fight. But in truth, he'd been glad they didn't.

She said, "Look at me."

He did. He felt her eyes deep in his heart and a pain squeezed his chest.

"What are you thinking?"

"I don't want to face battle again. I ..."

The words would not come out. They twisted in his throat. She waited, dark eyes watching.

In a rush of breath he finally spoke. "I fear ... I fear I'll abandon my friends."

There. It was out. More words came in a torrent. "I can't understand myself. When I was in battle, I wanted nothing more than to kill, but when it looks like I might have to fight, I want to run away, instead."

"Listen now to what I see for you in the water. The dreams are a testing. She will not take them from you at once, but in spite of that,

She expects you to remain faithful. If you remain faithful, the dreams eventually will be taken away."

The woman put a hand across her eyes. "This, too, I see in the water. If you remain faithful, you will not fail those who depend on you."

Was being faithful something more than just worshipping the Great Mother? He started to question her, but she reached for the bell, rang it, and her daughter reappeared instantly. The seer sat back in the chair and closed her eyes. The girl stood by his chair, clearly waiting for him to leave with her. Reluctantly, he rose. She let him out into the now dark street. He stood a moment, baffled. What did "be faithful" mean?

He found Laius and Trusis sharing a table with three strangers. He threw himself into a chair and took a swig of Laius's ale. A serving boy took his own order, but before it came, he'd had two more drinks from Laius.

The strangers were rowers of another Keftian warship, the *Black Crow*, whose winter port was the city of Lanithi on the island of Lemnos. The talk was of plans for what the men would do during the winter.

Trusis explained, "Our friend, Eumos, here," he pointed to a dark-bearded man with big ears, "is trying to get Laius or me to trade duty with him on this last leg home. He wants to winter in Alyris."

Big-eared Eumos turned to Alektrion. "They've both turned me down. What about you? Would you like to spend the winter in a pleasant town on a pretty island? My father, Cleos, has a fine inn there. For doing me this favor, he could give you lodging for practically nothing. *Black Crow* will return to Delos in spring, and your friends tell me *Sea Eagle* also makes a spring stop in Delos. We could trade back then."

"Why do you want to go to Alyris?"

"My father wants me to convince my uncle who lives there that they could do some good business in trading Keftian wine for jewelry made from Lemnos quartz. I need a winter there to set things up."

Alektrion considered the proposal. They would exchange ships, which rowers often did at the end of season, so Grimaldius would not likely object. Alektrion would go to Lanithi. He'd not have to see his father or mother. And if he stayed with the innkeeper Cleos, he would save a lot of money for his ship. But he also wouldn't see Alyris or his friends, and he had often thought of Leesandra and of bringing her to the dock to see *Sea Eagle*.

"It's probably not a good idea," he answered the man with big ears.

Eumos's face settled into resignation. "So, have you got a woman, too? Your friends seem to think at home there's someone, or two or three, who can't live without them for one winter."

"Alek is a half-breed," Trusis said. "And the best women on Kalliste are Keftian. You know how snooty Keftian women are."

The men laughed. A sudden flush of anger warmed Alektrion's skin.

For weeks now, he and Laius and Trusis had spent time together. Alektrion had thought that Trusis had put his half-breed status out of mind. But there it was. So long as Alektrion's world was Keftian, he would never escape this mark. Trusis was destined to rise as high in the Navy as his talents would allow, but Alektrion the half-breed could never rise beyond rank of squad leader. Which didn't really matter, of course. Though he loved sea life, he hated fighting and killing. But why should his birth be this never-ending curse?

Trusis added, "But then again, Keftian women take lovers as they will. You might not marry one, Alek, but that doesn't mean you can't bed as many as are willing."

Eumos grinned at Alektrion. "Well, Alek, that's another reason you ought to think of Lanithi for the winter. Few Keftian women there. We're mostly Thracean. Who knows. You might find a bride."

Drinks arrived, and Alektrion said to the boy, "Bring me another. Right now."

He downed half of his new cup in one long, soothing gulp. The conversation turned to the best way to catch lobster when a man is in a hurry. When the boy arrived with the new drink, Alektrion threw down his second ale with a gulp and started on his third. "Just keep the ale coming," he said to the boy. They drank, sang, played Skull and Bones late into the morning. Sometime along the way, much to Laius's vociferous protests, Alektrion agreed to trade ships with Eumos.

He boarded the *Black Crow* the following morning. Saying good-bye to Laius had been difficult, and he half regretted his bargain. But he would make the best of it. The last thing Eumos said was, "If you don't find any of the Thracean women to your pleasing, look up a friend of my mother's. She's Keftian. Served as hetaira, in fact, on Keftiu itself. She's a bit old, but very good. Her name is Philoxea."

Alektrion took the rowing seat the piper indicated. He had not yet lain with a hetaira. He would make a point to meet the woman Philoxea.

10

Meidra took her first lover within a month of our initiation. I sulked. I resented having to compete for her time. She had no patience with me. "Find a lover of your own," she protested with a silly grin.

I tried, but the moment any man gave me an inquiring look, I imagined his body intimately close to mine. My flushed gaze hurried elsewhere and I'd think, He's not nearly so handsome as Alektrion.

A week before harvest festival, I was in the storage room pouring milk for our house snake when the houseboy rushed through the door. "Your father wants to see you in his study. I think it has to do with a strange man who just arrived."

I bounded upstairs, full of curiosity, then on the landing I stopped a moment. Not an Achean, I hoped.

My father stood alone at a window. I assumed our guest was freshening himself in the bath. Father turned from looking at the harbor and nodded toward a couch. "Sit down, Leesandra."

I sat. His tone was unusually serious.

"I've been giving careful thought to your education. Next spring, you'll leave for Knossos. I want you to have every possible advantage."

For a long moment I sat like a sheep stunned from the butcher's blow, then I resolutely straightened my back. "I thought it was decided I could stay here. Meidra and I are ..."

"Leesandra, there's no point discussing this as if you, or your mother, or I, have a choice. Any Keftian who would rise high in Temple or government service must face the Bull Court. Don't let yourself imagine for a moment more your mother or I will fail in our responsibility! You'll go! And as hard as it may be to believe now, you'll find the experience to be wonderful."

I set my jaw and returned his stare.

"You'll not go alone," he continued. "Heebe will go with you. She's already agreed."

He looked at me clearly hoping for a favorable response. My lips thinned into a hard line. He continued. "I've arranged for you to have other companionship as well. You may remember when the Achean ship put into harbor after the big storm last year."

Dear Mother, I thought. *How could I ever forget?*

"She carried slaves and among them was an extraordinary man. I bought him and put him under indenture. Not only does he write Keftian and Akkadian, he speaks and writes seven other languages. In a year of working with him, I've grown to trust him. So much so, I've arranged for him to serve out his indenture as your tutor."

A private tutor! Disastrous! Probably less than one in a hundred Spider Clan children needed to know the ways of the world beyond Keftiu. My parents' expectations for me must be high indeed.

What tutor would let me spend afternoons at the beach or on the mountain? I clasped my hands so tightly in my lap my nails cut into my palm. "It's my duty to honor your wishes and the wishes of my mother." I picked my words carefully. "But I don't like school. I prefer the sky and fresh air. I'm most close to the Great Mother when I go to Her mountain. No matter how hard I try, father, I cannot imagine being a priestess. "

To my surprise, he moved to sit beside me, took my hand and held it. "I see a special light in you, Leesandra. Something very bright. A tutor will help you polish that brightness of mind and spirit. But Kalliste, beautiful as she is, is too small a place. Knossos is the center of our world. There, you'll have opportunities you could only dream about here."

I blinked back tears.

He patted my hand. "Let this remain just between us. I don't care what your ultimate choice is. Priestess or not. I care only that you be prepared to pick any path you choose. To have that freedom, you must have a proper education. Go to the Bull Court. Promise me to make your best effort to learn what's taught there. If you do that, you'll honor your mother and your family."

Any hope I'd had of remaining on Kalliste evaporated, a dream of cloud-mist touched down on lava. I felt dead inside. In a voice wooden-sounding even to me, I said, "I'll do as you ask."

He rose, strode to the door of the roof terrace, opened it and said, "Come in, Zuliya."

A man stepped into the library. I blinked. Before me stood the most extraordinary person I'd ever seen, his skin as black as a moonless night.

Something dreadful must have happened to him. A horrible fire, perhaps? But I was looking at flesh as smooth as a finished piece of ebony. Then I understood. The man who would be my tutor was Nubian, a man from the lands beyond Agyptos. Given the modest amount of gray in his tightly curled black hair and beard, I guessed him to be forty or forty-five. He was slender and a head shorter than my father. And father had already been most generous to him: he wore a red and gold robe resembling the saris of our priestesses and priests. Gold earrings dangled against his ebony skin and, most remarkably, one side of his nose was pierced by a slender gold crescent.

He bowed deeply to my father. He turned toward me and cocked his head to the side. *Inspecting me!* My father put a hand on his shoulder and led him across the room. I noted as I rose to greet him that he walked with a limp.

How should I act? He'd been a slave. Now he was indentured to father. I couldn't recall having been introduced to a person of such status before. I decided to treat him as I would any non-Keftian his age who was a teacher. I bowed my head half as deeply as he had done to my father.

He didn't bow to me at all. I stiffened. He expected me to earn his respect. He would never have ventured such bold behavior if my father hadn't given him leave. Just how much authority would my father give him?

"Zuliya of Memphis, I present my daughter, Leesandra."

The outrageous outlander offered me a small smile. "I have learned to admire your father's wisdom. I am deeply in his debt for the promise of freedom when my indenture is satisfied. I swear to do all in my power to serve you well."

Despite his small stature, his voice rang like a deep bell. At least when I listened hour after hour, I'd listen to a pleasant sound.

My father gestured to the Nubian to take the cushioned chair opposite the couch. "Come, let's sit."

I returned to the couch, and my father again sat beside me. Zuliya of Memphis moved to the chair and his limp called my attention to his feet. His boots were pointed and curled up at the toes, and of a most shocking bright red. He sat, crossed one leg over the other—astonishment piled upon astonishment. From the stiffness of his ankle, I realized one of his feet wasn't real. His left foot, and perhaps the lower part of that leg, wasn't of flesh. Someone had made it, perhaps from wood, or maybe metal.

Embarrassed lest he catch me staring, I quickly switched my gaze to my father's face.

Father was explaining my supposed merits. I scarcely listened. I couldn't keep from glancing at this Zuliya. His hair wasn't cut short in the fashion of mainlanders or curled like the Agyptian traders and diplomats. He'd braided it into a thick club that sat between his shoulders. Delicate, actually elegant, features gave him a refined air. I caught him studying me and took several deep breaths to keep from squirming under his gaze.

Finally, the full significance of the moment struck. Unless some circumstance that I could not now imagine intervened, for the next five years this man would be in charge of my education. What if I didn't like him? He was an outlander. Indeed, he was the strangest looking outlander I'd ever laid eyes on, and for some incomprehensible reason my father had chosen him to tutor me. Did he worship the Lady? Did he worship Poseidon? Did he worship one of the strange and sometimes repulsive lessor gods of Agyptos? I felt I might explode in anger.

"Do you understand me, Leesandra?" My father's voice broke through the whirlwind of questions spinning in my head.

"I'm sorry."

"Have you been listening?"

"Oh, yes."

"I've said in front of you both, so there'll be no question, that I expect you to spend four afternoons out of five with Zuliya. He is to determine what you'll study and how you'll study. When you're away from your mother and me, as you soon will be—"my father gave me a penetrating look signifying, again, that within the year I'd be in Knossos"—you are to obey Zuliya because he stands in my place."

An outlander to be my guardian! Was my father mad?

"Father." I attempted to smile at the strange black man, but my lips were as rigid as sticks. I turned back to my father. "What about Heebe? Won't this hurt her feelings? I'll gladly learn from Zuliya. But I'm sure concerning cares outside my studies, you'd intend for me to go to Heebe."

"I intend what I said."

Never! Never, ever. *This can't be.* "Does mother know?"

Father smiled at the outlander. "You see it's as I've told you. She's not easy to harness."

The Nubian cocked his head to one side again. Our gazes locked. His lips turned up in the smallest smile. "Ummm," he said. "The Mitanni, who prefer their women meek, have a saying. 'Beware a fire in the eyes. When there's fire in the eyes, there's fire in the heart.' I myself think fire is the most interesting and exciting of the four elements."

My father laughed. "Well put. And, yes, Leesandra, your mother and I have discussed your relationship to Zuliya. You'll find she agrees with me. Heebe would spoil you outrageously."

My father exchanged a final few words with the tutor, then left us alone.

"And so, Leesandra, what would you like to ask me?"

"I have no questions." With those words, a ludicrous lie because everything about the man, from his nose jewelry to his pointed red boots, provoked at least a hundred questions, I vowed to make his life miserable. I would drive him to distraction. Very soon he would refuse to tutor me.

His next few questions failed to soften my will. Seeing the pointlessness of continuing, he suggested a time for us to meet the following day. He wanted us to take midday meal together. "I have a friend. I meet her after school. Do you want me to tell her I can't?"

"Your schedule must eventually change, but it need not do so overnight."

I pinched my lips tight. I wouldn't return his smile or be won by pretty words. But to avoid antagonizing father, I agreed to meet him the next day on the roof garden after mid-afternoon prayers.

The next day we had no sooner exchanged chitchat about the lovely fall weather and found places to sit when Heebe appeared with a tray of sliced fruits and a pitcher of diluted wine. When she exhausted ways to busy herself with the refreshments, she watered my mother's plants. The white sea daffodils were blooming. I doubted they needed a drink. I'd never seen Heebe fuss so.

Switching to Akkadian, the most common language shared by outlanders, he said, "Do you like flowers?" He gently touched a daffodil and his dark eyes sparkled with pleasure.

"I like everything about the Mother's body," I replied curtly in that same harsh tongue. According to my teachers, my Akkadian was excellent.

In Akkadian, he posed questions about Kalliste's plants and animals and then, switching back to Keftian, he said, "You seem to have a way with the mother tongue of the people of Akkad. But your father tells me you do not speak the tongue of the pharaohs. As the world's greatest scholars are in Agyptos, and I would like you eventually to read their works, I suggest we begin our language lessons with that tongue."

Heebe caught my eye, and I knew she was thinking exactly what I was. Zuliya had said the world's greatest scholars were in Agyptos. Of just how much use could a tutor be who thought such nonsense?

I answered his questions with as few words as possible and asked none in return. My defiance sizzled between us. Still, he gave no outward sign of impatience. Maybe he thought he could outlast me. Perhaps win me over. Well, he would be wrong. I would be rid of him, and I had a good idea how to do it.

When my father returned from work, I went to his study. He was sitting behind his desk. "How did it go today with Zuliya?" he asked eagerly.

"He seems a gentle enough man."

He began rolling a stylus between his thumb and forefinger. I strolled to the couch, sat, and pulled my legs up under me in a way I hoped seemed relaxed.

"What did you talk about?"

"Oh, this and that. He tried to discover things I don't know."

My father laughed softly. "That shouldn't have taken him a lot of time. You are, after all, only thirteen."

His words stung. I hadn't imagined father's opinion of my learning was so low. Why was it that so often I didn't know what was going on in my own father's head?

Still determined, I said, "I'm sure you respect the tutor's skill with languages. But shouldn't a guardian be wise in the ways of the world?"

He tossed the stylus onto the desk and leaned back. "Of course. What is your thought?"

"Well. We were discussing which language I might study. Zuliya thinks it should be Agyptian."

"A sensible choice."

"But he said the reason was that the greatest scholars in the world are in Agyptos."

"He's quite right."

"But ... but ... didn't you say, just yesterday, that Knossos is the center of the world?"

"I said Knossos is the center of *our* world. One of the things you'll learn from Zuliya is that the world is a much bigger place than you've been taught to believe."

I sat stunned by yet another of my father's strange ideas. "Why this tutor, father? He seems too ..." I grasped for a thought. "Too old."

"Since when is being old a handicap for a tutor?"

I tried again. "He was a slave. Is it suitable for me to have a man who was a slave as my tutor?"

"Let me tell you a few things about Zuliya." My father's lips took a rigid, impatient set. "He's overcome great hardships. When he was too small to even remember it, he was stolen in a raid by the forces of Thutmoses. A Hittite scholar, traveling with Thutmoses's army, took him in, and at the end of the expedition, the Hittite took Zuliya to live in Memphis, the place the court at Hattusis had sent him to work. The Hittite adopted Zuliya, and Zuliya attended the school for scribes. He's been raised a scholar in a scholar's home in one of the world's great cities."

He's not that smart, I thought, blinking back tears of anger.

My father picked up the stylus again, pointed it at me as if to stick his point in my head for good. "Moreover, he has great experience of the world, which you currently do not. After years in Memphis, he and his father began a return journey to Hattusis. Unfortunately they encountered Phoenician pirates.

"Zuliya's father was killed. The Phoenicians sold Zuliya to the king of Mitanni. He was made a slave, for the first time, when he was only seventeen. He worked as a stable groom, but taught himself to train war horses. Years later, when the Mitanni lost a battle, Zuliya became the possession of a Sumerian general, and Zuliya's knowledge of horses was so extraordinary that he came to the general's attention. Unlike some people ..." my father paused significantly, "the general was shrewd enough to recognize a man of great talents. By the time the general retired to Ur, Zuliya was his personal scribe. Zuliya served with such distinction, Leesandra, that shortly before the general's death, he freed Zuliya. An exceptional act in that place."

"So how did he come to be a slave on the Achean ship?"

"He wanted to finish the journey to Hattusis that he'd begun with his father. He got no further than Lycia; and, two years ago, a pirate raiding party sacked the town. They killed his wife and sold him into slavery again."

This sad thought stopped me. How terrible to lose one's mate. My heart softened. But I reminded myself he was an outlander and probably didn't worship the Lady. It was possible, of course, for She was worshipped as Isis in Agyptos, but the Agyptians had so many goddesses and gods. I grasped one last hope. "Does Zuliya worship the Great Goddess?"

"And why are you wondering that?"

I felt myself softening. *Don't back down.* "Well, if he doesn't, I've been thinking it strange that mother would agree to have him be my guardian."

"Why are you questioning my will on this matter?" He threw the stylus onto the desk top. "Zuliya is gentle, very funny, very wise, and a man of high honor. I've never encountered a woman or man I trust more. You don't know him, yet you're digging in your heels. Why? Is it this foolish aversion you've developed to foreigners?"

I bit back what I wanted to say.

"Is it?"

"It's not my place to say who is to be my guardian. But I am Keftian and ..." Again I stopped my mouth.

"Your mother agreed at once that Zuliya should be your tutor. We disagreed at first about making him your guardian. Your mother, though, has talked with him for hours, and you're right in guessing he probably doesn't worship the Lady. In fact, he'll say nothing about his beliefs. He simply smiles and says, 'The quality of a religion is judged by the women and men it produces.' It's difficult to argue with such a statement. And as he's clearly no zealot and he's sworn to your mother he'll make no attempt to corrupt you, she's agreed with me."

I was standing in surf and the ebbing water had pulled all the sand of argument from under my feet. I fought hot tears of desperation. "I … I promised Heebe I'd help her take a weaving from her loom."

He dismissed me.

Within the week, Zuliya and I began tense, uncomfortable sessions. Under no circumstances would I let this outlander influence my thinking.

Some weeks later, the Temple declared the end to sea season. From our roof terrace, I checked the harbor daily for Alektrion's ship, the *Sea Eagle*. I needed to see him. When it finally came in, I forced myself to wait a day—so as not to betray my eagerness—and then went to the dock.

I learned that Alektrion had chosen to overwinter elsewhere, a town called Lanithi, a place so obscure I'd never before heard its name. Once again, my foolish heart suffered from keen disappointment. Why couldn't I just let him and my fantasies about him go?

A month later Heebe's first grandchild was born, and I attended the child's naming party. I loved naming parties. The cooks outdid themselves making sweets: candied pears and quince; wheat sticks soaked in mint; crushed almonds and dates wrapped in layers of thin dough and soaked in honey. Meats, too, were specially prepared, but ever since the boy's sacrifice, I couldn't tolerate animal flesh. After the feasting, I always reveled in the wrestling. Even into old age, Keftians love a good tussle, and until the previous year, I'd always been able to hold my own, even against boys. I wasn't built stoutly, but I was strong and agile. I was an initiated maiden now, though, so it was no longer acceptable for me to wrestle with males, boys or men. This suddenly suited me fine. After seeing the coupling, well, being so closely entwined with a man would be most uncomfortable. At least for me.

After the party, Heebe remained to visit. Zuliya and I walked in strained silence toward home. Suddenly the wine maker's son, Abramanthus, ran into the lane in front of us, his arms flapping as always. He passed us, mumbling. I greeted him with a touch to the heart and called to his demon to "leave this child of the Lady in peace!"

Zuliya stopped and watched a moment. When we resumed walking, he asked, "How long has he been thus?"

I told what I knew of Abramanthus adding that there was disagreement as to which demon had taken him and why. I started to elaborate on this subject, which fascinated most people, but Zuliya interrupted.

"Umm," he hummed dismissively. "There is a Sumerian healer who believes such conditions are caused in some people by eating foods that disagree with them. I myself witnessed a cure." He chuckled, a rumble deep in his chest which had an infectious quality difficult to resist—though so far I usually succeeded. "The man regained his senses, but the foods he was allowed to eat to maintain this balanced state were so boring, I half thought it might have been better for him to remain afflicted."

To say that Abramanthus had no demon when the Temple priestess had declared that he did verged, at the very least, on impiety. Zuliya had promised mother never to corrupt my religious views. Hope to be rid of him reignited. "Are you saying Abramanthus isn't possessed?"

He filled the remainder of our walk with a discourse on the effects of foods on a person's disposition. I scarcely listened. Once home, I rushed to mother's room anticipating triumph. I told her of Zuliya's irreverent disdain for the priestess's pronouncement. I told her of the silly notion that somehow food caused Abramanthus's behavior.

She laid her embroidery in her lap. Frown lines appeared on her forehead. I finished, breathless and sure of success.

"Did Zuliya say a demon *wasn't* responsible for Abramanthus's state? Remember carefully."

What did this matter? But I did as she asked and thought back to Zuliya's exact words. "He said the Sumerian healer believed this condition, in some people, was caused by what they ate."

She patted her footstool and I sat. "So isn't it possible that sometimes a demon is responsible and sometimes disagreeable food?"

Confusion left me silent.

"Or isn't it possible that perhaps a demon does its work by entering the body and changing the body so that when Abramanthus eats, his food addles his spirit?"

"Well. Yes. I suppose. But that's not what the priestesses say. And it's not what our healers believe or, otherwise, they would have tried to change what he eats."

"You certainly know, Leesandra, things aren't always what they seem. Two women may smile at each other warmly when in truth they're deeply unhappy about a tree that belongs to one that's dropping sticky leaves into the courtyard of the other. To gain wisdom, you have to look behind the surface of things. Always. I'm a seer. People come to me full of troubles and looking for direction from the Mother. I always look deeper than the surface. The Mother has taught me to listen, and She guides me, so I listen with more than just my ears."

"At Knossos, as you learn how the Temple works, you'll discover that priests and priestesses make mistakes. They can sometimes be very wrong. This doesn't mean the Lady is unclear, only that sometimes we don't listen carefully enough. Even your father and I disagree sometimes about what the priestesses say."

Seeing what had to be stunned amazement on my face, she laughed. "Oh, yes. Your father thinks I'm sometimes too willing to submit to the Temple's authority. But on the sort of thing we're talking about, your father and I agree. It's not necessary, or wise, when one is an adult, to let others make decisions for you."

My father walked in looking very tired, his shoulders stooped. She laid her embroidery aside, crossed to him, and embraced him. Unlatching the fibula securing his robe, she began to help him undress. "Leesandra and I have been talking about Zuliya."

Still dismayed, I rose and walked to the door. She caught my eye. "I've asked the Mother to guide you. I ask you to always seek Her guidance. More than that, I can't expect."

At evening meal I studied Zuliya with secret glances and gradually accepted that further attempts to escape his authority were futile. Days passed, and then one afternoon I decided the battle was finished. I had lost. He told a joke and I let myself chuckle. It quickly became easy to enjoy his wit.

One afternoon I laughed at a joke about the clever wolf and the dumb sheep. "Ah," he said, "a smile on the face of a woman whose spirit is foul can blot out even the sun." He paused meaningfully. "But a smile on the face of a woman with a beautiful spirit illumines even the darkest night."

I shifted uneasily. "My spirit isn't beautiful."

"I think it is. It is strong."

"Strong isn't the same as beautiful."

"Perhaps I disagree."

"Then we will always disagree."

"Perhaps."

I couldn't help myself. I smiled. "You are a strange and difficult man."

He only smiled back.

∾ ∾ ∾ ∾

In early spring of the next year, I spent several days with Meidra on her family's farm. No Zuliya. We milked goats, rode donkey-back, collected birds' eggs, and gathered bracken for me to take home to make cushions. We returned to Meidra's townhouse in Alyris. I was expected home, but now great sheets of rain were falling, so I lingered playing draughts, waiting for a clearer sky. My mother's messenger-boy arrived dripping and breathless. "Your mother says come at once. The prince from Anatolia arrived early. She needs your help."

We left immediately, each carrying a large bag of bracken tied around its neck with string. Because mother wanted me home quickly, I chose the most direct route. We passed through two outlander districts, both of which I'd avoided for months.

The first district was solidly Achean. As we passed their horrid temple of Poseidon, the icy rivulet that trickled down my back had nothing to do with the downpour.

The second district housed a complex mix of peoples. Before witnessing the boy's sacrifice, I'd loved to roam its streets, taking delight in the strange clothing, the exotic shops, the seductive smells of foreign foods, the pure energy and variety of life. Now, it's strangeness seemed threatening. Suddenly, I heard a woman shrieking.

Mother's messenger and I ran toward the sound. In a small public courtyard, we found two people. A man stood in the center, and at his feet lay a woman. His tunic was of rough animal hide, his sandals heavy-soled, like those of a laborer. In his massive hands he held a sturdy pole. The woman wore a cloak of equally crude design and was curled in a tight ball at his feet, still shrieking foreign words. To my horror he kicked her, then brought the pole down on her head in one monstrous blow.

The woman uttered an ear-shattering wail. I tightened my grip on the bag in my hand, ran at the man full speed, and swung the bag at his head.

The bag of bracken smacked into the side of the brute's face. The tightly packed fronds exploded into the small square. He roared some foul oath, then with one hand snatched the bag from me and with the other fist hit me in the right eye.

I flew backward and landed on my rear end in a puddle of cold muddy water, my vision wavering, my ears ringing. There I was, sitting next to the crouching woman, both of us absurdly draped with the scattered bracken.

The man leaned close to me, shook his laborer's fist and roared a guttural string of Khorgan. Drunken breath assaulted me. Bloodshot eyes glared from his unshaven face. The enormity of my folly registered. Thinking he'd thrash me senseless with the pole, I bunched up in terror.

By the Lady's good grace, he didn't strike me again. Instead, he grabbed the woman's arm and yanked her to her feet. He shook her. Her head wobbled on her thin neck and he grumbled another word, then spun on his heels and, half-dragging her by her arm, led her from the square.

The houseboy knelt beside me, his dark eyes as big as goblets. "My lady," he said—his use of formal address a sign of his terror that I might be badly hurt. "What should I do?"

"I ... I'm all right. I'm just ... Here, help me up."

He began to pluck bracken off my cloak. Cold water from my soaked kilt trickled down my legs. Black dots swam in front of my injured eye. Gingerly I touched it. It was already swelling closed.

From deep inside, the anger I'd stored for months swelled and churned. The heat of rage surged though my chest, neck and face. "The barbarian will not go unpunished." I pushed the boy's hand. "Leave them."

I spun around and headed for the government house, nearly running. Trotting with his full bag and my empty one, the boy kept pace.

Kalliste's government house stood on one side of a spacious park. As the ambassador from Keftiu, father had the finest rooms, located on the third floor with direct access to the roof garden. At this time of day he would be hearing complaints and soothing the spirits of Keftian traders, Kallistan residents, and a sprinkling of visiting dignitaries. Perfectly aware of my bizarre appearance—everyone we passed gawked—I wanted it no other way. My father should see exactly what had been done to me.

I stomped through the building's pillared entry and up the three flights of stairs, our houseboy trailing me. We swept into my father's antechamber, and perhaps twenty women and men stared at us, mouths agape. Stunned silence was followed by the buzz of speculation. The door to my father's office was closed.

Seeing my father's chief assistant in conversation with a Kallistan matron, I strode directly to them and greeted them with a tap to the heart. The assistant's jaw fell slack. I had intended to wait until they finished, but the matron touched my arm and said, "Whatever has happened, maiden?"

"I want to see my father."

The boy and I were driping muddy water onto a fine green carpet. My father's assistant signaled for an aide to see to the boy, then he ushered me inside the office. Father rose from a couch, blinking rapidly. "By Kokor, what has happened, Leesandra? No. Wait."

He asked the man with him to please retire for a moment, then rushed to me and bent to examine my eye. I told my story while he removed my soaked, muddy cloak, took it to the door, said a few words and handed it out to someone, presumably to have them scrape off the worst of the muck.

I expected him to grow an anger to match mine. He drew me to a sofa opposite his desk, snatched a rug from the floor and tossed it over the sofa's embroidered cushions. "Sit. I've sent for a healer."

I obeyed his command to sit. "My eye will be fine. When I hold the lids open, I can see. But I want you to send someone with me to find him. He has to be found and punished."

My father sat beside me. "You know I can't do that. Keftiu doesn't interfere with the domestic affairs of Kalliste. These outlanders have their own laws, and so long as they behave when they're in their own districts, the Kallistan government doesn't intervene, either."

"But I'm *your* daughter. It's not as if he struck one of his own."

"But you interfered in something that was none of your affair. And you were in the Khorgan district."

"But ... but he was kicking and beating the woman! It was horrible."

"Very likely the woman was his wife. Do you have reason to believe otherwise?"

"What difference does that make? What he was doing is loathsome. Even more so if she's his wife! And besides, I'm not asking that you interfere in a matter between Khorgans, father. It was me he hit in the eye!"

"But you were the first to strike." He smiled. "Though your choice of weapon leaves much to be desired."

A fist tightened over my heart. Teeth clenched, I stood. It was as if he had chosen an outlander over me. I had to get away before I said something I'd never be able to take back. I pivoted on my heel and, before he could even rise, I was halfway out of the room. Under full, angry sail I swept through the antechamber's entry door.

"Leesandra, come back!" he called.

The rain had worsened. I walked rapidly yet with no sense of direction or purpose. I would never forgive him. I passed beside a small park that beckoned to me with its peace and serenity. I suddenly felt drained. I turned toward the shelter of a colonnade in the middle of the park wondering if my unsteady legs would carry me that far when, from the corner of my eye, I saw the white light.

As always, it was at first small and on my right side, but it grew rapidly and filled my vision. The sweet smell blossomed. Dizziness struck. Moments before I'd been suffused with rage and hatred, now the calming warmth wrapped tender arms around me. I fell to my knees, and the Goddess spoke, as clearly as if She were my mother standing beside me. For the first time, I understood Her words. Her voice sparkled like gems, yet was soft.

"You are my child, Leesandra. Forever. Serve me obediently and I will never leave you."

Ah, such compassion in that gentle voice.

I must have lost consciousness because when I became aware again, I lay on my side, curled into a ball.

I rose, staggered to the colonnade, sat on one of the stone benches and pulled my legs up tightly and wrapped myself with my arms. I should have felt chilled to the marrow, but I felt warm. The Lady's presence still protected me. I couldn't have felt more secure. I thought of her words, and a strange and unfamiliar sense of power welled in my chest and spread strength to my limbs.

The stories of my birth rose up in my mind. I laughed, dazed but delighted. I was the last one to realize the truth. My mother knew. Heebe knew. Even my father had agreed I should prepare to serve the Lady. Though I felt unsuited by temperament to be a priestess, I was sure now, beyond doubt, that I was called. And with Her call She would give me the strength to do whatever She would require. I had heard Her speak and at last understood the words.

I stood, stiff in all my joints, but still warm.

I would have to leave my family and all that I loved on Kalliste, but on Keftiu, at Knossos, I would be at the Lady's heart. And if I sought Her aid and served Her faithfully, She would give me the power to do whatever She asked. If I couldn't be outdoors, She would come to me some other way.

For a moment I imagined telling my mother of the vision and the Lady's words, but if I told, I would instantly become the focus of agitated fussing by everyone. I repeated the wonderful words aloud. She'd said nothing about my telling anyone. I decided that, as Zuliya often said, "A wise woman keeps her own counsel."

I started walking. My puffed eye was completely sealed and throbbing hotly, but it was of no importance. Afloat in joy, I strode confidently all the way home, eager to leave Kalliste, eager to reach Knossos. Eager to meet my fate.

∾ ∾ Author's Note ∾ ∾

Having secured the Greek Pelaponnesus, Atistaeus's first major island victory was over the Saronic Gulf island of Aegina. Every shrine to the Goddess was razed and a temple to Poseidon, the third largest in the Mediterranean, was constructed on what had been the temple grounds of the Goddess. Hesiod reports that when Atistaeus wiped the blood of the temple's high priestess on his cloak, the people rioted; and virtually every man, woman, and child on Aegina was killed by the Red King's warriors. Atistaeus then installed families of his soldiers in what had been the homes of the island's inhabitants.

JRE

11

The muscles of Alektrion's arm burned. He bent over the bucket again and, clenching his jaw, scooped another pail of bilge water and hoisted it to Laius, who passed it up to the main deck to be dumped back into the Aegean. Beside Alektrion, four other men in similar agony strained and heaved and groaned.

During what should have been no more than a skirmish with a poorly armed privateer, *Sea Eagle* had been damaged at her water line, something the ship's carpenter couldn't fix at sea. She was taking water like a thirsty camel. With the captive privateer keeping pace, *Sea Eagle* wallowed in the early afternoon toward Palmaki, the largest town on Samos. Alektrion prayed they'd make port before their arms failed and the sea swallowed them.

Laius passed down an empty bucket. Alektrion filled it, swung the bucket over his head, ignored the pain and thought instead of the promise he had made to himself. Before they left Samos, he would visit the famed outlander Temple to the Great Mother. And he had made himself another promise, too. No gambling. Grimaldius had said, "We'll be shore-bound in Samos for at least a month." An entire month. Plenty of time for total disaster. At sea, Alektrion was relatively at peace and in control: few nightmares. But when they put into port the nightmares came frequently, and to avoid them, he drank. Or maybe Laius was right and it was the other way around, that in port he drank more and that brought the nightmares. Whatever the truth, if he drank and gambled, he lost. A month of drinking and gambling on Samos and he could lose his entire proceeds from the sale of the privateer. If he gambled, his dream of buying a ship with Laius would remain no more than a dream.

"No gambling," he muttered.

He thought of last winter and Lemnos. Drinking, unmemorable sex, stupid games of chance. He'd lost everything. The one good memory was the friendship of Philoxea. Eumos had been right about his mother's friend, the woman from Keftiu who had served as hetaira. Philoxea, though Keftian, apparently hadn't cared that he was a half-breed for she had never once brought it up. She lived as if being Keftian did not make her apart. She had also tolerated, without question, his drunkenness and dark moods; and she took over Laius's job of wakening him from dreams when he screamed. She was good company, a good lover, and a good teacher. Still he didn't miss her. His indifference bothered him. But he had a hunger for something he couldn't name, and Philoxea hadn't satisfied it. This season, back at sea, he'd decided the only thing that would bring him peace would be to own his own ship.

"Up oars. Prepare to beach," he heard from overhead.

Alektrion sighed. *Accept my gratitude, Merciful Lady.* They weren't going to sink. He changed his clothes. In his side-bag he packed what things he'd need: razor and comb; extra sandals, kilt, belt; and the pistatas and copper the paymaster had advanced each man upon boarding. The advance would have to last until the privateer was sold.

With Laius, he emerged onto the main deck, and a large hand clapped him on the shoulder. A deep voice said, "Don't forget, Breed. I've promised to teach you to fight."

He turned. A grinning Dolius beamed with his usual good nature. "And your young friend here, too," Dolius added, indicating Laius with a nod.

The grizzled Achean soldier-of-fortune had been hired after the battle with the Pylian ships. He seemed the very model of the awesome Achean warrior Alektrion had so admired during boyhood play. He was tall, powerfully muscled, a man at all times in command of his body and his moods. Three weeks ago, during a grim battle, Alektrion had saved him from a potentially fatal knife wound by shoving a shield between the descending knife and Dolius's back. Alektrion's all-consuming thought during the fight had been that if he planned to survive, he must learn to kill like the best. Later, Dolius thumped him on the back and said, "I owe you my life. I owe you a big favor or many small ones."

Alektrion said at once, "Will you teach me to fight?"

"Can you work yourself until you drop from exhaustion?"

Alektrion convinced the marine he was more than willing. When Dolius soon discovered that Alektrion was half-Achean, he'd taken to calling Alektrion "Breed." It was said with good humor and a feeling of shared blood. Alektrion couldn't bring himself to object. And he wasn't going to let anyone get the idea that the label irked him. Still the name ground repeatedly. Fortunately, no one else used it.

Alektrion grasped Dolius on the forearm and with his other hand he gripped the warrior's callused palm. "How will I find you?"

Laius cut in. "Do you know Samos, Dolius? Do you know a good inn?"Dolius chuckled. "I know Samos well. I'll show you a clean inn you can afford and the best bars in Palmaki."

They accepted his offer. Alektrion was three steps behind Dolius on the gangplank when the first urge for a drink struck. His mouth could almost taste the refreshing bite. He stepped onto hard-packed sand. The afternoon sun burned fiercely. A strong, hot Anatolian wind ruffled the curls at his forehead and carried the scent of the lands of the east. Samos lay so close to the mainland, he'd been told, that from a certain high point he could look across the strait lying between and see the Lydian coast.

Three of Dolius's outlander friends joined them. The activity on the wharf diverted Alektrion's attention from thoughts of bars and ale. Samos was the farthest he'd been from Keftian influence. The goods being hauled onto and off the ships weren't anything he hadn't seen many times in Alyris: cedar logs from Keftiu, bales of Agyptian cotton, ingots of copper from the mines at Melkos. The difference seemed to be the scent of something foreign in the air. And that almost all adult men wore beards. A band of cloth tied around the forehead kept their straight shoulder-length hair in place. He saw plenty of short, thigh- or knee-length Keftian kilts—Knossos kept a strong presence in Samos—but many men wore calf-length robes belted at the waist, and the working garb of laborers fell all the way to their ankles. There were more donkeys used along Palmaki's dock than he'd ever seen on all of Kalliste. And most remarkable, there were no women.

Their party of six turned into a narrow, curved and paved street leading inland. Tall shops cast the street into perpetual shadow. The variety of wares, from rugs to carved and inlaid furniture to jewelry to farm implements to exotic fruits, would have been impressive, even on Alyris. Laius stopped and stared at a shop selling monkeys, then at one selling articles claimed to enhance coupling.

"Not now," Dolius grumbled. "Later I'll give you time."

They passed a tavern. Alektrion smelled cooking lamb. His stomach growled, but the taste for which his mouth watered was ale.

Dolius let them pause only when they passed a sports field. He dropped back to Alektrion's side, pointed out the running track, indicated several men wrestling on a large grassy area and others practicing swordplay. "This is the nearest field to the inn."

A pod of young boys was watching a pair of wrestlers. At the edge of the grass, a vendor of boiled eggs had set up a stand. Laius leaned against Alektrion and whispered, "Loan me enough change to buy some gull eggs."

Alektrion fingered through his sidebag, found the pistatas, and handed them over.

"If we take rooms at this inn," Dolius said, "this is the place for us to meet." He touched his own weapon and eyed Alektrion's side bag. "Did you leave your sword at the ship?"

Alektrion nodded.

"Go back first thing tomorrow and get it. Your first lesson is that a warrior keeps his weapon near to hand."

Youthful laughter interrupted. The boys had encircled Laius. Laius waved his hands several times, then seemed to pull a brown-speckled bird egg from one boy's ear.

The boys cheered and laughed.

Dolius set off again, leading now through a residential section. Alektrion saw women now, but none assessed him openly as they would in a Keftian town. Laius stepped closer and with lowered voice said, "I need a favor."

"You need only ask."

"I've got myself into a bit of a corner again. About money."

Alektrion knew what had to be coming. Laius already owed him two month's credit. He mentally shook his head, but thinking of his own losses on Lemnos, decided he was no one to judge.

"I played Skull and Bones the night before we took the privateer. I doubt you'll be surprised to hear I lost most of my advance. Could you lend me enough for my room? Just until the privateer sells?"

Alektrion nodded. "We'll take a room together. If you're agreeable. I'll understand, though, if you don't want to sleep with me. I've enough money to get you a room of your own. Or with one of the others."

Laius grinned and thumped Alektrion on his bare back so hard his skin stung. "Your nightmares don't bother me. I go back to sleep as fast as a baby."

The Brown Ox was clean. Its owner, a thin man with a bulbous nose and eyes like polished lava pebbles, remembered Dolius and greeted him warmly. Arrangements were agreed upon for their rooms and meals. Before disappearing into the sleeping room next door, Dolius said, "There are no public shrines on Samos. You two will have to do your prayers in the temple or in your room or right in public with everyone staring at you. And don't expect the calling of the conchs. My suggestion is pray now. As soon as you're ready, we'll leave for the bathhouse."

Alektrion and Laius looked at each other. They were, indeed, very far from the Lady's heart. They washed hands and feet in the room's two small basins, said prayers together, then hurried to meet the others. It was late afternoon when the six marines approached a tavern, their bodies clean and freshly oiled. Just outside a wide double door, Laius whispered, "Swear you'll not let me within a stadia of a game of Skull and Bones."

Alektrion chuckled. "We're a fine pair. You keep me from screaming. I keep you from gambling. And whatever happens, I must not gamble either."

His pulse accelerated as he walked through the entry. He could not deny his urge for a drink now, not if the city caught on fire or a quake brought the tavern's walls down around him. The room vibrated with voices and the sound of laughter. The place was almost as dark as one of *Sea Eagle's* holds. His vision adjusted and he felt a sudden sense of the foreign, even stronger than on the wharf. He stood in a full tavern peopled only by men!

Near the back they found two square tables and shoved them together. Closer inspection proved his initial assessment wrong. Women were present, but greatly outnumbered. The men's clothing indicated they were laborers, lower-class merchants, and seamen. He nodded to four members of *Sea Eagle's* crew seated at another table.

A scraggly-bearded Samian youth ambled up. They ordered. The drinks came first. The sharp taste of the ale on Alektrion's tongue made his body relax like wax placed in the sun. Platters of meat, bread, cheese, olives and a gruel-like concoction of mashed cucumber, oil, and spices followed. Dolius showed how to eat it by scooping it up with the bread.

From a table halfway to the door, two women rose. Alektrion studied their clothes, looking for some hint as to why they were here among so many men. Each wore a dress that appeared to be a single piece of cloth that started at mid-calf, wound around the body several times, then looped across the breasts and over one shoulder. The colors were dull, cheaply dyed.

He expected them to walk to the door. Instead they turned and walked to the next nearest table. Two men leapt to their feet and fetched chairs. There could be no mistaking the meaning of the smiles and the batting of the women's eyelashes.

Laius leaned toward Dolius. "The women," he said, indicating the room with a gesture of his head. "Why so few?"

"They're not here to drink, boy. This isn't Kalliste, where a woman's free to go where she chooses. This is Samos, and these women look for men looking for sex."

"So why are there so few?"

"Because no woman of quality would put her foot in a tavern."

"Well, the patrons are a rough lot themselves," Laius continued. "I wouldn't expect to find the most refined ladies in town, but surely a working class woman needs a good toss now and then. Are you saying most women here go only to the temple for sex?"

"No, my very young friend. I'm definitely not saying Samian women go to a temple for sex. They're expected to go only to a husband."

Laius sat his beer down with a thud, slopping a bit over the side. "What?" The noise caught the attention of the other three men.

"Wake up, Laius," said a grinning marine from Eritrea. "We're practically in Lydia. Men here see their women a lot differently than you Kallistans."

Alektrion took another sip of his third ale thinking, "Men see their women?" The marine spoke as if women were something possessed. He felt again that intriguing sense of something wildly foreign.

Dolius popped a fat green olive into his mouth, severed it smartly with one bite, and washed it down with ale. "Samians aren't as wrong-headed as some places I been. But you best make sure before you get involved here that the woman's free. If she's married, you may have Kokor's own time with her husband. Why, with some races here, even unmarried women are off limits." He nodded and smiled toward the two women Alektrion had been watching. "They're the best. The tavern women are independent agents. And I say we invite some over."

As if they'd read Dolius's mind, the two women rose, excused themselves with smiles, and undulated toward their table. From a different direction two more women approached. All four arrived together. The six men leapt to their feet and drew up chairs. More food was ordered, and drinks. Alektrion felt the women's appraising gazes slide over his skin.

Not long into conversation, a marine leaned close to one of the women and said, "Would you like to take a walk?"

She nodded. With very little in the way of excusing themselves, they left.

Alektrion started on another ale. The pleasant-looking woman he caught watching him most often had used a hair dye that gave her black hair red highlights. She smiled. She had remarkably crooked teeth. He realized then that she didn't smile often.

He'd lost count of his drinks when the thought occurred that he'd like to bed her. There were no such women on Kalliste. There was no need for them because any man wanting sex without attachment could go to a hetaira and be assured of the best. He was fascinated by the strangeness of the concept of paying the woman for lying with her.

What else might be different? He caught her eye and smiled. She smiled back, taking care to keep her lips closed.

"Would you like to take a walk," he said. Laius kicked his leg.

The woman nodded. He rose and so did she.

"Don't forget, Breed." Dolius had an amused glint in his eye. "And you too, Laius. We meet tomorrow for your first lesson immediately after your prayers."

Alektrion shook his head. "I can't begin tomorrow, Dolius. I must do something I can't put off."

Dolius frowned. "If I'm to be your teacher, what I say becomes law. If you can't agree, say so now. Otherwise there'll be no point to the effort."

Laius, as eager as Alektrion to learn from the battle-wise marine, quickly said, "I'm free tomorrow. And I agree most readily."

Alektrion considered briefly that he might put off his plans. But he really couldn't. "I also agree to submit myself. And I'll not make any further exceptions. But I've promised I'd do something tomorrow. I try to keep promises."

Dolius crossed his arms and leaned back. "Keeping promises to oneself as well as others is as it should be for an honorable man. But from now on, make none, to yourself or to others, that you don't check with me. Understood?"

Alektrion agreed. Then, with the woman leading the way, he followed her swaying hips into the early evening. "What's your name?" she asked. Her Keftian, though serviceable, was ugly to the ear.

He told her his name and that he was from Kalliste, at the same time his mind was trying to decide what to do. Would the Brown Ox's innkeeper be upset if he brought her there? For that matter, did he want to take her back there? What about Laius?

"Your name?" he asked. Her straight hair hung lifelessly to her shoulderblades. He suddenly realized he had no idea what bathing customs she might follow and hoped her hair was clean.

"Kladia." She took his arm, and the warmth of womanly flesh sent a jolt of anticipation through him. He'd been away from Philoxea for nearly four weeks and his shipboard fantasies about Serena had been fueling his appetite.

He took a breath, prepared to launch into an exploration of what was expected.

Kladia said, "Do you like to go your place? Or we can go mine."

"Yours," he said.

She then turned them back toward the wharf.

Rather soon they turned into a narrow alley, and not far down they entered a three-story house. Kladia took him to the second floor. Another couple came down the stairs. The man's furtive grin suggested that he and the woman weren't man and wife.

One window high up on the wall opposite the entry served Kladia's small, sage-smelling room. She lit a lamp on a table beside the door. When he was inside, she lit two more tiny lamps. A bed, barely large enough for one, was pushed against one wall. Two tall cupboards stood under the window. A tiny table with three stools was arranged in front of the third wall. He faced her and saw a shrine beside the doortable. Inside it squatted some deity resembling a man with a goat's head.

Kladia stroked his arm. He was immediately arroused. "Drink?" she asked. "I have only wine." She looped his sidebag off his shoulder and sat it beside the flickering lamp.

"Yes. I'd like wine."

On a shelf of one of the cupboards sat a few plates, a few goblets, and crudely painted eating utensils. Another shelf held bread and some fruits. A perfume vial and cosmetics occupied another shelf, and he decided that perhaps she did live entirely in this small space. The other cupboard might be for clothes.

She poured two drinks, rather little in either cup, then swallowed her cup's contents in one gulp. He followed her example.

"Four pistata if you stay only long enough to come once. Ten for twice. Twenty for whole night."

The baldness of the transaction fascinated him. "Agreed."

She smiled her tight-lipped smile, took the cup from him and set both on the table. He reached for her hand and kissed the palm. He'd learned a lot from Philoxea. He might have only barely turned seventeen, and Kladia might have been with many men, but he would show the foreign woman he wasn't lacking in experience.

He kissed her wrist. She sighed. He let his hands drift slowly up her arms. Her skin was soft, warm, firm. She untied the belt of his kilt. He felt heat and movement in his groin. He took a deep breath.

Her dress was secured at the shoulder with a simple knot. He undid it, unwound the material to reveal her breasts. They stood high and had small, very pink nipples. He began to regret how long it had been since he'd bedded Philoxea; he had to slow himself more or he'd not have time to rouse Kladia to fulfillment.

"There," she said as his kilt dropped to the floor. She looked into his eyes. "What do you like?" She took him into one of her hands and he groaned. He was already on fire and ready to enter her.

"Should I ..." She started to kneel in front of him.

"No." He caught her shoulders. "No. Let me breathe a moment." He unwound the rest of the material of her dress and tossed it onto one of the chairs, then took her hand and led her to the bed.

She lay down and he lay beside her, propped on one elbow. He forced himself to breathe slowly as he let one hand play over her breasts, gently pinched one and then the other. She closed her eyes. He bent to her and licked the tip of a nipple. She smelled of cheap lily perfume.

He put his mouth close to her skin and blew hot breath onto the nipple. It tightened even harder. He took care that his fingers never left her skin. She moaned over and over. Her cries sent fire rushing under his skin.

He licked a trail from one breast to the other, began to suck the second nipple. The heat and throbbing in his groin filled his mind. He wanted in her now, this moment. *Wait, wait, wait.*

He moved his hand between her legs, slowly caressing, found her wet. With his hand and knee he opened her to him, and then slid inside. When the spasms came, fire rushed through him as his spirit fled to the Goddess.

He returned feeling out of breath. Feeling good. Had the Goddess taken Kladia too? He wasn't sure. Maybe Kladia didn't care. Her objective was money. Maybe the pleasure meant nothing to her. "I'm sorry." He lay back on the bed, his skin still warm and alive. "I couldn't wait any longer."

She stroked his face, then rested her hand on his chest. "I too had pleasure, Alek. I assure you. Great pleasure."

They lay in silence for a while, then his curiosity demanded satisfaction. "I'm a foreigner, and unaccustomed to your ways. May I ask something."

She sat up and ran her fingers over his chest, tapping lightly. Tantalizing. "Please," she said.

"If the giving of pleasure suits you, why don't you become hetaira. I know Cybele has a Temple here. Does the Mother's Temple at Samos have no hetaira?"

"Of course it has hetaira. But I not worship Cybele. My people worship Bamaalek. We have no custom of hetaira. And because Bamaalek is my God, they not take me at the Cybele Temple."

"You might convert." He glanced at the stark room. "You would certainly live better in the Temple of the Mother."

"But the priestesses would take the money. I need the money. No man of my people will marry me."

"Why?"

She blushed and said nothing. He'd stumbled into a sensitive area. He started to change subjects but she interrupted. "I slept with a man I thought I could not live without. But we not married. We were discovered."

So. She must belong to one of those races where a woman's sexuality was something pledged to one man. To have lain with another had made her an outcast. "I'm very sorry."

"My own sister discovered. She told my father. I had to leave my house. Now I have no other way to make my money."

"I still think you should consider converting to Cybele." He didn't add that he thought the image of Bamaalek in her shrine was one of the ugliest things he'd ever seen. "The priestesses would take the money, but you'd live well while you served. And hetaira may keep the gifts they receive. Many become wealthy before they leave the Goddess's service."

At this her eyes widened and her fingers stopped their delicious tapping. "Is truly so?"

"Yes. It is."

She considered that revelation for a time. "I could not serve false religion. I could not say I worship goddess when I don't." She quickly looked at him apologetically from the corner of her eye, realizing she'd probably insulted him. "Now I sorry."

The thought struck him it was her religion, which he thought false, that had separated her from her family. Why would she remain loyal to it? "No need. I'm grateful you answer my questions."

"I have a question."

"Ask."

Her gaze dropped to the rumpled cover of her bed, a gesture he would have described as shy. "Why did you come with me?"

Strange question. After all, she'd come with her companion to their table seeking business. "Why do you ask?"

"You are Keftian, no?"

This was no time to explain the significance of having a non-Keftian mother. By his dress, by his speech, by his worship, by his loyalty he would be judged Keftian by any outlander. "Yes."

"Then why you not go to hetaira of Cybele?"

"Is that so odd?"

"But of course. You are only the third Keftian man I ever serve. They always go to Temple or take a lover in town. Even many men who not worship Cybele go to the hetaira. I see mostly men of my religion or others who want nothing to do with Her worship. Why you come with me?"

"My friend said the women of Samos that come to the taverns are good to lie with. I trust my friend's judgment."

"I'm grateful to your friend. Tell him so." She touched soft fingers to the side of his face. "Keftian men are the finest lovers in the world. They are trained in the ways to please a woman."

Her comment answered conclusively the question of whether he'd pleased her.

"Like more wine?" She rose from the bed and he watched her buttocks, which he now realized were rather large. Then the significance of her question registered. She was inquiring if he'd stay to lie with her again. Maybe stay the night.

He rose and went to where his strap, kilt, and belt lay on the floor. "It's late and I have something to do tomorrow." He began to dress. She retrieved her simple cloth dress, wound it around her, and sat on one of the stools, her shoulders slumped, her eyes having lost all trace of sparkle. Her look tugged at his heart, but he couldn't imagine spending the night in this tiny room on that tiny bed.

Feeling enormous awkwardness, he withdrew some pistatas from his sidebag. He selected four and without the slightest awkwardness on her part, she opened her hand and took them. He felt a strange kind of sorrow for her.

He walked back to the door. She didn't rise. At the door he slung on his sidebag, feeling in the inside pocket for more money. He laid twenty pistatas on the doortable. "I thank you, Kladia, for your graciousness. I pray the Goddess lights your path."

He took the walk back to the Brown Ox at a slow pace. He felt as empty at this moment as he'd ever been. Coupling wasn't going to give him peace. He needed to be at sea. And he needed to be the owner of his own vessel, to decide to come and go as he chose.

He woke in the morning in a low mood, dressed, and left Laius snoring softly. From the proprietor he got directions to the Temple of Cybele. His walk toward the heart of Palmaki took him uphill a short distance, then the street widened and ran flat and parallel to the coast. From the sun's burn on his shoulders, he knew the day would be hot again, maybe even hotter as he felt no hint of yesterday's breeze.

The main street and many narrow alleys teemed with people. On Kalliste, most people went on foot. Here donkey carts, man-carried litters, and even ox-drawn carts, which on Kalliste were never seen in the heart of town, competed for space with foot traffic.

He passed prosperous-looking businesses and fragrant temples of modest size dedicated to an impressive variety of goddesses and gods. In what the proprietor had said was the town's most important square, he found the Temple to Cybele.

The outer wall ran along the entire length of one side of the square. His breathing quickened. He stood at last before one of the Mother's most renowned holy places. Here he would do something he could do nowhere else he'd ever been.

12

Never had Alektrion set foot in one of the Mother's Temples. In the world that lay within Keftiu's tight embrace, those permitted the most intimate worship of the Goddess were chosen by birth. No foreigners allowed. No "breeds" either. In the rest of the world full privileges weren't restricted, so in this foreign city, distant from his home and from the Lady's heart, he could enter.

His father had told him the Keftian Law of Exclusion was necessary to keep Keftian ways pure. Having no grounds except his own heart to argue otherwise, he had accepted this hard fact. Nevertheless, like so much about his half-caste status, if he let himself think about it, he bristled.

Sacred horns painted gold lined the perimeter wall, but their form here was more life-like than the angular, stylized form at home. And positioned between their tips was a moon disc, not the butterfly of regeneration.

Inside the wall, vendors in a park-like area displayed offerings. He purchased a barley cake and raisins. Another table displayed clay miniatures: hands, feet, a nose, torsos, or a woman's breasts. After making offerings and prayers and explaining their bodily complaint, worshippers could leave the token as a reminder. Or leave one in gratitude. Alektrion purchased a warrior in the attitude of reverence.

He washed his feet, then entered. Frankincense penetrated the antechamber. Beyond it he entered a dimly lit, hushed space, the distant corners of which receded into darkness. Black carpet covered the floor. Towering in the room's center, brilliantly lit by a ring of man-high candles, stood a three-times-larger-than-life statue of Cybele, a fearsome lioness on each side beneath her hands.

His breathing caught as he stared at Her face. Stern, somber. The Mother gave generously, but She also demanded obedience. The sinking sensation that he didn't belong struck him. For him to enter was to defile. He should leave.

But his feet seemed to have taken root.

Some moments more and the feeling of wrongness passed. Here the Goddess made no proscriptions. All were welcome.

The room held perhaps fifteen people, some standing, some kneeling. Tables of offering sat at the base of the candles, and beside each was a small lamp and twists of straw. He knelt, placed the raisins, cake, and figurine on the table, then used the straw twists to set the cake burning. In the position of reverence he stared into the face of the Mother of All. Silently he prayed, the prayer he thought she would most want to hear from him.

Creator of all life, Hear me, your son.
Look into my heart and judge me.
Forgive me where I have failed to follow your Laws.
Make me strong to obey.

The quiet of the room seeped into him. Calmness, soft as the softest woolen gown, settled on his shoulders, wrapped around him. Perhaps it was a trick of the subtle light, or the suggestion of incense, but in his heart he knew it was She.

You who see all, You know I'm troubled. So many things eat at me. I remember peace. And I have none. Your seer told me that I should remain faithful, and I failed. I am deeply sorry. I don't know what demon takes me when I drink too much. I tell myself it's to escape the nightmare. But it's a fool's path.

Her face was stern, but She was listening. Never had he felt Her closer.

I have such anger. At even small things. Say my friend Dolius calls me Breed. He means it kindly. I don't know why I can't accept that. But mostly I hate the Red King and the evil he's spreading. Give me the heart to fight if I have to. You know I sicken whenever it looks like I'll be in a fight. Mostly, protect me from the rage that opened my heart to a demon that loves killing. That isn't who I want to be. To know I had such a passion in my heart, ever, would kill my mother.

The stern gaze looked deeply.

Please. Let me fight bravely, but can you keep me from so much destructive anger. Can't there be something in between?

He heard the seer's voice, "If you remain faithful ..."

Aloud he said, "I want to. Make your servant strong. Strong enough to bear the dreams. Strong in heart in battle."

A woman knelt beside him. The sense of connection to the Lady evaporated. He remained a moment more in the position of reverence, decided that while on Samos, he would come to this place as often as he could.

He rose, bowed low, backed away twenty paces, turned and left. Even in the antechamber, the light was so strong he stopped a moment to get his bearings. Outside, he winced.

Dolius had ordered that he fetch his sword, so he set off for the wharf. He wasn't far from the entry to a wide boulevard when shouts erupted from one of the many uphill alleys. He spun in their direction. An unhitched donkey cart piled high with baskets careened toward him, its wheels bouncing on the uneven cobbles, its unsecured load jiggling like tossing-bones in a gambling cup. People jumped or dove out of its way.

Alektrion tensed; the cart was headed for a curtained sedan chair no more than ten strides away. The man holding the chair's forward poles saw the cart, blanched, froze. Alektrion dashed to him, wrested his hands from the poles. He pulled the man forward and the front end of the chair fell with a loud thump. The cart missed the man and the chair, only barely clipping the bearer's foot, then bounded across the street. Yowling, the bearer wrenched himself out of Alektrion's grip and grabbed his heel.

The rear man lowered his poles to the ground, bent close to the silk curtain and spoke to the rider. He then ran to his companion. A crowd gathered while the two bearers inspected the damaged foot. Though gashed, the man could walk. The cart driver trotted up, red-faced. Leaning next to the curtain, he apologized to the chair's occupant. A soft, feminine voice dismissed him, and he rushed off to his cart.

The crowd dispersed. The bearers returned to the chair and grasped the poles. When the rear man signaled to lift, Alektrion stooped to help the injured man take up his burden. The man nodded his thanks.

The bearers took two steps when the soft voice behind the curtain said, "Wait."

A ringed hand pulled back the drape to reveal a copper-haired, fair-skinned woman with startling green eyes, the color of shallow sea. "My thanks to you for aiding my bearer," she said in flawless Keftian.

"I was there."

"You acted with great speed."

What a feast she was. He found himself at a loss for words. The heat was suddenly stifling.

"I haven't seen you before. And I'm familiar with a great many faces."

The last thing in the world he would do is tell this woman he was a lowly rower. "I serve on a Keftian warship, the *Sea Eagle*, from Alyris. We arrived yesterday."

"Ah." She made it sound as if, by some magic, she understood everything about him. "And what is your business here, away from the docks and the sea?"

"I came to honor Cybele."

She smiled, and his heart stumbled from the radiance of it. "I, too, worship the Great Mother. It's nice we have that in common. I am Belamena Sonaria. May I ask your name?"

"Alektrion, son of Meela."

"Well, Alektrion, I'm giving a party tonight. Many interesting people of Samos will be there. You bring fresh news from Alyris. Would you like to join us?"

"Yes."

She gave directions. Then, after treating him to another of her heart-stopping smiles, she signaled the bearers, who whisked her away.

Only when he started walking toward the wharf did he realize he hadn't thought of Laius, Dolius, or the others. "Kokor take me!" Laius especially would be hurt he hadn't arranged for them to go together. And he hadn't asked permission from Dolius. Dolius had said Alektrion's evenings would be his to spend as he pleased, but he should have made certain this was acceptable.

The woman would probably never miss him if he didn't show up. Perhaps he shouldn't go.

He envisioned Belamena's eyes and smile. Cool. Inviting. Like the interior of the gymnasium on a hot day. Again he swore. He'd have to face up to Laius's displeasure. And maybe that of Dolius. But no man in possession of his senses would throw away a chance to see Belamena Sonaria of Palmaki again.

∽ ∽ ∽ ∽

A pair of sedan chairs whisked past Alektrion. Torches flanking massive entry gates of a home on his left created quivery chair-shadows on the street as the bearers trotted toward the next entry.

He fingered the bronze lion's-head fibula at his shoulder. It was borrowed from Dolius, along with the richly brown tunic that hung a bit too loosely. Their innkeeper had insisted that Alektrion's inexpensive white tunic would be the wrong thing to wear to a party in Palmaki's wealthiest district.

Again he tugged at the fibula. He suddenly felt the perfect hayseed, come to town and invited to a party where he'd doubtless do something wrong. For a horrified moment he wondered if that had been Belamena's reason for inviting him: amusement for wealthy guests. "Kokor take me for a fool!" The moment he stopped having a good time he'd leave.

Impressive homes lined the street, their outer walls conjoined. The sedan chairs entered the gate of a brightly-lit mansion on the hill's crest, and he guessed their occupants might also be going to her party.

Stone gateposts there bore an incised garland of poppies, her family insignia, Belamena had said. Pottery lanterns illumined an entry garden, and beyond, the door of the house stood open. Brightly gowned figures talked in clusters. Flute and cythera music drifted into the warm night.

He'd barely stepped inside when a male servant presented a tray. "The short cups are sweet wine, the taller cups are dryer, the small fat cups are pear nectar."

Dolius expected him to be fit tomorrow. He chose nectar.

The interior courtyard buzzed with the talk of half a hundred men and women. He overheard Keftian, spoken with disastrous accents, and Akkadian. The talk seemed to be of art and politics. He searched for Belamena. A statue of a seated Cybele dominated the courtyard's center, and flowering plants hung from the second story. Behind the supporting columns on all four sides, doors led to more rooms.

He strolled toward an opening at the courtyard's far end. It led him into yet another and even larger court. His assessment of Belamena's wealth doubled, tripled, quadrupled. Laughter exploded from a circled group to his right. She was there, the center of attention.

She caught his eye, nodded, and smiled. Fully revealed, she was of medium height, slender, with a long graceful neck. He judged her to be about ten years older than he. Her burnt-umber robe was worked with gold and silver flowers, and the jewelry holding her upswept copper hair and the girdle at her waist were also gold.

A familiar, hungry longing gripped him. He wanted to touch her in the way he'd recently touched Kladia. But that wasn't exactly right, either. He wanted … he couldn't name exactly what he wanted. His limbs suddenly restless, he turned away.

A table heaped with food and surrounded by guests stretched the length of the courtyard. He selected from four kinds of braised fowl, roast suckling boar, fresh clams, spiced and oiled squid, platters overflowing with cut and uncut fruits, five different cheeses, sweets, and a variety of breads.

A hand gripped his forearm. A buxom matron with a lined face and irregularly colored skin, almost like a pied cow, said, "Aren't you Jamal's son? Oh, no." She let go. "I see now you're not. How very silly of me. You must forgive me. But you look a great deal like the son of one of my late husband's business partners. But then, I'm forever making such mistakes. Do, do forgive me."

The woman, who reminded him of a pleasant but silly cow, continued to babble, all the while either touching his arm or catching his eye. On Kalliste the gestures would suggest interest in a liaison. He needed to escape.

A servant bearing a drink tray walked up behind her. The woman waved her arm in a gesture of explanation. Her hand smacked the tray. It clattered to the floor at the feet of a portly man sauntering from the table with a full plate. He slipped on the spilled wine. His feet flew forward, he plunked onto his rear end, his hairy legs and knobby knees exposed to the tops of his thighs, food arcing into the air. His plate landed and, in the room's sudden silence, made a spiraling sound as it circled faster and faster on its base until, fully spent, it settled.

Alektrion bit his lip to keep from laughing.

"Oh my, oh my," said the pleasant but silly cow.

Alektrion knelt next to the man. "Are you hurt?"

He heard the patter of sandals accompanied by the scent of lilac. "My dear Menaxamus."

On the side opposite Alektrion, Belamena knelt by the man named Menaxamus. Another man knelt to help her and, aided by both, Menaxamus stood. She drew her guest away to see what her servants could do about the wine on his robe.

"Took quite a spill, didn't he?" said a male voice.

The pied cow had disappeared, no doubt embarrassed, and a strikingly handsome young man stood at Alektrion's side. "Lucky he didn't break something."

"My name is Lormaximander. My friends call me Lormax. I don't think I've seen you at Belamena's before."

"I've only recently arrived in Palmaki."

Lormaximander smiled. "Then you're not one of Belamena's regular friends?"

"I met her only today."

Lormaximander offered to introduce Alektrion to other guests. The handsome youth slipped his arm in the crook of the arm in which Alektrion held his wine and drew him toward a cluster of men. Something about the gesture struck Alektrion as odd, and the feeling of being a hayseed returned.

The circle of five wedged open to admit them. The first words he heard came from a gray-beard wearing rings on every finger. "Only a Keftian sympathizer would think it reasonable to pay a tax for something we'd be better off doing for ourselves."

Keftian sympathizer? The man's tone held disgust. Alektrion stiffened.

"And I say only a simpleton would think we could mount enough protection ourselves." This from a man with a large chin wart who stood opposite gray-beard. He had more to say. "The Keftian navy is enormous and still can't stop all piracy. How could a private navy hope to succeed? The tax paid to Knossos is worth every pistata."

"I think you're being naive," gray-beard countered. "What about these increasing attacks? Don't you find it odd, if the Keftians are so powerful, that we're losing ships to what we've been told are small rogue operations? Who's talked to witnesses? The Keftians claim they find all aboard dead. Who's to say what really happened?"

He wanted to tell them of his encounter with Atistaeus's ships, of the dead he'd seen with his own eyes, of his hunger for revenge and how *Sea Eagle's* other men shared his loathing for The Red King, but a third man addressed gray-beard. "I agree the tax is high. The confederation ought to petition Knossos to lower it. But you're wrong about their navy being involved in the piracy. I don't believe it. They know our willingness to pay the taxes depends on believing that they serve our members reasonably honestly. If it were proved they were robbing us, there would be a revolt. And besides, I hear rumors that are quite different. I hear that Atistaeus, that grisly bastard from Pylos, is itching for still more conquests and these so-called pirates are really under his orders."

Alektrion decided he was grateful to the Lady that he'd worn Dolius's Achean tunic, not his own, the cut of which screamed "Keftian." Here was an unprecedented opportunity to hear what outlanders thought of his navy. And he might learn more about Atistaeus. He clamped his jaw tight.

"Who could revolt against the Keftians, Semus?" a fourth man said. "The idea's absurd on its face. Who has the power of Knossos?"

The man with the wart shook his head. "The Keftians can sometimes be hard to stomach, I admit. They seem to have this notion that the rest of us don't know how to wipe ourselves."

This observation evoked billowing laughter. Having suffered, himself, from this Keftian sense of superiority, Alektrion winced, but privately agreed.

"But I've been to Knossos," continued the man with the wart. "And you have not, Semus. There's no city like it. Its streets are broad and run with fresh water. The vast underground sewers keep it astonishingly sweet smelling. Public gardens and beautiful baths are everywhere. Its people, a bit effete I'll admit, are the most cultured in the world. Giving allowance for the exceptions you'll find when you deal with men or, in the case of the Keftians, with women ..."

Several of the men chuckled and gray-beard interrupted. "That's another thing. What man wants business dealings with a people who listen to the advice of women?"

"Now there, Semus, I know you're wrong," said the third man, who had originally agreed with the beringed gray-beard. "Man or woman, the Keftians are as shrewd in businesses as any race you'll ever meet. They live for the bargain."

"Let me finish," insisted the man with the wart. "Whatever you may think about the Keftians personally, they provide the strength needed to keep piracy at sea to a minimum and have done so for as long as anyone remembers. No private navy could do this. And there are, in my mind, few if any races, run by women or by men, I'd trust with the task. Knossos has never broken faith with the alliance, and I defy anyone to show me proof they're doing so now."

Gray-beard snorted. He launched into a diatribe about Keftians as bigheaded traders who'd just as soon cheat you as look at you. Alektrion clenched a fist. He'd heard enough.

He didn't know what the local custom was for disengaging from conversation—and didn't care. To Lormaximander he murmured that he had to piss and walked away. He was nearly to the front entry when the scent of lilac announced Belamena's presence. She took his arm. A renewed rush of male interest burned in his groin. "I was look-ing for you. And here I find you leaving."

"I have to meet friends."

"But we haven't talked at all. I apologize for not finding you sooner."

Her hand still rested on his arm, its warmth like the rays of a mid-day sun. "No need for apology. Thank you for your hospitality." He hesitated, than added, "As you suggested I would, I've found the people and the conversation most interesting."

"I can tell you're unhappy." She drew him out of the path of a laughing man and woman. Her sea-green eyes were beautiful, but his gaze kept slipping to her lips, heavy with invitation and red with the color of a fully ripe pomegranate. "If I can't convince you to stay now, will you join me tomorrow for midday meal? There are far too many people here tonight. I promise, tomorrow we'll be able to talk."

He very much wanted to see her again. But then he thought of Dolius. During the day, Alektrion's time belonged to the art of war. "I, too, am sorry we didn't talk tonight, but my days are fully occupied."

"Come then to a light supper tomorrow. Our custom is what you're used to. We take our main meal at midday. Now I think of it, having your company at supper would be even more pleasant."

"Yes. I could come to supper."

She squeezed his now throbbing arm. "Excellent." Keeping him firmly in her grasp, she walked him to the door and through the gar-den to the gate. "I'll wait eagerly to see you, Alektrion of Kalliste."

She let go. He traveled on light feet into the street. Oh how he needed a drink, the quicker the better. Just one. It was early. He could still find Laius.

He strode downhill, wondering. If Belamena Sonaria gave parties for two hundred or more, how many might she have for a light supper?

13

Alektrion's mouth tasted like the dregs of a brewer's tub. Where was he? He remembered the Brown Ox. Remembered last night, Laius, drinking, gambling, and—

Gambling! He snapped his eyes open, threw off the thin coverlet and swung his legs to the floor. Fool! In three strides he reached his sidebag. His fingers tore at the thong that laced closed the pocket in the bottom and, finding coins, he pulled them out. He counted them. He'd lost very little. He sighed with relief.

He glanced at the bed. "Laius, time to meet Dolius. Get up."

A shake of Laius's shoulder elicited a muffled, "A bull kicked me in the head." No movement.

That's how it always was after a really wild night: Alektrion awoke with little more than a foul mouth while Laius wished he'd died and the Ancient had taken him.

The room's single window stood open to the dawn. The Anatolian wind, hot and still blowing strong, played with the edges of the drying cloth on the wash basin. The wind raked his mind. So many days of hot winds set his teeth on edge.

He finished shaving, then called again to Laius. "You want me to tell Dolius you quit?"

Laius sat up, held his head between his hands. "Kokor's little brother, Alek. My head is splitting."

While Laius bathed, then threw on his roughest tunic and a rugged pair of sandals, Alektrion sat on the edge of the bed polishing his sword's hilt. Dolius could teach him the skills he needed to keep alive until he and Laius had enough money for a merchant ship, but the old marine had little patience with fools or slackers. Well, whatever Dolius required, Alektrion would do.

The mercenary sat in the common room nursing a cup of warm celery-root juice, a decoction he drank to relieve joints that ached from old injuries. He grinned a satisfied smile over an emptied plate. They started to sit. Dolius stood. "You're not eating yet. First a small, brisk run."

Dolius ran them to the park and then around and around the dirt track until Alektrion thought his chest would explode. Finally Dolius gave the command to stop. He watched their breathing and how long it took them to recover. Alektrion's feet felt tied to anchors during the trot back to the inn. The skimpy breakfast Dolius allowed—olives, goat cheese, and bread—tasted better than any delicacy he'd nibbled at Belamena's party. The honeyed mulberry tea pumped new life into his legs. Unfortunately they returned immediately to the park, Dolius carrying a javelin and he and Laius weights. "I intend to teach you the Achean way," Dolius said somberly. "So let's see what you children can do."

How far could they jump, how far could they heave the javelin, how quickly could they catch a dropping weight, how many times could they lift the weights before tiring? Not once did the old warrior smile. Several times he grunted in disgust. He cursed Laius, saying Laius wasn't trying hard enough. "You give me everything you've got, Wishful, or I'll wash my hands of you." Dolius had taken to calling Laius "Wishful" because, whenever he gambled, Laius always thought he'd win big. Twice Dolius cursed Alektrion, bellowing similar complaints about slacking. Much as he wanted to learn from the Achean, the continual flushes of anger Alektrion suffered took even more energy from him to keep under control.

They ate a painfully light midday meal on a grassy hillock in grim silence. Alektrion imagined the possible foods Belamena might serve at supper: a stew of crab and mussels or maybe spicy lamb, dripping with hot juices.

Below them, other men were practicing with twanging bows or clanging swords. Dolius found fault with all. Alektrion forced himself to remember each criticism. Then Dolius said, voice heavy with sarcasm, "The Red King's forces could wipe out the likes of this lot even after being blinded by staring into the sun. Knossos knows where to get her warriors. From the mainland."

Laius objected. "The Lady's People serve as Her defense."

Dolius snorted. "Keftian fighting men would be nothing without the training they get from mainland mercenaries like me."

Alektrion stiffened, but locked his jaw tightly closed. Laius wasn't so controlled. "The Keftian navy is the greatest fighting force in the world."

"But who provides the expertise for the navy, Wishful?"

"Keftian officers."

"Ah. But Keftian officers schooled by Kallistans. Kallistans who are born to the sea. And besides, Wishful, I wasn't talking about the navy. I was talking about warriors. And it's mainlanders like me who train Keftian officers."

"That's not so." Laius's protest echoed Alektrion's thoughts.

"Wishful, you've a lot to learn. And not just about how to fight. It's well known that mainlanders teach the skills of war at the Keftian academies. And something else you may not have figured out. Keftiu's defense depends more on the sea than even on the mercenaries she pays so very well. What defeats greedy mainlanders like The Red King is the difficulty of getting past the navy on the Great Sea. If any halfway decent mainlander force could conquer the sea well enough to get past the navy, Knossos would fall."

Alektrion had had enough. "You're wrong, Dolius. Not all Keftian marines are at sea at all times. There'd be plenty of warriors on land to fight. Our ships could return with reinforcements. And the People would arm themselves."

Dolius laughed.

Alektrion bridled his anger and managed to say, softly, "My father is Keftian. He would fight to the death in defense of Keftiu."

"But would he fight well, Breed?" Dolius leaned back on one elbow, an arogant gesture that sent blood pounding into Alektrion's temples. "Could he kill even one of Atistaeus's warriors? Your father wasn't trained to fight from his youth as my people are. And is it true, as you believe, that the Keftians would take up arms? Your father makes weapons. He's familiar with war and men of war. I assure you, most Keftians haven't the faintest concept of battle. I've been to Knossos. Have you? Keftians are a people of commerce totally unsuited to killing. They live in secure isolation. It's even against their law to fight among themselves. You'd do well to learn to mind your tongue unless you're certain of what you say."

Alektrion sat in grim silence. Dolius had voiced two astounding thoughts. That the success of the Keftian navy actually lay in the skills of mainlanders and Kallistans. And most astonishing—because Alektrion would have thought it virtually unthinkable, let alone something to be said aloud by some mocking mainland mercenary—that if the sea could be breached by anyone—by the Red King!—Knossos would fall.

Knossos had existed forever and would remain forever. A tremor, a kind of panic, ran through him. He jammed this astonishing heresy into a deep corner of his mind.

Dolius rose, and the punishment began again. In the late afternoon they returned to the Brown Ox, and Alektrion forced his feet up the stairs so tired he wished he didn't have to go to Belamena's. By morning his muscles would be howling. With Laius and two shipmates, he dragged himself to the nearest bathhouse. Soaking with ten other men in the hot basin, he closed his eyes. Every fiber of his body yearned to tell Dolius he hoped Dolius would live forever in the underworld. But he wouldn't quit. He wouldn't give the barbarian the satisfaction.

Laius said, "I'm near to death. After we finish here I'm going to eat and go straight to sleep."

Alektrion imagined throwing himself down on the bed. "Wish I could."

"Send her a message that you had sudden urgent business."

"I promised."

"So? You don't really have to keep a promise to come to dinner."

Alektrion had long since noted, with discomfort, Laius's too flexible approach to commitments. "Can't do that." Alektrion hated a liar and had difficulty respecting anyone who could break a promise. He hoped Laius would never break one made to him. He didn't want to find out what it might do to their friendship.

When he arrived at Belamena's, the prospect of good food and the desire to see her did battle with his exhaustion. He thumped the door's knocker several times. A servant—or was she a slave?—answered. He followed her lithe figure through the first courtyard and into the second. The house was remarkably altered: no torches, only a few lamps, no music, no tables groaning with food, and most conspicuous of all, no people.

Belamena received him in a windowless room where the walls were softened with tapestries displaying the symbols of Cybele, and the space was discreetly lit by floor lamps in the corners. Belamena sat alone on one of two curved couches that faced each other across a lamp-lit table. Lilac perfume lingered in the air.

The servant girl said softly, "Alektrion, son of Meela," then backed out the door.

Belamena rose. The room felt very close. He was alone with her when he had not expected to be. She glided to him in a light green gown so thin he could see hints of her nipples and woman's hair through it.

She took his hand and the warmth of hers flowed up his arm. "I am so very happy to see you." She tugged his arm. "Come. Sit with me."

If a Kallistan woman invited a man to her house and entertained him alone in such a provocative gown, the evening would have to be considered an invitation to an affair. But this was Samos. Maybe the same rules didn't apply. "Last night," he said, "I must not have been paying close attention. I imagined there would be other people."

Belamena glided onto the couch and pulled him down with her. He sat stiffly, one of his knees no more than a thumb's width from one of hers. She released his hand. "Are you disappointed, then?"

"Of course not." How could he carry on a conversation with her? What could he say that was entertaining? And why would this beautiful woman want to talk to a lowly rower on one of the Lady's warships? Well, he hadn't actually told her yet he was a rower. "Just surprised."

"I hope not unpleasantly surprised."

"Being able to dine alone with you, Belamena Sonaria, will be a pleasure."

She laughed softly. The sound ruffled the hair on his arms. Maybe the same rules of entertaining did apply on Samos and she had more than talk in mind.

"What would you like to drink?"

"I'm on a training regimen. May I have watered wine?"

With a cloth-tipped mallet, Belamena tapped a small bronze disc. In an eye blink a different serving girl appeared. Belamena said she would have nectar and Alektrion watered wine. The girl returned carrying a decanter and their drinks in two crystal goblets of astonishingly thin workmanship. She set the decanter on the table and, at a wave of Belamena's hand, vanished.

"Tell me about your ship, Alektrion. May I call you Alek?"

"Alek is fine."

"Where does your ship winter?"

The question seemed innocent enough, yet it made him uncomfortable. Maybe just because Belamena's way of asking was so direct. She asked what ports he'd visited. He answered her questions, but all he seemed able to think about was the way the gown clung to her body, how her hands were so graceful, how round was the curve of her breasts.

His body responded in a way that, if she noticed, would be embarrassing. He quickly swallowed the remainder of his nearly full cup and handed it to her. "May I have some more wine?"

"But of course." She turned her attention to the table and the decanter.

Alektrion shifted to make his arousal less noticeable and took several quick, deep breaths.

The serving girl returned, with two companions. They placed light food on the table. Belamena had reddened her lips slightly with something that glistened, and he found himself fascinated with her mouth and the sensual way she had of placing food in it, especially the grapes.

"Now I want to know how fate has brought such a handsome youth to Samos."

He told her of the run-in with the raider. She seemed particularly interested in the details of how *Sea Eagle's* marines responded to the challenge of battle. He ended by explaining that they were likely to be in Palmaki for a month.

"I'm pleased to hear that, Alek. In a month we could get to know each other quite well."

He asked her questions while stealing glimpses of her breasts. She had, she explained, been born to a wealthy family. She'd caught the fancy of a wealthy man and married him. Because he was Carian, he, not his family, held rights to his wealth; and when he died prematurely, before she'd given him even one child, his money had become hers. "I've chosen not to marry again. Do you find that a disharmonious decision?"

She was perhaps thirty. And if Samians were anything like Kallistans, she'd be considered already too old to marry again. She'd chosen what seemed to him a lonely life. "It doesn't bother you that you won't have children?"

"Will it shock you if I say no?"

He thought of five dead women lying in their own blood. "Nothing shocks me too much any more. Do you have family here?"

"Exactly so. I have four sisters and three brothers."

She struck the bronze disc again, and the three serving girls whisked into the room, removed the remains of their meal, and deposited a large platter of sweets. "Tell me," she said when they were again alone, "do you like the life at sea?"

"Yes. I'm at peace there, like no other place." He felt a moment of panic, fearing she would ask why he used the word peace. He certainly wouldn't tell her about his nightmares, and he suddenly realized he didn't want to be evasive with Belamena.

Green eyes peered at him intently. "You think of the sea as a peaceful place? Strange. My sister's husband, a sponge diver, drowned off Lesbos. He spoke of the sea as temperamental, unpredictable, dangerous. I myself find that Poseidon is a fierce, fickle, and demanding god. So many seamen worship him, though. Do you?"

He blinked, startled that Belamena, who claimed to worship the Goddess and who had met him coming from Cybele's temple, could imagine he might also worship another deity. "I'm a man of peace, one of the Mother's children."

"Ah. Then it's somewhat surprising that you serve on a warship. How do you feel about the battles you've fought? I should think combat would make the strongest impression possible on a man."

She put the last bite of a sweet in her mouth and licked her fingers. A wave of pleasure swept lightly over his shoulders and down his sides. Merciful Goddess, Belamena was beautiful. "Such things make for poor supper conversation." He would never, ever, speak to any woman—save a priestess—of the horror of battle.

"You needn't think you'll offend or shock me." She cocked her head to one side. "I want to know what I can about you."

The topic needed changing. She changed it for him. "I apologize if I seemed to pry into things you wish to keep private. Tell me then, do you intend to make your life on the peaceful sea?"

He told her he would someday own a ship of commerce.

"You mustn't think just one ship, Alektrion. Think of a fleet of such ships."

He liked the idea.

A serving girl brought mulled wine. He declined. As Belamena drank hers, the smell of the spices alone seemed to intoxicate him. The day was, at last, taking its toll. He felt his shoulders slumping, his eyelids drooping.

Belamena rose from the couch. In a slow glide to the rug, she lowered herself to sit at his feet. She put her hand on his naked thigh. Weariness evaporated. "You look tired, Alektrion. Have I bored you?"

His mouth went suddenly dry. He shook his head a bit too vigorously.

With a small smile she said, "I'm not afraid to tell you that you please me. But I am afraid you'll tell me that I don't please you."

"How could you not? You're beautiful." His tongue still seemed unable to speak his mind. "And … and gracious," he added, short of breath.

"It's possible we'll not have much time together, you and I. Would you wish to spend tonight with me?"

He hesitated, thinking of his possible nightmares. She misunderstood. She rose and retreated to her place on the couch, hurt written in her eyes but pride showing in her straight shoulders.

He moved swiftly to her and took her hand. "No, Belamena. The Goddess knows I'd gladly stay. I know I must look tired. The truth is I'm utterly exhausted. I fear I'd be a poor match."

She gave him a long slow smile. "Then you're willing to stay?"

"Yes." He quickly added, "But I can't stay the whole night."

She frowned.

"I'm in training. At dawn's light I have to meet other men, and I need enough rest to function."

"Ah. Yes, then I understand."

The significance of his commitment to stay with Belamena settled into his bones—soon he would join his body with hers. He suddenly felt he'd already had a full night's rest.

He stood, took her hand, pulled her to her feet. "Lead me to where we'll sleep."

Her hand in his, Belamena led him into the now darkened courtyard. Only the sounds of their sandals accompanied them across the flagstones and into a softly lit bedchamber. She stroked his cheek and the edge of his jaw. He put his hand over one of her breasts, and she sighed. As she began to unwrap his belt she said, "I intend eventually to know all of your secrets. Including why you find the sea so peaceful."

∾ ∾ ∾ ∾

His days settled into a simple pattern: Dolius drove his body and his mind to increasing levels of fighting skill during the day and Belamena drove his body and spirit to increasing heights of pleasure during their nights. Being with Belamena was nothing like being with Kladia. And, unlike what he'd felt with Philoxea, with Belamena there was genuine passion—and satisfaction—for the both of them. He couldn't remember ever being happier. He had no nightmares. The gnawing hunger seemed a thing of his past.

Two weeks after their first night together, Alektrion arrived at her mansion and, for the first time, Belamena wasn't home. The girl took him to the sitting room, directed him to assorted fruits and breads and nectar, and told him her mistress should soon return.

He examined the weaving on her loom: two octopi in the center with running spirals on the edges. He found himself tapping his foot. He studied a set of gold cups. They depicted the Mother's eight obedient daughters and sons and her eight disobedient children as well, their demon forms looking like something from his nightmare.

Still Belamena hadn't returned. He swallowed what drink was left in his cup and poured another.

Finally she swept into the room. She made a great fuss of kissing him, then said, "I was shopping for tiles to pave a section of the garden."

Only later, after they had twice made love and two lamps had already burned out, did he ask if she had another lover. His cheeks burned as he spoke the words. He knew the question was unacceptable, knew the possessive fire raging inside was a danger. The Law said, "The desire to own one of the Mother's children is forbidden." He'd never felt jealousy before, had never expected he would, but beyond question he knew this feeling for what it was.

She curled her naked body close, placed her palm over his heart. "Would it bother you if I did?"

"I know it's not proper for me to ask."

"You're right. It is not. Such questions too often lead to discord."

"It's just that you fill all of my thoughts, and I wonder if I fill all of yours."

"You're here every night. Isn't that good enough?" Her warm palm moved to cup his maleness.

He returned her hand to his chest. "Will you answer my question?"

"What will you do if I don't? Will you threaten to force the answer from me? Will you pin my arms over my head and take pleasure from me against my will? I'd like that, Alek."

Why try to divert him with thoughts of sex games? Her refusal to answer only added to his suspicions. Couldn't she see that? "Tell me if I fill your thoughts."

She sat up beside him, bent over and let her coppery hair spill like the softest silk onto his chest. "This bothers you a great deal, I see." Her fingertips traced a hot trail down his abdomen. "You are the only one, Alek. Yes, you fill all my thoughts." She sat up again and gazed straight into his eyes. "I want no other man but you."

She straddled him, bent so her nipples touched his skin, pressed warm lips to his. Did he believe her? He needed to believe her. But the power of her exposed presence made thought difficult. She moved her hips and his doubts ended their nagging.

He didn't question Belamena again, but sometimes he had the odd experience of looking at her and feeling that same great hunger he'd had the first time he saw her at the party. The nameless longing had come back. Not as strong, but there nevertheless.

With his days and nights filled, even overfilled, the time approached when *Sea Eagle's* repairs would be finished. Laius had found his own ways to entertain himself in the evening. Alektrion suspected lots of gambling and was relieved when Laius gave him his share of the money for their room and also repaid his debt. And still better yet, Dolius offered Alektrion a crumb of praise. "Your mother's Achean blood shows, Breed. You have promise. If your heart's as strong as your body, you might make a half-decent warrior."

Alektrion thought it ironic that Dolius's backhanded compliment also hinted at his deepest dread—that in the face of fear his courage might, in fact, fail him.

Then, on a dark night of new moon, when he was returning to the Brown Ox from Belamena's, he turned into a winding residential lane and suddenly felt as though he were being followed. The lane was so narrow that little starlight penetrated it, and it was well past the hour when residents were required to keep a torch lit. He stopped and glanced as far into the darkness behind him as possible, expecting at this late hour to find the lane empty. It seemed to be so.

He increased his stride and listened. From behind he heard the definite scuffle of sandaled footsteps. Once again he stopped and turned. Did he see a movement beside a door two houses away, as if someone had hurriedly stepped off the path?

He was in Palmaki. He had no reason for fear. Still, the hair had risen on the nape of his neck. Dolius and the other widely traveled soldiers loved to share gruesome stories of cutthroat crime in ports like Piraeus, Ugarit, and Byblos. Were he in any of those depraved cities, he'd be carrying his dagger—his beautiful piece of booty from that first sea battle. Though Palmaki was considered safe enough that a man or woman might travel its streets at night unarmed, Alektrion knew no place was crime free.

Not ten strides further on he heard running feet. He spun sideways. A man of Dolius's build lunged toward him. The lane was dim, but Alektrion still saw that his attacker clenched a dagger, it's blade's length twice that of a man's hand.

14

The knife slashed toward Alektrion's chest. "Keftian spawn!" his attacker hissed.

Alektrion lurched backward. Heart thudding, he grabbed for his attacker's wrist, missed. But his dodge worked so that only rough knuckles, not slicing iron, raked the skin of his chest. The man yanked one arm back. Alektrion again grabbed for the wrist of the knife-wielding hand, but the man rammed his free fist into Alektrion's gut.

A ball of pain exploded in his belly. He gushed air. He grappled again for the knife. The man twisted toward Alektrion, showed him a darkly bearded face and deep, hooded eyes. Again the assailant pulled his arm back, and where before he'd spoken in a menacing whisper, now he bellowed something unintelligible.

Alektrion grasped the man's waist, hooked a leg around one of the man's ankles, yanked the leg forward, threw the man onto his back, crashed onto him. A burning sensation slashed down Alektrion's side.

He's cut me! Alektrion lost concentration. In a protective reflex, he bent left. Fast as a sun-warmed lizard, the man elbowed off the ground, slammed himself against Alektrion, his weight a sixth again heavier than Alektrion's own.

Locked chest to chest, they rolled over and over with Alektrion's left hand clenched around his attacker's knife wrist. Lights sprang up in several windows. *Hold on! A bit longer. Someone will come!*

Grunting, his attacker halted their tumbling with himself on top and his weight pressed like a stone anchor on Alektrion's chest. The man's face was contorted with effort, lips pulled back from clenched teeth, brow deeply creased.

"You there!" a quavery male voice shouted from one of the townhouses. "What's going on here?"

Alektrion's attacker, distracted by the sound, relaxed for an instant. Alektrion leapt upon the opening and shoved the man back as he swung his knee toward the man's groin. His assailant was too fast. Alektrion's knee struck short, but the man was rattled. Alektrion wrenched free. He scrambled to his feet, staggered back against the townhouse wall, and gasped out, "Why do you attack me?"

Again the man rushed forward, raised arm ready to strike.

Alektrion focused on the knife hand. Time slowed. He grabbed the wrist and, as precisely as if Dolius were giving instructions, he twisted it down. He turned the knife toward the man's chest and at the same moment spun him so his back was pressed to the wall. He rammed his whole body against his attacker, focusing all his energy down his own arm, through his attacker's hand, and into the knife.

A soft, "Uugh," spilled from the man's mouth. His body stiffened, then, like an empty sack, he sank to his knees, the knife sticking out from his chest. Alektrion stepped back. His attacker collapsed forward onto the knife, then rolled to his side.

"What is this outrage?" said the same quavery male voice. The indignant and frightened resident stood in the street, a flickering candle in his uplifted hand. He was accompanied by two women. All three wore sleeping gowns and their eyes were the size of platters.

"This man attacked me," Alektrion said between labored breaths.

"I saw that, fool. But what caused this madness?"

An elderly woman and her husband in the townhome opposite peered out, a candle in each of their hands.

Alektrion studied the dead man's face. "I don't know. I … I've never seen him before."

The elderly couple came to stare. The woman said, "I've sent my slave to fetch the king's guard."

"Good," said the first man. "We will all wait." His voice had lost its quaver and had taken on a tone of authority.

Six men from the king's guard arrived at a fast trot. Alektrion couldn't explain who his assailant was or why he'd been attacked, and the corporal in charge ordered that Alektrion accompany them to the barracks. The now calm townhouse resident assured the corporal that he had indeed seen the dead man attack Alektrion and he'd definitely heard Alektrion ask the dead man why he was being attacked.

Every step on the walk to the barracks drove Alektrion's pulse ever faster. He'd killed a man. He was in a strange city. And none of his friends knew where he was.

At the barracks a guard shoved him into a small room with straw on the floor. "Wait," the guard said.

"Can I send word to friends?"

The guard slammed and locked the door.

Shortly, another soldier arrived. What was Alektrion's name, why was he in Palmaki, where he was staying, why had the dead man attacked him? When Alektrion had no answer to the last question, the man stomped out giving the door an even louder bang, but he returned with a basin of water and rough linen. Without comment he left them.

Alektrion cleaned his wounded side, then bound it. The gash wasn't deep. He prayed it wouldn't go sour. When he was released—surely they would release him for he'd not been at fault—he would go at once to Serena. Bad enough that he'd have another scar, but if the wound went sour, his attacker might yet succeed in having killed him.

The small oil lamp burnt out. He sat in darkness, his heart a knot in his chest, his stomach a knot in his gut. How could he alert Laius and Dolius? He'd made no enemies in Palmaki. Why had the stranger attacked him? What penalties might be exacted on Samos for killing someone?

He thought about the fight. He'd been frightened, but he'd functioned. *I am grateful, Mother.* Perhaps this was Her sign that in the heat of real battle he'd also find courage.

He marveled at the relative ease with which he'd killed. The weeks of submitting himself to Dolius's grueling training had fully repaid him.

He paced, trying to relieve his growing, unbearable tension, then sat again, avoiding the straw which stank of sweat and urine. The knots in his innards had only tightened all the more. At some point during the night, he must have collapsed into sleep because the next morning he was startled awake by a soldier shaking his shoulder.

A new guard nodded toward a bowl by the door. "Somethin' for you to eat." Alektrion smelled barley porridge.

At what he guessed must be midday, he performed *soutas* devotions. Shortly thereafter the captain of the guards arrived. "You're free to leave. You're lucky, the town's most respected poet witnessed the attack."

For a moment relief left him breathless. "I'm charged with nothing?"

"Nothing more than keeping bad company, I guess."

"Who was the man?"

"Name's Gulddrath Sednartha. Least, that was his name. One of Belamena Sonaria's lovers. In fact, she was seeing him most evenings before you put into port."

Alektrion envisioned Belamena in the arms of … of … Crushing weight settled onto his shoulders. He fought to let nothing show in his face. "She's a very … a very powerful presence."

"Oh, I've no doubt of that. I know her well by reputation. I see occasional fistfights over women, but a knife attack is rare. Then again, apparently Gulddrath is—was—a known pirate and troublemaker. Some say a spy for the Red King. And, as you've said, Belamena Sonaria is a woman over whom a man might make trouble.

If I were you, I'd watch out for the man she's seeing during the day. He's not the kind of fool to attack you himself. He'd pay a professional."

"What you do mean, the man she's seeing during the day?"

"My sources say he's a banker."

A stifling blanket of silence settled over the tiny room. Alektrion forced in a breath. "I'm free to go?"

"Exactly. I understand you're wounded. Do you know you're due recompense from the dead man's family if you care to seek it?"

"I only want to get out of here."

"Don't blame you."

One of the guards walked Alektrion to the door. Outside, high thin clouds streaked a blue-white sky so painfully bright it hurt his eyes. A cool breeze stroked his skin. The back of the miserably hot weather had been broken.

None of what the captain said is true. She said to me, 'There is no other.'

He retraced his path to Belamena's door, stopped, inhaled slowly, and then knocked. A boy slave he didn't recognize answered and led him into the reception area.

The boy bowed and said, "Please wait," then began to walk away.

"Is your mistress home?"

The boy stopped, nodded. Alektrion brushed past the child, who quickly ran around and tried to block his path. "You must wait," the boy whined.

Suddenly realizing he didn't know where Belamena might be, he said, "Tell your mistress Alektrion, son of Meela, awaits her."

The boy hurried through the first courtyard toward the second. Alektrion followed. The boy disappeared in the direction of the sitting room. Alektrion heard the young voice speak his name. He was barely halfway through the door to the second courtyard when the boy rushed back into view followed by Belamena.

She pushed forward, smiling and frowning at once. "I was so frightened to hear that Gulddrath—the man was a fool. A fool! How relieved I am to see you. The Goddess has been good to us."

"Can you dismiss your lover so easily, then? I was told he was your lover. Right up until my arrival here."

Her smile disappeared. "I had wanted, for a long time, to insist that he leave, Alek." She put her hand on his arm. "But having you gave me the courage."

"I was told—" His voice froze. She'd lied. To him. Only with the greatest difficulty did he stop himself from striking her. How many lies had she told him?

"I'm so relieved you're all right. That's what's important."

She tugged on his arm, turned him back toward the entry door, and began walking him toward it as though she intended for him to leave.

He stopped. "The man who investigated the attack said—"

From behind him a refined male voice said, "So who is your friend, Belamena?"

He yanked his arm from hers and spun around. In the passage between the two atria stood a man he recognized from her party. Tall, thin, elegantly dressed in gray silk, just as he was then. A man introduced to Alektrion as a banker.

A metal door in Alektrion's head clanged shut. Oh, how she'd lied. And he'd played her fool. Her entertainment for the evenings.

In a voice as cold as his blood he said, "As I was saying, Belamena, the captain who investigated Gulddrath's death informed me that you have another lover. A man you see during the day."

She smiled awkwardly. Her hand fluttered to her throat. "You mustn't take such things so seriously, Alek. I can't see how—"

"So it's true." Perhaps all she had ever wanted from him was information about *Sea Eagle*. If that were the case, she had essentially failed for he'd never told her anything of real significance.

The banker intruded again. "I think we met," he said with a leering smile. "It's Alektrion, isn't it? From tiny Kalliste."

Belamena touched Alektrion's arm, her gesture a kind of pleading. He brushed her hand away and stared hard into her eyes. "I see I am indeed altogether too serious."

He strode out her door, buoyed by rage. But his pace quickly slowed. His neck grew warm under his tunic. What a colossal child he had been. The strange hunger he'd felt when he first saw Belamena at the party struck in full, gut wrenching force. He'd thought Belamena had sated it, but he was wrong. It was still there and feeding at this very moment on his spirit like a greedy pig.

ⵗ ⵗ ⵗ ⵗ

Within days he returned to sea duty. He visited the Temple a last, sad time. In its shelter he found calm, but the calm fled the moment he stepped outside. Dolius said his skills with knife and shield were now impressive, his skill with a sword rapidly improving. He'd learned not to care too much for a woman. Betrayal awaits. As he told Laius, "In the future I'll confine myself to hetairas."

At first his body craved Belamena constantly. He relieved himself in the way a solitary man can, but physical relief didn't dull the spiritual hunger. Rumors had it that the Red King had succeeded in uniting forces with kings from two smaller, but militarily significant, Peloponnesian cities that also had strong navies. Alektrion longed for *Sea Eagle's* next engagement. He'd have another chance to wound the Pylian monster. He'd take booty to add to his savings for his ship. He would turn his heart from love to war.

∾ ∾ Author's Note ∾ ∾

The Red King's first wife, taken in his twentieth year when he returned to Pylos from Delphi, was Leahsa, the daughter of the king of nearby Messene and one of the Goddess's seers. After Atistaeus razed the shrines of the Goddess on Aegina, Leahsa broke her vows and the Law when she tried to kill him with a knife while he was bathing. She failed, and Atistaeus had her skinned alive. It was said that he personally wiped her blood on his infamous cloak.

JRE

15

Accompanied by Heebe and Zuliya, I arrived at marvelous Amnissos, the principal port of Knossos, in mid-summer of my fourteenth year after two days on the sea. The sails of our passenger ship were furled and the rowers edged us in as the lower rim of a brilliant pink sun touched the western horizon.

I stood at the railing bubbling with impatience to finally be at the Mother's Heart. Impatience and fear. All the things I now hoped for, all the things my mother and father desired, depended on my success. To fail at the Bull Academy would end my dreams.

A pang of regret struck and I looked around the *Asphodel* thinking I should try to memorize her feel. I closed my eyes and listened to the creaking of the deck. I inhaled salt air. Knossos was so far inland that from the Bull Academy, I would not see or even smell the Great Sea for months.

I walked to the railing amidship that ran alongside the rows of passenger benches. My fingers traced the design chiseled into the wood: a field of asphodel full of bees and hives. From the moment I'd seen the engraving, only minutes after stepping onto the ship from the dock at Alyris, I'd felt at home. And I soon discovered that I loved being on the water. I thought of Alektrion, wondered where on the Great Sea he might be. I told a gull to carry a message to him, that he should remember me.

The first night out of Alyris, while we slept on the deck, a school of flying fish catapulted onto us. Heebe and nearly all the other passengers screamed with terror and disgust. To me the fishes wriggling simply seemed full of life. And earlier this very morning when a squall battered us, I was among the few passengers who hadn't gotten sick. I had stood near the bow and let spray and wind hit me full force. I felt oneness with the Mother and an empowering rapture. In two short days my feelings had shifted profoundly. I knew I belonged to the sea as I once had believed I belonged among the bees and hives, and I was certain I would serve the Mother by returning to the sea.

"Up port oars!"

The captain's command pulled me from reverie. I walked to where Heebe and Zuliya stood beside our belongings. The *Asphodel* bumped against the wharf. Zuliya grabbed Heebe's arm to steady her. The ship's crew seemed to scurry in every direction but with practiced purpose.

Zuliya said to me, "Run ahead to the dock. Bring back three porters."

"We'll need four, Little Bird," Heebe countered. She grinned at Zuliya. "The packets weigh more than you suspect."

I made my way forward weaving past passengers and their belongings, and I'd started past the palanquin of Ninarin, the ship's priestess, when she called out, "Leesandra, come a moment!"

Ninarin was tall, with large bones and a large smile full of big teeth. Her saying of the prayers was the most beautiful I'd ever heard, her voice deep and resounding, like breakers on boulders. She gave me one of her big smiles. "Were you going to just slip away without saying goodbye?"

A blush warmed my cheeks. "My teacher sent me to fetch porters."

"You go to the Bull Academy, don't you?"

"Yes."

"Are you looking forward to it?"

Ninarin said something else, but I didn't understand because a sudden wave of dizziness unbalanced me. Then came the white light. Just as it exploded I heard the familiar murmuring.

ᴄᴠ ᴄᴠ ᴄᴠ ᴄᴠ

Heebe was speaking as if from a far distance. "It happens to her once or twice a moon cycle."

Strong hands went around my back. "Welcome back, Leesandra," Zuliya said softly near my ear. He helped me rise.

Ninarin's face, tanned and deeply lined from years on the water, was now wrinkled with concern. "Are you all right, maiden?" I assured her I was. "Your companion, Heebe, tells me when this happens the Great Mother speaks to you. Can you tell me what She said?"

Not since the day in the park had I ever again heard the Mother's actual words. But I'd never forgotten. "She tells me that she loves me, reverend one. And that I must serve Her obediently."

Ninarin took my hand, smiled, and nodded. "I am pleased, very pleased, to have met you, Danae's daughter."

Ninarin touched her heart to Heebe and Zuliya and then stepped back into her palanquin. Two bearers lifted her, carried her to the loading ramp, and she disappeared from view.

"I'll get porters," I said. "I'll bring them right back."

The day approached evening, and we wanted to reach Knossos and the rooms waiting for us before night fell. Following the porters and two torchbearers, their torches still unlit, we began a walk that would take almost an hour.

Amnissos was merely a port for Knossos, yet it was enormous. Ship-supply, repair, and import and export buildings lined the main street. The air was sharp with the smell of fish and the sounds of squeaking cart wheels. The road, full of people even in this late hour, was half again as wide as any on Alyris and its paving stones so smooth that carts traveling over them scarcely bumped.

Zuliya strode a bit in front of Heebe and me, limping in the way I now regarded with fondness. Full darkness fell. The boys lit their torches. Finally Zuliya stopped at the top of a gentle rise. He waved excitedly for us to join him. "The sight is astonishing."

And so it was.

Heebe clasped her hands to her chest. "Why, there must be a thousand torches!"

The Temple of the Great Goddess at Knossos, a sprawling labyrinth, stood three stories high with torches lining its roofs and set into cressets on its walls, so many one might imagine the place was afire.

Unearthly. Beautiful. Frightening. Even from here, the building's height dizzied me, but in some places I knew the walls rose to six stories. And my destiny lay within.

Heebe pointed. "See the sacred horns. The roofs must be lined with thousands."

Zuliya shook his head. "I've seen nothing like it since I left Sumer. It might rival or even surpass the Mother's Temple in Memphis."

The porters were far ahead of us. We hurried to catch up, but I looked again and again at the Temple until we reached the city's outskirts where two- and three-story buildings blocked the view. The porters turned off the great main road onto a narrower street. This modest avenue led to an inn where we would live until Heebe and Zuliya found permanent lodgings and I was received into the Academy.

Within the week, the two of them took rooms in a boarding house close enough to the Bull Dance Academy that Heebe could visit easily and Zuliya and I could meet daily. In return for a part of the cost of her room, Heebe would help the boardinghouse owner with cleaning and meals. Three days later Zuliya was welcomed as a teacher in a non-restricted section of the Temple, at the tablet house for the training of scribes. The scholars were delighted to have a man who could write eight languages, including that of Agyptos.

Twelve days later we went to the Academy barracks. The Academy head sat in his office at a desk of age-darkened wood. We exchanged pleasantries then he looked first to Heebe and then Zuliya. "She's not allowed to leave the premises or see anyone, not even you, venerable teacher, for the first three moon cycles. That will be a period of testing. If she remains thereafter, time for tutoring will be made available each day in the late afternoon."

I tensed. Doors and walls were about to close on me, a maiden who loved the sky and sea.

The time came to part. We three stood at the massive gate. Heebe hugged me tightly. "You'll do just fine. Only remember to make a smooth path. Sometimes you tend to stick out." All I could think was that I didn't want to let go of her.

Zuliya, as always, mixed practicality with philosophy. I'd discovered, sometimes with consternation and sometimes with amusement, that concerning nearly everything, these two friends, though profoundly fond of each other, gave me contradictory advice. For one thing, Heebe agreed with my mother and me that I should be a priestess. Zuliya had several times hinted that, like my father, he thought other possibilities awaited.

Zuliya caught my gaze and held up one finger in emphasis. "The Academy is the door to your future. Make sure that door is pushed wide open so all choices are available to you. No slacking. The Sumerian wise ones say, 'By his choices a man creates the life he lives.' The same certainly applies to a woman. I say, do not willingly let anyone outdo you."

Zuliya didn't hug me. He didn't kiss my cheek. Rather, he lifted my hand and made a brief gesture as if to kiss my palm. He'd explained to me once that for Hattians this gesture represented affection. If the doer also wanted to indicate respect, his lips would touch the skin of the hand. And the duration of the gesture always indicated very carefully the degree of both affection and respect felt.

We parted, and a girl in her second year of training, a *stameidoi*, took me to the maidens' sleeping quarters, on the way pointing out to me the corridors that led to the youths' sleeping rooms, the principal training court and gymnasiums, the classrooms and refectory.

"How many *dolmeidoi* are there?" I asked.

"We begin with a class of just over three hundred youths and nearly four hundred maidens." She laughed. "Those numbers will fall a hundred each, though, and soon. It's one thing to be told your time isn't yours anymore. It's another to have every minute of your life regimented, to be made to eat in unfamiliar ways, and to never speak unless spoken to. And not all who are sent by their family really want to be here. The weak of spirit leave quickly."

That will not be me.

We entered a room where half a hundred silent young women were making up narrow beds. The silence was daunting. My guide introduced me to a stern-faced woman, the room matron. "For the next three moons," she said, "I'm the only person to whom you may speak, and then only in emergencies. If you need to ask a question, approach and open your hand, palm up, to receive permission."

She led me to a bed, showed me a chest for my belongings and said I should unpack. I was free to smile at, or touch, the other girls, she said, then told me the names of the maidens nearest me. One exquisite girl, shorter than I with a tiny waist and delicate features, had the longest lashes I'd ever seen. With a confident, conspiratorial sideways glance, she smiled at me. A tiny cupful of my apprehension drained away. The maiden's name was Galatea.

In the following days I experienced everything the second-year stameidoi guide promised. Strange foods, unfamiliar daily routine, the aching desire to speak. I missed Meidra, and though Galatea was unlike her in that Galatea was strikingly beautiful, she had Meidra's same happy-go-lucky spirit. We took to holding hands and exchanging smiles and hugs.

In our second week, we met our dance instructors. Our class gathered in the Academy's main bull dance court where light from clerestory windows beamed down on a red clay floor. Cedar planks darkened by the lamps of ages lined the walls. This was the oldest building in Knossos, erected in days so ancient there was not yet a Temple and the Goddess was worshipped only in Her sacred caves and at mountain shrines.

The leader of the dancers, Hopthea, entered at the court's north end and climbed the steps of a wooden platform. Her assistants wore white exercise kilts but Hopthea was too old to look dignified in one. She and the other older instructors wore white, skin-tight blouses and tight-fitting, wrapped leggings that extended to calf length. Galatea and I had heard rumors from several stameidoi that Hopthea had been the finest leaper of her day. She had a high brow, erect bearing, thin tight lips.

"Tomorrow you begin training," she said. "If you finish, you will participate in one of the most sacred events of the People's life. The bull's horned head symbolizes the feminine essence because it resembles the horned womb, the source of life. His strong body symbolizes the generative male power. In the totality of the sacred Bull, the two essences are in perfect harmony. To dance successfully with the bull so you bring no harm to yourself or to him means you will have so disciplined your spirit and body that you, too, are, in that moment, in perfect harmony. Here you'll learn to submit to the Lady's laws and how to lead others to submission. Only then will you be able to dance with a proper spirit."

At first my days went well. The demanding, even grueling, exercises suited me. I enjoyed discovering how to control my body. But in my fifth week, my section was jump-tumbling over low bars in an outside court not far from the bull barns, and a number of children had gathered to watch. Some were also tossing a ball. A wagon caught my attention.

Bumping along the road next to the exercise field, the wagon was transporting several giant storage pithoi for wine destined for the temple cellars. At the very moment I saw one of the containers begin to slip free, a small girl chasing a rolling ball ran out onto the road. The container would hit her.

I didn't even think to call out. I dashed past Hopthea and two other instructors, sprang over a bench and then over a waist-high fence. I barely reached the girl in time to shove her out of the way. As it was, the huge vessel struck my shoulder and knocked me to the ground.

I regained my feet. The girl hugged me. I started to speak but remembered the rule. We looked at the container, which had split open, then laughed, and the child thanked me. My silent classmates beamed approval. Galatea patted my shoulder, worry in her eyes, and I smiled to assure her I was unharmed.

Hopthea and the two other instructors strode up. The youngest, a woman, hugged me and then turning to Hopthea said, "Did you see her run? Did you see her leap over the bench and fence? Hopthea, what promise she has! She may outshine you."

I looked to Hopthea expecting to see a smile, to perhaps hear a word of praise. Her thin lips did smile—stiffly—but she said nothing. Instead she took the child's hand and tugged her away from me.

"The little one is fine," Hopthea said. "The Goddess is merciful. All of you, back to tumbling."

There was an awkward pause. The instructor who had praised me blushed.

I couldn't imagine what I'd done that displeased Hopthea. I'd even refrained from speaking to the child. For the rest of the day I felt an uncomfortable tension coming from Hopthea but by the next morning, I'd put it out of mind.

Weeks passed and an evening came when Galatea and I crowded into the main torchlit bull dance court with all the other dolmeidoi, maidens and youths. The Academy head joined us. Bearded, as befitted his age, he wore a brown sari embroidered in silver. He said, "I release you now from the discipline of silence. Tomorrow you are free. Go into Knossos. Visit family. Or go to the beach. Whatever pleases you. You may even eat what you wish."

He smiled, crossed his arms, and waited.

I thought, the Great Silence is over. *I have survived*!

The entire body of the dolmeidoi began to jabber. Galatea and I hugged. "You are amazingly quick of body, Leesandra. You'll make a first rate bull dancer." Her voice was as softly alluring as her almond eyes.

"And you, Galatea. What eyelashes you have! You'll have many lovers."

She laughed at my jest as we both knew the penalty for violating the prohibition against liaisons of pleasure with anyone in the Academy: immediate expulsion in shame. For me this discipline seemed no problem at all. I'd not be troubled because all my energy would be focused only on learning whatever I must to succeed.

We questioned our companions. The bursts of laughter and conversation of nearly five hundred youths sounded as beautiful to me as a rushing mountain torrent. Stameidoi brought light food and drink. All too soon it was time to return to the dormitories.

Galatea linked her arm in mine. "What do you want to do tomorrow?"

Had nothing else been involved, I would have chosen to go near the sea. But for three cycles of the moon I hadn't seen or spoken to Zuliya. "I want to go to the Temple, to visit my tutor."

"Ah. The mysterious Zuliya. What do you think Hopthea meant the day she said to you 'Your tutor, Zuliya, is a man out of harmony?'"

I remembered the day vividly. Hopthea was giving training assignments and seemed angry with me.

"I can't imagine. I don't know how Hopthea could even know about Zuliya. He's never been here to see me. You'll like him, Galli. He's very witty. He's Nubian, and he looks wonderfully ... exotic."

She grinned, rather wickedly. "I think if Hopthea doesn't like him, I most definitely will." She straightened the front of her pleated kilt. "I want to see the Temple, too. So we will visit your tutor."

The olive harvest was less than half a moon cycle away, but the next morning's air was still so warm we wore our lightest tunics. The Amnissos road took us first past private residences and townhomes, but as we approached Temple precincts, government buildings crowded the street.

Galatea suddenly asked, "Have you had lovers?"

"No." I didn't want to explain that I had once been drawn to someone who had not even kissed me and who had undoubtedly by now forgotten Leesandra of Kalliste. I quickly asked, "Have you had many lovers?"

She fluttered her long eyelashes at me. "Many."

"Tell me," I said, eager to hear.

She talked all the way to the edge of the Temple where streets gave way to gardens. The center of worship of the Mother of All sprawled, unimaginably tall and rambling, before us.

Galatea stopped walking and made a sweeping gesture with her arm. "I want to be a priestess, Leesandra. And that's where I want to serve."

By day the Temple was as breathtaking as it was at night, just in a different way. The walls glistened an otherworldly white, covered with something that made me think of the magical snow said to cling to Keftiu's highest mountains, even in summer.

I took Galatea's hand. "I will serve the Mother at sea. But here is where we will train." I squeezed her hand. "We will take our first steps inside together."

We reached the northern portal by way of a public court and a shallow flight of steps. We asked one of two doorkeepers—an imposing man of warrior age in a remarkably brief kilt—where to find the tablet house. He directed us to the northeast entry. We hurried through the gardens and past the Academy for gifted outlander youths.

The splendid view from the northeast entry looked hundreds of feet down from the hilltop into a ravine through which the Kairatos river flowed toward the sea. Boats carrying passengers and cargo dotted the water or were docked at the foot of a path that zigzagged uphill to the Temple's entry. Porters and travelers trudged up and down.

I craned my head back and looked up at five stories of white wall. The stairs were steep and narrow, an arrangement less one of grace than of practicality as the Temple's east side perched on the edge of the valley. We slipped out of our sandals, washed our feet, and ascended. Several times the steps leveled, then turned and rose again. At the top I took Galatea's hand. We stepped together into a roofless reception area.

Water from some higher level fell in a sparkling pattern into a cut-stone channel along one wall, then gurgled into a drain and disappeared. Citrus scented flowers hung from pots and trailed the walls. On the horizon, far to the south, I could see the notched peak of sacred Mount Juktas.

We passed quarters dedicated to a variety of crafts and eventually located the rooms of the tablet house. Zuliya was teaching, but when he saw me at his door, he came outside. He was polite, but was clearly rushed, and said he would come to me the next day. He recommended several artisans who didn't mind if people watched them work, especially a jeweler. "He uses the most ingenious polished crystal lenses to help him see the delicate work on seal rings. Be sure to see the lenses." He turned to go.

"But, Zuliya, before you go. Have you met my instructor, Hopthea? She mentioned you."

He shook his head and frowned. "I did not meet her, but I know of her."

"And?"

"I received notice a month ago, as your guardian, that you were to be transferred to the bull-raising farm at Phaestos." He saw my shocked look. "Yes, yes. I was sure that was how you would feel. I went immediately to the Academy head. He said this instructor, Hopthea, had recommended the change."

"But I would never undergo the dance training! I would have no chance to perform. All would be lost."

"I asked the man if this decision was because you had broken discipline or were incapable of the physical demands of the dance. He assured me it was not. But apparently your instructor made the recommendation. I objected strenuously. When I said that if the decision was not changed, I would contact your parents, he said he would inquire further. Within days I was told your training would continue. I don't know why the woman wanted you transferred, but that is how she knows me, I'm sure."

Zuliya left us. Galatea and I strolled, hands clasped, past the clanging sounds from the room of a bronzesmith. "Why would Hopthea want me transferred?"

"It is odd. You're good at the training. But your tutor resolved everything. Hopthea is just a cranky old woman. Don't let it trouble you."

"But if I'm ever to be admitted to study here," I gestured to indicate the whole Temple, "I must succeed at the Academy. Being sent to the raising farm is something they do with dolmeidoi they have decided can't achieve the dance."

Galatea frowned. "Who said that?"

"I don't remember. But ... well, there is something very wrong if Hopthea wanted to send me to Phaestos."

Galatea patted my arm. "Don't fret. It's nothing. Look. It's nearly midday. I'm starving. Let's go into town."

Still troubled, I let Galatea lead through crowded streets. She explained that she'd lived away from the Mother's heart for many years, just as I had. Her father, a merchant, had business in Pylos, but their family had recently returned to Knossos. "I've been into town many times." She talked of her father, Minyas, and of his business, and I could tell she cared for him at least as much as I cared for my father. Her talk brought sadness as I thought of Alyris and both my parents and Meidra. All so far away.

At a large central square I spied a cluster of tables at an outdoor tavern. Galatea picked a table. A stout, jolly woman had just finished serving us the tavern's meal of the day—a steaming soup of mixed shellfish, hard-crusted bread, and a platter of sliced dates and pears—when people sitting behind Galatea looked in surprise toward the square. My gaze was drawn to a man dressed in a bright blue mid-thigh tunic. My lips fell open in surprise.

He was grotesque. His body seemed normal enough, but his head was huge. It sat on his shoulders like some great boulder. A leather headband held a wild mass of dark curls off his face. He seemed to be heading directly toward Galatea and me, and I sucked in my breath.

Galatea heard me. She turned to look at what had surprised me, then said in a whisper, "Oh, no. Lynceus."

16

"A good day, sister," the man said. Despite being astonished that he'd called her sister, I noted that the dark eyes in the grotesquely misshapen head twinkled with humor and his voice was gentle.

"Good day, Lynceus," she snipped. "What brings you here?"

How had such a monstrosity come to be? What had caused his head to grow so large? His lips were thick, his brows heavy.

He said he'd been with Minyas, their father. Then said, "You are forgetting yourself, my sister." The monster looked at me, and I saw curiosity in the twinkling eyes. "Shouldn't you introduce your lovely companion?"

Galatea performed the formalities and, without being asked, the monster named Lynceus pulled another chair to our table and sat.

The woman who'd brought our food hurried to us and gave Galatea's brother a wonderful smile. "Young Lynceus. We've not seen you for some time. How can I impress my friends with a new bit of poetry if my favorite poet never visits me?"

"Your daughter Kitta just had her first child. Yes?"

"She did. A boy."

"Then, to celebrate the arrival of a little one, give her this bit of verse. I've only just finished it. I'll title it, 'A Song to Kitta.'"

The serving woman glowed.

The poet spoke.

> *Hear the Great Mother sing!*
> *This child's spirit I charge to you,*
> *A precious thing.*
> >*To cherish and nourish,*
> >*To protect and shape,*
> >*Beware, lest you wound or crush it,*
> >*Beware lest you warp or betray,*
> *Fail this small spirit,*
> *Heed well, mother, what I say,*
> *Fail this small spirit, and your spirit will pay.*

The serving woman nodded. "I like it, poet. The Great Mother does expect much from us when we care for Her children. In exchange for your wisdom finely put, I'll pay for your food." She patted Lynceus on the arm, then hurried off.

Galatea scarcely seemed to listen; she was using her knife to skin a grape. Lynceus appeared not to notice her rudeness.

"Your verse is shapely done," I said. "You've given the new mother a fine gift."

"I love the sounds of words." His thick-lipped smile made me want to pull away, but again I saw the twinkle in his eyes. What should I say? I didn't want to stare. Caught in this dither, I dribbled a spoonful of soup down my chin and onto my tunic. Swiftly, my face warm with embarrassment, I wiped my chin with a bit of cloth from my sidebag, then succeeded in making a bad effort at blotting it from my tunic.

I decided his deformity must have been from birth, and I couldn't imagine why his mother hadn't returned him to the Goddess immediately after his birth, as the Law requires.

Galatea returned her attention to her soup. Her dislike of him crackled in the air. He was terribly ugly, but he was pleasant and his poetry spoke of a good mind. Her response seemed unfair if based simply on his tragic appearance.

"We visited the Temple this morning," I offered.

That friendly gaze stayed tightly on me. "Galatea wishes to enter religious service. Do you feel the same?"

"I hope, with all my heart, to serve the Lady."

We shared a plate of sweets, then Galatea and I parted from him amicably. But once we were out of his hearing, she said, "I don't know why father lets him work at our business. He scares people away. And as for being a poet, I think he's a dreadful bore."

I didn't like to hear Galatea speak this way. She was usually so light hearted. After the briefest talk, I liked Lynceus, and the serving woman had treated him with evident affection.

"He's not my father's son anyway, and my father knows it. I don't understand why Minyas is so fond of Lynceus."

I began to suspect she liked her father so much she was jealous of Lynceus. One of Heebe's sayings popped into my head: "Jealousy, a great destroyer, eats the soul."

"My mother had a lover and she refused to take precautions," Galatea continued. "Metis can sometimes be such a silly woman. She should have told the midwife to leave him for the Goddess, but she didn't."

Nearly that very thought had earlier crossed my mind, but now the idea shocked me. "I like him, Galli. He looks terrible and people stare at him, but he doesn't seem to let it bother him. And his poem was pretty. And wise."

"Oh, let's not talk about Lynceus. Come. Let me show you a jeweler who makes clever anklets." She began talking about Hopthea, warning me that I should be careful not to offend her, but I wasn't listening. I'd had a startling thought. Perhaps the Law of Returning was wrong if it meant that someone like Lynceus was not allowed his chance to live.

I suddenly felt spiritually cut off, a feeling I hadn't had in a long time. Of course, even small physical flaws detract from body harmony. And a serious defect is far worse, a curse from the Demon Children that shackles its bearer for life. Everyone knows that keeping a child with a profound physical defect, no matter how badly that child is wanted, is a selfish cruelty. Yet for some reason Metis had done just that, and the result had been Lynceus. Galatea chattered on about Hopthea, but I couldn't really pay attention. Down deep, I wasn't certain Metis had been wrong.

∾ ∾ ∾ ∾

Our instructors moved us from exercises to increase stamina to actual leaps, handstands, and forward and backward flips. By midwinter we'd begun to use a springboard. My body seemed to know just what to do. For hours after training sessions, even when my muscles groaned, my spirit floated. I occasionally warned myself that to be humble was the Lady's way, but from the beginning I more closely followed Zuliya's word that I let no one outdo me.

We were a moon cycle from sea season when Hopthea presented us with our "baby bull." It was nothing more than a low stuffed hide that represented a bull's back. A real bull would be many hands taller, and the ability to even attempt leaping such a height lay half a year in the future. A year beyond that would pass before we'd practice with a real bull, and then an old one trained to do nothing but stand and toss his head properly.

The day finally came to combine a leap from the springboard with a backward handspring off the stuffed hide. Older students demonstrated. "You'll note," Hopthea said, "that though these students do these flips from a baby bull unaided, you'll use two catchers. I don't want anyone hurt, so wait until your catchers are in place."

Hopthea lined us up. I stood tenth. As I watched the others, a craziness overcame me: I'd do the highest and cleanest backflip of all. And do it without the aid of catchers.

The dolmeidoi maiden in front of me finished. I stepped onto the springboard and, without waiting for the catchers to get set, I took the two steps, sprang into a forward leap, hit the baby bull's back solidly with both palms, did what felt like a good back flip, and felt a solid burn on my feet as I hit the floor.

I didn't expect praise. But I stood flat-footed on the floor, staring at the far wall of the court, and I knew I'd done really well. A perfect flip.

I turned. Hopthea strode toward me, her eyes as hard as stones, deep lines in her cheeks. "Do you think it's your place, Leesandra, to show everyone how leaping should be done?" Everyone nearby fell silent. "I teach here. Your place is to learn and to submit. If you ever disobey the directions of an instructor again—ever—you will leave this house."

A knot pulled tight in my stomach.

"You are under penalty of silence until the next quarter moon."

Blood hot as lava rushed to my face. I was so close to yelling that she was being unfair, but I bit my lip hard. So hard I tasted salt. I'd done a fine leap and flip. I hadn't been hurt. Zuliya would have complimented me for attempting to stretch myself. Submit! The thought stuck in my head like a dagger-thorn in a bull's hoof. I couldn't learn to submit. I didn't want to.

When Galatea learned that I couldn't speak for over a week, she turned white-faced and teary-eyed.

Of course Heebe found out. She'd developed a circle of friends and took just as much pride in her gossip here as she ever had on Kalliste. She came to visit, and I was sure she was pleased to find me under a vow of silence. She clucked and scolded. She harangued me with how disappointed my parents would be if I were dismissed. "Oh, Little Bird, haven't I taught you not to stick out? That we must submit to the ways of the Lady and to those who have authority?" I squirmed, unable to say a single word in my defense.

Zuliya at least waited to speak until the penalty time passed. We sat side by side at a table in the library, windows for reading behind us. He quoted an Agyptian saying: "A man must do what his heart commands, and the strong man is willing and able to bear the resulting bruises." He lifted my hand and, to my astonishment, actually touched his lips briefly to my palm. "I hear you leapt well." He gave me a wicked smile that showed fine white teeth against his black skin. "Although we should perhaps discuss when it is or isn't wise to follow the commands of one's heart."

"Was I wrong to want to be the best? To do the best?"

"Wrong is perhaps not the proper word. The thing you must answer first is whether you wish to remain in the training."

"You know I want more than anything to be a priestess. To do that I have to finish at the academy." I'd been looking straight ahead, but now turned my face to Zuliya. "I love leaping, Zuliya. I feel free as the falcon when I do well."

"Then the question isn't whether to excel or not, but to understand how one can best achieve one's goal." He shook his head and one of the gold earrings flashed in a shaft of sunlight. "Among the People it is not considered desirable to, as you Keftians say, 'stand out.' But you know I have told you there are races in which excellence is valued above all else."

Zuliya continued speaking, but something stirred in the back of my mind, scratching to be heard. Suddenly I remembered. I saw Alektrion and the admiring light in his gold-flecked eyes when he'd talked of the Achean warriors' pursuit of excellence.

"And I must add a final word—a warning," he continued. "I sense strong opposition to you from your instructor, Hopthea. Watch yourself carefully with her."

Two days after my punishment ended, all enterprises in Knossos closed, even academy training. A remarkable event was to take place. A man had killed another man out of jealousy—not by accident but by plan. Today he would be sentenced by Damkina herself. The Lady's Voice! Would she be fearsome? Would she be beautiful? Would I be afraid when I saw Her?

I agreed to go with Heebe and Zuliya, and Galatea asked to come with us. We found an excellent vantage point in the paved area of the Temple's northwest court and sat on our folding chairs to wait. I saw Lynceus standing with friends in a garden just off the Amnissos road, and I waved. Galatea ignored him.

Zuliya questioned Heebe about the sentencing. Hopthea and three other instructors arrived and sat not far from us. Zuliya and Galatea both made sour faces in my direction. I felt jittery having Hopthea anywhere near me.

Zuliya quickly returned his attention to Heebe. "This man has been convicted by his city's council," she explained, "but he has come to Knossos to be sentenced because banishment to a tiny island with no water and no food is a death sentence. Banishment to Lissimos island can be pronounced only by the Lady's Voice."

That was the reason I was here. Not really to see the murderer. To see Damkina. Only rarely did the Lady's Voice appear before the People. A murmur rippled through the court. The People stood. A tiny stooped woman with extraordinary fair skin stepped through the portal. She wore the most remarkable blouse and sari I'd ever seen—completely white, not touched by a stitch of embroidery or flash of color. She'd draped one end to cover her head. Two priestesses glided alongside her, I wasn't sure whether to show honor or to catch this fragile creature if she fell. I knew at once she was one of the seven Wise Women, and a wave of murmurs confirmed my guess.

She shuffled to an elevated section of the courtyard where three ebony chairs stood in a row. The Wise Woman took the right-most chair. Her attendants stood behind her. I was so close I could see two dark moles on the pale skin of her neck.

The moment she sat, a man dressed in the red sari of a council member appeared at the portal. He mounted the platform steps with another man following him. The second man, plainly dressed, was startling. He had a hunched back.

"The current Speaker," Zuliya said as his gaze followed the tall man in red. Zuliya was always more interested in the affairs of the council than the Temple.

A Speaker talks with many people and must have accurate knowledge of many events and what was said. The second man had to be the Speaker's Memory. The Memory would hear and remember and, when necessary, whisper in the Speaker's ear. He was the first person of this breed I'd ever seen. Everyone knew the malady was the price many Memories paid for their astonishing ability. It ran in their lineage. I wondered if even living a life of service and high honor could make up for being so deformed.

From the direction of the portal came the tinkling of bells that precede the Lady's Voice, and with the rest of the crowd I turned toward the gate. Twenty bell-girls dressed in red and black winter tunics emerged and lined the portal.

Then, at last, Damkina.

The People took the position of reverence. The High Priestess of the Goddess glided to the central chair. She wore full formal dress: tall hat wound round with a charis, jewelry symbolizing the Great Mother in all Her aspects, an open-breasted robe cinched tightly at the waist and covered to the ankle with a flounced skirt. Her features were regular, though I thought not beautiful. It was hard to tell because her look was so stern: lips pulled thin, eyes hard.

She sat, and the crowd relaxed.

Galatea whispered to me, "Why does she look so angry?"

Heebe overheard. "This isn't a holiday, daughter of Metis. Today she sends a man to his death. The weight on her spirit must be enormous."

I heard a disturbance at the Temple portal. A burly man of middle age stepped out, his hands bound behind his back. The sight of him made my flesh creep. My heart missed several beats and began a rapid thumping against my ribs.

The man stood tall, shoulders squared. He blinked several times, whether amazed at the enormous size of the crowd or simply from bewilderment, I couldn't tell. Four guards brought him before Damkina. I could see the side of his face.

The Speaker rose. He recited the man's offense. The man's shoulders slumped. The Speaker finished with the words, "Hear now the displeasure of the Goddess."

Damkina rose. I heard the rustle of her skirts. The guards forced the man to his knees.

"We live under the gracious Law of Our Mother, who gives life, sustains life, and after She takes life, brings renewal." Each word falling from her lips had substance. Her eyes were focused somewhere far off. She didn't seem to speak loudly, but I knew her words would carry to the most distant ears.

"The world She has created lives in harmony. Each element—plant and animal and fish and tree and river and ocean—has life, and the worth of each must be respected. That is the Law. We, her People, must act so harmony will not be broken. When any of the People disobey, balance is upset and the Demon Children are unleashed and use every disharmony to foment evil. Kokor, who brings disease and pain. Shilat, who is the enemy of all that grows. Dilgoratha, who deranges the winds and rains. Small disobedience leads to small disharmony, but the small failures of many magnify into great harm." She paused. "And if done by many, great disobedience can be seized upon to do incalculable harm."

"You," Damkina said. Her gaze shifted to the man. Her brows lifted and beneath them were eyes ablaze. My breath stopped short. The man began to teeter as if the earth were crumbling beneath his feet. "You have broken one of the three Great Laws. You allowed yourself to be deluded that a woman belonged to you when the Law says all of Her children belong to the Goddess alone. And when you accepted that delusion, you acted on it and took a life. This can never be permitted. Only the Mother, the Ancient, can take life. You must leave the body of the People forever."

Damkina raised her right hand and held it over the kneeling man's head. The crowd waited—breathless—silent. "I say you shall be taken this day to the island of Lissimos, there to be left alone. In one year a boat will return to look for you. If the Great Mother wills, She may yet spare you. But if your offense is too great to be tolerated, She will take you. That, too, is the Law."

Damkina lowered her arm, and the wretched man began to wag his head. Tears streamed down his cheeks. His teetering body began to sway as if he were caught in some downward spiral.

From my left a woman's agonized voice cried out, "He's my son. Have pity." She began to wail. Murmuring swept the assembly, and for some reason I glanced at Hopthea. She glared at the man with a hatred so intense I physically recoiled; she would doubtless willingly row him to Lissimos herself.

Two guards yanked the man to his feet. His eyes were downcast, unable to look into the face of the Goddess's Voice, but through his quivering lips, I heard him whisper, "Mercy."

The guards turned him toward the portal. His knees gave. The guards stopped his fall. I watched, nauseated and shaken, until the man disappeared inside the Temple.

"All that is good and beautiful comes from obedience to the Mother's laws," Damkina said, her voice mesmerizing. Before, she'd been speaking to no one in particular. Now her gaze swept the crowd and, perhaps it was a trick of my mind, but I felt her look at me. "Disobedience brings disharmony, prolonged disharmony brings disaster. The Goddess is a wise, loving Mother. But her wrath falls hard on the disobedient."

Damkina's words rang in my head: *Disobedience brings disharmony, prolonged disharmony disaster*. I felt a strange disquiet run through me. The Goddess had looked into my heart and said, "Leesandra, learn to obey." But something felt wrong.

"Wasn't Damkina magnificent?" Galatea said as we four began our return to the boarding house. "And how very awful to know when and how you are going to die."

Hovering on the edge of tears, I silently agreed that such knowing would be awful in the extreme. And with every step I grew more distraught. The man had broken the Law. And not just any law, one of the three Great Laws. But how could the Lady's Voice condemn him to die all alone?

"If life is so precious," I looked at Heebe, "how could Damkina send him to his death?"

"It's the Law."

"But ... I will never forget the man's face."

Zuliya asked, "Do you know the face of the man he killed?"

"No. Of course not —"

"Then you cannot have all the information needed to make a judgment, can you?"

"I don't want to make a judgment. I want to understand."

"It seems what we are considering is the offense of murder. To take another person's life with intention."

"I know what he did was terrible. But when Damkina spoke his sentence, I was shaking. The punishment seems so brutal. I don't want him to have to die. Slowly. All alone."

"Do you understand that among other peoples this offense of killing is not the unthinkable thing it is here? Killing, in my experience, is rare only among the People."

"Surely that can't be."

"But it is. I believe the Lady's People may be the least violent race in the world. Keftians have the Law deep in their hearts. They raise their children by it. This is the only place I have lived where if you are pushed, you are forbidden—not discouraged, but forbidden—to push back. It is virtually unthinkable to push back."

I glanced at Heebe, thinking of the day she and I had watched the Achean women and her two sons in the bird market. "What has this to do with Damkina's pronouncement?"

"My countrymen, the Hittites, have many virtues. But in general we are a violent race, descended from warriors. We practice war and we raise our children to believe in the warrior virtue of killing to serve one's king. We have penalties for offenses, large and small, far more severe penalties than what you know. If a man steals another man's property, say a storage pithos, he can be sentenced to be the wronged man's slave. Permanently."

"But that's horrible."

"Dreadful," Galatea echoed.

"You may say so, but it prevents theft. In the end, every race finds the means to keep order. I know places where, for this man's offense, they would stake him between poles, allow the victim's mother to cut open his belly, and when his screams grew faint, they would cut off his arms and legs. This man will simply be sent to the island without food or water. True, it is virtually impossible for him to survive, but as Damkina said, his fate is in the Goddess's hands. No one of the People will take his life. And because violence on Keftiu is so rare, the banishment itself is so offensive it will prevent other murders. Do you understand, Leesandra? Something must always be done when people behave in destructive ways, and the more serious the offense, the greater must be the punishment. Otherwise the offense will be taken lightly and will spread. In my opinion, the Lady's Law in this matter is both fair and wise."

We reached Heebe and Zuliya's boarding house and as Galatea and I continued toward the Academy, Galatea said, "Did you notice Hopthea? She seemed positively eager for the man's death."

I agreed. And I decided that though Hopthea was unquestionably a very good dance instructor, her spirit was sick. And she disliked me.

Spring festival was less than half a moon cycle away. Afterward, at last, I would train with a real bull. He'd be old, but at least he'd be breathing and his flesh would be warm.

The dolmeidoi were in a fever because immediately after the festival we'd also be assigned to a *compathos*. The instructors would group us in teams of six, three girls and three boys each, chosen to have the balance of strength, agility, and height to control a bull and perform the leaps. For my remaining academy years, my compathos would be the most important people in my life.

The instructors reminded us often that our dance bull still ran free. "His heart will be wild and unless you pay close attention, your bull will more likely kill you than dance with you."

Among all the dolmeidoi, maidens and youths, none were more agile than I. Always aware of Hopthea's probing gaze, I never again flaunted my skill, but somehow I simply couldn't help but do each movement just a little better than what others could do.

"I know now why Hopthea is so stern with you," Galatea said one day. "She's jealous."

I couldn't suppress a chuckle. "Why?"

"She could tell from the beginning that you'll be an even better leaper than she ever was. She doesn't like it."

∾∾∾∾∾

All students had two days free prior to the beginning of spring festival. Galatea went to her parents. Her mother's family owned a huge farm outside Knossos. On the first festival day, the Temple priests presented the youth chosen to represent Velchanos for the next year. On the second day a high-ranking priestess would perform the annual mass marriage.

Heebe, Zuliya and I began in the twilight before sunrise and arrived at the shrine about mid-morning.

I wasn't often out with Zuliya in public, and it made me chuckle to see how everyone stole looks at him. Given his black skin, his nose jewelry, the distinctive club of hair at the nape of his neck, and his truly remarkable red shoes, Zuliya was a rare entertainment. I'd asked him once why he didn't assume Keftian dress so he could blend in. "Blending in is a Keftian practice," he'd said in a carefully neutral tone.

At the shrine Heebe and Zuliya decided we should use a canopy to protect us from the sun. I was anxious to find Galatea, but first I helped to set it up. I was positioning a corner pole when from behind me a woman's voice said, "They were driving goats into a pen." I shifted to see her. The woman had a sharp chin and a mouth full of large square teeth.

She continued. "I'm sure it was to kill them for sacrifice."

"They're a blood-loving people, all right," said a thin stick of a man who appeared to be her husband.

An elderly man in a wine-colored robe, who was with a different family, added his opinion. "There are too many of them on Keftiu."

Who were "they?" A woman I took to be the wife of the man in the wine-colored robe said, "There are too many foreigners altogether, but the Poseidonists are the worst. Sometimes I don't understand how the Law can allow them to kill in order to worship. It is a terrible breaking of harmony."

I hadn't thought about Poseidonists since entering the Academy. I remembered the slave boy, felt myself in that narrow, leafy tunnel again, sitting beside Alektrion. Oh how I sometimes ached to see him. To feel his hand on my back. To hear his laugh. I would lie awake and wonder at how the memory remained so strong.

"I don't mind having them here," said the sharp-chinned woman with big teeth, "so long as they do whatever they do in private. The Lady knows devotion can't be forced. She says they can do as they wish. That's the Law. Just so it's in private."

"But," insisted the second woman, "they're becoming more bold."

All at once their heads turned toward us, doubtless realizing Zuliya would have overheard them, and as he was clearly foreign, they couldn't know what god he worshipped. "Isn't it fortunate that the rain occurred yesterday and not today?" said the thin husband, blushing like a child caught lying.

The woven canopy was raised and secured. Heebe shooed me off. I found Galatea near the shrine gate. I told her what I'd overheard.

"Who cares what the Poseidonists do? I don't." She tugged me closer so we could see. We watched the mothers bring gifts and pray for the fertility of their daughters. I would never have little ones. I would never have a husband. Lovers, yes, that was permitted a priestess, but not the commitment of family.

"Are you sorry you won't have children?" I asked Galatea.

"Not really."

After the mass marriage, Galatea walked back to Knossos with Heebe and Zuliya and me. She and I talked about the Sacred Marriage, only days away. "We'll carry honey," she said. She spoke with surprising authority. "All bull dancers carry the symbol of valor. And we'll follow the officers of the navy."

"How do you know?"

"My father's told me everything. Minyas was Velchanos."

I stopped walking and stared. "You never told me!"

"We've never talked about the Sacred Marriage before."

"But a man can have no greater honor."

She gave me a satisfied smile. We started walking again. "He's told me many times everything he's allowed to tell. You know all sacred servants must participate in the Great Procession at least once in their lives. Nearly three thousand of the People will take part."

"What else?"

"Well, at last, my dearest Leesandra, we'll go inside the sacred part of the Temple. We'll spend the night in the Central Court in fasting and prayer."

My empty stomach growled. "Speaking of fasting, do you want to eat with us tonight?"

"I'm expected home."

I had a disturbing thought. "Did your father couple with Damkina?"

She shook her head. "When my father was Velchanos, Sosuma was still High Priestess. Two years after he served, I was born and the next year he took our family to Pylos. Damkina was chosen the Lady's Voice the next year."

Pylos was an Achean town under the thumb of a man so thirsty for blood he was called The Red King. "You must have hated living in Pylos. The Acheans are such barbarians."

She pulled her arm from mine. "What a terrible thing to say. My father says, and I agree, this attitude of superiority some of us Keftians have towards the Acheans is foolish."

"But—"

"The Acheans are a remarkable people. Proud and fierce. And very handsome. To say what you did just means you don't understand them."

I understood Acheans all too well. They were indeed handsome. Alektrion had resembled his mother. But were Galatea's wrong-headed ideas her own? I thought more likely they were her father's.

Her eyebrows arched in a most haughty look. "Isn't your tutor always trying to teach you tolerance for the ways of others?"

I started to tell her what I'd seen that day with Alektrion, but those arched brows stopped me. I turned our talk back to the Marriage.

On the day before it, a list was posted outside the refectory door with names of students who, for one infraction or another, had been denied the privilege of attending. Grabbing my hand, Galatea tugged me to it. "Look. Oh, Leesandra, look," she said, pointing. "Your name is right there."

Panic squeezed my chest so hard I felt dizzy. "It has to be Hopthea."

"Absolutely. I wonder what she has done. You must go to the overseer. Say you think it's a mistake. Find out the reason."

I agreed and took leave of Galatea and rushed toward Netta's chambers. But then I stopped to think. Zuliya had taught me never to act without thinking. If I complained or questioned, I would only add fuel to whatever Hopthea was already saying about me. I returned to Galatea.

We were working in the stable, and very soon she said, "I can't bear this, Leesandra. I'm going to talk to Pressla. She likes me. She'll tell me the reason."

"Don't let her think I'm complaining."

"I promise. I won't."

She returned within the hour.

"So?" I said.

"She seemed very surprised."

"What did she say, exactly?"

"Exactly?" She said, 'I believe Leesandra's spirit is goddess-touched. Something seems amiss.'"

My heart beat faster hearing Pressla's strong and favorable words.

I slept miserably, woke sick at heart. Then the room matron said, "Go to Netta's room. At once."

Netta was the overseer of student participation in the Great Procession. In her rooms I found Hopthea and two dolmeidoi instructors, Pressla and Nomialis.

"You will have seen your name on the exclusion list by now," Netta said. "I've called you here to tell you that your name has been removed. You may attend."

I fixed my eyes on Netta's plump cheerful face. I dared not look at Hopthea.

"Hopthea felt your spirit isn't correct this year. That you're too eager to shine, to show your abilities. She felt it would be better for you to wait for next year."

So! I was right!

Netta continued. "Pressla and Nomialis have spoken in your behalf."

Both instructors smiled, though Nomialis, a shy man who had been an excellent catcher in his day, looked uncomfortable. I'd never had any idea they took enough concern with me to overrule a decision by Hopthea.

"I've told Hopthea we'll let you attend the Marriage this year, Leesandra. But you must promise me you'll guard your spirit well, making sure it is humble at all times. Can you do that?"

I nodded. "I am most grateful, Netta. I promise I'll not fail your confidence. And that of Pressla and Nomialis."

"You are all dismissed, then."

I stole a hurried look at Hopthea as she turned stiffly toward the door. Hard eyes looked back at me, eyes that said she would not forget. I felt as if I stood naked in a winter storm.

When the day of the Marriage arrived, my first thought on awaking was how I must be careful to keep my spirit humble, to honor Netta's faith in me. Then I remembered how the Goddess had sounded that day in the rain when She'd spoken clearly to me. My memory of the wonderful voice was so faint. My Hearings were less frequent now and I had a fierce yearning to hear Her beautiful voice again.

The mood in the crowd gathered at the Temple was eager and expectant. Priestesses and priests milled with Temple craftsmen, scholars and artists, the hetaira and hetairon, speakers from Keftiu's many districts, military men and merchants. Clutching my vessel of honey, I lined up with Galatea and the rest of the dolmeidoi.

At midday the conchs sounded, and the People streamed into the Temple from the north and south. In single file, with Galatea directly behind me, we passed down a corridor decorated with a fresco of the Bull Dance and then out into the Temple's Central Court. In the center, with the Law chiseled on its rounded surface, stood The Tree of Life, and to the east of it, Velchanos sat in a chair elevated on a dais. I reminded myself again that it was my duty to keep all my thoughts focused tightly on prayers that this union be successful and on nothing else. The energy of all of our prayers was an essential ingredient for success. Beside him sat an empty chair for Damkina. She was praying now, in her sanctuary behind the Mother's Womb.

The midday sun spilled light directly into the court, and when I passed the God, I looked up at him. The fair color of his hair struck me. Uncommon and extraordinarily fair. Like Alektrion's. My concentration broke. I was several steps past the entry to the Mother's Womb when I suddenly realized my inattention. I was draining precious energy from the ceremony. *Stop at once!*

By the time I ascended the west staircase my spirit was right again. Galatea and I poured our libation into a receiving pithos as tall as a man, then retreated back down the staircase. Finally the Central Court could not hold even one more worshipper. Witnesses crowded the second floor balconies. The resinous scent of frankincense was so heavy it cloaked my shoulders. The music ceased, and those closest to the entry to the Mother's Womb gave a great cry of happiness. Damkina appeared. "The Lady! The Lady! The Lady!" we shouted as one.

17

Fear and joy shot through me like shooting stars in the night. She was beautiful. She was terrible. She was the Great Goddess. Giver, Sustainer, and Taker of Life.

Damkina walked with outstretched arms, a living charis twined along each. The snakes, taken from cooled pottery before being placed on her arms, seemed content, drawing in her body warmth. She ascended the dais, and Velchanos rose. His eyes were fixed on her beautiful breasts with their red-rouged nipples, the symbols of the Goddess's nurturing of life and of Her gift of coupling that fosters and maintains harmony among the People.

Only after Damkina sat did Velchanos take his seat again. The Goddess let her arms fall and the snakes obediently flowed off her hands into the warmed baskets that were their homes.

A hush swept the crowd. All eyes turned as a Wise Woman descended the east staircase. In her unblemished white sari, she was a riveting point of purity amidst so much color. She proceeded to the dais and climbed its stairs.

The Goddess and the God rose.

The Wise Woman took them each by the hand, then, moving slowly, clasped their hands together. The crowd sighed in approval.

Raising her voice, she chanted the marriage hymn, giving first the God's words, then those of the Lady:

Let me plow your field, the God requested.

And how deeply will you plow it? the Goddess asked in return.

As the Wise One continued, time stopped for me, and when the recitation was over, the Goddess and God retired to the Lady's chambers.

Now and again I shivered with the cold during the long night vigil, even though Galatea and I sat thigh to thigh for warmth. But not once did I feel the pull of sleep. Twice I had lost concentration. Might I have done damage? Was Hopthea right about my spirit? At dawn the Wise Woman emerged and said the union had been successful. Apparently my small failings had caused no harm. No other Sacred Marriage remains so vivid in my mind. I couldn't have imagined, not even in my strangest of poppy dreams, that one day I might defile this most sacred ritual.

Shortly afterward Hopthea assigned all dolmeidoi to a compathos. Happily, Galatea and I were kept together. Tall, strong Gleantha was the third maiden of our team, and the three youths chosen for us were Kronos, Dromalis, and Renon.

Bull Dancers enter the bull court in the same way maidens enter the mother's womb for initiation: veiled. In the Leap, the first movement in this dance of life, the veil is used for seduction. Three of the compathoi must turn the bull sideways, and the veil is used to lead and distract him. Two dancers then hurl the leaper in a single flip over the bull's back. In the dormitory, in the park, Galatea and I practiced flicking and twirling the blood red cloth until it was heavily marked with patches of dirt and sweat. Just one day before we were given to our bull, our instructors announced that our performance with the veils was satisfactory.

Our bull's name was Thunder, and unlike most bulls, which have patterned hides, Thunder was as dark as night. I saw him, and my heart faltered for the span of several beats.

"He's ... rather large, isn't he?" Galatea said as the six of us studied him in his holding pen.

A stunning understatement.

Thunder stared back at us with glaring, angry eyes.

"We will become one with him," Gleantha said. Gleantha was, by any measure, the most courageous—or foolhardy—of the six of us.

We lived with Thunder. We fed him and watered him. When finally given permission, we shooed him into the close box to feed him, and while he ate, we stroked him. During those days Thunder heard our voices often; we were always gentle, always soothing.

I couldn't imagine a time when we would have tamed wild-eyed Thunder enough that he'd lower his head on signal and allow us to grasp his horns. Even more important, we had to train him to toss his head straight, not to the side. A bull that swings his head so that he tosses to the side is terribly dangerous.

More dangerous than the Leap is the Toss. In the Toss, the companions position the bull with their veils, then the dancer approaches him head on, grasps his horns, and when he raises his head, does a back flip away from him.

But the most dangerous move of all, the climax of the dance, is the Vault. The dancer waits, heart pounding, with her back to the approaching bull. The two grapplers must lower his horns, and at the very moment the bull's head goes down, two hurlers thrust the vaulter upward into a back flip. She lands on her palms on the bull's withers, does a back-flip onto the bull's flanks, and then another off his back into the waiting arms of the catcher.

If Thunder were to rear his head too soon or throw it right or left, the vaulter might be impaled on a horn. Were he to charge or back up, the vaulter could fall and be trampled. And if we failed to tame Thunder, any one of us could be gored.

I started to dream of doing the Vault. To think of that wonderful moment caused my pulse to quicken. And only one of us would be chosen for that glory. I wanted this honor with such passion, I knew my desire was in itself dangerous. Though practiced with the leather bull until the vaulter's dreams are full of nothing else, the Vault is never practiced with a live animal. That would drain its power. The Vault is done only once, for the bull and for the vaulter.

Months passed. Thunder's spirit did meld with ours. He was in us, we in him. This bonding was the goal of the dance: to harmonize all life forces and, especially, to tame for good those that can be destructive.

In mid-winter, during the Silvanos festival, training slowed. But immediately afterward we began work on the Vault. By tradition the Vault would be done by the team's harmonizer. We would choose this person from among us by casting secret lots. If for some reason the harmonizer couldn't perform the Vault, the harmonizer would decide who would do it.

The day came to choose our harmonizer. I boiled with indecision. I wanted to be chosen so passionately I nearly picked myself, but the training in submission was working; to pick myself would be pridefulness of the worst sort. Gleantha and Renon weren't suited because, though very strong, they weren't sufficiently flexible. And one of the harmonizer's responsibilities was to make sure team members worked well together. Hopthea made several pointed comments about how helpful Kronos was. I agreed. Kronos did bring out our best. So I picked a blue stone for Kronos though my fingers almost refused to let it fall into the counting jar.

When Hopthea strode into the court the following day, I was in agony. She called out the names of the bulls and, after the bull's name, the name of that team's harmonizer.

"Thunder," she said at last. Her lips pulled into a sour line.

I shut my eyes and held my breath.

"Leesandra."

Quietly, as names of other teams were still being read, each of my compathoi embraced me, their happiness evident in the warmth of their smiles. Galatea's smile was even bigger than mine. I wanted to shout. To sing. I would do the Vault! On the glorious day when we performed in front of the Reverend Speaker, a Wise Woman, and the People, my mother and father would see me fly.

That afternoon, when Zuliya came for my geography lessons, I rushed to him and for the first time embraced him. His eyebrows shot up and, blinking, he held me at arm's length. "What is this, Danae's daughter?"

"I've been chosen harmonizer, Zuliya! My companions picked me."

"Ah. Good news, indeed. They would not have cast the stone for you if they didn't feel you are concerned for each of them. I am proud."

Pride. I suddenly realized just how bloated I was with anticipation of glory.

"This means, does it not, that you have the right to choose to make the Vault?"

I nodded.

"Your father will be very happy when I write him about this."

"It's not wrong of me, is it, Zuliya, to be so pleased?"

"What are you thinking when you say wrong? Are you thinking of pride again?"

So often it seemed Zuliya and I were the only ones who felt this urge to excel. I felt as though the weight of all others—my friends and family and teachers, to say nothing of the Lady's laws—were set on a balance against Zuliya and me, and yet most of the time his council and my own spirit weighed more.

"If I'm to serve as a priestess, I have to put down this need to assert myself."

"If submission is contrary to your nature, perhaps serving as a priestess is not the path for you."

"I want to serve in the Temple with all my heart. It's just ... hard. I think this would be easier now if ... well ... if I weren't quite so good at the dance."

He smiled. "Yes, even I have heard what they say about you."

"What do they say?"

"That Leesandra of Phaestos, daughter of Danae, is one of the finest bull dancers ever to train in the Bull Academy."

I glowed to the tips of my ears.

"It's not my task to decide your path, only to throw as much light as I can so you see all possibilities. Heebe and your mother, and apparently you, believe you are called to the religious life. But if you walk that path, you must eventually give your intellect, and your will, to the Goddess. If you do this thing, if you give up your identity this way, it is no longer you, Leesandra, who will choose your steps. Others will choose for you." He stood, came around behind me, and placed his hands on my shoulders. His grip was firm and warm, and he gave me a little squeeze. "I think now you should just continue to study and to experience fully each of your days. Later will be the time to decide. When you have tasted more of what life offers to those strong enough to make life's decisions for themselves."

Immediately after he left, I went to the academy shrine. I chose a figurine of a bull dancer in the posture of reverence, and after burning incense, I placed it on the offering table. *Help me, Mother, to remain humble and obedient.* I stayed there a long time.

Winter that year was wetter than any Heebe or any of her growing circle of friends could remember. Street drains often overflowed, and Keftiu's packed dirt roads became rivers of mud so impassable that communication between the seven cities was at times hopelessly bogged down. The pattern of my life, except for breaks during festivals, was as constant as moon cycles. In training I'd moved beyond Hopthea's specialties so I saw her less often—a blessing. But I didn't forget her.

Finally spring approached and with it the moment of the dance. My mother and father arrived early and, after briefly visiting me and Heebe and Zuliya, they left to visit mother's family in Phaestos. A week before the festival they returned to Knossos, but I wouldn't see them again until after the dance because we dolmeidoi were back in seclusion.

I could think of practically nothing else but my Vault. Each night in sleep I imagined myself sailing over Thunder's back, but during each day my insides roiled because I knew the consequences of failure: four dancers had been injured so severely they'd left the academy. Sometimes I imagined myself fatally gored, and I'd go to Thunder and caress him and whisper words of love.

On the night before the Dance, after mealtime ended, I followed Galatea into the hall and a stameidoi touched my arm. "The Mistress of the Dance wishes to see you right now." Looking pointedly at Galatea he added, "Alone," then went on his way.

Galatea said, "What could she possibly want?"

"Do you think—but I can't imagine."

"Go!" She gave me a little shove. "You mustn't keep her waiting."

The cedar door to the Mistress's chambers bore a carved relief of a bull with a dancer flying over his back. I arrived just as Hopthea came out.

Surprised, I said, "I've been asked to attend the Mistress." Silly. That was obvious. Why else would I be there?

She nodded, her face devoid of expression, told me to go right in, then hurried off.

The Mistress, Aristala of Gournia, who was in charge of every aspect of the training of maidens, sat on a couch. A light incense, pear-scented, freshened the room. She smiled and gestured for me to approach and sit opposite.

"I'm drinking pear nectar." She indicated a flask carved from rock crystal and several engraved gold cups on the table between us. "Would you care to share with me?"

My heart was pounding, my stomach had been unable to take much food for days, but I couldn't imagine refusing her offer. I nodded.

"Help yourself, then, Leesandra."

With the sound of my name ringing in my ears, I poured a very small amount into a cup. The Mistress of the Dance knew my name!

By the time I'd backed to the chair and sat, I'd begun to wonder if Hopthea had just told her my name.

"You've done well in your years here, Danae's daughter. You're eighteen now and a credit to your family. I've been told you show great promise."

How should I respond to such praise?

"I understand your parents have come all the way from Alyris to see the Dance."

"Yes." I took a sip of the nectar to moisten my dry mouth.

"And I imagine that they're pleased that your compathoi chose you as harmonizer."

I nodded and managed to say yes again.

"I have something of great importance to say to you. It won't be easy for you to hear."

My fingers tightened on the cup's engraved stem.

"We both know pride is a danger in those who would be fit vessels for the Lady's service. A leader must think first of the good of all, not of self. Your instructors have noted in you a tendency to push yourself forward."

My face fell; I could feel it start to flush.

"I'm putting a choice before you. You will listen to what I say, then I'll dismiss you. We'll not discuss the matter, but I'll know tomorrow what you decide. Do you understand?"

I nodded.

"I want you to pick Galatea to do the Vault. She has prepared to take your place in case you became sick or injured. I expect you to otherwise participate in the dance, just as you've practiced. But I want you to tell Galatea when you rise in the morning that you don't feel well enough to perform the Vault."

This isn't happening.

"When you and your companions enter the Bull Court, I will hope to see Galatea enter first. And you are to tell no one—I mean absolutely no one—of my decision or what we have said here. Only you and I will know the nature of your spirit."

The face before me was serene, the dark eyes level. I sensed she would say no more and that I was dismissed.

I felt as though Aristala of Gournia had casually asked me to cut out my heart.

I shut the heavy door behind me, pressed my hands to my eyes to keep back tears. No one would see the daughter of Danae crying.

I won't do it!

Torchlight flooded the hallway. I stumbled to the dormitory. The room was dark, the dancers already put into bed in anticipation of tomorrow's dangers. I lit a hand lamp from the night light and made my way toward my bed, but halfway there the tears won.

I fled the bedchamber for my favorite sanctuary, a tiny shrine located next to the maiden's bath. Heedless of the rule that I first do reverence, I sank to the floor, shoulders shaking, tears wetting my hands and face.

I cried and hugged myself and rocked. A moment came when the salty river slowed and then an image of my mother and father, disappointed in me, set the torrent loose again. One by one, the three lamps burned out. I huddled in darkness. I finally stopped crying, but couldn't gather the will to return to bed.

∾ ∾ ∾ ∾

"Whatever are you doing here?" The girl whose job it was to rise before dawn and light the lamps had spoken to me, her eyes big and round.

Startled, I rose, muttered something, and fled to the dorm. I slipped into bed and pretended to be sleeping. Not long after, Galatea shook my shoulder. "Wake up, sister." Her voice brimmed with anticipation. "Today is our day."

I rolled over and sat up, my head in my hands. "I ... I'm not feeling well."

Was I going to obey Aristala? I thought, amazed at my words. Absolutely not!

Galatea shook her head and tugged on my arm. "Don't be silly. What can you mean, not well?"

She knelt and took my hands in hers, searched my face until I lifted my eyes and met her gaze. I thought she might notice and comment on my puffy eyes. Instead she said, "You aren't afraid, Leesandra. You can't be. You're too brave."

A new pain shriveled my heart. I withdrew my hands. If I didn't do the Vault, would they all think I was a coward? That possibility hadn't even entered my head. I'd been thinking mostly of my parents and their disappointment. And my desire. My face stiffened with anger. Aristala's test was unfair. If I danced, but didn't do the Vault, how could I ever hold my head up in pride before my companions?

Pride.

Galatea tugged on my hand again. "Come. I want you to curl and bind my hair."

I helped her, and then fumbled through the routine of oiling my body. One moment I'd think maybe Aristala would send for me. She'd tell me she'd changed her mind. Though my head said I should be asking the Lady for humility, instead I begged Her to cause Aristala to relent. But no messenger came. I fumed, determined to defy the Mistress of Maidens.

Then I considered again what would happen if I didn't submit. She'd said the choice was mine. But when the day came for the Temple to consider accepting me as a novice, they would surely seek knowledge of me from the academy. If I did the Vault, Aristala would know beyond question the depth of my pride. That was the whole point of the test. I stepped into my kilt, secured the belt.

"Whatever is the matter with you?" Galatea asked as she fastened my headband in place.

"Nervous."

The moment when we would leave to assemble grew closer. Still no reprieve from Aristala. I secured the leather thongs of my dancing sandals.

"It's time," the room mistress said. I straightened just as she spoke and my knees turned to water. I grabbed onto a dressing table, feeling as if I were standing at the edge of a precipice with my back to a cliff. If I did the Vault, as every fiber in my body longed to do, the price would be forfeiture of any chance to become a priestess.

"Leesandra!" Galatea whispered. She'd put her arm around my shoulder. "You're so pale."

"I still don't feel well." My pulse beat in my ears. The Mother had called me. I must not, would not, fail. I forced the words out. "You'll have to do the Vault."

She stepped away, eyebrows raised.

"I don't know why, but I feel weak. If I try the Vault, our dance may be ruined. You're as able as I. You'll do it beautifully."

"But ... I know how much this means to you."

"The dance is more important." Oh how I hated to say those words. But if this sacrifice was what the Great Mother demanded, I would submit.

"Go now, maidens," the mistress of the room said. She'd come up behind us.

"I'm feeling weak. I've told Galatea she will have to do the Vault with Thunder."

I expected the room mistress to show at least as much surprise as Galatea had. She didn't. She felt my forehead, asked me just how weak I felt and if I thought I should dance at all, and, having apparently satisfied herself, hurried us off to the assembly area.

When the great moment arrived, Galatea led our compathos into the arena. I avoided looking toward the place where Aristala would be sitting. Nor could I bring myself to hunt for father and mother, or Heebe, or Zuliya—those who loved me and who would now be very surprised. Zuliya would also be deeply disappointed.

Thunder was beautiful, not only because we'd spent hours washing and brushing him, but because he was now part of my spirit forever. Before we released him into the court, we placed a garland of white peony and holy thistle around his neck.

In the end Galatea vaulted well.

When it was all over and we stood to watch Thunder being ceremonially bled from a cut on his neck, I clenched my hands so hard trying to fight back tears that my nails cut crescents into my palms. Hopthea had had her revenge.

I'd never seen Galatea's eyes brighter or her body more energized. Beaming, she said, "Did you see my father's face after I did the Vault? He looked at me in a way I've never seen before. I'm sure he was trying to be humble, but Minyas isn't by nature a humble man. I could see he was happy enough to fly himself."

The feasting and dancing in the academy garden stretched late into the night.

Zuliya, who now knew me better than anyone, drew me aside. We found the embracing canopy of the plane tree said to have sprouted when the world was created. The fragrance of blooming purple hyacinth sweetened the night air. He sat me beside him on a stone bench and crossed his wooden leg over his good one.

"Is it true that a little feeling of weakness caused a fierce heart to fail?" He studied me, his fingers playing with one earring.

I couldn't meet his gaze. "I did what was necessary."

"Necessary?" he echoed. "You do not seem weak now, nor did you look weak during the other parts of the Dance. Am I right to suspect that the decision not to Vault was not made by you?"

I said nothing.

"One of the lessons taught here is submission, is it not?"

"You know it is." He's angry with me, I thought. Zuliya valued excellence and an Akkadian notion for which there was no word in Keftian, but which meant roughly "to walk alone." He had told me more than once that he was pleased I would do the vault because then I could "catch the glory and enjoy its sweet taste. It will be an important lesson."

He tapped a finger to the side of his head and gave me a sly smile. "To catch the big fish, we must often let the little ones go, is that not so? I know you are disappointed. Perhaps only I among the family know how much. The teachers here have keen eyes, and they read you rightly, my Leesandra. They put a hard challenge to you. This time you were wise to submit. To have refused would have put unnecessary barriers in your life path." He leaned toward me and patted the back of my hand. "But be careful of the lesson you learn."

"What lesson would you have me learn?" My question felt sufficiently neutral. I hadn't broken Aristala's command of silence.

"Others will teach you to submit to higher authority *always*. I say submit only when your head as well as your heart tells you to do so. And never to submit otherwise."

Dear Zuliya. I wanted to hug him. To have him hug me. I loved him. But that wasn't his way. I said nothing further, and he seemed satisfied. He changed the subject to how, as my training would shift emphasis to the Bull Capture, our lesson schedule must change. Beginning tomorrow he would come in early morning. His eyes had the twinkle they showed when he told stories. "If you demonstrate courage in next year's Bull Capture as well as you have shown discipline to learn the dance, I will begin to think my time teaching you has not been altogether wasted."

Zuliya's praise that my choice had been wise helped to soothe my spirit. That I faced a new challenge, the Bull Capture, also helped lessen some of the sting of disappointment and divert my attention. In one year, my companions and I would face a wild bull. No bull capture had ever been accomplished without dancers being maimed— a bad enough fate—but in some years dancers were killed.

18

A summer sun scorched Siros's rooftops as Alektrion entered the alley of the One-Eyed Donkey. Two hours ago a leather merchant had shown up at the inn where he and Laius were staying demanding to see Laius. Since then Alektrion had looked for Laius in all the obvious places: the nearest public bath, the rooms of the tavern-woman Laius was seeing, the tavern where the woman worked.

The One-Eyed Donkey was the last possibility. Maybe he had joined their old teacher for a few ales. Dolius's ship, *Lion's Heart*, was in port—a year ago the old marine had been transferred—and the Donkey was Dolius's favorite tavern.

Alektrion reached the tavern door just as one of the nine men under his command strode out. The marine saluted and the eagerness of his smile reminded Alektrion of his own eagerness when he'd first put to sea. How very changed things were from that first year. Two seasons of rowing had been good for him. He was in his fifth season now and though he no longer rowed, most of the muscled bulk he'd put on in those early years remained. At twenty-one, he'd also reached what he expected would be his full height.

Because of Dolius's superb training, Alektrion and Laius had fought well at Marisostos and at the end of their third year were accepted as marines. Then came the incident at Impios. At Impios he'd followed his gut instincts, rallied the men, and captured for Knossos a pirate vessel bearing enough copper and tin to outfit a small army for half a year. He'd been elevated to the rank of squad leader, the highest rank a non-Keftian could ever attain—the same rank as Dolius.

That had been a heady day. Klemonair, still second in command, pinned the treasured patch of a sword crossed over the butterfly of regeneration onto Alektrion's sleeve. The moment had been marred only by Trusis. Alektrion had been basking in the pleasure of his elevation in rank when Trusis walked up and said, "Enjoy it 'breed.' It is, after all, as high as you'll ever go." Through the months, the Keftian Alektrion had once thought a friend had grown increasingly hostile. Trusis would leave at the end of that season to go to Knossos. He would enter the Naval Academy. His future held much promise. Alektrion could not understand the source of his sour personality and animosity.

Laius had said simply, "He's jealous. You're bigger, faster by far, the men like you better, and so do the women. It's not hard to figure Trusis out."

Alektrion stepped into the dusky, cool interior of the One-Eyed Donkey and scanned the room. No Laius, but Dolius sat at a table with two men Alektrion didn't know, presumably shipmates from *Lion's Heart*. With them were three women.

"The Scorpion has arrived," Dolius said, giving Alektrion a toothy grin. He gestured to one of the women to fetch Alektrion a chair. That was another change. Since Impios, where he and Dolius had fought side by side, Dolius had stopped calling him Breed. But the old warrior now called him Scorpion, a nickname with a different but equally uncomfortable association. Many of the men used it.

All three women turned greedy eyes on him. They smiled. He thought, *You're wasting your charms, sisters.* His ability to attract women was a curse akin to boils.

"Have you seen Laius?" he asked Dolius. To the tavern boy he said, "Ale."

"Not today. Why?"

"A leather merchant claims Laius ordered a specially made sidebag. He hasn't paid for it."

"Strange."

"I've checked the bath, his woman, and his favorite tavern. Any other ideas?"

"He'd better not be gambling."

"Laius has his gambling in check. It took him forever to repay me. He says he's not going to get into that kind of fix again."

"Well, we've all been warned." Dolius sat his cup on the table and ran his tongue across the damp ring over his lip. "And in my opinion, once a gambler, always a gambler."

The warning about gambling had come from all ship captains. Atistaeus used agents to trap a man into debt and, once indebted, a man could be forced to cooperate with the enemy.

The boy brought Alektrion's ale, and right behind the boy came yet another woman. This one had an especially determined look. Alektrion downed a hefty swig. And thought of Belamena. He took another swig, and thought of Helene, the Keftian girl who'd caught his eye when he'd finally returned to Kalliste his fourth winter. She'd wanted to take him as husband. He was a half-breed, though, and her parents had turned him down. He almost wished there were a way he could hang a message around his neck that said in five languages, I intend never to marry and the only women I bed are hetairas!

The woman drew up a stool and sat so close she touched his arm. One of the other women asked Dolius, "Why do you call this handsome one Scorpion? It's not a pretty name."

"Ah, but it's an accurate one. I've seen Alek fight."

Alektrion flinched. Dolius sounded as if he would tell about Impios again. Most of the time Alektrion could control the killing rage, but at Impios a marine named Eteocles had been wounded, his guts ripped out. He'd screamed the scream from Alektrion's nightmare, and Alektrion's discipline had collapsed and the rage had taken him.

"You don't ever want to rile up a scorpion," Dolius began. "You get in their path when they're riled and they kill with a single thrust, quick as an eyeblink. Fast. That's how Alek fights. And kills."

Gazes shifted to Alektrion. One marine smiled. Two of the women looked shocked. A third raised a jaded, skeptical eyebrow. Alektrion prayed fervently Dolius would shut his mouth.

The woman pressing against his leg smiled seductively. "Tell us more about how the Scorpion fights."

Alektrion took another swig and from behind the cup, shook his head at Dolius. His teacher grinned back mutinously, but spared him. "Well enough to survive."

The conversation drifted. Alektrion's thoughts returned to Laius. They could have enough saved within the next five years to buy their first trader. The very dark cloud on the horizon, though, was Atistaeus. The Red King's marauding had grown ever more serious, and the Keftian fleet continued to obey the Law to do no more than defend the sea's commerce. Unless Damkina took the battle to the barbarian's door, Keftiu would never stop Atistaeus. But the High Priestess remained unwilling to invade Pylos.

Klemonair strode up to their table. "Need to talk to you, Alek. Privately."

Alektrion left his ale. Outside, a breeze promised some relief come evening from the oppressive heat.

"Grimaldius's orders. Find your squad. Have them report one hour before dawn. We ship out in secret. The men must tell no one they're leaving."

The crew had trained to leave secretly, but *Sea Eagle* had never done so in Alektrion's five years aboard her. "Where are we going?"

"No one will know until we're on the water. By the way, don't say anything to Dolius. His captain will contact him. I can't stay. I have to find the other squad leaders."

Alektrion returned to finish his drink. Then, under the pretext of a continued hunt for Laius, he went in search of his men. Most were at a bathhouse. He'd found all of them in time to return to the inn to eat an over-cooked dinner. Laius arrived in the middle of the uninspired meal. After explaining that they would be leaving early, Alektrion mentioned the sidebag and asked where Laius had been.

"Nothing important. You know Siros is famous for carnelian beads. My mother wanted me to buy some. I spent the whole cursed day looking for the best and then had to bargain with the dealer."

Laius set to eating with extraordinary attention to his food. Alektrion studied him. He'd never known Laius to lie to him, but beads? The story felt peculiar.

In the middle of the night he awoke screaming, with Laius shaking him. *Kokor be damned*. His pulse drummed in his ears. He'd been free of the dream for almost a year.

Laius put a steadying arm around his shoulder. "You're fine, Alek. It's only because you know something big is going to happen. Anticipation stirs old memories." Laius let go, scooted across their bed and sat with knees up, his back against the wall.

Alektrion, still sweating, used the edge of his bed linen to wipe his face and chest. "I get the two of them mixed up, now. Eteocles and the man on the ship. They're both screaming at the same time."

"Belly wounds. Ugh!" Laius shuddered. "About as bad a way to die as a man can. I want to go fast. Preferably at the moment I plow the field of the most beautiful woman in the seven worlds."

Alektrion rewarded Laius's attempt at humor with a weak chuckle, then added, "I'm not going to be able to go back to sleep."

"Nor I. I say we dress and go to the beach now."

They weren't the first to arrive early; half the crew was already stowing supplies in *Sea Eagle's* hold. The ship carried mostly replacement weapons and the tools, hardware, and sailcloth needed to keep the ship fit and running. As for food, warships ran lean. They fished while at sea and, each night when they put ashore, sent out foraging parties.

Near dawn the rowers took them to sea, and as soon as they cleared the lee of Siros, they raised sail. Serena offered blessing, then Grimaldius called for attention. Their captain stood on the aft deck, spread-legged and shifting with the ship's pitch and roll.

"I know you wonder why we left under cover of darkness. The Great Goddess has given us an extraordinary chance to strike a heavy blow to Atistaeus. We make for Lanithi. We assemble there with other ships under the direction of admiral Sarpedon." Murmurs of approval rippled across the deck. "With the Goddess's blessing, we're going to cut off Atistaeus's manhood and stuff it down his throat."

Cheers went up. Laius crowed, "It's about time!"

Alektrion felt a nervous tingling in his hands that spread across his chest and shot down his legs. Might they at last actually do something more than swat at the swarms of gnats the Red King had spread over the sea?

The men found their assigned places and flung themselves down on their sheepskin cloaks. They were in for a long run. Laius said, "You'll see Lanithi again. If I recall, you weren't exactly at your best the winter you spent there."

"Drunk most of the time. A foolish, rude, miserable slave of Kokor. And still, most of the people were kind. I hope this battle doesn't spill onto the land and involve the islanders."

Laius shrugged. He knew what every experienced warrior knew: battles, once begun, made their own rules.

The sun came up to find the sky cloudless. A westerly held strong and they ran with it. After mid-afternoon prayers, Grimaldius summoned Alektrion. "What do you see on the horizon?" He pointed.

Watchman wasn't Alektrion's official duty, but he had the reputation of having the best eyesight among the crew. He squinted where Grimaldius indicated, into the sun. "It's a ship all right. Impossible to tell whose or what kind. The light's bad."

"I think it's running parallel to us."

"You think she followed us out of Siros?"

"That's my worry."

"Maybe it's *Lion's Heart*."

"No. *Lion's Heart* left well before us. This ship is running alongside or slightly trailing. I'm afraid she'll hang to, eventually figure out where we're going, and if she's a Pylian fastship, she can outrun us to Lanithi and warn the seal dung. Surprise is critical for us."

In the late afternoon Grimaldius surprised the crew: they would run during the night. Alektrion could remember doing such a thing only a handful of times—always in open water. Grimaldius was going to risk running in darkness when Klemonair couldn't see navigation hazards. Knossos must be eager, indeed, to make this strike.

After sunset they changed course. The sea was in a glowing season, and for some time after darkness fell, he and Laius watched in a companionable semi-trance as twenty-five port oars dipped into the water to be raised and spray behind them gossamer veils of shimmering green that hypnotically disappeared and reappeared with each cycle of the oars. At some point Alektrion noted that the ship troubling Grimaldius had disappeared. Still, the captain ordered that the men light no lamps and that the lamp Serena kept lit at all times be taken into her cabin. Klemonair ordered another course shift, one that once more put the wind behind them. They raised sail. Grimaldius ordered half the men below to find some half-comfortable place to curl up. With Laius, Alektrion was among those left to sleep on the main deck.

Laius wrapped himself in his cloak and Alektrion did likewise. "I'm glad it's Sarpedon who'll lead us," Alektrion said.

"The man does have a reputation for being clever in battle."

"Even better, he seems to be the only admiral who understands we're going to have to make war on Pylos."

Laius shook his head. Softly but firmly, Laius spouted the official line that what the Keftian navy was doing now and had been doing since the beginning of time was correct. That the Law against making war was the only way to keep harmony.

"Things can get too far out of balance," Alektrion protested. His eyelids felt heavy. He burrowed deeper into the wrap. "Damkina has to stop Atistaeus soon or there will come a time when there'll be no stopping him."

Laius yawned. "Nothing changes that much, Alek. The ways of the Mother are forever. You worry too much."

∾ ∾ ∾ ∾

Alektrion sat up, momentarily disoriented. Something had awakened him. He quickly realized he was on *Sea Eagle's* deck and that Laius wasn't beside him. The ship was still running with the wind, the men around him slept. He looked aft. Klemonair stood at the steering oar.

Something moved at the corner of Alektrion's eye. He looked toward the bow, behind Serena's cabin, and was amazed to see what he took to be a small but bright light flicker out. He squinted and blinked several times. Had Serena, for some mysterious reason known only to priestesses, disobeyed Grimaldius's order to maintain darkness?

He looked aft. The mast stood between the navigator and the spot where the light had seemed to be. Even had there been one, Klemonair wouldn't have seen it.

He waited some moments more. Nothing. He decided his eyes had tricked him. Glowing sea spray must have come over the bow.

Where was Laius?

Almost as if in answer to the question, Laius, wrapped in his cloak, eased around the corner of Serena's cabin. He made his way with quiet steps to Alektrion's side. Alektrion felt a turning lightness in his gut. "What were you doing?"

"Had to piss." Laius's tone was unnaturally sharp as he settled beside Alektrion.

Alektrion tried to sleep again but his mind kept racing forward to tomorrow, to battle, to doing Atistaeus some real damage. An uncomfortable feeling needled him. Battle nerves, he decided. He couldn't have seen a light. Laius had been at the bow. Laius would have seen it and told him about it.

∾ ∾ ∾ ∾

By the next afternoon, a hundred armed marines and the crews from three ships—the *Hunting Cat* and *Strong Fox* and, arriving last, the *Sea Eagle*—had rendezvoused on the smallest landing beach on the west side of Lanithi. Alektrion was disappointed *Lion's Heart* wasn't one of the ships. Dolius wouldn't be at his side in this fight.

Grimaldius, the most senior of the three captains, prepared to speak to the men. Standing on a hastily assembled trestle table, he projected his voice so all could hear. "We've time now only to eat cold rations. After you eat, you march over that mountain." He gestured toward the string of peaks that halved Lanithi. Having spent his first sea winter on the island, Alektrion was familiar with the terrain. The town and the port lay on the island's far side.

"It's already late afternoon. The main body of our ships is gathering behind an islet several stadia south of Lanithi City. Tomorrow at dawn they'll move to pin the Pylian admiral's flagship and twenty other ships in the harbor. Your task is to keep the Pylian scum from escaping out the back door. You absolutely must be across the island and positioned behind the town by dawn."

Guarding the back door. Alektrion sagged. Kokor's ass! Aware of his men, who stood around him, he pulled his shoulders back, but his disappointment only served to revive the sinking feeling he'd had in his gut all night. A child's task. Only one route led out of the town, a route easily guarded because it wound through a narrow pass. Nor was anyone likely to flee. He was going to end up with nothing more than a good seat from which to watch others pick off the Achean ships.

Klemonair strode up to him. "Put your squad at perimeter watchpoints. I'll send someone to relieve you to eat before we march." The second in command strode off toward the circle of officers.

Alektrion paired the men, partnering Laius with one of two new marines and himself with the other. A band of scree rimmed the landward edge of the beach, a bouldered slope behind the scree. The boulders could easily hide a hundred men. He walked the squad to the beach's north end, dropped one pair there and others at roughly equal intervals as they walked back toward the south end, telling them, "Search your area, then keep watch."

His partner was a Keftian of twenty-five, older than he was by four years. Though uncommonly young to be a squad leader, he had never felt resistance from his subordinates. For this the Scorpion could thank his reputation as a wild man in battle.

He and the Keftian crunched across the scree, began to climb the bank of boulders. Uphill and to the right, he heard the staccato clacking of tumbling pebbles. He gestured for silence. Again the sound, from exactly the location he would have picked as a good place to spy. He glanced at the Keftian, who nodded.

Alektrion waved. They moved upward. Someone wearing a fisherman's tunic flushed and scrambled up the slope. Alektrion scrambled after him. The man made a misstep on the loose stones, yelped, fell to one knee. Alektrion caught him by the back of his tunic.

"Let me go!"

From behind, Alektrion pinned the man's arms to his sides. "Why were you hiding?"

"Let me go!" The man yelled again, now at the top of his voice. "I've done nothing wrong."

Holding an arm each, Alektrion and the Keftian walked their protesting, squirming captive to Grimaldius. "Who are you?" Grimaldius demanded.

"A fisherman. Just a fisherman. What do you want?"

"A lone fisherman has no need to be on this isolated beach so late in the day. Where is your boat? Where is your fishing gear? I ask, again, who are you?"

Twice more the "fisherman" repeated his answer. Grimaldius signaled for Menelopolox. Alektrion's stomach turned over slowly. The dark-eyed, heavy-browed Thracean had watched the questioning intently from its start. Like a cat stalking prey, Menelopolox eased his way to Grimaldius's side, never for an instant taking his eyes off the cringing man.

"I want to know who he is," Grimaldius said. "And I want to know quickly."

Menelopolox smiled. A tiny light at the back of his cold eyes had turned on. The marines from *Hunting Cat* and *Strong Fox* and even *Sea Eagle* had watched Grimaldius and the fisherman with only modest interest. Now the men from *Sea Eagle* stopped eating and stared at Grimaldius, then at Menelopolox. Of all of *Sea Eagle's* crew, Menelopolox was least liked. Almost despised. He had a strange and frightening temperament. He had no friends, only three Thracean companions who always followed his lead.

Menelopolox signaled and his three companions joined him. Elbowing Alektrion and his watch partner aside, two of them grabbed the fisherman's arms. With Menelopolox leading, they dragged the man back toward the north end of the beach.

"Here. What are you doing?" bellowed the fisherman. "Stop!"

A cold shudder brushed across Alektrion's shoulders. If the man was nothing more than a fisherman … But why, as Grimaldius had said, would a fisherman be here without fishing equipment?

To Klemonair, Grimaldius said, "Hurry. I want all of you out of here within the hour."

Klemonair turned to Alektrion. "You did well. Demos's men have already eaten. Tell Demos to have his squad relieve your men, and get your men fed."

Alektrion was bolting down cold lamb and dry bread when a baleful howl, as from some great wounded sea creature, echoed down the beach and out to sea. His chewing halted. Not a soul within earshot moved. Then another scream, more human this time, stabbed the early evening and then stopped, cut off without even an echo. For a moment, in the reverberating silence, everyone remained frozen. A shout from Grimaldius set everyone once again in motion.

Men from his squad approached the table. Alektrion forced down another bite of half-chewed meat. If this was the last time they were to eat before a long hike, then eat he must. No more screams disturbed the air. Menelopolox returned to report. The fisherman wasn't with him. Alektrion moved closer to hear.

"The man is a Pylian spy," said the Thracean.

"How could he possibly know we'd be here?"

"He says he was on a fastship. Followed us out of Siros. They knew we were coming to Lanithi, so the fastship dropped him here and dropped two other men on the other two likely landing beaches on this side of the island. He was ready to run into town and report. They also dropped someone at Lanithi City."

"How could they know our destination?"

Menelopolox's thick lips twisted into a chilling smile. "He says last night someone on the vessel *Sea Eagle* used a lamp to signal them. Three flashes of light meant Lanithi."

It's not true. Alektrion's gaze flicked over the warriors. He did not see Laius among them.

Let it not be true! Not Laius. Sweet Mother, not Laius.

19

As if someone had mentioned the dreaded wasting disease, the warriors from the other two ships shrank from anyone wearing *Sea Eagle's* distinctive brown and red trim on the arm of their tunic. A wave of nausea shook Alektrion. He searched the crowd again. Still he didn't see Laius. He brushed past the man beside him and grabbed the arm of the man with whom he'd paired Laius. He fought to keep panic out of his voice. "Where's Laius?"

The man looked at Alektrion's hand on his arm and shrugged. He looked over his left shoulder, then his right. Shook his head. "Don't know. Thought he came in for food." He grinned. "Maybe he's watering the rocks."

From behind, Alektrion heard a disturbance and turned to see Grimaldius vault onto the trestle table. Nearly choking on panic, Alektrion once more scanned the crowd and then the beach. But he knew he wouldn't find Laius. Laius had run.

"We've been betrayed, men."

Alektrion had never seen such a look on Grimaldius's face. Not when demanding that they charge in battle. Not when burying men Grimaldius had known for years. Not even moments ago when ordering torture. His eyes were cold; the deep sun-dug lines in his face were stiff with loathing. "Somehow, someone used a light to signal an enemy fastship. I want to know who this traitor is. I want to know now."

No one moved, not the faintest rustle of human sound disturbed the lapping of water against the shore. Even as bitterness of betrayal twisted his spirit, Alektrion prayed Laius was running fast. The life his friend had known was over. There would be no shared fleet. The two of them would never so much as share food again.

Why Laius? Why?

Laius would never cheer Alektrion with his jokes. Return to Kalliste was out of the question; word of what Laius had done would soon reach home and his parents would be banned. No one would speak to them or trade with them. And if Laius didn't run fast enough now and find some way to get off Lanithi, he'd soon be found and punished on the spot as the Law stipulated for traitors in battle.

The voice of Kleos sliced the silence. "It must have been Laius. He's missing."

Klemonair muttered softly, "Your friend is a fool of a gambler."

Yes, Alektrion thought. Perhaps a gambling debt. But ... *How could he betray friends? Not Laius.* And the Goddess knows he could have borrowed from me. Then another thought, *Will they suspect me?*

Alektrion glanced across the faces of *Sea Eagle's* crew fearing to see suspicious looks directed his way. He found none.

In deep murmurs, speculation rippled among the warriors. Grimaldius cut it short. "What's done is done. This betrayal is a bad turn. No question." He set his jaw. "If a fastship has warned the Pylian ambassador, our ships are in danger. At least you have a nearly full moon to light your march. Keep to quick pace. You can be to the outskirts of Lanithi City well before dawn. We can't know yet how this treachery will play out, but we won't fail in our part. Get to Lanithi at top speed. But with caution. They know you're coming."

The men readied their gear. For a moment, anger overwhelmed Alektrion's sadness, the bitterness, even the fear of impending battle. He clenched his sword hilt. A man he had trusted—his friend—had betrayed them. Whatever fate the Goddess decreed, Laius deserved it.

Grimaldius and the two other ship captains relinquished command of the marines to their second officers: the captains would stay with the ships. Klemonair, as most senior second-in-command, led *Sea Eagle's* marines out at quick speed. The crew from the *Hunting Cat* came next, followed by the men from *Strong Fox*. The path wound between cliffs strewn with rubble and boulders. Klemonair sent four scouts ahead warning, "Keep a sharp look up. This terrain is an invitation to ambush from above. And keep an eye out for the traitor."

Why didn't he borrow the money from me? It could only be money. He knew Laius's heart and it could never side with the Red King. Laius's debt must have been huge. The moneylender must have said, Pay or you are a dead man. *Maybe I'm partly to blame. Did I make paying his debt to me so painful he risked this disaster rather than ask for money again?* He began to feel that whatever went wrong this day, it would weigh on his spirit as well.

And if they caught Laius— An unbearable image flashed into his head. *Merciful Mother, please let him escape.*

For several hours Klemonair allowed only an occasional slowdown, no halt. The brightly lit trail grew steeper and so narrow only two men could advance shoulder to shoulder. A scout returned. A contingent of Pylian marines was coming out to meet them. "They have only half our strength, but if they reach the top of the pass first, they can hold it indefinitely."

"How far to the top?"

"A fifth the width of the mouth of Knossos harbor. But they're closer to the crest."

Klemonair ordered increased speed. The sound of one hundred battle-dressed men running, shields hooked over their shoulders and light packs on their backs, bounced loudly from one rock wall to another. With his left hand, Alektrion steadied the hilt of his sword to keep the weapon from banging against his thigh. With his right, he reached to the small of his back and patted his short sword to reassure himself he'd not lost it. His dagger was snug in its sheath at his waist.

The line labored uphill. His heart felt on the edge of bursting, and the vision of Pylian warriors advancing to meet them now dominated even his worry that Laius must somehow escape.

"That's it," the scout shouted to Klemonair. "That's the top."

Alektrion expected Klemonair to halt the column and send out scouts. Instead the column continued its upward thrust. Though hot and sweaty, Alektrion felt a mental chill. They were rushing headlong into the unknown.

In what seemed only moments he found himself at the crest. Klemonair ordered a halt. We've made it, Alektrion thought, and apparently before the Pylian forces.

From halfway down the length of the column behind him came a sharp, clacking sound. Every nerve in his body twanged. Booms followed in rapid succession. The unmistakable sounds of a major rockfall. Screams rattled the night. The mountain sounded as if it were coming down. From both sides of the trail, undulating cries shrilled out of the semi-darkness. Figures of men rushed toward him, night-blurred shields raised, swords drawn.

He drew his sword, dropped his pack, racked his shield.

Clang!

His first blow, against his opponent's sword, jolted a shock up his arm and across his chest, like a dousing of frigid water. He bellowed. Inside his head he heard only, *Him or me, him or me, him or me.* The man stumbled. Fell. The Scorpion stung him in the heart.

The night rang with the sound of metal, cried out with groans and shrieks. The moon looked on with an unblinking eye. He killed. Others killed. Men were maimed. Harmony ruptured. Some part of beauty slipped forever from the Mother's face.

As suddenly as it began, it was over. Alektrion stood gasping. On the ground at his feet lay an ugly man three times his age with a deep cut across his sword arm. The man made the gesture of spitting. "Go ahead, Keftian bastard. Do it."

Alektrion snatched up the man's sword and hurled it end over end into the ravine's darkness. Finding no other weapon, he turned and surveyed the field. The Pylian commander who'd declared surrender sat on the ground, hands pressed hard against a bleeding leg wound. Sounds of continued struggle rattled up the canyon. The Pylians had evidently set off a rock-fall that cut the Keftian line in half, and on the other side of the now blocked trail, the battle still raged.

Threading among the warriors, Alektrion checked his squad. None dead. Five untouched. Three wounded, one seriously. Serena was on the other side of the slide. He looked around. "Where's Kleos?" he asked a man of Kleos's squad. Kleos was also good at tending wounds.

"Don't know."

Searching for Kleos and Klemonair, he found Klemonair flat on his back with six men, including Kleos, hovering around him. Their first officer lay with closed eyes, his helmet gone, a swelling wound across the top of his head. The men looked to Alektrion, an odd look that gave him an eerie feeling. "He's unconscious, Alek," Kleos said. "I don't think he'll die. But I'm not sure."

Why are they all looking at me that way?

A marine wearing the *Hunting Cat* insignia stepped forward. "Fifteen of us are separated from our mates. Our two senior officers are dead."

The strange looks started to make ominous sense.

Kleos said, "You're in command, Alek."

"No he's not."

Alektrion recognized the dissenting voice, low and gravel rough, at once. He turned to find Menelopolox and his three Thracean companions. "I outrank The Scorpion by two moon cycles."

The warriors fell into a tense silence. Their eyes shifted back and forth from Alektrion to the disliked Thracean. Alektrion could imagine what they were thinking. He couldn't easily stomach taking orders from Menelopolox himself. But rank was rank, rules were rules. "Menelopolox is right, Kleos. He outranks me."

Those demanding eyes now shifted to and fixed on the Thracean.

"We'll leave all the wounded here, including Klemonair." Menelopolox spoke quickly, eager for command. "If our forces on the other side of the rock-slide prevail, they'll climb over. Serena will be with them. She can treat the wounded. Our job is to get to Lanithi. Secure the enemy wounded. Then we move out. But I promise we'll be back to collect them. We'll have much profit when we sell them."

"I want to stay with our wounded," Kleos said with force.

"As you choose."

From the trail to Lanithi came the hum of voices. All turned to find two scouts walking toward them. And secured between them, hands bound behind his back, was Laius.

Alektrion's legs went soft at the knees. "Well, well," he heard Menelopolox say.

Alektrion thought he couldn't bear to look at Laius's face—a traitor's face—yet couldn't tear his gaze away. Cool moonlight showed Laius's skin pulled thin with fear, the face of the already dead. The scouts stopped. Male voices that had hummed in questioning now grumbled with anger.

"You've done well," Menelopolox said to the scouts. "As for you, Laius of Kalliste, we have little time for you. You see your commander on the ground. He may die because of you. Others already have." Menelopolox gestured to the scouts. "Strip him!"

They won't do it, was Alektrion's desperate thought. But the scouts moved quickly to obey. With what seemed incredible swiftness, before Alektrion could loosen his tongue, they'd unbound Laius's corselet. "You can't do it!" he finally heard himself shout as the scouts threw the corselet to the ground.

"You stay out of this Scorpion," Menelopolox said, his voice low and menacing. "Or were you in this with him?"

With their short swords, the scouts cut away Laius's tunic. Alektrion's friend—his brother—stood in only boots, loincloth, and cold moonlight. Laius finally glanced at Alektrion. His terror-filled eyes seemed to both look at Alektrion and through him.

Searching frantically for mercy in the faces of the men around him, Alektrion begged, "You know this man. This is Laius. He's a friend. I say, ban him."

Demos's hand gripped his arm, fingers tight and firm. "It's the Law, Alek. He's a traitor. He will die alone."

"You bet it's the Law," Menelopolox said. "This man, this friend"—Menelopolox raped the word friend—"has betrayed us all. The Ancient demands him." Turning to his closest companion, Menelopolox grunted, "Get on with it."

Short sword drawn, the man stepped toward Laius. Alektrion threw himself toward the executioner, but strong arms from both sides yanked him up short. He twisted but was held fast. "The Law is wrong! Great Mother, the Law is wrong! You can't do what's wrong!"

The executioner's arm moved fast. Alektrion could see the swift stroke as he cut into Laius's gut. Laius's eyes, which looked surprised, blinked rapidly as he fell to his knees. Then it started. The scream of his nightmares.

Alektrion began to shake. He clenched his fists in an attempt to stop the shaking.

Without letting go their hold on him, Demos and someone else yanked him away from the killing site. The screaming changed; for the first time, the agony of his nightmares had words. "Alek," the screaming man cried. "Have mercy, Alek."

The men began to troop downhill toward Lanithi. "Let me go, Demos," Alektrion demanded as they pulled him along. He was amazed his voice sounded so calm. His ears rang like a cymbal had been struck beside his head, and Laius's continued calling of his name was so loud he wasn't sure if he was hearing it or imagining it.

"It's done, Alek. It had to be done. If we let you go, will you promise not to attack Menelopolox or that other Thracean oaf? I don't want to lose you, too."

"I give my word."

He felt Demos's fingers loosen a bit.

"I'm asking you again. You swear?"

"Yes."

"Let him go," Demos said to the recruit holding Alektrion's right arm as Demos himself let go of the left.

Alektrion spun on his heel and started back. "By Kokor! Alek," Demos yelled, "What are you doing? You come back here! The Law says he's to be left to die alone." Demos yelled again, but he didn't come after Alektrion.

After stumbling several times, he realized he couldn't see because he was crying. He rubbed the back of his fist across his eyes. He ran toward what was now only an animal-like wailing. Laius lay on his side in a moonlit murcurial pool of his own blood, clutching his belly, entrails between his fingers. Alektrion collapsed beside him and pulled Laius into his arms.

"Alek. Alek. Make it stop." Waves of nausea doubled Alektrion over and he clutched Laius even tighter. *Mercy*, he pleaded.

"Make … make it stop, Alek." Laius was panting now with the pain and the fingers of one hand dug into the flesh of Alektrion's upper arm. "How long?"

Yes, how long? Half an hour. An hour. Half the night. A moment longer was too long.

"Don't leave me."

"I won't."

"I'm sorry, I …" Laius halted. Blood dripped from his mouth.

"Don't talk."

A strong spasm, which Alektrion felt as though it were attacking him, cramped Laius's chest and belly muscles. His legs jerked twice, like a dog running in his sleep.

Is this how a man's life ends? This is wrong!

With his sword hand, Alektrion fumbled to pull his dagger from its sheath. Another spasm shook Laius and he shrieked another animal cry that seemed to sear the very marrow of Alektrion's bones. He realized, with surprise, that his own body was trembling more violently than Laius's. *Make my hand steady.* Tears still blinded him, but he knew exactly where to place the knife tip and his fingers found the way. The beautiful blade, his very first booty, slid in like a razor cutting butterfat.

Laius seemed not to have even noticed, not even when Alektrion withdrew the blade. Long, breathless moments passed. Then, "It's better now, Alek," he said softly just before the life faded from his eyes.

"What are you doing here, Scorpion!" The angry voice belonged to Kleos. "What have you done? You're a fool."

Kleos shoved Alektrion away from Laius, and Alektrion was astonished to realize he was too weak to protest. He sat paralyzed, staring at Laius's face.

Kleos bent over and felt Laius's neck for a pulse. Silly, Alektrion thought. The dead always look dead. No need to look for the sign of life. Tears no longer blinded him. They'd stopped the minute he'd withdrawn the dagger.

Still squatting, Kleos pivoted to face him, his lips thinned. "Get away from here. Anyone finds out what you did, and you'll be banned. Who do you think you are to interfere with the Law?" He shook his head. "It won't matter that he was your friend if anyone finds out." Alektrion watched as Kleos's face shifted from anger to pity. "You keep your mouth shut and I'll hold mine. But get away from here. Right now."

"I don't think I can move."

Kleos stood, closed the two strides between them and yanked Alektrion up by the arm. The marine spun him around toward the trail leading steeply downhill to Lanithi. "Git," he said, and shoved Alektrion hard in the center of his back.

Alektrion walked. He didn't know exactly how long he walked, a man with a chest that no longer felt like it had a heart, but eventually he realized that if he was to catch up before the column reached Lanithi, he'd have to run. He started running, and the pounding of his feet, the jolting of his joints, the need to watch the trail carefully lest he put a foot wrong on a rock or in a hole absorbed him almost as if he were completely drunk. The running allowed him, for a time, to ignore pain.

∾ ∾ ∾ ∾

"So how bad is it for Keftiu?" Menelopolox asked the informant. The man was breathing hard having been forced at the last moment to leave Lanithi City by a circuitous route over a nearly impassable hill. He'd run a winding goat path to meet the Keftian contingent at the appointed place by dawn.

"I need a drink," the informant said.

It took time for water to be brought and for the man to ease his thirst, and in those empty moments, Alektrion's thoughts wheeled to Laius. The weakness in his legs and a rolling in his gut struck again. He squeezed his eyes shut. The only antidote was to think of the cause of all this grief. The Red King.

Like a volcano—like Kalliste herself—his hatred for Atistaeus would lie dormant for months, but it was always hot in his core. And when something new happened—a brutal raid or word of a Keftian ship lost—his anger erupted again. In the time between leaving the mountain pass and rejoining *Sea Eagle's* marines, he'd discovered that when he thought of Laius and the weakness of his muscles struck, he could think of Atistaeus and how sweet it would be to kill him. The image of Laius would lie quiet a moment. Only hate seemed able to keep him moving.

"The Pylians were warned in time to move ten ships out of the harbor and around the north point," the informant said, "apparently without anyone warning Sarpedon. When your ships attacked, they thought they had all the Pylians pinned in the harbor and went in to pick them off. But the Pylian ships swooped in from behind, from the north. Pinched your forces in a vise. Picked the Keftians off from front and rear."

From behind the inner ring that circled the informant, Alektrion said, "What about Sarpedon?"

"Took him prisoner."

"Where?" Menelopolox said. He threw a sour look at Alektrion, fully aware that his right to lead hung on the slim seniority of a mere sixty days.

"Got him in the best house in town. The Pylians have been here for weeks. They've taken over all important buildings—and that includes the townhome of the Keftian ambassador. That's where they've got the admiral."

Alektrion felt a jolt of hope. To free Sarpedon would be the most perfect way he could imagine at this moment to revenge himself on Atistaeus. He stepped forward. "I don't know the ambassador's townhouse," he said, "but I know the townhouse directly behind it very well.

20

The faint light stealing between the closed slats of a single window barely served to let Alektrion stumble through the dimly lit obstacle course that was Philoxea's attic. His guides as he felt his way past boxes and baskets were the soft padding of her sandal-footed steps, the familiar peony scent of her perfume, and the still youthful movement of her body.

He swore as he tripped over the end of a rolled-up rug.

"Just a bit farther," she said.

He edged between a tall cedar closet and a covered chair. The attic was crowded with treasures Philoxea had acquired during the years she'd served as *hetaira*.

Outside, the sun blazed. The day was hot with no wind and was growing hotter. Though he'd changed from military dress to the simple kilt of a litter bearer, he was sweating as hard as he ever had under Dolius's most brutal drilling. The tightly shut window throttled even the hope of a relieving breath of air.

"Here." She stopped by a ladder and turned to him, took his hand. "It leads directly onto the roof. Do you want me to check for guards?"

"No. I don't want anyone to be able to say you were home."

She leaned close. He felt desire wash off her. It flowed over him and he sensed it strongly, but he didn't share her passion. Except at the very beginning, he never had. Still he dropped the rope and the bundle of woman's clothing she'd given him and put his arms around her. She pressed tightly, curled under his arm, and he remembered how many times that grim first winter, when he'd been drunk and sad, Philoxea had taken him in, let him sleep it off, fed him, and provided good company. He squeezed her shoulders. "I hate causing you this risk."

"I've made it my business to make friends with the Pylians. Or at least to appear to be friends. When I leave the house, I'll take my sister with me. Except for the two cooking women, there'll be no one else here and, if they stay in the kitchen as they should, they won't see you and they'll have nothing to report. My sister and I will make a great show of stopping at the bath. Don't worry, Alek. I'd do this even if I felt great risk. I hate the Pylians. I want them out of Lanithi."

"Getting Sarpedon out of their clutches won't get the Pylians out of Lanithi."

"No. But it'll be a good start. I know the admiral's reputation."

She stepped back, put her hand to his face and cupped his chin. "You are so very handsome, my Alek. I'm glad you came back to see me, no matter what the reason. Old eyes love to feast on the young."

He kissed her—because he felt her need, and because he remembered her kindnesses.

"I'm off now," she said when the kiss ended. "The trap door opens toward the ambassador's roof. You'll be able to peek around to see if they've posted guards. As of two hours ago, when I went up to water my flowers, they hadn't. And as I said, that house's matron leaves their storage window open all summer." She arched an eyebrow. "In my opinion, a very dusty habit."

She started to leave and he grabbed her hand and kissed her palm. He had few friends—even fewer now, he thought with fresh pain. Philoxea was one of them. "Leave the house straight off. I'll wait until I hear the conchs announcing afternoon prayers. You should be well into your bath by then."

With a warm hand she stroked his cheek. "Don't worry. I'll complain to the skies that anyone should invade and use my home for ill purpose."

She left. Alektrion settled to wait. He tapped his foot, cracked his knuckles, drummed his fingers, tried to keep his mind on Sarpedon and away from the Lanithi pass—and Laius. Finally he heard the conchs. He stood and flexed his fingers. Down the inside of his kilt next to his skin, he wore the dagger—his only weapon. Waiting in the street outside were the two men he'd brought with him, similarly dressed but unarmed. The three of them must seem to be nothing more than litter bearers.

Menelopolox had vigorously protested this scheme. "Only three men," he'd scoffed. "Three men can't possibly free the admiral."

Alektrion suspected the Thracean resisted mostly because it galled him Alektrion would be the one to act. "Offer us another plan, then," Alektrion had said, careful to keep his voice friendly.

Menelopolox had fumed in silence. When Alektrion asked for volunteers, fifteen of the men swiftly stepped forward. The two waiting below were brothers—New Moon and Full Moon they were called. One was thin, the other plump, and their skin was remarkably light in color.

Judging that, at last, the time was right, he grabbed the coiled rope from the floor and slung it over his shoulder. Climbing to the trap door was easy: the much-used ladder was sturdy, its square rungs thick. With his heart thumping against his ribs, he raised the door and poked his head high enough to see around its edge.

There were no guards on the flat roof of the Keftian ambassador's townhome. He searched the rooftops of adjacent buildings. This hour was the time of prayer; householders should be at their shrines. All he could see were gardens and aviaries. He had to move fast. He must be back inside Philoxea's house before observance was over.

Just as she'd described, a gap separated her roof from the ambassador's. The window to the ambassador's storage room lay just below the roof and, again, as she'd predicted, the window stood open. He walked to the edge of the townhouse and the air slipped out of his confidence. Philoxea was wrong about his being able to jump the gap. A waist-high wall rimmed both roofs. There was no way to get the running start that would have made the leap possible.

He estimated the distance between the two walls, then had a thought. The ladder! He fished it onto the roof and laid it like a bridge between the two buildings. Less than the length of a man's thumb supported the tips at each end. The slightest shifting, and it would fall.

He studied the three-story drop and his heart rate hitched up a notch. *So, just make very sure it doesn't shift!*

He climbed onto the wall. To avoid flipping the ladder up with his weight, he stepped over the first rung and squarely, but gingerly, onto the second. Placing each foot like a man using mossy stones to cross a stream and with his arms spread for balance, he crossed his make-shift bridge.

On the other side, he tied the rope to the base of a trellis, let himself over the edge of the wall and into the storage room. The room was, as Philoxea guessed, filthy with dust. It was also stuffed with even more furniture, tapestries, candle holders, rugs, cooking utensils, and assorted flotsam than Philoxea's. How could anyone possibly hope to find anything?

Stepping fox-like, he crossed to the door. The urge to sneeze seized him. He contorted and tensed every muscle. When it came anyway, mostly muffled, he felt as though his insides had exploded. He listened to the house. Philoxea's sister had used her friendship with the ambassador's cook to learn that the Acheans held Sarpedon in a third floor chamber. When you leave the storage room, she'd said, go to your left two doors.

He pressed his ear to the storage-room door and, detecting only quiet, opened it and looked into the hall. Empty.

Quick strides brought him to the second door. He opened it. Lying in a bed was a man in the Keftian dress of an admiral. Alektrion stepped inside and closed the door.

"Kokor's prick," the man said. "Who're you?" The lower half of the officer's leg lay at a sickening angle.

"I'm from the Lady's ship *Sea Eagle*, and I've come to get you out of here."

"How did you get in?"

"I've just realized we have a problem. I walked to get in. I'd expected you to be able to walk your way out. How bad is your leg?"

"Can't move it. Can't walk."

Alektrion swore.

"I ask again, how did you get in here?"

"I came from the townhome behind us. Across the roof." Alektrion studied the great admiral Sarpedon. True, he was injured, and no man lying in bed looks as big as he does when dressed. It still surprised Alektrion that the Sarpedon, whose career he had followed and whose lion's spirit he'd admired, was a very small man.

"Then you'd better get yourself back out the way you came because as soon as prayers are over, I'm due to be questioned again."

"Do you want to get out of here?"

"What kind of fool's question is that?"

"I can carry you."

The admiral hitched himself higher on the bed. He studied Alektrion with the same measuring eye Alektrion had just used. "How far?"

He described the route he'd taken.

"Let's get on with it then," Sarpedon huffed. "You can't stuff me out the window, but people have been using a stairway to the roof at the far end of this hallway."

Alektrion dropped to one knee beside the bed, and Sarpedon mounted his back like a child playing pony with his father. With Alektrion half-running, they made it without incident as far as the ladder. At the ladder Alektrion stopped. He was breathing and sweating hard. The overheated afternoon air didn't move enough to lift a feather.

"The ladder will go down if it's jiggled at all," Alektrion said. "Think you could crawl across it?"

"Boy— What's your name?"

"Alektrion. Alek."

"Well, Alek. I said before and it's still true. I can't move my leg at all. Either you carry me over or you dump me here."

"Then I'll crawl. I don't trust myself standing up."

With Sarpedon still straddling his back, Alektrion crept out on all fours onto the makeshift bridge. His heart boomed in his ears. A knee and a hand at a time, careful to shift his weight slowly, he snailed his way to Philoxea's wall.

"Wasn't sure you could do it, Alek," the admiral said when Alektrion let him down onto the roof garden's floor. His amused voice sounded like he was simply out for an afternoon stroll. "What next?"

Alektrion replaced the ladder. Getting back into Philoxea's store-room with Sarpedon on his back was easy, but when he unrolled the bundle of woman's clothes, the admiral sniffed. "Surely you're not serious. Dress as a woman?"

"It's the only way. Because you can't walk, it's actually fortunate the plan was to take you as a woman in a litter. But we have to hurry. We must be away before the mistress of this house returns." No harm must come to Philoxea. He handed Sarpedon his knife. "Carry it under the blouse."

The admiral wasted no more time. Alektrion called for the brothers. Full Moon and Half Moon lifted Sarpedon, and they left the house without being seen. The Moon brothers lowered the admiral into the litter, closed the curtains, took up the poles. With Alektrion trotting behind them, they headed toward the southern edge of Lanithi.

When they were well away, Sarpedon stuck his hand out from between the curtains and waved for Alektrion. Full Moon and New Moon slowed from fast to a slow walk. People on the lane ignored them. From behind the curtain Sarpedon said, "What now, friend Alek?"

According to plan, Grimaldius should be in the middle of bringing *Sea Eagle*, *Hunting Cat*, and *Strong Fox* to this side of the island. Menelopolox had told Alektrion that today he would take the marines to the beach.

Alektrion explained the plan and then added, "*Sea Eagle* will wait at least through tomorrow for me to come with you. The three of us will carry you to the beach."

"I hate to create a problem, but I've started bleeding." Sarpedon raised the skirt and gestured to his leg. Blood from his wound soaked the litter's cloth. Sarpedon nodded to indicate their surroundings. The road was solidly lined with small homes. "Where can we find privacy to bind it without drawing attention?"

Alektrion thought at once of Cleos, the owner of the inn where he'd stayed that most unhappy winter. It wasn't far ahead, a bit off this narrow road and somewhat isolated. "I know a place. We should be able to go to the back and do it inside the privy without attracting any attention, though we'll have to leave the litter at the front."

"How far?"

Alektrion described the distance.

"Fine. But how do you propose we get a crippled and veiled woman attended by three men to the inn's privy?"

The image set them both to laughing. The first time, Alektrion thought, that he'd felt the slightest mirth since ... a crushing weight replaced the pleasant sensation fizzing in his chest. He fell silent.

They completed the tricky feat of closing the wound, and Full Moon and New Moon, carrying Sarpedon, approached the litter prepared to lower him back into it. Three Pylian soldiers strode out of the inn's front door. Loud and swearing, they marched to Sarpedon. "Let's have a look at this high-born lovely," one said.

The soldier reached out and pulled the veil from Sarpedon's head.

Alektrion rushed the closest of the soldiers, pulled the man's sword, spun him around, grabbed him across the chest, and pressed the sword's blade to his neck, intending to yell that if the two others didn't disarm he would kill their companion, but the Pylians were already in a whirl of action. One ripped away the woman's dress covering Sarpedon's uniform and yelled, "It's an officer," in the same moment his companion charged the unarmed Moon brothers.

Beneath Alektrion's arm, the soldier squirmed, but took exquisite care to hold his neck very still against the sword's blade. New Moon howled, then clutched at his left side. Sarpedon fell, moaning as he grabbed his wounded leg.

Chaos! One soldier hooked an arm around New Moon's neck, trying to pull the wounded man to the ground. Howling, Full Moon jumped onto the third soldier's back.

With one leg, Alektrion hooked the ankles of the man he held, then leaned hard. Together they toppled forward. When they hit the ground, the man took Alektrion's full weight and let out an "ooof." With one smooth move, Alektrion drove the sword deeply into the man's side.

Sarpedon had crawled to Full Moon and now clung to one leg of the brother's opponent; the Achean soldier hopped on one foot, locked arm in arm with Full Moon and half-hobbled by the little admiral. Alektrion shoved himself to his feet. Cleos stepped out of his door. His scowling wife and several patrons followed. He stopped, eyes wide, but seeing Alektrion, a smile of surprised recognition lifted the corners of his mouth.

He launched a determined step to give assistance. Alektrion shook his head hard. Cleos halted. Alektrion gestured toward the inn's door and prayed his old acquaintance would understand. He wanted no help, no witnesses.

"Back inside, everyone," the innkeeper said loudly. "This isn't our business. Let the foreigners fight their own fights." He grabbed his wife's arm and pulled her inside the door. Doubtless seeing the wisdom of remaining uninvolved, the others followed.

New Moon lay curled on his side. The soldier above him kicked his head. Alektrion crashed into the soldier. They hit the ground. Pain seared its way through Alektrion's shoulder. Over and over in the dust they rolled. They hit the donkeys' water trough. Warm water slopped onto Alektrion. They rolled back the other direction. The dust on Alektrion's body became a skin of urine-smelling mud.

With a sudden jerk, they halted. Alektrion had the soldier's back pinned against one support of a rickety leanto meant for shadiing pack animals. The man tried to bring up his knee. Alektrion socked him in the mouth. His lip split. Blood flowed. He went limp. Alektrion rolled away, leapt up.

Perched on the back of the no longer hopping Pylian, Sarpedon held the knife with which he'd cut the man's throat. Full Moon knelt beside his brother. Alektrion ran to them. "Can he move with us?"

Full Moon shook his head. "He's bleeding bad, Alek. I have to get help." Full Moon stood and turned toward the inn.

Alektrion laid a restraining hand on his arm. "I have to get Sarpedon away from here. Fast. Someone in the inn may report us. I trust the Lanithians. They hate the Pylians. But you can never be sure."

"I can't leave New Moon."

"Of course not."

"Then how will you carry the admiral? Maybe someone from the inn?"

"No. I don't want to involve the innkeeper. Or his patrons. But I've an idea. We'll tie this Pylian. Then you go ask someone to send for help for New Moon. All I ask is that, before you let anyone come out here, you give me a few moments. Tell them they'll be safer if they stay inside. Then they can honestly say they don't know what happened. For me to get us away, I'll need a good head start. At least the time it takes to do evening prayers in a hurry."

Full Moon nodded.

From rope used to tether donkeys, Alektrion cut a length. Full Moon tore a strip from the dress and in quick time the Achean was gagged, bound, and stashed in the inn's animal shed. Alektrion dragged the litter behind the shed.

He clasped Full Moon's forearm. "The Goddess light your path." Full Moon nodded then loped toward the inn's door.

Alektrion returned to Sarpedon, who said, "You obviously have something in mind, young Alek." He sounded amused.

The more he saw of Sarpedon, the more Alektrion liked him.

"That I do." He reached a hand to the admiral, who still sat in the dust. Fortunately his bandage showed no signs of bleeding. "Ride my back again so I can run." Sarpedon used the water trough as a step. Alektrion hoisted him and took off at a trot toward the rear of the inn. He knew the family on the adjacent sheep farm. Covered as

he was with caked mud, though, he wondered if anyone would recognize him.

Again the Goddess favored them. The farmer, Bemis, not only recognized Alektrion, the man greeted him with enthusiasm suitable for
a returning family member. "Penthea will be very sorry she wasn't
here," Bemis said while he hurriedly cinched a riding blanket to his
family's donkey, a beast called Flop-Ear. "She's married now. Will have
a child of her own soon."

Alektrion remembered the young daughter well. She'd been but
twelve. Whenever Alektrion was at the inn or the nearby beach, she'd
followed him like a pet duck. He'd treated her as a younger sister.

Together he and Bemis lifted Sarpedon onto the animal's swayed
back. "We need water. And something to eat."

The farmer filled two travel bags, one with water and one with
dried fruits and bread, and these he looped across the animal's withers, in front of the admiral. "When you've finished with Flop-Ear, just
tether her near the trail—in a good patch of grass. I'll look for her day
after tomorrow."

Bemis pressed onto Alektrion a final few directions for how to avoid
the most-used trails, then Alektrion set off at a fast trot, leading the
donkey. For support he'd roughly bound Sarpedon's leg between short
poles, and he glanced back to see how the admiral was taking the
bumpy ride. He was gritting his teeth. They made good time. The
goat path wound up and down one hill after another. Alektrion had
no trouble keeping himself in a fast trot. It helped to imagine Pylian
soldiers close on his heels. The air offered not the slightest breath of
relief. The heat beating down from the heaven and rising off the ground
seemed to suck Alektrion dry.

By late afternoon he decided there was little likelihood they could
make the rendezvous beach even if he tortured Sarpedon all night.
Better to let the admiral rest. Mud clung in brown streaks to his sweating body. He looked for a way to reach the ocean. He would find a
sandy place where Sarpedon could sleep on something other than
hard ground and where he could wash. It was unwise to use any path.
He led Flop-Ear across rocky terrain and through a small forest of sea
juniper onto a heat-smothered, white-sand beach backed from one
end to the other by a thick hedge of tamarisk. He halted the donkey in
the shade of one of the feathery trees.

"Looks like a good place, Alek. First get me off this poor beast,
then check for footpaths. The place doesn't look much used, but let's
be certain."

Alektrion tethered the donkey and verified there were no nearby
trails. He returned to Sarpedon, swigged down several mouthfuls of

water, then ran to the sea and walked straight in until the beach fell away and he dropped completely under. He came out thinking that the feeling of being clean was itself enough to refresh him.

For now they were probably safe and soon it would be dark.

He returned to Sarpedon just as the admiral popped a date into his mouth. "If you want, I'll carry you to the water," Alektrion offered. "No reason you can't bathe."

The admiral shook his head. "Too much trouble. I'll wash when we reach your ship. I'd rather eat."

The beach at its far end curved sharply and a short finger of boulders ran like a small jetty into the water. Alektrion sank his teeth into the date's sweetness as the sun's tip touched the top of the tallest of the boulders. The illusion was perfect: a large pale-red ball poised exactly on the tip of a black stone surrounded by a blue-green sea. For a few moments he chewed silently, letting the beauty wash his mind as the sea had his body.

He thought of Kalliste, of being young, and of having young eyes that looked at the Mother's face without feeling sad with the knowledge of how much ugliness competed with the beauty. He remembered the simple joy of talking to a spider and listening to a very young, very pretty girl's giggles. He thought of Leesandra—and of Laius.

He stopped chewing, his mouth suddenly bitter. For the hundredth time he wondered if somehow he'd done or said something that made Laius unwilling to ask for money. He swallowed hard against a painful lump. No matter what Laius did, or why ... But, heart of the Goddess, how could he have betrayed them? Still, no one should die that way.

He held his breath a moment, then let it out slowly. Something sat in his chest like a boulder. Guilt? Anger? Both? No rationalization would ever dissolve this misery. He would never again see Laius's face.

"I'm glad to be alive to see the sun set again." Sarpedon's voice cut into Alektrion's thoughts. "Tell me who you are, Alek."

Alektrion gave up the information that he was from Kalliste, that he'd started as a cook's helper and that, within five years, he had been promoted at Impios to squad leader.

The admiral grunted in surprise. "I know all about Impios. How did it result in your promotion?"

Alektrion was midway through the telling when Sarpedon interrupted. "I hear a sadness in your voice and I don't understand it. You fought well. You were promoted."

Alektrion hesitated. Something about Sarpedon's face—the level, non-judgmental eyes—loosened his tongue. "I thought, when I was a boy, that I'd love the life of a warrior. I admired Acheans. For their strength. For their determination to win. But I no longer feel that way. If I could, I'd go home to Kalliste now and never again set foot on a warship."

Sarpedon nodded. "Yes, the Acheans don't understand the art of compromise." His gaze fixed Alektrion's. "Why then, don't you go home?"

"A friend and I … I … I'm saving my booty until I can buy a merchant vessel. I plan to own a fleet. It's the Lady's way of peace I want. But I need a stake."

"I see. Finish telling me about Impios."

Alektrion explained that the depth with which a particular ship sat in the water suggested to him she must be carrying an unusually heavy cargo. Alektrion had insisted they follow and take her instead of a larger ship that turned out to be carrying little but men. She'd been heavy with copper and gold.

Sarpedon smiled. "Clever. So you were the one. Even old hands sometimes miss important clues. At this rate, young Alek, you'll soon be a captain." Sarpedon threw another date pit over his shoulder into the tamarisk thicket.

"I can rise no higher, admiral. I'm Kallistan, but I'm not Keftian. My mother is Achean, born at Korinthos."

"Ah. Too bad. I myself think restricting high office to Keftians is foolish policy. But then, I think much that Knossos does is foolish."

This frank blasphemy sent a spasm of disquiet up Alektrion's back. One did not question the Law aloud to virtual strangers. Alektrion felt as though he was sitting beside something a bit frightening. Though he agreed with Sarpedon about taking war to Atistaeus's door, Alektrion suddenly understood, as if he'd been struck in the head, why it would be so hard for Sarpedon to persuade anyone to listen to his warnings about the Red King.

"As you say you don't relish the warrior's life, Alek, I'm puzzled. Why were you picked to rescue me?"

"I volunteered."

"Why would you volunteer for such a risky task?"

" I know Lanithi. I spent a winter here. It didn't seem so risky."

The admiral snorted and tossed another date pit over his shoulder. "Of course it was risky. And you don't look a fool. Why did you fetch me out of there?"

Again the open look in Sarpedon's eyes invited the truth. "Is it true you want to make war on Atistaeus?"

Sarpedon's eyebrows shot up. He laughed. He bit into another date, and his gaze became distant. Finally he said, "I owe it to you, Alek of

Kalliste, to be honest. Yes, I want to make war. I believe with my whole being that if that bloody Pylian mongrel isn't stopped soon, he'll only grow stronger and the day will come when we Keftians find him on our doorstep."

"Well, I rescued you because I agree." Bitterness sharpened Alektrion's voice. "And you're the only military man of high rank who seems to see the truth. Seemed a shame to let you die. Or let Atistaeus silence your voice with captivity."

Sarpedon raised an eyebrow again. "That anger sounds personal. What could possibly lie between the twenty-one-year-old squad leader of the warship *Sea Eagle* and the king of Pylos?"

"I've been at sea for five seasons. I hold Atistaeus guilty for many things." In spite of the still sweltering heat under the listless tamarisk, gooseflesh rose on Alektrion's arms and his hand felt again the knife cutting into Laius heart. He shook himself.

"You say you plan to leave the military. Save enough to buy a trading vessel, maybe a fleet. But if you think to escape Atistaeus that way, my young friend, you're sadly mistaken. I tell you, unless Knossos acts, Keftiu will lose control of the sea. Traders will soon answer to Pylos, not to the Lady's Voice. The raids we're experiencing will only get worse because Atistaeus needs money to wage his wars."

Darkness erased the last of the light and the Lady's daughter, Diktynna, lit the evening star. He and Sarpedon were still discussing Atistaeus and the prospect of war when the moon rose full. "Tell me, Alek," Sarpedon said, "do you speak Achean?"

"Yes, of course."

"When I was taken captive, my Achean translator was killed. I'll need another. Clearly, for the reasons we've discussed, I can't promote you any higher for having rescued me. But I can hire you as my translator."

The idea struck Alektrion as funny, but he kept a straight face. "I'm a fighting man, nothing more. I'm no kind of scholar."

"I don't need a scholar, Alek, I need a translator, one with military experience, one I know I can trust because he agrees with me. More importantly ..." Sarpedon hesitated, readjusted the position of his broken leg. Alektrion waited.

"More importantly, even my best officers don't support my views. You speak Achean. No one can protest if I take you on. Not after your having rescued me. And I've a plan. I'm going to gather men who are like-minded." He leaned toward Alektrion. "Men I can trust. Then, when I'm strong enough, I will return to Keftiu and press my case. If you want to stop Atistaeus, give me your help. What I'd ask of you is less exciting than serving on a warship. And perhaps for you much less satisfying than watching the sunset from the deck of your own merchant vessel. But it'll be more important than either."

In Sarpedon's offer, Alektrion felt as if the Lady Herself was calling to him. The thought that he might do something to take the battle to Pylos made his spirit feel light. Still, he hesitated. What would happen to his dreams?

Laius was dead; did those dreams have meaning?

He felt Sarpedon's hand grip his forearm. "You think of your own plans, don't you? Of saving enough to buy your ship and escape the conflict. But trust me, Alek."

The hand withdrew. "You will never have your own vessels and ply the sea in peace unless someone stops Atistaeus."

"I've wanted to do that for years."

"Then join me."

For the dead women and the nameless man of my nightmare, he thought. For Menapthus and Prian and Eteocles. And for Laius. Alektrion nodded. "How soon do you think we'd return to Knossos?"

In the moon's light he watched Sarpedon smile broadly. Alektrion received two sharp thumps of welcome on the back.

"We'll go within the year."

∾ ∾ Author's Note ∾ ∾

At least twelve years before the final conflict between Pylos and the Keftians, seeing what he perceived to be a rapidly encroaching threat from the mainland, the Keftian merchant Minyas of Knossos began to explore ways and means to secure his survival and ultimate ascendency.

JRE

21

The year of training following my dance with the bull was more strenuous than any spent preparing for it. We wrestled, ran, boxed. Using tame cattle, we netted, roped, and tied.

My body grew stronger, but my spirit suffered. Submitting to let Galatea do the Vault ate at me until my insides felt hollow. I lived with a hunger nothing satisfied. Galatea took a lover. When I did not, she accused me of clinging to a childish memory of Alektrion and said, as many did, that I was quite beautiful and should have many lovers. She claimed my refusal caused my unhappiness. I thought her silly.

I tried to fill the emptiness with passion to become a priestess. One hour of every day I dedicated to prayer and four days each moon cycle I fasted. Unreserved dedication to the Lady's service, I thought. Surely in that harbor I would find peace.

It troubled me, too, that the Mother now came less and less often in the light.

Zuliya was cheered. "It is a sign your body is maturing."

Heebe was also cheered, but for quite a different reason. She said less frequent visitations showed my strength in The Lady's love. "She no longer needs to touch you so obviously."

Neither explanation soothed me. I believed I'd lost the Mother's favor. I had submitted, but the Goddess knew I hated Hopthea who was, in fact, responsible for my being denied the Vault. Zuliya said the decision was a fair test of my character. But try as I might, I couldn't cleanse myself of anger as the Mother required.

Three times Galatea and I were able to go to the beach at Amnissos. I collected some shells and looked at them when I wanted to remind myself of my goal to serve the Lady at sea. When the aching longing for that indefinable something saddened me, I touched them.

Well before I felt truly ready, first fruits festival and the bull capture was at hand. The sacred bulls were bred and left to run wild in the vast plain that lies a three-day journey south of Knossos. With all participating Academy students and teachers, I traveled in a great caravan to the capture site. The crowds encamped beneath the trees in an oak-dotted meadow. Local people came every year, but families from far places also came to support their participating children. The air vibrated with prayers, laughter, and songs. It also hung heavy with the knowledge that what would be done was dangerous.

Phaestos, my birthplace and the place of my family's land, nestled on the plain's western edge. We had a day to visit before the capture, and I was hugging aunts and uncles and cousins I hadn't seen since I was five, when Galatea spied her mother, Metis. Galatea kissed my cheek and said, "Perhaps I'll see you at tonight's dance."

Many people, drivers and beaters, work to round up the bulls and channel them to the nets. The drivers begin the day before, far from the capture site. They flush the summer-fattened males and head them in the right direction, a task of little danger. But on capture day itself, once the bulls approach the oak grove where the nets hang between trees, the beaters must make sure the animals remain on course. The beasts are funneled into a small area and they're frightened by the driver's shouting and pole-brandishing, so the panicked animals became a danger, even for beaters.

I was playing the bull for my nieces and nephews, who were pretending to be a capture team. This game reminded me of Alektrion and the day he'd told me about playing at the Bull Dance with his friends. I was wondering if he was, at this very moment, at sea and wishing I were at that moment on a ship like *Asphodel* when Galatea came to our cooking area with an imposing older man. I went to her.

"Father," she said, smiling at the man, "I wish to present to you my finest friend, Leesandra."

The extraordinary Minyas! He wasn't tall, not more than a thumb's height taller than I, but he had what Zuliya called "presence." I decided this effect was created in part because his head was large in proportion to his body and large dark eyes dominated his face.

The corners of his lips turned up, so when his face was at rest he appeared happy, as if about to smile. He seemed pleasant. Then he did smile. The strangest sensation went through me, as if I'd swallowed a chunk of mountain ice. Those great dark eyes lacked any mirth. So unlike the joy in the eyes of Galatea's half-brother, Lynceus.

"Will I see Metis and Lynceus at the dancing tonight?" I asked.

Minyas plucked a piece of lint from the sleeve of what I now noticed was an ostentatiously expensive robe. "Metis will be there, of course. But Lynceus had to take care of business," he said coolly. "He's not with us."

Apparently Minyas, like his daughter, didn't care for Lynceus. Minyas looked back at me with those big empty eyes of his, and the ice in my stomach gave a turn.

I introduced him to my family and to Heebe and Zuliya, then watched him afterward as he walked away with Galatea. Zuliya appeared at my side.

"So we've met the great Minyas," he said.

"I don't like him."

My tutor muttered non-committally.

"Galatea thinks he's wonderful."

"It's natural for a daughter to admire her father. And he is a man of great talents. He is, unarguably, the richest man in Keftiu. Imports and exports practically any items of value not the sole province of the Temple. Timber, spices, unguents, gems. The man's traders go everywhere." As was his manner, my clear-thinking Zuliya presented the facts—good, bad, or neutral. We interrupted talk of Minyas when the children encircled Zuliya and begged for a story. By late afternoon, sounds reached us now and then from the distant drivers. The air hummed with anticipation.

That night I wriggled on the ground, unable to sleep. I thought of my parents and their hopes. I imagined myself wearing a sea priestess's blue and green robe and standing on the bow of the *Asphodel* with the sea's fresh breath on my face. Would I be hurt? Might I disgrace myself? Might I fail my companions?

I am truly sorry, I whispered silently to the Goddess. I love You with my whole heart, and I will try again to let go of my anger. I know it does my spirit no good. Surely that's why You demand that Your children learn to let hate die.

I shifted and suddenly found a comfortable position, as if the Mother had heard me and approved. *Give me a brave heart for the Capture so I can honor You. And I understand You sent Hopthea to be a test, and so I shouldn't hate her.*

∾ ∾ ∾ ∾

We assembled immediately after rising prayers. The highest ranked priestess from the Phaestos Temple blessed us, and the crowds assembled in the grove of oaks from which they could watch in relative safety. I walked with my companions to our two trees. Galatea and Gleantha would tend the net, and so they carried it. We embraced each other one by one saying each time, "For the Lady's service."

Galatea and Gleantha set to work securing the net between the trees. It was made by our own hands out of cords of woven tree root and would stop the bull. If we did everything correctly, our team would bring this embodiment of the male and female essences to the ground smoothly without harming him—or us.

The sounds of the beaters rattled ever closer now; the bulls were nearly with us. My already rapid pulse fluttered in my throat and I took several deep breaths while fidgeting with the noose in my hand, making sure it draped at just the right angle and that the loop was just the right size.

Then I saw him. A great pied bull rushed toward us. He veered left. Waiting beaters rose and crashed cymbals above their heads. The beast veered again, but too late to avoid entrapment. He plunged into our net. I heard shouts from the crowd. The net stretched and swayed. The bull bellowed and kicked.

From the corner of my eye, I saw Galatea and Gleantha pulling at the net's ties. They flung the net over the bull's head. Our two strongest, Dromalis and Kronos, leapt onto him, each of them grappling one horn. They must bring his head nearly to the ground. The bull reared his neck, lifting both grapplers high into the air. The animal took two steps back and bawled again.

As we had rehearsed a thousand times, Renon and I hesitated, waiting for the correct moment. Again I heard the shouts and cheers of onlookers. Again the bull's head came down. Dromalis and Kronos hung their full weight onto the beast's neck, but he must have been incredibly strong; he merely shook them back and forth. Dromalis's arms were slipping.

"Dromalis is going to lose him," I shouted.

As one, Renon and I rushed forward. No matter the danger, we must loop the bull now and add our strength to that of Kronos and Dromalis. He stank of the pungent cattle smell of sweat and dung. His hoofs seemed enormous. The moment he lifted his right foot, I threw myself forward, slipped on the noose and pulled it tight. A hoof struck my right leg.

"Pull his head to the left!" I heard Galatea yelling to Kronos and Dromalis as something stung my face.

I started to rise so I could back off and pull on the rope. Pain like liquid fire raced from my right leg to the center of my back. Shrieking, I fell.

From behind me, I heard a loud thump, an animal grunt, then a bellow, as the bull went down.

"We've got him!" Renon crowed. "We've got him!"

I imagined my companions binding those big hoofs so the animal couldn't move.

Within a heartbeat Galatea was at my side, then the rest of the companions. The pain in my leg seared, throbbed.

"Let me see her," said a commanding voice.

The Temple observer for our team knelt beside me. For some reason I couldn't understand, he took my chin in his hands and studied my face. The fire was in my leg. Why was he looking at my face?

Heebe and then Zuliya appeared beside the observer. Heebe knelt.

I said to the observer, "It's my leg that hurts."

"Where. Show me." I pointed, and he fingered his way down my leg. He reached the injured place. I bit back the scream that balled in the center of my gut.

Zuliya frowned with concern, but Heebe had started crying. For some reason her tears frightened me far worse than facing the bull had. She was looking at something on my face. I reached toward the place on my cheek where I'd felt the sting.

Catching my hand the observer said, "Don't touch it. The healer will be here in a moment. Touching it may only do more damage."

Damage? *Dear Lady.* Something was wrong with my face! The world seemed suddenly to have started spinning, small black dots circled before my eyes, my vision tunneled down to a tiny point of light—and blinked out.

〰 〰 〰 〰

The sanitarium at Labena is built around a healing spring that wells hot out of the ground. No finer home of healing exists anywhere in the world, and it took less than the time between mid-morning and midday prayers to carry me there by litter. To ease my pain, they gave me a strong potion. I remember little of the trip.

My leg was broken. A healer soon fixed it in place with specially shaped slats and said I mustn't put weight on it for some time. While he fussed with my leg, a woman with gentle hands examined my cheek. The whole time I fought the urge to break into sobs. Heebe had told me since childhood that I was beautiful, but beauty had never seemed as important to me as it did to most girls. Now? I was certain any small beauty I'd had was marred forever.

The woman of gentle hands soon confirmed my fear. "I can do two things for you, Leesandra. And you must choose. If I merely clean the wound and cover it until it heals, I'll not have to hurt you much. But the scar may be large and wide. Or I can take a small needle and very fine thread and sew the ends of the cut together. I can't say you won't have a scar, but it will be thinner. Less noticeable." She looked at me with eyes as gentle as her hands. "But it will hurt."

"Sew it."

Heebe squeezed my hand the whole time the healer worked, and the potion given me didn't mask the pain.

Were it not for worry about my face, I might have enjoyed the sanitarium. Perhaps fifty others were there for treatment, but I was told Labena could easily care for a hundred sufferers. After a period of diagnosis, which for many ailments involved the study of dreams, the healers chose foods to harmonize the person's spirit and body. I remembered Zuliya's comments about Abramanthus. Zuliya was a very learned man. Daily, we were bathed and massaged with great tenderness, the closest thing I could imagine to the pleasures of Elysium itself. And the library was so extensive that, could I have let myself forget, I'd have found both entertainment and enlightenment. But all I could think about was the scar.

No Keftian man wanted a scarred woman—for lover or wife. I still hadn't tasted the pleasures of the bed and had been thinking more and more often that I must take a lover. Now men would look at me with either pity or disgust.

The day the covering was removed, the healer offered me a mirror. I refused.

"It's not all that bad, Little Bird," Heebe said. But she didn't insist that I look.

For three days I avoided mirrors. Finally Zuliya set his jaw. "This is foolishness, Leesandra. Your heart is strong. You're not afraid of anything. Your behavior the day of the capture was noted and you can be proud. You can't show cowardice now. Here."

He stuck Heebe's polished bronze mirror in my hand.

I raised it. A long red streak the length of my forefinger traveled in a straight line down my right cheek.

"You know that with time it will grow white and will be less noticeable." He spoke uncommonly gently.

I nodded. Tightness in my throat warned of tears. I swallowed hard.

"I'm sure you know your father is proud of his scar. Have you ever thought why?"

I was afraid to speak. I shook my head.

"Your father is a man who has seen more of the world than most Keftians, who are much too isolated. He feels, as I do, that the Keftian passion for physical perfection is a kind of denial. Life is not perfect. Life can be very hard. His wound was received honorably. It is a permanent reminder of life's hardness. But also of his courage. He wears the scar proudly, Leesandra. I recommend you do likewise."

I resolved several things. I would never complain about the scar. I would never speak of it unless asked directly. And I'd never put myself in a position where a man could turn away from me because of it.

The latter resolve soon became a heated matter of contention between us. We were in the sanitarium's library. Zuliya put a hand over a portion of scroll he'd had me reading aloud, a passage describing a Sumerian woman's required subservience to her husband. He pushed the scroll away. "This will never do. We must talk."

I'd never seen such an agitated glint in his eyes.

"I know you still plan within the year to submit your name to the Temple. I want you to be in a position to consider other possibilities. When you leave the academy, you must be in a position to choose something other than the religious life."

Knowing his strong feelings about this, I said nothing.

"You never spend time, as Galatea does, talking with the young men at the festivals. To my knowledge, you've never lain with a man. You are not giving yourself any feeling for being married or having a family. This is not good."

His intent was so transparent I smiled. "Are you telling me, teacher, I must take a lover as part of my lessons?"

He chuckled, folded his arms, and leaned against the cushions. "Yes."

"I will consider it," I said, a small lie. I wanted no lover. I knew my memories of Alektrion were now only a young girl's dream. And I had long since hardened my heart against having children. I told myself that a lover would only complicate my life.

Zuliya snorted. "I want you to do more than consider. Once you commit to be a novice, choosing any other path will become exceedingly difficult. Time grows short. I must be clear with you. You have a brilliant, insightful mind. And without effort on your part, others look to you for leadership. For one having your gifts, the religious life is too narrow. It is too cut off from experiences that lead to full maturity."

His remarkable statement left me breathless.

"You could have so much more. Promise me you will look with a hungry eye on the young men you meet and take several to bed. Expose yourself to something other than dusty studies with me or the disciplined confines of the academy and the Temple."

"You've never before said anything so openly opposed to my desire."

"I promised your mother never to dissuade you. But I also promised your father I would see that all paths will be open to you. I fear I have failed him. You are too withdrawn, too focused on doing well at the academy. Such discipline is demanded in the first three years, but not now." An earnest frown wrinkled his forehead. "Take a lover. Several. Follow Galatea's example. Go more often to dinner when you're invited. Please. For me."

Thinking of my scar, I pulled the scroll to me again. "Let's read some more." I might offer Zuliya small lies, but never large ones. I was never going to subject myself to rejection. It was also pointless trying to explain to Zuliya, who was after all raised with non-Keftian eyes, just how ugly my scar was.

∾ ∾ ∾ ∾

Two cycles of the moon passed, and on an afternoon shortly before Heebe, Zuliya and I would return to Knossos, a new patient arrived. I was soaking naked in a large tub of hot spring water along with eight others when the newcomer, a rather handsome outlander from Cos, perhaps three years older than I, settled in directly opposite. He brought news of a shaking of the earth along Keftiu's northern coast. My soaking companions questioned him about deaths and damage, and then he said that Poseidon worshippers were insisting that their god alone could shake the earth and that Poseidon had caused this shaking as a warning.

"A warning of what?" someone asked in a tone expressing my own puzzlement.

"The Poseidonists want to do their blood sacrifices of sheep and goats and pigeons in public."

Something brushed my ankle. No doubt someone's foot. I moved my leg slightly to avoid the touch.

"One particular priest, Oenopion by name, has taken their plea to your High Priestess," said the youth from Cos. I felt that same foot brushing against the calf of my leg. He continued talking, but he gave me a slight, intimate smile. "Actually, it's rumored the man's tone when he spoke to the Lady's Voice was more demand than plea."

"Shocking," said the plump lady soaking next to me.

A merchant from Samos said, "I heard similar talk during the few days I spent in Knossos."

I felt a strange thrill from the youth's touch. Still, I moved my leg away again.

His foot followed.

My face had to be red with the heat of the water. I was probably blushing on top of that. The scar on my cheek had to be screaming, but clearly my ugly scar wasn't deterring this outlander. I thought of Zuliya's order that I take lovers, and for a moment imagined myself taking the first step on that path. My body urged me in that direction: I wanted him to touch my leg again.

But good sense stepped to my defense. He was an outlander, not forbidden, but a most unsuitable choice for a woman who hoped to be a priestess of the Great Mother. Gently enough so the face of the water wasn't disturbed, but firmly enough that he knew my feeling, I kicked his foot away.

"But why all this agitation now?" asked the plump lady.

The farmer from Lasithi was quick with an answer. "It's because too many are allowed to live here. We should send half of them back where they came from."

The conversation continued until one of the men said other rumors held that the agitation was political, not religious. That Acheans were behind all the ruckus, backed by Atistaeus, the King of Pylos. "Many think he has eyes on the Keftian hegemony."

The laughter this evoked sent rippling wavelets of water across our soaking tub like a small storm. The idea of some minor mainland king, or anyone else, posing a serious threat to Knossos was preposterous.

I rose to leave and felt the Coan youth's hungry gaze follow me, and as I wrapped a linen sheet around myself and walked away, I felt a strange emptiness. I had chosen the right path, but at that moment I felt lonely. Well, in three days I would leave Labena. I decided to avoid him. The empty feeling would pass.

Later Zuliya and I walked on a beach of pale pink sand by a lake near the sanitarium. The two of us, limping along side by side, made an odd pair. I asked, "Do you know a priest by the name of Oenopion?"

"A rabid Poseidonist."

"What do you think of the rumors circling around his name? Some say an Achean king, Atistaeus, is using the Poseidonists to create disharmony."

"They may be right."

"But to what end?"

"Keftiu is perhaps the richest land in the world. Only Agyptos rivals it. The Achean king is thirsty for conquest, and he grows stronger every year."

I ignored Zuliya's oft-stated notion that Agyptos might have wealth equal to Keftiu. But what of the even more outlandish notion of conquest? Coming from Zuliya and stated so seriously, the idea that someone might contemplate conquest of Keftiu took on substance. Still—Unthinkable. "I know—or at least I've guessed—that you don't worship the Goddess. I can see how, that being the case, you might think, well, you might imagine such a thing could happen. But it can't."

"Why do you think it cannot?"

"The Lady would never allow such an unbalancing of the world."

"I have lived in many lands. In some places the numbers of deities worshipped is staggering. Enough, if you tried to learn them all, to set your head spinning. And their natures are amusingly diverse. The divinities of Sumer are so spiteful people there spend most of their time worrying about which god is angry with them. Much of their wealth is spent buying gifts to appease some goddess or paying a sorceress to coax an evil spirit to leave them in peace. They have no concept of the Great Mother's love that gives Keftians such a sense of calmness."

"What has this to do with—"

"Bear with me." He stopped walking. "Let's sit. Walking in sand tires my good leg."

A few steps up from the water lay a natural bench. Slipping my hands under one of his arms, I helped him sit, then joined him. The sand was made of tiny shells, whole and broken, and seemingly without thinking, Zuliya sorted through them. While he talked, he picked out perfect ones and placed them in a pile.

"The numerous gods and goddesses of Agyptos are more friendly as a rule than those of Sumer. Nearly every town has its own divine patron. But amidst all this confusion, one who has eyes sees a pattern. In all lands some deities are much more important than others. And among them there is always a supreme pair. The king of the gods, if you will, and his consort, the queen or the great mother."

"But these gods are false, Zuliya. Truly. Those people have turned away from the Mother of All."

"I'm coming to my point. The Agyptians call the Mother Isis and Her consort is Osiris. Just as here in Keftiu the Lady has her consort, Velchanos. But in Agyptos, Osiris is, to most of the people, a god of power equal to the Mother. The spheres of influence of Isis and Osiris are simply different. Cybele is one of the Mother's names in Anatolia, but there she also shares worship with other gods, especially Poseidon. It is only here, in Keftiu, Leesandra, where only the Mother, and She alone, is worshipped."

"Of course. I know all of this." I was growing impatient. "What has it to do with some dreadful Achean king wanting to attack Keftiu?"

Zuliya had created a small mountain of tiny shells. With the palm of his hand he flattened the mountain into the sand. "I think if the worshippers of Poseidon aren't stopped, the numbers of their followers will increase, they will continue to agitate, and the worship of the Lady will be pushed aside. She will have to share her power here, as she does in other lands."

"But, Zuliya, that can never be. As Galatea is always saying, 'The Lady is who She is.' She would never allow some false god to usurp Her place."

Shaking his head, Zuliya scattered the shells with one finger. We sat in silence.

"In a test between Poseidon and the Lady," he finally said, "I do not think the winner will be decided by which is the true divinity. The winner will be decided by which faith produces the more aggressive followers." He pushed himself to his feet.

I did likewise and, brushing the sand from my tunic, said, "Then why do you give any serious heed at all to this talk of the Achean king?"

"Because, as the Hittites say, 'Might wins all.'"

"I don't like the way the saying is put, but I don't think I disagree. Surely if you believe that's true, then Keftiu has nothing to worry about."

We walked to where the trail led from the beach to the sanitarium. I thought the matter was finished, but Zuliya said, "I'm not a military man, and I know the might of Keftiu's navy is renowned. But I have been worried for some time. I have found no place where women and men live in greater harmony than here. In all my travels, I have found no place with laws more conducive to serenity of life. Though the Agyptians most definitely have a better sense of humor, they cannot touch the Keftian love of peace. On Keftiu there is no war between the cities. There is no holding of people in slavery. I believe I appreciate your people even more than you can. And I worry a great deal when I hear rumors that Atistaeus has not yet satisfied his hunger for conquest."

We talked about the Keftian navy. Zuliya agreed there was no other navy to rival that of Keftiu, but he kept repeating that the Red King troubled him.

On my bed that night, Zuliya's words ran through my thoughts over and over, always ending with the phrase, "Might wins all." I felt reassured. I agreed with the Hattian saying. And it meant that the Lady, the Mother, the Creator who gives life, takes life, and gives life again would keep the balance of the world forever. We would have harmony. So long as the People remained faithful.

22

The scar on my face—a vertical slash of white the length of my little finger—healed as well as could be expected, and I learned to ignore looks of pity. My leg healed so well I soon forgot it had ever been injured.

In the following year, during olive harvest, Galatea and I were accepted as novices. Our tasks were menial, given to teach us modesty, obedience, carefulness, and selflessness. For months I simply carried messages from one part of the labyrinthine Temple to the other, and I became familiar with every storage area, bath, classroom, shop, shrine, and refectory. I held in front of my eyes a vision of me on a passenger vessel like the *Asphodel*, the wind and sea spray, gulls and dolphins my solace and companions. My path for the next three years would be direct. Nothing would deter me.

Galatea's greatest difficulty was that in our first year we once again weren't allowed lovers. "It's the worse discipline of all," she complained at least weekly.

I thought it a blessing. I didn't have to deal with any awkwardness about my scar. In the past Galatea chided me with comments like, "Why are you so shy? You're beautiful. Men are always buzzing around you, but you act like you're afraid." Now she said nothing. Oddly, in a way this felt worse.

I would have insisted I was happy. But in truth, emptiness underlay all my moods. Only during festivals, when we danced into ecstasy, did elation take me, sometimes for days and nights in succession. My body throbbed with excitement; I lost myself in the joy of uniting with my sisters and the Mother. But when the dancing ended, the fire of joy died.

The danger to a priestess of taking a lover and caring too much for him was brought forcefully home when two sisters, in their second year, became so attached to the men they were seeing that they left the Temple to marry. "I've never met any man sufficiently compelling to steal my heart from the Lady," Galatea said. "I never will."

I agreed wholeheartedly.

I had been a novice for four moon cycles and was eighteen, beyond the age of tutoring, when father sent the paper granting Zuliya his freedom and a letter offering him the opportunity to work again in Alyris. We met in Zuliya's empty classroom. With sadness, almost desperation, I took my seat at the table: Zuliya was no longer bound to me. Soon his strength, his wise humor, would be gone from my days. I was determined, though, to make our parting light. I was one of the Mother's novices. I could bear anything.

His gaze searched my soul. "My years of teaching you end. Others will take my place. But if you would honor me, I beg you never to forget what I have given you that is of the most lasting worth. That you think for yourself."

"You know I will." A lump warning of tears formed in my throat. I handed him the parchment—his freedom. "I'll miss our daily meetings." His eyes skimmed my father's strong markings. "Father says he's asked you to return to Kalliste. Is that what you'll do?"

He rose and, from the opposite side of the long writing table, moved with his characteristic limp around the table's end. I thought he was leaving the room, but he came all the way around to me. He knelt on one knee at my feet. He took my hand, opened the palm, and gave it a long, lingering kiss.

My hand would never forget the warmth of his lips. The sharp, foreign scent and the alien gold crescent at the side of his nose struck me powerfully with his otherness. I caught my breath, remembering what he'd said long ago about this special kiss of honor.

"I ask you, Danae's daughter, to let me serve you as a free man for the rest of my life. If you turn me away, I will return to your father. I will, in fact, do whatever you ask of me. I do not ask you to pay me— I earn sufficient keep with my work here. But I offer my service. If you will accept it."

I sat stunned, flooded with joy and relief, and collecting my composure, I nodded emphatically. "Zuliya. Dear friend. Here. Please." I stood and helped him to his feet. My heart singing, I embraced him, but knowing he was uncomfortable with embraces, I pulled away sooner than I wanted. "I'm honored and I accept. But why?"

He glanced aside as if suddenly uneasy. I sat and gestured to a chair, which he took. " I am a man of words, but it seems at this exact moment they fail me. Ummhumm. Let us just say, as the Midians do, that 'the morning star is happiest when closest to the moon.'"

"Zuliya, nothing will make me happier than having you with me. What can I do to show you how happy I am?"

He grinned and twisted an earring, pretended to be thinking. Then, "You can promise me something."

"Anything."

"It might not be an easy promise."

"I can promise whatever you ask."

"Promise, then, that though you have become a novice, you will keep open to the possibility of a life outside Temple service. You are still very young."

His look was so earnest. For a fleeting moment I considered making the promise. I didn't want to hurt him. "I don't want to lie to you. But my heart is set on serving the Goddess. I can't say honestly I would consider any other path."

"Would you just promise, then, that you will never let your mind close. That you will continue to learn and grow by considering new things."

I smiled. "That I can promise."

He hesitated, crossed his arms and uncrossed them.

"You don't believe my promise?"

"I want to, but I know you better than even your parents. With kindness, but frankness, I say your greatest fault is rigidity of thought."

"Zuliya, that's not so. What makes you say that?"

"You have great curiosity about the world. That is good. But you always filter what you encounter through the fabric of the Keftian Law in a way that limits."

"Filter?"

"If an idea is not encompassed by the Law or if it seems to contradict Keftian ways, you dismiss it."

"No I —"

"Yes, you do, Leesandra." He smiled. "This unwillingness to compare honestly and perhaps change your views is, I assure you, a crippling flaw. For many, such a mind set may not become serious. After all, most people, once grown, do not question what they have come to accept as true, and mental rigidity need not have serious consequences for them. But I believe—I hope—your life will weigh more than that of the common person. Promise me you will strive to keep an open mind."

He had just sworn to remain with me as my friend and confidant. And what he asked seemed simple and reasonable. How could I not promise? I rose, went to him, knelt and put my hand on his knee. "If you see me fail, you need only to tell me."

He patted my hand. "Then I put my spirit at ease. If you hold fast to the treasure of an open mind, nothing can harm you."

I returned to my seat and, because lessons were no longer appropriate, we talked of when and where to meet for discussion. We agreed to enjoy herbal tea twice weekly in the south garden.

Later, though, as I brushed my hair before sleeping, I turned his odd comment in my mind. From exactly what harm did he think a promise to remain open in thought would somehow protect me?

∾ ∾ ∾ ∾

From the beginning of our second year, we were allowed to use the poppy. I ate the cakes and, for the first time since I'd stopped seeing the light, well over a year ago, I felt the Mother beside me. She didn't speak, but I felt the beating of Her heart: I was certain, once again, that I was on the right path. We were allowed the poppy once a month, and each time I drew strength from it.

My fifth work assignment was caring for the incense burners and lamps in Damkina's quarters. I picked up information here long before other novices knew of it. A persistent worry was that the Poseidonists wanted to worship in public, and Damkina's advisors were sure they meant to eventually perform their dreadful sacrifices in the open. Every one of these reports brought back evil memories. I heard the name Oenopion—the Poseidonist priest—regularly.

"I agree with father," Galatea said when I first reported this to her and two other novices as we settled into bed. "Minyas says he doesn't understand all the fuss. Why shouldn't they worship openly? Damkina stays silent and she shouldn't. By her silence she indirectly supports all this agitation against the Poseidonists."

One of my roommates drew a sharp breath at Galatea's rebuke of the Lady's Voice. Galatea blew out our single candle. I said, "The Voice of the Goddess knows the Law. Damkina is right."

Galatea said nothing.

I spoke into the darkness, "Do you know what they do when they worship?"

"I don't really care. It breaks harmony to have all this bickering over whether they can do what they do in secret or out in the open."

"But what they do is horrible, Galli."

The Temple gong sounded, signaling that novices were to begin silence.

"How do you mean horrible?" whispered our roommate from Matala.

"They ... they kill animals," I whispered, painfully aware we should not be speaking. "Sometimes they even kill people."

Galatea's voice, sharp with scorn, raked the darkness. "Oh, Leesandra. Killing people. What nonsense. That's what their enemies say. They don't do any such thing."

My heart was thumping hard in my throat. We should not be talking. "I tell you, they do!"

"My father would know, and he would tell me. I'm sure I would know. We lived for years in Pylos, and the Acheans there worship only Poseidon."

"How can you know what they do in their temples? Have you ever been to one of their ceremonies?"

"Well, have you? Of course not. None of us have. But my father says—"

"If he says they don't make human sacrifices, your father's wrong."

"My father is no fool, Leesandra." Her voice bristled.

Our little room fell silent at last. I took a deep breath. She must understand. I must tell her I myself had seen such a killing.

In that same chilled voice she said, "If I believed what you say, I guess I'd agree with you. That would be a loathsome break of harmony. But my father knows the Acheans well, and he says all such talk is a lie. A very malicious lie, Leesandra." The word "malicious" held so much venom it stung.

I put my fist to my mouth. Should I call her father a liar or a fool? And I wasn't supposed to be speaking at all.

I kept my secret, this time for friendship's sake, but I remembered Zuliya's charge to me and thought Galatea, too, would be well advised to learn to think for herself.

∾ ∾ ∾ ∾

In my third and last year of trial, the great admiral Sarpedon returned to Keftiu. Galatea and I were watching the grand parade from a roof garden when I spied a tall, intense man of great presence walking beside the mounted admiral. My heart skipped several beats, and my attention lingered on the tall man for long moments. He cut such a dashing figure: he was deeply tanned, powerfully built—as many rowers are, and possessed of strikingly fair hair for a Keftian.

"Look at that one," I said to Galatea, and pointed to the man.

"Handsome, isn't he? You can tell that even from here. He's Sarpedon's translator, I hear, a half-breed marine they call the Scorpion. Seems he's a terror in battle."

The admiral and his aide moved beyond my view, but the marine had so impressed me I looked for him that evening at the admiral's welcoming banquet, only to be disappointed. A few days later Galatea told me Sarpedon had sent him to Phaestos. As for Sarpedon, a man greatly admired for his battle sense, he was openly advocating the heretical notion that Knossos should invade the mainland to rid the sea of Atistaeus of Pylos, an idea that evoked either laughter or outrage. He was certainly free to speak his mind, but I was confident no one would pay him much attention.

My first assignment in this third year was doorkeeper to Damkina's audience room. Galatea assured me this task was given when someone in the Temple believed a woman a suitable candidate for high position. Zuliya continued to pressure me in ways calculated to deflect me from religious service. He proposed a trip together. He would take me to Kyprus, to Byblos, to Agyptos itself.

Such a temptation! A bit to my surprise, even Heebe approved. Through the years she and I met regularly to exchange gossip, to shop, or to dine. I described the idea and she said, "What a great adventure that would be." Her eyes had a wistful look.

I might have taken the trip and perhaps never returned to the Temple had it not been for what happened when I attended the Second Birth. To teach me humility, I had been assigned to assist the butcher—backbreaking, stinking, bloody work, made doubly disgusting to me because, since the day I had seen the boy sacrificed, I'd never eaten animal flesh. One morning the Mistress of Tasks called me into her presence. "You know that in two weeks there will be a Second Birth."

I nodded. This would be the first such ceremony in fifteen years. A wondrous event. At any given time only nine serve as Wise Women and, at the Second Birth ceremony, a girl who might someday be chosen to join that holy sisterhood would be presented to the People. All such chosen are born in darkness. Immediately they are taken to and kept for the first nine years of their first life in the mountain cave of Silpos, less than a day's walk from Knossos. For this small girl's entire life, her only communion had been with her single caregiver and with the Mother. It is through this extreme isolation that the Wise Women attain their special closeness to the Goddess. No ritual was of greater importance because it is the Wise Women who directly counsel the Lady's Voice. And when all nine Wise Women speak on matters spiritual, what they say is the Lady's Law.

There wasn't enough room for more than a few hundred witnesses, so attending was a great honor. The Mistress of Tasks said I had been chosen and Galatea as well. I fairly floated out of the room. We went with twenty other novices, men and women. A rumor spread that the Wise Woman, Kishar, would be there. Kishar was thought to have almost as much influence in Government House and the Temple as Damkina. Damkina wouldn't be present—the Voice of the Goddess never left the Temple.

We carried flowers of the season—mine were blue hyacinths— and while we waited outside the cave mouth, we were told to be very quiet. Without warning, a young girl appeared, just inside the cave. Dressed only in a white kilt, she wore a garland of purple spider orchid. She was quite small, but most astonishing was the color of her skin—a shocking white, like the underbelly of a flatfish. The strangeness of her life suddenly became powerfully real. To achieve special closeness to the Mother, the Wise Women were made to endure such great sacrifices. Dark curls fell to the back of the girl's knees.

A Wise Woman stepped forward and turned to the crowd, and Galatea leaned close to me. "Kishar," she whispered so softly I could barely hear.

Though dressed in the undecorated white sari that de-emphasizes differences, this Wise Woman could never go unrecognized. Stark white hair pulled into a bun framed a face that seemed too young for so much gray, and running through her hair on one side was a vivid stripe of black. She raised a hand for silence.

No one moved. No one spoke. At this most precious moment, what the girl must experience first was the Goddess. She stepped from the cave's mouth. Beginning at the east, she looked around as if touching, with her gaze, every part of the Mother's body. I listened for the sounds she'd be hearing: wind whistling in the cedar trees, the murmuring of the stream. She would be smelling the pungent fragrance of cedar, too. A raven croaked. She raised her head, clearly having heard it, but didn't break her ritual searching, east to west.

She completed this seeing and hearing of the world for the first time and returned to the cave's mouth. We lined past, singing, to present our flowers. "Move quickly," we'd been told. "She's unused to the sun and can't stay out long."

I placed my bouquet at her feet, smiled, and to my pleasure she smiled back. I thought, *What a heavy weight those little shoulders one day will carry*, so naively grateful that no such burden would ever be put on mine.

After all the flowers had been given, her caregiver led her back into the heart of the cave, and the crowd began to stir. From behind me a woman's voice said, "Wait a moment, Leesandra."

I turned to find the Temple Vizier and the Wise Woman. "I know your mother, Danae," Kishar said to me. "And I knew your grandmother, Ninkasi."

I bowed my head low, which afforded a moment to recover from my astonishment. "This is my best friend, Galatea," I said, my pulse dancing. "The daughter of Metis of Knossos."

Kishar introduced the Vizier, a man of piercing eyes named Nothos. Not long after beginning Temple service, Galatea and I had nicknamed him "The Badger" for his stout frame, religious zeal, and legendary temper.

"Once a week I invite young women and men to my home," Kishar said, looking at me. "We talk of life, we sing, we read poetry.

I live half an hour's walk south of the Temple, just off the Phaestos road. I've watched your progress in service. I'd like you to join our circle."

From the corner of my eye I noted that Galatea frowned and tensed her shoulders. "I'm honored," I said.

"Come to Damkina's small audience chamber this afternoon. I'll give you directions."

If I alone were honored, Galatea would be terribly hurt. "Is it permitted to bring a friend?"

Kishar smiled at Galatea. "Forgive me. Of course. By all means, Galatea. Please come, too. I know both your mother and father, and I have also seen that you progress well in service."

Galatea smiled in return, but with shock I noted that the smile didn't reach her eyes. She looked exactly like her father Minyas.

Kishar returned her attention to me and said solemnly, "We are in perilous times. You will need great wisdom."

I felt the back of my neck prickle. Galatea's frown returned.

Galatea and I tapped our hearts, then Kishar and the Badger left us.

"She seems very familiar with you," Galatea said. "You are getting quite a reputation, you know. For skill in languages. And for being so unswervingly dedicated." Her lips turned down in a pout. "Inviting me was the merest politeness. Perhaps I shouldn't go."

"Don't be silly. We'll go together. And we'll sing and read poetry and talk. I wonder who the others will be?" My protest sounded strong, but of course I understood Galatea's hurt feelings.

Galatea gave me a sharp look. "Did you notice what she said at the end?"

"That thing about us being in perilous times?" I felt that odd prickling again.

"No. She said you will need great wisdom."

"Well, I suppose if we're in perilous times, we will."

"No, Leesandra. She looked right at you. She said that *you'll* need wisdom. What do you think she meant by that?"

I shrugged and put the thought out of mind.

∽ ∽ ∽ ∽

Galatea and I went to Kishar's each week. Her dinners were a feast of food and music and dance and meditation. Thoughts I had entertained of traveling with Zuliya vanished.

Kishar was so totally unlike him. Her teachings weren't of striving and searching and questioning, but about how to achieve harmony. Where Zuliya insisted that I reach out of myself in a struggle to know and understand, Kishar encouraged me to stop questioning and simply "be" in the spirit of the Mother.

It wasn't long before I saw clearly, and with dismay, that Kishar was leading me deep into the way of the Lady's Wise Ones—and that Zuliya's ideas were foreign to that path. At first, I continued to follow Zuliya's training. I questioned. I tried to understand the differences between their teachings. I tried to determine their relative merits. But it was so difficult to resist the tranquillity of simply letting go and submerging myself. So comforting not to be obliged to question.

Zuliya sensed I was changing. He had given up hope of coaxing me on an adventure trip, but he wasn't accepting my refusal without what sometimes appeared to be anger. "Haven't I warned you that it is easier to let others think for you and that the easy path is easily taken and appeals to sheep," he said, along with, "Let others drive your cart and you never know what miserable ditch you may end up in."

One day, a few months before I would take final vows, he sent me a message. I should meet him at his boarding house. I felt uneasy. Only two days earlier we'd had one of these uncomfortable exchanges. Wearing an enormous grin, he took my arm and tugged me into his room. "Come in, come in."

On a table, placed under a window where it could catch the best light, lay a partially unrolled manuscript. A quick inspection of his bed revealed four more lying still rolled up.

"What makes you so happy?"

He steered me to the table. "It's mine. I bought it. I used the money your father sent and saved enough more to meet the dealer's price. I own this work."

I bent over the partially unrolled script. It was Agyptian. The workmanship exquisite. The pictographs were done in rich colors—mostly red, yellow, brown and blue—and symbols belonging to one of the major gods stood out boldly on the margins.

"It's breathtaking, Zuliya." My father must have been very generous; Zuliya's work as teacher would never have earned enough money for such a prize.

He limped to the bed and picked up another of the scrolls. "I own the complete work, Leesandra. *The Sayings of Saramsett.* She is a priestess of Thoth. One of the wisest of women."

"I'm so pleased for you. Has Heebe seen it?"

He uttered an amused snort. "You know Heebe. She said it was pretty enough, but not the sort of thing for her to trouble her mind with." He moved to the table and began to roll up the scroll. "I've already read this one. You can take it with you. I'm anxious to hear what you think."

"You ... I'm ..." I searched for the right words. I felt my face heating. "You know I'm soon to be dedicated. Last week at Kishar's, I decided I'd begin now to observe restrictions. You know the Lady's holy servants aren't allowed to read anything other than what's necessary for Temple service. I won't be able to read Saramsett."

His body stiffened. Tears formed in his eyes. He spun away from me and straightened his shoulders. "So. It begins." The bitterness of his tone cut like a knife.

"I'm sorry, so sorry, to disappoint you. But—" A brutal weight pressed on my heart. A clear, unequivocal fork lay in my path. Were I to take the final step and become a priestess, I couldn't hold to the ever-critical mindset Zuliya adopted. In this I could never please him.

His shoulders slumped. "You will never know how great my disappointment is."

The shared joys of our years together flooded my heart. And, for a moment, I held them in my mind's eye to give them honor. But my course was set. I walked around him, took his hand. "You knew the time would come when I wouldn't be allowed to read what I wanted any more."

"Do not do this, Leesandra. There is still time to choose another way. I have friends in the Council. Heebe has a friend whose sister is highly placed at the Bull Academy. You could train dancers. There are other possibilities. This religious path ..." He looked deeply into my soul. "The Temple way is too narrow for a truly great spirit."

What a strange thing to say. Kind in its way. Flattering. But not true. Why did he say such things? "There is no greatness here, Zuliya. It's just Leesandra. And this is what the Lady has called me to do. And I'll do it as best I can with my whole heart. "

He looked away. "Do you wish me to leave you?"

I would rather have him cut off my arm. "Never."

For a moment we said nothing.

"Then I shall stay." He pulled his hand away. "And I will hope you continue to listen to me, at least sometimes."

For a while we talked of other small things. He never once looked at or referred to *The Sayings of Saramsett.*

23

Late one afternoon, less than three moon cycles before my vows, I stepped from Kishar's door to find a dark sky threatening Knossos's first winter rain. A cool and moist southern wind whipped my robe around my ankles. Ordinarily I'd have remained hours more to enjoy the fellowship, but my current duty required that I be in the bakery before sunrise. I flipped up my cloak's hood to keep the cold off my neck and set out, my thoughts on my dedication. My pace was brisk and my heart joyful. Only a few weeks more and the goal of years would be achieved.

A pomegranate orchard lay both left and right, and I'd just crossed a planked bridge over a stream when a fat raindrop tapped my cheek. The Temple lay a full hour ahead. The sky hung heavy with its burden. I hurried forward and had passed the dirt road leading to the hamlet of Kulos when the sky burst. My sandals quickly soaked through. How fortunate that, at this point, the Phaestos road was still paved! Otherwise I would be wading in mud.

A shout caught my attention. Peering through heavy sheets of rain, I saw a horse standing in the road a short way ahead and, beside the horse, three men in a circle. Horses were used only during military parades or by Temple messengers, so I assumed one of the men was a messenger. As I drew near and saw what they were doing, an icy chill ran along my skin. The three were beating a boy who lay on the ground. I'd heard the rumors recently about attacks on Temple messengers. No one was as yet certain who was responsible.

As if lightning flashed through my mind, I remembered that day on Alyris when my mother's houseboy and I had come across an outlander beating a woman. Not since then, not in all my years on Keftiu, had I ever seen one person strike another.

I ran toward them. The man kicked the messenger, and the boy let out a pitiful cry.

Looking toward me the kicker yelled, "Hey, look at what's a 'comin!"

"Stop!" I shouted, my pulse pounding so hard I could barely hear. A second brute kicked the messenger in the back. The other two turned toward me.

I tried to push past the largest man, my thought to throw myself over the boy, but a hand the size of a lion's paw wrapped fingers around my upper arm. The man yanked me toward him so hard I lost my footing. He grabbed my other arm, lifted me off the ground, shook me like a doll. My head snapped back and forth, my feet dangled.

"S-st—op!" My protest shook in the air like my body.

My head spun. I thought I heard running feet. Then suddenly the villain dropped me. I fell onto the road on one ankle. Pain shot up the calf of my leg, and I realized someone had struck my attacker from behind.

Above me two men struggled, entwined like wrestlers. The dolphin and sacred horns on my rescuer's scarlet cloak marked him as Keftian navy. I curled into a protective ball, but another blow sent a ripping pain from my back to my chest. I gasped for breath.

The two men spun halfway around. I saw my rescuer's face. Had I been the object of his fury, I'd have fainted with terror. His grimly twisted mouth and clamped jaw signaled a rage eerily absent from his hard, empty eyes. He raised his fist like a club—an enormous club—and brought it down onto the side of my attacker's head producing a sickening crack.

The brute slumped to the ground.

I lay in a pool of water expecting my attacker's friends to come to their companion's defense. Instead I heard the splashing sound of retreating feet.

Every breath caused fire to flash in my chest. Kneeling in front of me, my rescuer put the palm of that same enormous hand lightly on my side. His eyes caught mine. Rain had matted his hair. Water streaked down his forehead, over high cheekbones, and off a square chin. Only moments ago his eyes had been frighteningly cold and dark. They still held only neutral interest. But I knew those gold flecks.

"Are you all right?"

With age his voice had changed. It had a deep, resonating quality, as if the sound were coming from the depths of a mysterious well. And I'd heard those very words from his lips once before. With a thrill of recognition, I felt a warm ball of light explode in my heart. Alektrion!

I willed my face to hide my swirling emotions and said, "I'm not entirely sure." I started to ask about the messenger, but again heard the sounds of running steps, now coming toward us. Panicked, I whispered, "They're coming back."

I began to uncoil, to stand. Stabbing pain struck my chest again.

"If you hurt, don't move suddenly," said Alektrion of Kalliste. "Those bilge slugs aren't coming back. These are my friends."

A confident, smooth but higher pitched voice said, "The demons got away, Scorpion."

Scorpion was the name of the aide to the admiral, Sarpedon. Could it be? If so, I, myself, had just seen the famous Scorpion strike. And I knew him. I eased to a sitting position in the middle of my puddle.

"Too bad you've killed the other one," continued the same smooth voice. "We're not going to get anything useful out of him."

"Kokor's breath, Anchices. I barely tapped him. How's the messenger?"

Alektrion was speaking to the taller of his two companions, and with a voice of authority that surprised me, because both men were older than he and their tunic insignia indicated they held higher rank. The tall one, Anchices, reminded me of a very hungry cat. "Badly hurt," he said in that refined voice. "Looks to me like they intended to kill him. These filthy Poseidonists are becoming more vicious. He needs a healer's attention. Quickly."

Alektrion addressed the shorter man. "The horse?"

This man's nose was twisted as though broken many times; and three large scars, jagged for lack of proper treatment, marred his brow and chin. One eye was missing, its lids sewn shut. So ugly was his face that I couldn't suppress a shiver.

"Leg's broken. I'll put her down," said the old boar—in a whispery voice that hinted at still more horrors in his life.

Alektrion nodded. The man strode toward the stricken animal. Both men looked to Alektrion for direction. If he were the Scorpion who stood next to Sarpedon, his half-breed origin would certainly explain his lower rank. And if he were that warrior—but how could such a thing be?—it would explain their deference to him.

Alektrion turned to me. "Can you stand?"

"Of course." But when I tried again to move, I couldn't keep a grimace from my face.

"Where do you hurt?"

I reached across my chest to touch the focus of my pain, a place high on the ribs on the left side of my back. "Uugh," I said, struggling to smother another grimace.

"Let me see if anything feels broken." Without asking permission—as a civilized man would—he leaned forward and slid his hands under my cape and over my thin linen gown feeling through it and my corset for my ribs.

A delicious liquid fire raced over my skin. I looked deeply into his eyes wishing I might melt into them and disappear, but he looked straight ahead as he felt gingerly over my sides. *He doesn't know me!*

"Nothing's broken, but you're badly bruised. You're going to be very sore for a few days. Here. Let me help you stand. It's urgent we get the messenger to the next inn."

He slid his arm around my back, strong fingers grasped my waist—the fingers of the fist that had just killed with a single blow. I reached across his chest to hold his free arm, and when he tugged me to my feet, arm muscles like tough cords of leather tightened across my back.

I settled to my feet, and a sharp band of fire seared my left ankle. I jerked my foot up and moaned. Alektrion shifted so the length of his body supported me. I sagged against him. "I've also hurt my ankle."

I glanced around. The one-eyed man was wiping his knife blade, red with the horse's blood, on the saddle blanket. The horse lay in the road, its legs still jerking. The messenger lay on his back, his eyes closed. Anchices pulled the body of the dead attacker to the roadside.

Appalled by so much violence, I swallowed hard. "Leave me," I said. "Take the boy to the inn."

"Rig a field litter, Talos," Alektrion commanded the ugly man. "I'll stay with the woman."

Talos nodded. He and Anchices strode into the orchard.

"I can walk," I insisted, determined to do just that. I pushed myself from Alektrion's body, amazed at how much doing so drained me. "There's no need for you to stay."

"Let's see you walk."

He released my arms—freedom from him felt like being lost. I took a trial, limping step, bit the inside of my lip to hide the pain. "See," I muttered. "I'll just come along behind you, slowly."

Anchices and Talos reappeared, each carrying a thick pole.

With one swift move Alektrion picked me up, again without asking permission. Either he didn't understand convention or he chose not to follow it. Either way, I should have found his impudence upsetting. Instead it intrigued me. He carried me toward the low stone wall circling the orchard. "You'd never make it to the inn."

He plunked me down, then turned and strode to his companions. Together they used the two poles and their cloaks to fashion a litter. They lifted the messenger into it, and the two soldiers took off at a splashing half-trot through he rain toward the inn. Alektrion strode back to me and I stood up.

I didn't like having separated him from his companions. "Perhaps a farmer will come along soon with a cart. Perhaps you could go on."

"Not likely. It's too late in the day. Where were you going?"

We stood face to face, both soaked to the skin. My gaze dropped and lingered on the large, beautifully shaped—and deadly—hand. Then I studied his face again, its bones starkly emphasized by the rain. Nose straight and finely sculpted. High cheekbones. High, intelligent forehead. His eyes were the same gold-flecked color I remembered, but what lay behind them now wasn't the curiosity or gaiety of childhood or even that cold rage sparked by a fight. Indeed, I'd taken training on reading mood in the eyes and, with a pang of disquiet, I realized I could read nothing in Alektrion's. What could have happened to turn a gentle boy who loved to talk to spiders into a man-killer named Scorpion?

"We know each other," I said.

One eyebrow went up. "I don't think I'd forget you."

I remembered my years of yearning, my pining over Alektrion, and a sudden, terrible disappointment clutched my throat. He clearly didn't remember me. Better to let the past be past. Before I could stop myself, though, I covered my scar.

He seemed not to notice. "Our Mother was watching over you," he said. "I and my friends were late coming here. I've no doubt those Poseidonist scum would have killed the boy. And probably hurt you badly."

Why was he on this road? Where had he been these many years? And most of all, what had taken the light from his eyes?

"You can't walk to the inn." He glanced down the road then back to me. "We certainly can't spend the night in this rain. My friends and I were heading to a shepherd's hut. Much closer than the inn. Are you expected somewhere?"

As I was wearing street clothes, Alektrion couldn't know I was a novice—and for some impulsive, inexplicable reason, I didn't want to tell him where I was expected to sleep. Twice I'd spent the night unexpectedly at Kishar's, so my failure to return to the Temple wouldn't cause any disturbance.

"I'll not be missed."

"No husband or children waiting?"

I shook my head. Alektrion picked me up again, this time with noticeable gentleness, and plodded back toward the lane to Kulos. I clung to him, wishing myself lighter, acutely aware of his heart beating not far from mine.

When he carried me through the door of what appeared to be a humble shepherd's hut, his mud-caked boots touched a fine wood floor. How peculiar that Alektrion and his friends were meeting so far from Knossos in a shepherd's hut that was, in fact, furnished more like the home of a prosperous tailor or carpenter.

I said, "We're dripping and making a mess."

The house wasn't so fine that it had running water. He carried me through a small common room. The pantry floor was of flagstone. He sat me on a tall stool beside a finely hewn table. "I'll find something for us to wear."

He removed his boots, then I listened to the pad of his bare feet in the common room and the opening and closing of chests. I shrugged out of my soggy cape and dropped it to the floor. Alektrion returned with two simple tunics of fine, light-brown wool—a much better quality than I would have expected from a shepherd's family—several belts of different lengths, and two towels. He put the tunics and towels on the table. "Get into one of these. I'll start a fire."

I untied my skirt and then reached behind to unlace the strings of my corset. A stabbing pain shot up my back. I sat breathing shallowly for a few moments, then tried again with the same result. My pulse raced. I couldn't undress myself.

In the other room, a log thunked as it was dropped onto the hearth. Footsteps. Rustlings. Flint being struck several times. Footsteps in my direction.

"Are you changed?"

"I … well …"

He walked into the pantry. My face flared hot with indignation. For all he knew, I could still have been undressing! In many situations, to be seen undressed would be quite natural. To be intruded upon when one is in the act of undressing wasn't. Alektrion seemed not to care.

"Shouldn't you …" I began, but caught myself and said more firmly. "You should have waited before entering."

"Can't you undress?"

More heat rose to my cheeks. "It seems not."

"I'll help."

I clung tightly to the seat of the stool suddenly reluctant to have Alektrion's hands moving over my body. "No," I whispered, so softly I don't think he heard.

He walked behind me and his fingers tugged on the corset's laces. My waist relaxed and the pain lessened.

"That should make your breathing easier. Stand." He moved beside me and slipped his arm under mine.

I stood on my good leg. With his free hand he dropped my skirt, pulled the girdle free from under my blouse, and began to loosen my inner skirt.

Though I knew I had to get out of the soaked garments, my mind shouted, *Stop him!*

But too late. My inner skirt joined the outer one on the floor and my blouse fell partly open. I snatched it closed, so aware of my half nakedness that flesh pebbled over my chest and belly.

Again he moved behind me. He reached over my shoulders to the front of my blouse as if to remove it. "Let go," he said, his tone sounding amused.

My fingers seemed to have become woven into the blouse's fabric. Warm hands skimmed my collarbones, rested on my shoulders. He turned me to face him. Gold-flecked eyes held my own captive. The sound of my anxious beating heart filled my head. He loosened my fingers, and a warm palm brushed over one of my nipples. He peeled the blouse back, slipped it down my arms, and dropped it to the floor.

We stood fixed for a moment that way—me naked, him fully dressed in sopping tunic.

"By the Goddess," he said softly, "you are astonishingly beautiful."

Years of anguish over my scar congealed into a suffocating lump in my throat. My gaze dropped from his eyes to his chest. Better I should have died from the bull's kick than be given pity by Alektrion. I turned to the table and with shaking hands picked up one of the tunics. "You're kind."

His fingers closed gently on my upper arm, and I clutched the tunic to my chest as he once more turned me to face him. "I'm not being kind. You're a beautiful woman."

With his eyes he held my gaze captive, and something inside me broke loose, floated away. He looked at my scar. I said, "I know it's ugly."

"That's in your mind. I say it's only barely visible. And I assure you, it doesn't mar your face."

Something hungry in his look made me shudder. Uncertainty, fear, excitement? Desire?

Without warning he released me. He backed away a step. "I've … I've started a fire. You're shivering. Here. Let me help." He took the tunic and with quick movements slipped it over my head, even though I'd not yet dried with the towel. I was sure he'd sensed my desire— my need—to hide myself from him.

"Way too big," he said and smiled, the first real smile I'd seen.

I'd been standing in a dark night and with his smile he had opened a door to reveal the brightest summer day. I didn't think Alektrion smiled very often. He said, "Let's see if I can tie it so it won't fall off."

Using two of the belts, one around my waist and the other criss-crossing my shoulders, he secured the tunic.

"My turn. And by the way, my name is Alektrion."

So the impossible *was* true. He reached to untie his belt and I left, half limping, half hopping to the brazier in the common room. I lowered myself cross-legged before the fire on a soft white rug of sewn sheepskins. My childhood fantasy was only steps away, now a warrior, and a rather famous one at that.

If I breathed gently and didn't twist, nothing hurt too badly, though my ankle still throbbed. He joined me and nodded toward the pantry. "Something to eat or drink?"

I nodded. He disappeared into the pantry.

Perhaps he didn't see my scar as a true Keftian might. He was partly Achean. Acheans had very different views toward such things. My embarrassment subsided a bit and curiosity resurfaced. I called out, "Have you been here before?"

Without answering, he returned with wine, bread, and cheese. The food was simple, but of exceptional quality.

"Tell me about the sea," I asked. "I love the feeling of being on a ship. What's it like to live at sea?"

He spoke about the ocean and the freedom of flying with the wind. His mouth suggested a smile and the firelight produced astonishing effects with the gold in his eyes. After awhile—perhaps distracted by thought of how remarkably good the wine was in this shepherd's hut, rather than whether I was asking about something he might want to explore—I said, "You must have fought many battles."

He turned from the fire. His eyes lost their sparkle. "I've seen my share."

The room lost all sense of life even though every sound intensified: the crackling of the fire, the thrumming of the rain on the shutters and roof of this puzzling shepherd's hut—if there was a shepherd.

"Who owns this place, Alektrion?"

"My friends call me Alek." He laughed, an unsure sound. "I can't imagine why I said that."

"All right, Alek. Who owns this hut?"

"This land belongs to the family of Sarpedon of Mallia. I work for him."

Everyone knew that Sarpedon was speaking openly against the Red King. "Why were you and your friends coming here, so late and to a place so isolated?"

"Are you always so direct?" He attempted a disarming smile.

"This is no simple shepherd's hut."

"My friends and I travel a lot. We often need a place to stay. I think it much stranger that you were on the road alone. Where were you going?"

He clearly wasn't going to answer my question. And I couldn't any longer keep the truth about me from him. "I'm a third-year novice. I was returning from a friend's home to the Temple."

Wide-eyed, he sat his wine cup on the hearth and leaned back on his palms and studied me as if seeing me for the first time. "You will be a priestess?"

"Yes. I'm to be dedicated next festival."

"Less than three moon cycles."

I nodded again.

"For some reason ..." He took his wine and drank a long sip, watching me over the cup's rim as if making a decision.

He sat the cup down and drew the board holding the cheese to him. His hand found the knife, all without taking his eyes from me. Then he looked away as he slowly and deliberately cut a wafer-thin slice of the cheese. I watched him put the bit of cheese on the pad of his middle finger.

He can't be thinking that!

In the ancient gesture of solicitation for coupling, he raised his hand palm up and offered the cheese to me. My heart beat as though it wanted to be free from my chest. He looked directly and boldly into my eyes. If I accepted, I would put his finger in my mouth and take his offering. From the top of my head to the tips of my toes, my entire body ached to take his hand, to guide his finger to my lips.

Instead I said, "I can't."

A flicker of something unreadable passed over his eyes. He pulled his hand back.

I touched my scar. "This has made me ... I feel like a misfit ... unacceptable."

He leaned forward and, with his free hand, grasped one of mine. Using his thumb, he forced my palm open, and to my amazement raised it and stroked it under the cloth of his tunic sleeve along his left upper arm. I felt and then saw, for the first time, a long, vicious-looking white scar. What horrible pain he must have suffered! My heart melted.

"I, too, am scarred. Who is to care? What difference do scars make? My friend Talos has many scars, but his spirit is fine and still unbroken." He released my hand and traced the white line on my cheek. Where his fingertip moved, fire burned. "You are beautiful. I know too well what it means to be a misfit, and it's no reason to deny oneself the pleasures of the Goddess."

Yes, I thought. Alektrion surely knows even better than I what it is to be unacceptable. Again he moved the finger bearing his gift toward me. You don't want to say no! My heart fairly shouted as it hammered against my ribs. *For years you dreamed of just this moment.* I drew in a deep breath, and stabbing pain must have registered on my face.

He slid close and put his free arm around my shoulder while he brought the piece of cheese close to my lips. Male scent—powerful, enticing—came off his skin and hair. "I want you, and my heart tells me not to believe your refusal."

I grasped his hand, the killing hand, and guided his finger to my mouth. The cheese melted on my tongue. He thrust his finger deeply, then, as I tasted him along its full length, he pulled it out slowly. Warmth pooled deep in my belly.

He kissed my neck. His hands stroked my side. I took a deep breath and stabbing pain again paralyzed me a moment, but I couldn't stop myself now. I didn't want to stop him. No matter what happened.

His hand covered my breast. Warmth and an insistent pressure reached through my tunic. I saw the two of us locked in the creating embrace.

What was I doing! I had no experience with the arts of the bed. I was about to make a fool of myself with the man I'd dreamed of since childhood.

I pushed against him, and a cascade of jabbing sensations jolted down my side and back. The look on his face only added to my embarrassment. Puzzlement? Amusement? Keen disappointment?

He eased away. "Have I done something wrong? Does it hurt too much?"

"Yes." I grasped at this excuse. "It's really much too painful. I'm sorry."

He drew a deep breath. "Not as sorry as I." He eased back still further. "You're sure I've not offended you?"

I couldn't stop myself from touching him. I rested my palm over the balled fist that lay on one knee. "It's just that my side hurts so much."

"Then I'll make a bed for myself. You will have the shepherd's." He rose, leaving my hand feeling as though the finest thing I'd ever touched had slipped forever from my grasp.

The wonderful moment was gone. The magic was gone. Galatea had always hinted she thought there was something wrong with me because I took no lovers. Clearly she was right. How could I have turned Alektrion away? There was no part of my body that didn't ache to join with him.

I limped to one of the chairs. With quick efficiency, he made a place for himself on the rug in front of the fading fire. When he finished he turned to me. "Shall I help you out of the tunic, or will you sleep in it?"

I still couldn't think straight.

He stepped to me and, again without asking for permission—evidently that was his way—he untied the two belts. "When I'm not in the field, I sleep naked. It's best when you're wounded, though, to be covered but comfortable. Keep the tunic on."

"Have you cared for many wounded?"

"I've been in many battles. Battles always have their wounded, and I've done my share of caring for them."

Something in his tone reminded me that this man, my long-lost friend, Alektrion, was also the Scorpion. He slipped his arm under mine, and we hobbled to the shepherd's bed. What had so hardened him?

I turned and sat on the side of the bed and looked up at him. "Will you tell me sometime about war?"

"Sleep well," he said. A chill washed over my injured ribs.

Sometime in the dark of the night I awoke, terrified by the sound of agonized moaning. Where was I? What was making the sound?

A shaft of moonlight fell across the bed in which I lay. I recognized the furry cover. I was in a shepherd's hut. And Alektrion was nearby.

The moaning grew louder. He began to scream.

24

"Alek, Alek. Please! Wake up."

Alektrion opened his eyes and realized the face hovering over him did not belong to Laius.

It was a woman in a shepherd's tunic on her knees beside him, anguish in her eyes. Moonlight backlit her form. She used a corner of his sleeping cloth to wipe sweat from his forehead.

He sat up and grasped her wrist. "It's all right. Truly. I'm awake now."

He felt himself shaking slightly. The fight and the woman's troubling questions about war must have torn loose something inside him. He hadn't had the nightmare since he'd left the stage of physical battle on the sea for the political war on Keftiu.

"By the Lady, Alek! You were screaming." She started to sit back, but he kept his grip on her wrist. He didn't want to let her go. The rain had stopped and moonlight filled the room. The fire was only glowing embers. "I'm all right."

"I feared a demon might be taking your spirit."

"Thank you for freeing me from the dream." By the Mother's grace, this woman was so astonishingly beautiful and yet so unaware of it. He wanted to taste her lips, join with her so she would never forget him. The pulse in her wrist beat fast and strong. He inhaled sweet scent from her still slightly damp hair. He tugged her, urging her closer.

Alarm flashed in her eyes—that same hesitation he had seen before. "I …"

He put a finger against soft lips. "I promise I won't hurt your ribs. I want you."

She blushed but didn't pull her arm away. "It isn't my ribs." She looked down at the sheepskin beneath them. "I … you …"

He tugged her again. She didn't resist. He rose to his knees and his cover fell away, leaving him naked in front of her. He kissed her, being gentle with her back and side. He found her lips and with his tongue, pushed, and she let him come in. A breast, warm beneath the tunic, filled his hand and she moaned. The soft sound crawled under his skin, brought him to full arousal.

Slow, slow, he thought. He drew kisses over her neck and throat and felt tension drain from her until she was limp. He slid his hands under the tunic, lifted it, raised it over her head and tossed it aside. She lay motionless, as if paralyzed, nipples tight. She looked at his shaft but quickly looked again to his face. And she had reddened, as though she were an unawakened maiden.

Strange.

They lay down on the fleece, and with his lips and hands he sought to pleasure her. Still she lay unmoving, reminding him again of an unsure maiden. Impossible! Perhaps he'd made a mistake; perhaps she didn't feel the same need he did.

His put his mouth to a nipple. She moaned, a long agonized sound. Her arms and body surged into life.

Soon she was panting. His doubts vanished. "I never knew, I never knew," she said, her voice urgent with surprise. Her hands pressed hard against his back, eager, urgent, insistent.

He struggled to wait. He should linger over pleasuring her, but a strange sense took him, as though she were his first, the woman he could never remember. His body throbbed. Almost pain. *Slow, slow!* But he was losing the ability to listen, to think, to wait.

It has to be now. He rolled onto his side and pulled her to face him, spread her. She surprised him again. As though she were a girl, she didn't guide him. He thrust to make the joining. His conscious mind let go and he released himself to the Goddess, and he thought, *Sweet Mother, I think I'm the first.*

Afterward he lay beside her, tracing his finger over her breast and belly. "Have I pleased you as much as other lovers?"

She rose on her elbow and studied him. Her hair draped like a waist-length cape in curls around her shoulders. Stray ends ticked his belly. Her eyes were enormous, their long lashes hiding them in shadow. She touched his lips with her fingertip. He would never forget the touch.

"You're my first, Alek. My dear Alek."

I was right! He shook his head. "I can't believe you've let that inconsequential scar keep you from the pleasuring gifts of the Goddess. You're so beautiful."

"The scar is not inconsequential."

"You aren't choosing to be a priestess because of it, are you? I know Keftians. I know making a marriage would be difficult, but you've obviously never even given yourself a chance to find a husband."

"I was called to be a priestess years before I got this scar."

"How did you get it?"

"The Bull Capture."

He saw her bravely confronting long horns and sharp hoofs and smiled. This woman was extraordinary, especially for a Keftian. On

the Phaestos road he'd watched in astonishment as the small lone
figure had closed in on the three Poseidonists, determined to stop the
attack. Most Keftians in her place, seeing violence which was so foreign to them, would have been weak with fear. *She has a falcon's fierce
heart.* She would likely challenge even a demon. "I'd bet a pistata or
two you did something reckless."

She laughed, warm and soft, a sound that would soothe the most
troubled soul. "Not really."

"Not many Keftian women, or men for that matter, would do what
you did on the road." He reached up and took a handful of the silken
black hair.

"Alek."

He let go of her hair and studied her face.

"What I said is true. We've met before."

He smiled and twisted a strand of her hair. "When?"

"We were children."

"I'm from Kalliste."

"Yes. I lived on Kalliste as a child. You are Alektrion, son of
Meela."

He nodded.

"We met at my pool on the mountain."

Her words halted his hand. It couldn't be possible. He touched
her waist. "Leesandra?"

She nodded.

He sat up, stared. "By the Goddess, you were but a child. How
you've changed. How incredibly beautiful you've become."

She touched the scar. He pulled her hand from it. "It makes your
face interesting, Leesa. Distinctive. I like your scar."

"So you remember me?" Her gaze was fixed on his eyes, as if looking deeply, all the way to his heart.

"I never forgot you."

The room fell silent. A white fire flared in his chest. It spread to his
limbs.

She crossed her legs as if settling in to attend to him with care.
"Then tell me about your scars, Alek."

"They're nothing."

"Please tell me."

He began to describe the superficial events associated with each,
but as he talked the weight of all the killing settled on him hard. He
stopped in mid-sentence, touched her cheek, the unscarred one. She
smiled.

Something strange was happening—had already happened.
Leesandra made him feel clean. New. As if he'd just washed in her

spring on Kalliste and all the rest had never happened. His throat tightened. He wanted to speak, to tell her how long it had been since he'd felt anything like this peace, but the words stuck in his chest.

Her face clouded. She took his hand. He flashed on the vision of that same hand putting the knife into Laius and pulled away, gently so as not to offend.

"I'm sorry, Alek. I think I've been wrong to ask—about something so obviously unpleasant. Forgive me."

He needed space. "I want wine. And I'll start a new fire." He rose quickly.

"I'll make me some saffia tea."

"No. Stay off your leg. I'll make it."

When he returned, she'd added two logs to the hearth and from the embers rekindled a blaze.

They talked. She wanted to serve as a priestess on merchant or passenger vessels. At first the idea of his wild mountain girl becoming a priestess sounded all wrong, but then he thought of Serena and began to think Leesa's idea not at all strange. He shared his dream of owning a merchant fleet. Revealing himself to her was so easy.

"If that's your dream, how long will you stay with Sarpedon?"

This was dangerous ground. Some of what he was doing for Sarpedon was plain and simple treason. He chose his words carefully. "The admiral's of the view that unless Atistaeus is stopped, the piracy we're experiencing now will be remembered as a trivial inconvenience compared to what will happen."

She frowned. How much did she know? What did she understand? He had the insane urge to tell her everything and forced himself to count to four twice. "We have to convince Knossos to stop Atistaeus. When I do own a fleet, I don't want my livelihood at constant risk."

She pressed. "What exactly do you do for Sarpedon?"

He evaded. He only lured her away when they talked again of the pleasures of life at sea.

Dawn eventually pushed light into the corners of the room. She tried her ankle. It was better. They rummaged through the pantry. She made hot porridge while he cut fruit and bread. He added another log to the fire, and they ate in companionable silence. Not since Laius, not for a long time, had he felt such ease.

He was completely at peace when she glanced toward one of the room's windows. From the light's quality he judged that the birds had been out of the trees for at least an hour.

"I have to go." She slid close, circled his chest with her arms and lay her head over his heart. "I don't want to leave, Alek. All these years my friends have said that coupling is wonderful. But I never imagined. It will hurt to leave you."

Ordinarily such a passionate tone from a woman he'd bedded would have alarmed him. But she was to be a priestess. She'd not be seeking marriage. And she was so intriguingly different. "You can't go. Not yet."

He kissed her, explored beneath the loose tunic, felt her nipples harden. This time her spirit wasn't shy. What he did, she returned. Her body burned. Her hands held him to her as if losing him would cost her dearly. As she approached the moment, her skin turned slick. Her distinctive cry of release seared its way into his mind.

Afterward they dressed quickly. They walked to the inn, but he insisted on, and she accepted, a litter ride back to Knossos. He walked beside her, glanced at her over and over. He simply couldn't absorb enough of her. "I want to see you again, Leesa. Are you allowed free time?"

She didn't answer.

His stomach clenched. Might she be entering a period when the novices were forbidden lovers? Not seeing her again was suddenly unthinkable.

"I don't know, Alek. I want to see you. But I'm afraid to see you."

"But can you see me? Are you allowed to?"

"Yes. I have free time every day, and we're allowed to use the baths and rooms in the hetaira quarter."

The tension in his gut unwound a bit. "What's to fear? This is new to you. Perhaps that's what you fear."

She shook her head, so slightly he only barely saw it.

The litter bearers stopped outside the Temple's southern portal. He helped her descend, wanting nothing more than to take her again, right there on the street. He didn't let go of her hand. "Say you'll see me again. Promise."

She smiled. Warmth flushed beneath his skin. The light of the Goddess Herself shown in Leesandra's smile.

"Yes. We can meet. Come to me after mid-morning prayers in three days. I'll meet you in the hetaira garden. I'll have arranged a place for us."

∾ ∾ ∾ ∾

Leesandra watched Alektrion walk away. Don't leave, she thought. Her insides shook, as though he were taking with him the sun, the moon, and all the stars.

A large donkey caravan was winding its way uphill from the river. Alektrion crossed its path and disappeared from view. She turned away, washed her feet and, carrying her sandals and limping, entered the colonnade to her quarters. If she was to see Alektrion again, she must begin at once to take fennel. No child could come of their union.

Suddenly stunned, she halted. She cared too much. She could even imagine, with pleasure, bearing his child. This feeling, this passion— this unnamed longing that had gripped her for hours—had to be the passion against which hetaira and novices were warned. The hetaira because they must never interfere, on pain of banishment, with the marriage vow. And the novices because if they became too close to any man, they might grow a desire to marry. She remembered two ruined sisters and how Galatea had said, with convincing assurance, that she'd never found any man sufficiently compelling to be dangerous.

But I feel danger.

She shouldn't see Alektrion again. She hugged herself. She *mustn't* see him again. She should send a message at once that she wouldn't meet him.

Yes, that's what I'm required to do.

ov ov ov ov

Heavily into sleep, Alektrion nevertheless heard the knock at his door. He struggled to consciousness. The knock came again, louder. He sat up, put his feet to the cool floor. Last night he'd gotten drunk again, a habit he'd acquired at some point he could no longer recall. He wrapped a towel around his midsection and sat on the bed again.

"Enter!"

The door opened part way and the housewoman peeked around it. "I have a message for you."

"So tell me."

"It's written." She stepped inside and handed him the rolled piece of parchment.

"Seems it's from the Temple," she said, grinned, and waited, hoping for him to open it.

Noting the seal he replied, "Yes. Seems it is." He stared at her. She blushed, turned and left him alone.

His pulse had taken wings. Three days ago he'd found Leesa. This afternoon he would see her. He broke the seal and found himself staring at graceful characters that looked to be from a feminine hand. He glanced at the bottom. It was from her.

> My dearest Alektrion, dear friend. How happy I was
> to meet you again. How grateful I am to you for sav-
> ing me from who knows what fate. Every moment we

spent together was unexpected delight. I will treasure those moments, always. Sadly, though I said I would be able to see you three days hence, it will be impossible. My work here is ever more consuming of my time. I am certain you will understand. Now that you are in Knossos, perhaps we will some day have another opportunity. Do forgive me that I break a promise, but I made it without sufficient thought.

I remain your friend, always.

Leesandra of Kalliste

He stood, read the note again.

He did not understand. Most emphatically he did not.

An hour later he left the lodging house, a sealed note of his own for Leesandra nestled inside his tunic. At the Temple's southern portal, where foreigners and other non-Keftians were received, he delivered the note to a porter and asked that it be delivered to her. He was assured she would receive it within the day, perhaps within the hour.

In it he had asked, insisted really, that he must see her, if only to talk. That her explanation wasn't adequate. That she should give him a time and place where they could meet. He spent the afternoon writing letters Sarpedon expected to see before they were sent, but attending to the work was nearly impossible. He should have a reply from Leesandra by late afternoon.

None came, and he started drinking early.

By mid-morning the next day, he still had heard nothing. To calm himself, he had a drink. How was he to see her? He could not go inside the Temple. He was forced to depend on her to respond. By late afternoon, he was fuming. What rudeness!

He rose the next morning with a plan. She had said she went to that same place on the Phaestos road once each week. Presumably she went at the same time. Day after tomorrow, at dawn, he would position himself at the place where they met. At some point she must come along. He didn't care if she thought him a fool. If she became insulting, perhaps he would tell her how rude he thought her, and then leave. But if she were as he remembered her from the other night, as he remembered her from childhood, then he would ask, Why? He was nearly certain she had felt the same powerful force he did. If so, her note made no sense.

Dawn had crept past less than an hour prior when, two days later, he saw her coming toward him on the road wearing the same brown cape. Another woman walked beside her. He could tell she recognized him at almost the same moment he recognized her.

She and the other woman reached him, and she stopped. "I had not expected to see you again so soon, Alek." She nodded to a creature with exquisitely delicate features and long eyelashes. "This is my very dear friend, Galatea, daughter of Metis of Knossos. She serves with me as novice. Galli, this is Alektrion of Kalliste. He is the aide to Admiral Sarpedon."

The woman eyed every hair and pore on his body. "A great pleasure," she said in a low, seductive tone. "I have heard much about your exploits with our Admiral."

He acknowledged with a bow, then said to Leesandra, "I received your message. I wonder if you received my reply?"

"Why don't you walk with us? We are expected at a friend's house. I don't want to be late." She took her friend's arm, and he fell in beside her.

"Did you receive my message?"

"I'm sorry I didn't respond. But as I said, I have been extraordinarily busy. Haven't we Galli? I'm working in the bakery, and we're making extra sweets for celebrating the naming day of one of the Wise Women."

Galatea just looked at him and smiled.

He said, "I very much want to see you again. We've been away from Kalliste a long time. The other night, we had no good chance to talk of family or home."

"We take this path," Leesandra said, and the three of them turned off the paved road onto a well-trodden lane through an olive grove.

Galatea said, "So you're the man who rescued my Leesandra. How fortunate for her that you and your friends came along."

"Yes, it was."

The woman talked about the increasing hazards to Temple messengers. How could he get Leesandra alone? Surely her life couldn't be so busy she had no time at all to see him!

The orchard opened out into a field and sitting in its middle was a modest two-story home. The house was not remarkable, but the garden was. Unlike the usual Keftian home flower garden, laid out with precision, here the flowers grew with their own will, where they would. The effect was as if the house's owner wished to recreate a natural scene of the Mother's body, one where the plants were the most interesting or beautiful.

They reached the door. Leesandra and her friend turned to him.

He wasn't going to beg. But by the very fact of his being here, she had to know how important this was.

Her face somber, she said, "I apologize again for not replying, as you requested. I will write as soon as I return to the Temple."

Behind the two women, the door to the house opened. A young girl stood waiting. He would have to be satisfied with the promise of another note. "I'll look forward to hearing from you."

Galatea tapped her hand over her heart, turned and entered the house. Good! He would have his moment alone.

But Leesandra also tapped over her heart. "Thank you again for my life, Alek. I'm sorry. I really must go."

She hurried inside. The girl closed the door.

∾ ∾ ∾ ∾

Leesandra walked next to Galatea down Kishar's short hall—she could hear the voices of others already gathered in the library—but instead of going forward, Galatea stopped, grasped her arm, and grinned. "Sweet Elysium, he is devastatingly handsome."

Leesandra felt her neck growing warm. What would Galli say if she knew she had coupled with Alektrion? That he was crowding out all other thoughts in her head?

"What is this about being too busy to see him?"

"I just didn't want him to … It's hard to explain."

"Is it your scar?"

"Galli, I don't want to talk about him."

"Well, is it your scar?"

"No. Absolutely not."

"Then why don't you see him? He obviously wants to see you. Look how far he came to find a way to talk to you."

"It's probably not me as a woman. It's as he says, he wants to talk about Kalliste."

"Well then, see him."

Galatea grasped her arm again and shook it. "Silly hen. See him. You've always said you mooned over him for years, that he was so funny and so gentle, and here he is and he wants to see you. For your spirit's sake, Leesandra, see the man."

She knew Galatea was thinking that something was wrong with her, that she was afraid to be with a man or, worse, didn't want to lie with a man. Once that might have been true. But not now. Never again. Making love with Alektrion had changed everything. She'd wanted to couple with him the minute she saw him on the road.

Galli let go, slipped her arm through Leesandra's and tugged her toward the library. "Well, it's not really my business. But I think if you don't write to him and make a time to see him alone you are the silliest woman in the world."

ক ক ক ক

The day after meeting Leesandra again, Alektrion stepped out of the door of his lodging into bright, midday sun, the smell of freshly baked bread, and heavy human traffic. He turned left and found himself facing the most remarkable man. Most certainly Nubian, with gold ear and nose rings, a blue and orange sari, and shockingly red shoes with curled up toes. The man stepped in front of him and said, "Are you Alektrion of Kalliste?"

"I am."

He handed Alektrion a parchment. A pleasant scent that hinted of lemon hung about him.

Warily, Alektrion glanced at the seal. It was from Leesa. He returned the stranger's sizing-up. The Nubian's face had handsome, delicate features. How interesting that Leesandra would send him a note through such strange means.

"I am Zuliya, Leesandra's friend. I am happy to have met you, Alektrion. I wish you good day."

Without another word, the stranger walked past Alektrion, who turned to follow his progress and was further amazed to see that the man limped. Most extraordinary.

He broke the seal, his nail ripping a bit of the parchment in his haste.

> My Dearest Alektrion. You must think my behavior odd. I realize that. I assure you I have been so happy to see you. I will be happy to see you again. Come to the hetaira quarters in the afternoon the day after tomorrow, after prayers. I am free for two hours.
>
> Leesandra

Two hours! Much could happen in two hours. He re-rolled the parchment and squeezed it with a triumphant grip, as if he'd just won the most risky game of Skull and Bones he'd ever played.

Someone bumped against him, mumbled an apology. He became aware again of the street and people. Where was it he was going? Oh, yes. To the docks to meet Talos. He set off, steps firm and spirit full of anticipation. At his first opportunity he would send her a note agreeing.

Two days later, sweet-scented beds of mid-winter narcissus welcomed him as he entered the garden of the hetaira quarters. No woman since Belamena had so consumed his thoughts. He'd even avoided getting drunk at night. He wanted nothing to dull his remembrance of being with Leesandra.

He found a stone bench overhung by a branch of a red-fruited koumaria, sat, and fidgeted. One by one, four men and a woman arrived. Each was met and disappeared through the distinctive red door found at the entry to every Keftian hetaira quarter in the hegemony.

Leesandra appeared at the head of a path. He sprang to his feet, pulse racing. She rushed toward him.

As if his mind and hers were one, she reached out her hand at the exact moment he did. "I've had a hard time waiting to see you."

"You have been much in my thoughts, Alek."

For a moment he lost himself in the simple pleasure of looking at her. Then, "I sent word that I'd walk you to The Lady's Chair. Show you the harbor. The fleet's flagship is in port. You can see it from the promontory."

"I've hiked to the Lady's Chair many times. And as much as I might like to learn about the fleet, I thought you wanted to talk."

"I want much more than to talk, Leesa."

She blushed. Her scar became stark white against her skin. "I think of you, Alek, with every breath I take."

Glorious words! He took her hand. "Have you arranged for a room?"

She nodded.

"Can we go there now?"

Again she nodded.

At first she seemed once again shy, but that quickly receded. For the next two hours, in their moments of oneness, the unfamiliar sensation thrilled him that his spirit didn't simply flee from his body, but entered into hers. And he was safe there.

Afterward she walked him to the stone doves that flanked the garden's entry and they parted with the simple embrace appropriate in public for lovers. He had made her promise that she would see him again. He headed with reluctance toward the Boar district, the feel of her still on his arms. Sarpedon expected him to report on the secret recruiting in Phaestos. He tried to focus on numbers and names, but his heart led his mind to Leesandra.

Talos and Anchices already sat in the den of Sarpedon's townhouse, cups of ale in hand. The admiral waved, indicating that Alektrion should help himself to ale. Anchices grinned. "So how did it go with the scar-faced priestess?"

Heat rose on Alektrion's neck at Anchices's callousness. "She's not a priestess yet."

"But soon, no?" Anchices persisted. "At Silvanos? Less than a couple of cycles of the moon. It's the same thing."

Sarpedon gestured, with annoyance, that Alektrion should sit and attend to business. Alektrion forced Leesandra to the back of his mind. He reported with painful disappointment their problems in Phaestos, explaining that both the vizier and presiding Temple priestess were against Sarpedon and any notion of mounting war against Pylos. He and Talos and Anchices had been followed, and not very discreetly. "We made little progress. I have the names of only five men who can be counted on."

The telling continued, and Sarpedon's face grew darker and darker.

In the next week Alektrion saw Leesandra every day. Sarpedon said nothing. Then on the eighth day, again at a meeting at the townhouse, the admiral said, "Tomorrow I need one of you to make a trip with a message to Arhanas. I want Talos and Anchices on board ship in the afternoon. You take it, Alek."

Alektrion spoke without thinking. "Could Talos go? Tomorrow afternoon I'll do whatever he needs to do for you."

Sarpedon's eyebrows shot up. "I said, I want Talos on the ship tomorrow. Wasn't I clear? What's happening to you, Alek?"

"Well ... um."

"Don't mutter, man. Is it that scarred priestess?"

His skin grew hot. At the corner of his vision he saw Talos purse his lips and stare at the ceiling with his one good eye.

"You've been seeing that woman nearly every day. I don't like it."

Never before had Sarpedon interfered in Alektrion's private life. Why now? Leesandra was none of Sarpedon's concern. "I'll take the message. But how does your liking or not liking a woman of my choosing prove relevant?"

"You want to argue with me about this? It's not the woman. It's what she is. I don't like priestesses. They're a scheming, intriguing lot. Never met one I'd trust. I say you're wasting valuable time with her."

Alektrion held tight to the arms of his chair. His face must be flaming. "I'll not let her interfere in any way with my service. But I intend to continue seeing her."

The admiral rose, a blood vessel pulsing at his temple. Suddenly he turned his back to them and stared out his window to the fountain in the square below. "By Kokor, be very pissing sure you tell her nothing of our business." He faced Alektrion again, eyes blazing, gaze level and hard. "Is that understood?"

"Very clearly," Alektrion said, keeping his own gaze hard and steady. "You have my oath."

25

Eight weeks after finding Leesandra on the Phaestos road, three weeks before she would take her final vows, he waited for her in the public square adjacent to the gold district. He intended to buy her a gift and wanted her to make the final choice. This shopping trip meant, though, that the two hours she was free must be spent surrounded by people. Two small hours! It wasn't enough. It would never be enough.

A cold mid-winter wind whistled around corners. Leesandra wore the same hooded cloak she'd worn the day he'd come upon her in the rain. She looked so small, her eyes bright, her hair a mass of dark curls. She embraced him modestly, but even her light touch raised hair on his arms.

He took her hand. "Come. The shop is only a few steps down this lane."

The jeweler—short, round, with long ringlets that looked ridiculous on a man of his age—he fetched a box holding the hair pins Alektrion had selected and led the way to the shop's front where the light was strongest. Deluging them in chatter about the skill required to craft such wonderful works of art, he removed the three decorative pins and laid them on a black cloth.

"The eyes of this lovely gold snake are of amethyst," he said to Leesandra. "The best quality. From Agyptos. I understand from your companion that you are Snake Clan. But of course you are." The little man was practically purring. "I see from your dress you will soon become a priestess. How very impressive. So I could see how you might like such a beauty."

Seeing her frown slightly he hurried on. "But then, these two leaping dolphins are very, very special. See how elegantly they arch. They will seem to be leaping from your hair into the air. And the inset of mother-of-pearl into the black of the onyx is exquisitely done, is it not?"

Alektrion ran a finger down the side of one of the sleek beasts. "Dolphins have totally free spirits. I picked them because they remind me of you."

She smiled and squeezed his arm.

The jeweler purred on. "And then we have this absolutely lovely recreation in gold of a sea eagle, its wings outspread and partly raised."

"The sea eagle could remind you of me," Alektrion said.

She looked surprised. "Why not a scorpion? Scorpion is your nickname, isn't it?"

He frowned. How had she learned that name? "It's not a name I like. I picked a sea eagle because that was the name of my first ship. I rowed her with the best friend I ever had."

Leesandra picked it up and turned to the portly merchant. "The sea eagle." She studied the pin a moment then handed it to the jeweler, who put it in the box, wrapped the whole affair, and ushered them from his shop with a continued stream of assurance that she would be so very pleased with the pin and that they must return to do business with him again.

On the far side of the fountain, sun bathed the street. He said, "I want to see it in your hair." He steered her to a warm bench. She unwrapped the pin and let him set it above the mass of curls bound up at the back of her head.

"I don't have mirrors to see it."

"It looks pretty."

She reached her hand to the golden bird and fingered it. "It's so hard for me to be away from you, Alek. I miss you and think of you—often. I'll treasure the pin. When I miss you, I'll touch it."

Her words rubbed his sore spot. "I want to see you for longer than two hours of a day, Leesa. Our time together isn't enough."

"I believe ... I fear I shouldn't be seeing you at all, Alek."

"Not at all?"

"We ... I ... all of us are warned. We mustn't care too much for a lover. It's dangerous."

Even a week ago any talk of her not completing her vows for his sake would have alarmed him because it implied marriage. But suddenly he had the astounding thought that he'd like it very much if she didn't take that final step. "I don't understand."

"If a woman cares too much, she may be seduced from taking her vows." Again she touched his pin. "And I do care for you." She touched his hand. "Perhaps too much. Sometimes it frightens me." She looked away. "And then there's the problem of your allegiance to Sarpedon."

"Problem?"

"Even my very good friend Galatea says she doesn't understand how I can consort with a man who works for someone who advocates war."

He clenched his teeth.

"All the talk lately is about your admiral, Alek. What he says is folly. My friend Galatea—her father, Minyas, was ambassador to Pylos and he knows the Acheans well—she told me her father says that even if the Law didn't forbid wars of aggression, we could never defeat the Acheans. And he says we shouldn't start a war we can't win. Couldn't win! Have you ever heard anything so foolish?"

"Minyas may not be wrong."

"But of course he's wrong! No force can defeat the Lady's navy. But that's entirely irrelevant. Please, Alek. Tell me you don't agree with your admiral's blasphemy. Defense of Keftiu and the Great Sea is one thing. Making war is completely another. I'm sometimes amazed Damkina continues to let Sarpedon speak."

"Any Keftian is free to speak. There's nothing in the Law against speaking or thinking."

"Maybe so. But I worry that Sarpedon is stirring up trouble on Keftiu between Keftians and Acheans. I don't want you caught up in something dangerous."

"The trouble in Knossos isn't coming from Sarpedon, Leesa. It's the Poseidonists who are spoiling for a fight."

"Oh, Alek. I don't like this talk of anger and war. It's spreading everywhere. Even at Kishar's. We always talk about poetry or life. We sing or dance. This last week war was mentioned. We were all sickened at the very thought, but the subject can't be avoided. Kishar says for Knossos to make war would make us no better than the barbarians, to say nothing of the imbalance it would create in the world. If the People abandon the Law, Alek, who would keep the world in harmony? All human life would descend forever into strife and darkness and pain. Your admiral should respect the Law. All of the People must."

"Sarpedon sees things as they really are, Leesa, and he knows what I do. Atistaeus must be stopped. He is evil."

"I don't disagree. But the Law is the heart of the People's life. It must be our guide. What it says we must do or all is lost."

But, he thought, the Law is wrong about this. Once before he'd had that same conviction—when the Law demanded Laius's death by such cruel means.

Leesandra's eyes brimmed with concern, but her jaw was set. Certain as he was that in this instance the Law was wrong, he was equally certain she wouldn't agree. "Knossos doesn't understand how powerful Atistaeus is becoming."

She put her hand over his. "I'm worried for you, Alek. Eventually you, too, will come under criticism if you stay with that warmonger. I know you travel for him, that you are his voice at dinner parties and other gatherings. Please tell me that's all you do."

He wanted to tell her the truth. He needed her to understand. But he heard Sarpedon's warning: "Whatever you do, don't tell her what we're actually doing."

His silence wasn't a matter of choice. He'd taken an oath. "I do what I must." His heart was thudding. "Do you want to stop seeing me?"

She looked close to tears. She shook her head. They sat in silence. It was nearing the time when she had to return. Miserable at the thought of parting, he said finally, "It's getting late. We have to go."

They had passed the temple of Poseidon when he saw, at some distance, a wall of people rushing down the street toward them. Well in front of the crowd ran a lone man, and when he passed, Alektrion caught his arm. "What's happening?"

"They're coming! They're going to burn a sacrifice in the open," the man gasped, pointing toward the nearby temple. "There will be trouble. The anti-Poseidonist faction's heard about it. They're coming to stop it." He pulled out of Alektrion's grasp. "Got to tell the Council," he said and sped off.

Alektrion tugged Leesandra in the direction of the jewelry shop. "Let's leave."

"I want to see."

"Absolutely not!" He'd half-dragged her back to the front of the temple when the swirling mass of people overtook them. He smelled unwashed bodies; elbows and shoulders battered him from all sides. He pulled Leesandra into a niche in the low wall surrounding the central fountain.

"Oh, Alek. They've brought goats for sacrifice. Four of them."

The goats' bleating added to the churning confusion. A stick of a man in black priestly robes, with hair of a remarkable bright red, bounded up the temple steps. He waved to catch the crowd's attention. The noise subsided slightly.

"Oenopion," Alektrion told her.

"Ah," she breathed, a sound of disgust.

"The great God demands sacrifice in the open and without fear," the priest said in a booming voice. "Let nothing stop us."

Two large altars of gilded wood materialized from the crowd. Alektrion heard Leesandra suck in her breath. Six men carried each up the temple steps and placed them on the upper landing before the temple's door. From two directions anti-Poseidonists arrived yelling, "Shame! Blasphemy!"

"I have to do something, Alek."

What was she thinking! "You can't do anything. These people are beyond reason."

"I have to try."

Before his shocked mind could guess her intent, she climbed onto the fountain wall. For all the crowd to see, her robes proclaimed her a

third-year novice. Her voice amazed him: strong, clear, and as confident as his own admiral's. It reached out. "People of Knossos. Hear
me. Let this disharmony cease."

Her hands trembled but her voice gave no hint of fear. She radi-
ated only determination. "The Great Lady has welcomed you to Her
home." The crowd swiveled its attention from Oenopion to her.
Alektrion stiffened.

"The Lady is generous to guests. Our Mother wishes you to live
here in happiness. She expects only that you respect Her Law and
that you worship in—" A stone struck her on the shoulder.

Someone yelled, "Silence!"

"—that you worship in private," Leesandra finished. A stone struck
her on the forehead.

From somewhere to Alektrion's left came cries of "Stop them!"
and "The barbarians have harmed the Lady's servant!"

He yanked her off the wall, pulled her close. Her body was quivering, tip to toe, like a struck gong. The crowd's attention switched
back to the priest, who directed that a goat be brought forward. Bleating cries cut off abruptly, and Alektrion looked back to where the priest
and altars stood. Blood covered the altar. The beast's legs were thrashing and the priest was bent over it, collecting the red life spurting
from its neck.

A howling, animal groaning of rage erupted from the crowd and
anti-Poseidonists surged toward the temple's entry. Bodies heaved
into him; he and Leesandra were swept out of their niche and carried
forward in a human wave toward the temple steps. She gripped him
so tightly around the waist that her fingers dug into his flesh.

Suddenly three men in front of him withdrew stout wooden clubs
from underneath their cloaks. Poseidonists, he guessed. Other men
brought out more clubs. Demon's Breath! The miserable confrontation was escalating.

"Hold tight," he yelled.

She pressed even closer.

Heretics and objectors collided. Like a bull in the capture net, he
shoved and pushed and kicked as he battled to maneuver them out
of the mob's center. Thuds and screams filled the air. A club struck
him on the back, drove out his breath.

"Alek, oh sweet Goddess, Alek!"

He caught his breath again. "I'm all right."

The thudding of running feet announced the arrival of the Temple
guard. Clubs disappeared under cloaks. Oenopion had long since
vanished, and now the Poseidonists slipped away down side streets
like mist fleeing a stiff breeze.

He hugged her tightly. "Leesa, my Leesa."

Her body shook beneath his hands.

"Let me see your face," he said holding her to arm's length. There seemed to be no serious damage, but a lump was rising on her forehead.

"Are the two of you all right?" a guard asked. To arrive so quickly the guards must have come at a full run, and they had come armed with spears.

"Fine," Alektrion said.

The man moved on.

"You may be fine. But I'm not," Leesandra snapped. "Never! I'm never going to be fine until this heresy is stopped. Kishar must convince the Wise Ones to speak out to Damkina."

"This isn't a matter for the Wise Ones."

"Yes, it is."

"This doesn't deal with the Lady's worship. It's beneath the Wise Ones' concern."

"No, Alek. Public killing is an unforgivable insult to harmony." She paused, her brows pulled tightly together, her face awash with conflicting emotions. "Things have really gone too far. A terrible spiritual sickness has taken root in our island's very heart. Damkina must be made to see that Poseidon worship must be forbidden. Their temples must be closed. At least until this madness passes."

He drew her away from the street. They walked rapidly toward her quarters. Finally he said, "This isn't a religious matter, Leesa. Oenopion's pressuring is politically inspired."

"Politics?"

"Don't you find it remarkably odd that people came to make a sacrifice carrying clubs? There was a plan to make a riot of this."

She nodded. "Yes, yes. I see that. And Damkina must stop the Poseidon worship. Then the rest will stop."

"Leesa, I think the heretics are too strong now for Damkina to stop them. Even if she could finally rouse herself to do so. Damkina is a fool."

Leesandra halted, her jaw dropped in shock. "How do you dare speak so of the Lady's Voice?"

He wasn't about to take his words back. "You've said you don't agree with the admiral's conviction that the Achean, Atistaeus, is behind all this agitation. But I serve Sarpedon because I agree with him. Forbidding Poseidonist worship on Keftiu won't stop what's happening. We have collaborators within, but the threat is from outside, and ultimately Damkina will either come to her senses and agree to an invasion of Pylos or we'll have Acheans treading the Temple."

Her lips had drawn into a thin, determined line. "You've always admired the Acheans haven't you? Do you really think they're better than the People?"

"Not better, Leesa. Absolutely not. But Atistaeus is a vicious, brutal butcher and Damkina shows no comprehension of the nature of his threat. Either that or she has no spine."

"Don't, Alek! Don't ever again speak with such disrespect for the Lady's Voice in my presence."

He'd crossed a line. And maybe Leesandra could never understand.

She turned and started walking. "Damkina has the power to do anything she wishes," she said in a tone that tolerated no argument. "I'll concede to you this much. As frightening as it is to think it, I think Damkina is being somewhat... somewhat... well, wrongheaded. She must be convinced to act." She stopped. Her level gaze met his. "But she needs to act within the Law, Alek. Not break it. Only enforce it." She looked away again. "Perhaps Kishar, through the Wise Women, can convince her to close the Poseidonist temples."

All of them were blind. From Damkina to the Council to the Wise Ones to the masses of the People, so securely isolated on Keftiu for so long they had no conception of the nature of the enemy creeping up on them.

He took her arm. She didn't protest and laid her hand softly over his. What if Leesa were somehow hurt by all this? A different feeling shook him, snatched his breath. He didn't want her to take vows. He wanted to ask her to marry him. He would take her from Keftiu and the violence and pain he could see coming, and they would live in happiness somewhere else.

He risked a sideways glance, and quickly looked away again. By his mother's life, he wanted her. And he wanted her for himself, alone.

His mouth felt suddenly dry. You're thinking like a man with no wits!

Another painful thought. He would never put her in the horrible position of having to say no to a half-breed or subject himself to the pain of hearing her say it.

She embraced him to take leave, and he simply couldn't let go. If he didn't take her away at once, by force if necessary, he would lose her. He was sure of it.

She pulled away. Her smile was tentative. "It hurts me that we argued."

He took her arm again and then clutched one of her hands in his, feeling suffocated by a sense of losing control of something vital to his life. "We'll not argue again."

"No, love, we'll not."

She squeezed his hand, pulled hers free, and then was gone. He felt sick. And more enraged than he could ever remember being about the inescapable fact that he wasn't Keftian. Marriage to the only woman he would ever want as wife was impossible.

∾ ∾ ∾ ∾

Six days later, Alektrion threw his cloak over his shoulders, hurried out into a chilly evening to meet Talos and Anchices. He was already late. They were invited to a dinner where Sarpedon, though not present, would be honored.

Alektrion's time to meet with Leesandra had changed; their two hours were now in the mid-afternoon and she could see him only four days of seven. His every waking moment was haunted by the approach of her dedication, but he couldn't think of a way to stop it.

His stomach growled. He'd had no midday meal, and no time to eat after his meeting with her. He would leave the reception as quickly as decorum permitted. Tomorrow he would carry a message from Sarpedon to their key supporter in Mallia, a journey of several days. Long days spent away from Leesandra.

Tonight he might see perhaps fifty of Knossos's residents. Their host, Nickomon, was a cedar exporter whose ships had suffered major losses from Atistaeus's raiders. Though not yet converted, Nickomon had a sympathetic ear.

Talos and Anchices waited near the gate to the Bull Academy. He set off with them down the Amnissos road.

Nickomon's villa was two stories and large, even by generous Knossian standards. The entry mural set the tone, a tranquil scene of waterfowl in a marsh. Curved eating couches sat in seven intimate circles of eight guests each. The hostess had scattered the most important personages among the clusters to de-emphasize rank. He found himself separated from Talos and Anchices and sharing his couch with a gaunt, sharp-eyed woman who served on the Council. "She's very close to the current Speaker, Kryson," his hostess whispered as they approached the group,

She introduced him as Sarpedon's chief aide, and the ensuing brief conversation about his admiral was polite; he didn't expect to hear candid opinions. The talk shifted to the riot at the Poseidon temple. Remarks sharpened. The Keeper of Travel, the man responsible for maintaining Keftiu's roads, jumped in. "The Poseidonists brought weapons. That means someone's spending pistatas on spreading this foul religion. I travel to the seven cities often, and my sense is that the Poseidonist proselytizing is meeting with astonishing success."

"I agree," said a long-nosed man opposite. "If you mingle in the right places, you'll find misguided Keftians who think the Poseidonists should be allowed to worship any way they want, anywhere they want."

Keftians like Leesandra's friend Galatea, thought Alektrion.

The Keeper of Travel continued. "It's my conviction that there are Keftians of substance involved now."

The gaunt woman, friend of the Speaker, leaned forward. "What Keftian of power do you think is with Oenopion?"

Abrupt silence fell. Alektrion strained to hear, then the Keeper said, "I travel. I listen. But I can't honestly admit to hearing a specific name."

Alektrion let out his breath. Quite a letdown.

The conversation returned to Sarpedon. Specifically to the recent, controversial speech in which, for the first time, he'd publicly advocated war.

The sharp-eyed councilwoman turned to Alektrion and smiled. "You may tell your admiral he may expect a visit soon from someone from the Council, but tell him also that he's in no trouble so long as all he does is speak his mind." Her smile remained the same, but her eyes narrowed. "I'm very sure the admiral realizes the decision to act on such ideas could come only from the Lady's Voice."

"I assure you, Sarpedon knows and obeys the Law." It was definitely time to leave.

The servers brought sweet, after-dinner wine. The tables were cleared from the room, and music of harp, lyre, and flutes began. He told Talos and Anchices he was going, thanked the hostess and host, and was halfway across the patio when the councilwoman caught up to him.

"May I speak with you, Alektrion of Kalliste?"

He was embarrassed that he had not caught her name. "Of course. It is …?"

She smiled, softening somewhat her sharp look. "Semlena of Kato Zakro, daughter of Zelia."

She took his arm and walked them toward the garden. "Let's speak where we can't be heard."

His senses went on alert.

She drew him well into the night and the earthy-smelling garden. Then, "I understand you're close to the admiral."

He nodded.

"Tell him I'm with him. Tell him I have Kryson's ear and I'll begin to fill it."

He stopped walking. They clasped hands, and she wrapped two fingers of her free hand around his wrist, the signal used among those who could be trusted. He suddenly felt a surge of fresh hope. She added, "I have other good friends who wish Sarpedon well."

"Excellent." Perhaps this woman could move Kryson to their position. The Speaker could potentially have tremendous influence on Damkina.

He turned back to the verandah, but she put her hand out. "I've something else. I want you to tell Sarpedon that he should watch the merchant, Minyas." She leaned close, her eyes intent. "I've known Minyas since he was a boy, since before he served as Velchanos, and I don't trust him."

"I didn't know Minyas served as consort to the Goddess."

"Oh, yes. More importantly, he served ten years as ambassador to Pylos. It's logical to assume he knew Atistaeus."

"Does that necessarily make him suspect?"

She drew a long breath. "Minyas is my sister's nephew. Quite brilliant. He charmed my brother. Especially with his poetry and wit. But I never liked him." She tugged Alektrion toward a stone bench. "Please. I need to sit."

"Something happened that changed Minyas the year he became Velchanos. After serving, he emerged embittered. Sousuma was High Priestess and, in an unguarded moment, he said to me, 'Sousuma is a fraud.'"

Alektrion found this outspoken blasphemy impressively shocking. "What did you take him to mean?"

"With passing years, I've made friends inside the Temple. I've learned what the People weren't told. Minyas failed to perform on the night of the Sacred Marriage. Sousuma disdained him afterward and the feeling was mutual. During his year, the Temple people served him only with reluctance. I think since then Minyas has wished the Temple ill. I strongly suspect he may have made an alliance with Pylos."

Alektrion thanked Semlena for being so candid, wished her well, and left. He retraced their conversation as he walked his way back to his quarters. He couldn't think why, but for some reason her suspicion of Minyas was easy to accept. Then he remembered. Galatea, Leesandra's friend, was the daughter of Minyas. And more than once Leesandra had told him that Galatea tended to minimize the Poseidonist controversy. That Galatea thought the Poseidonists should be able to freely worship as they wished.

The trip to Mallia he made with great impatience, and immediately upon his return, he went to Sarpedon and repeated Semlena's warning.

The admiral nodded solemnly. "Fits in with other things I've heard. We'll do as she suggests. We'll watch Minyas as if he were under a jeweler's glass."

Alektrion left, heading for the Temple, his thoughts on Leesandra. Demon's breath take all! In five days she would take vows. He couldn't sleep. He barked at Talos and Anchices—at people he scarcely knew. He ate little. When he thought of her, his bones ached.

Life couldn't go on this way. He had to do something.

26

Some moments in our lives remain as vivid as when they happened, kept bright forever by our willing reliving of them. I've relived many times the days when I first understood the depth of my love for Alektrion.

He had left me at my quarters after we stumbled away from the first riot in Knossos, and I remembered how he'd held and protected me. I'd felt between my own shoulder blades the blow he'd received from a club. I caressed the hairpin he had given me with my fingers and eyes. I wanted to go to him, sleep in his arms, but instead, I would sleep alone. In five days, seclusion for my vows would begin, and I would not be able to see Alektrion again until after taking them.

The moment for which I'd planned and dreamed, which would give my mother and Heebe such joy, stood at hand. But for the first time since I had heard the Great Mother's call so clearly on Alyris, I felt unsure.

The next day at Kishar's I drew her aside. "I've committed a serious breach of rules," I began hesitantly. I told of meeting Alektrion on the Phaestos road and confessed how I'd continued to see him. "I knew, Kishar, even from the beginning, that I cared perhaps too much."

She frowned, her eyes darkened. She took my hand and led me to a cushioned bench. She continued to hold my hand. "Why do you tell me this?"

"I don't know." I could barely force the next words out. "I think if I could, I'd leave the Temple and marry Alektrion."

She tightened her grip. "Has he asked you to forsake your calling?"

"No."

"Do you think he will ask you?"

"I can't marry Alek. It wouldn't be accepted. His mother is Achean."

Clearly shocked at the depth of my foolishness, her frown deepened further. "Where is the problem then?"

I pulled my hand away, twisted my fingers together like the confused thoughts tangling in my mind.

"I'm desperate, Kishar. He's in my head, always. He's in the air I inhale. When we're apart, I live for the moment I'll see his face again and I can touch him. And I think I'd rather have my heart cut out than never see him again."

She sighed. "You want me to tell you what to do. But that isn't the way, Leesandra. Look within. The Mother will guide you." She squeezed my hand as if to emphasize her next words. "I have great personal faith in your calling, Danae's daughter."

"I have prayed. I assure you. But I still don't—"

"Do you doubt your calling?"

"Never!"

"Then let nothing deter you. Go to Her again. This complication may be a test of your determination. Maybe She'll ask you to make the sacrifice of letting him go entirely. Maybe she'll cool your passion so it will satisfy you to have him only as lover. Maybe She'll arrange for his path to take him away until your passion cools. Whatever She does, you know it will be right for you."

I spent that night prone and in prayer. The next morning I still had no peace. I knew only that to betray my call would be to betray myself, to betray the People, to betray the Goddess and everything I had ever believed.

To make matters worse, Zuliya came to me after mid-morning devotions. "We must talk." He looked concerned. We walked a short distance to Damkina's aviary and sat. He stretched his artificial leg at a comfortable angle and sighed. "The day of vows approaches. I know you better than anyone in this world. You are troubled. Is it the dedication? Or is it the man?"

I told him what I'd told Kishar.

"You need not take the vows. You can still change your path." I detected hope in his voice. "You could marry this Alektrion."

"I can't marry him. Even if he would ask me."

"Why do you say you cannot?"

"I assumed you knew. Sarpedon's right hand is half Achean."

"You cannot marry him and stay happily in Knossos. But Knossos is not the whole world."

My mouth fell so wide open Heebe would have said I could catch moths.

"Why do you look surprised? You and he have never thought of leaving Knossos?"

Such a possibility had never entered my mind. Leave Knossos! Impossible.

But was it? Hadn't there been a time as a child when the thought of leaving Alyris to go to Knossos had been so unpleasant it had cost me tears and sleepless nights? Yet now I was happy here.

That evening I even let my guard slip with Heebe. One of our favorite places to meet was the public bath near her boarding house. I sat behind her in the mint-scented hot water, massaging her back with a sponge. "I will meet Alektrion tomorrow at the Lady's Chair," I said. "It's the last time I'll see him before seclusion. I've been thinking strange thoughts."

"What thoughts?"

"Marriage."

She scooted around so she could stare at me. "Whatever are you saying, Little Bird? He's a half-breed. Worse. Everyone knows he's doing Kokor-knows-what for that warmonger Sarpedon. You can't possibly think of giving up the sacred path for such a man! For any man."

I touched the sea-eagle pin I now wore in my hair at all times. "It's only that now that I know how much pleasure there is in coupling. I ... I ..."

"You what?"

I finished lamely. "I can see better why my mother enjoyed being married to my father." Sweet Mother of All, I prayed silently, my spirit quaking again. *Make me strong. I know he can't be mine, but I have so much pain.*

"Of course. I always took great pleasure in seeing your mother and father's happiness. But surely, my dear Little Bird, you wouldn't turn your face from the Temple because of a man?"

"No." I took her hand, thinking how very much I loved her. "Of course not."

We spoke of other things, but my mind scarcely followed the conversation. That night I tossed on a hard bed.

In total contrast to my spirit, the next day was serene. Alektrion and I were nearly alone at the Lady's shrine on the promontory called the Lady's Chair. Only one old woman tended the votive stall. We bought clay figurines and offered them to the Goddess. Alektrion led me to the stone seat and we sat side by side, and for a while we studied the view while he held my hand and explained about the ships in winter harbor. Even at this long distance he recognized some well enough to know their names. He pointed out Sarpedon's flagship. He began to caress my hand with his thumb, though, and heat soon ran like liquid fire under my skin. "If you continue that, Alek, we'll have to go back to the hetaira quarter at once."

"I don't want you to go back to the Temple at all."

My heart did a little double leap.

"I can't bear it, Leesa. I want you to come with me now. To my rooms. I want you to ... to ..."

"You are my heart," I whispered. His fingers tightened over mine. "But I must go back. Today. And always."

He shook his head. "It's not enough for me."

"It has to be enough."

"It will never be enough, Leesa. I can't live like this. Marry me, Leesa. Come away from Knossos. Become my wife. I know a place. Samos. We could live happily there."

"No, Alek." The sound of racing blood hummed in my ears. "Don't ask me that."

"Is it because of my mother?"

"Never, Alek." I threw my arms around him, clung to him, I didn't care what the old woman might gossip about. "Surely, my love, you know your mother's blood means nothing to me."

"Then come away."

I pulled back to see his face. "The Great Mother has called me to serve Her here. I can't deny Her call. Would you have me betray my whole life?"

The lines pulled tightly around his mouth conveyed such pain I felt as though I'd stabbed him. He let me go.

"We will still have each other as we do now, and I will have no other lover, Alek. Never. I promise. On my life I swear it. Only please don't ask me to do what I can't."

"I won't stay in this situation."

I took his hand, pleading with my eyes. He turned away, toward the harbor.

"Everything will be all right." I was desperate to convince myself too.

A muscle at the corner of his jaw tightened. He balled his fist. "I beg you, one last time. Come away with me."

What could I say? He had to understand. Had to.

He waited.

The silence grew.

He turned dark, saddened eyes to me. "Tomorrow you enter seclusion. I'll seek word at the Temple on the day of vows. I beg you to send a message or come to me before then. If I hear you've taken your vows, I'll leave Knossos, Leesa. I can't stay. Once before in my life I felt the pain of great loss. I thought nothing else could ever match it. I was wrong. But if you take your vows, I'll leave. I can't share you."

My heart seemed to fall into a bottomless pit. "Then you would leave me?"

We sat staring at the view of the sea. Go with him, a part of me whispered. *Leave everything.*

The conchs sounded the hour.

I said, "I have to go back."

On the way, we came upon a swallow with a broken leg and wing. I picked up the poor tiny thing. The small body was very warm, and my fingers easily felt a racing heart beneath soft black feathers.

"Have you any idea what they eat?" I was thinking I might take it back and try to mend its bones.

"They can't be hand fed."

"I can't leave it here. It must be in pain."

"Give it to me."

He took it. He covered its head and eyes with one hand and immediately the tiny thrashing legs stilled. With the other hand he felt under its wings for its sides and squeezed.

He saw my distress. "This is quick, Leesa. I've talked with men who've nearly died from suffocation but lived to tell. For a moment there is panic because you can't breathe, but then you simply drift into sleep. Sometimes you have to do things, unpleasant things, to accomplish a good end." His words sounded cold, but to my amazement I saw the glint of tears in his eyes.

We placed the dead swallow in the crook of a tree so it would be nearer the air where it had spent its life. Before long others would find it, and its body would return to the Great Mother.

We returned to the hetaira quarter, and when we made love his hands touched me as they always had but his spirit was distant. Or was the barrier within me?

∾ ∾ ∾ ∾

I entered seclusion. I took my vows. I wrote mother and father a letter filled with details I knew would give them joy, but my heart was desolate. One day followed another—empty, flat, colorless, pointless.

From Heebe I learned that Alektrion had left town the day after my dedication. "He went with a party of six going to the east. The gossip is, they intend to spread their foolish disaster warnings to as many cities as they can."

I had made my decision, the most final of my life. Alektrion of Kalliste was mine no more. I would accept my fate. I would trust that the Mother would give me strength to live.

"You'll get over him," Galatea said, hugging me. She spoke with an assurance that made not the slightest impression on my grief.

The only fire that now and then burned hotly at my core was anger over the riot. The next time Galatea and I went to Kishar's and the three of us were alone, I told Kishar what I'd seen. I suggested she must talk to Damkina.

Galatea frowned.

Kishar asked, "What would you have me tell the Lady's Voice?"

"She must denounce the Poseidonists. She must close their temples."

Kishar shook her head. "The Wise Ones do not concern themselves with religious affairs of others. Only those of the People."

I described the butchery of the goats. "I know this religion, Kishar. It's evil! Their breaking of harmony can be horrific."

Still frowning, Galatea said, "I think what Damkina is doing is exactly right. Leesandra, for some reason, just doesn't understand that the only way to have harmony is to stay out of the religious affairs of foreign guests! Actually, if anything, Damkina ought to speak openly against further attempts to suppress the Poseidonists. If they sacrifice goats in the open, people will be offended for a while, but nothing of real consequence will have changed."

I clenched my teeth to hold back my anger. Kishar only smiled. "Let's not talk of this unpleasantness," she said. "Experience teaches that this storm of controversy, like others before it, will pass."

Later, as Galatea and I walked back to the Temple, she reached out and took my hand. "You're angry at me, aren't you?"

"Yes."

"Let's not argue over this foreign religion. We are best friends. I promise I'll not say another thing about Poseidonists."

"I hate their religion, Galli. But I agree it's wrong for us to argue." I slipped my arm around her waist. "What they do has nothing to do with you and me. We'll not argue about them again."

She hugged me back. "We will always be best friends."

As months passed other riots occurred. I heard nothing but disturbing rumors. I struggled not to express my worries and anger to her. Then, on the day guards found four sacrificed goats on the steps of the southwestern portal of the Mother's Temple, disgust and alarm drove me back to Kishar. I went alone.

She sat me down and spoke earnestly. "You may have thought I didn't pay heed when you spoke before. But I did. I respect your instincts. I believe they are guided. So I sought out and listened to others as well, and I agree now that the damage being done to harmony here is severe. I've asked for a private audience with Damkina. I want you to come with me."

How wonderful! Kishar agreed and was prepared to use her influence! But I found it hard to imagine myself in a direct confrontation with Damkina. "You must convince her, Kishar." I lowered my voice, almost afraid of what I was about to say. "Surely you've heard the rumors that sometimes they sacrifice people?"

"Rumors, yes."

"It's true."

She cocked her head.

"When I was a child, I saw with my own eyes. I was twelve and found a secret way to watch their ceremonies."

The boy in white, the black-clad priest, the gushing blood. With such sudden force that for a moment I couldn't speak, I lived that long ago horror again. And just as suddenly I realized that our present troubles must be the reason the Lady had let me see the boy's death. Yes. At last all was clear. Because of that day with Alektrion, nothing, no one, could ever strip from me awareness of the full extent of the evil growing in Knossos.

"To celebrate their salvation from a terrible storm while at sea, the barbarians cut a young slave boy's throat."

She spoke softly. "It is a great agony to know the depths to which people hurt each other. I'm sorry you saw this thing. But from great pain we often learn great wisdom, and so I'm not surprised the Mother led your feet on that path."

I resolved not to tell Galatea about the audience with Damkina, and during the five days I spent waiting for it, I tried to pretend it was natural not to tell Galatea absolutely everything. But it wasn't. A barrier, impenetrable as a thorn hedge, had been planted between us and was growing as fast as the Poseidonist heresy itself.

When Damkina's doorkeeper ushered Kishar and me into a cozy room, Nothos, The Badger, was already present. His stocky body looked uncomfortable even in his sari, a garment acclaimed for easy wearing. Despite Nothos's outward stiffness, Damkina and he were drinking salepi tea and conversing in warm tones.

The room smelled of lavender, and over the wide door opposite me a fresco of leaping dolphins adorned the wall. Observing custom in the presence of Wise Women, both Damkina and Nothos rose. Up close Damkina was a frail-looking creature with slender arms exposed by a short-sleeved, scarlet and yellow sari. She waited for Kishar to approach. The two of them embraced and exchanged the formal kiss on the lips shared only among Wise Women and the Lady's Voice. Kishar took a chair placed prominently opposite Damkina. The doorkeeper gestured for me to sit on a cushioned bench to the side. I reminded myself to keep silent unless spoken to.

Kishar made no polite conversational gestures. She plunged directly into the reason for our visit. She stressed the increasing frequency of public disturbances, the horror that the Law has for killing

262 Judith Hand

for any purpose other than food. She reminded Damkina of the brutality of spirit required to take any creature's life.

Damkina was listening with patience. Or was it indifference? Suddenly she interrupted. "I hear your concern, Wise One. But I see this problem differently. Your interest is with the People's spiritual good, as is mine. But I must consider also the wide implications of interfering in other people's religious affairs. Knossos hosts literally thousands from other lands. Trade with these guests is our life blood. Temple policy has always been not to interfere with their practices so long as what they do is done in private, and this policy has served the People well. I intend to continue it."

Kishar drew a breath preparing to continue.

Damkina raised a protesting hand. "Far more serious matters trouble my mind. The mainlander King, Atistaeus of Pylos, is wreaking havoc on the Great Sea."

Nothos, his gruff voice sounding very male in this delicate room, spoke for the first time. "What do you think of the arguments of Admiral Sarpedon that the agitation in Keftiu is supported by the Red King? A tactic to divide and weaken us from within."

Kishar said, "I've seen or heard nothing to prove such a claim."

We were getting away from my purpose. *Tell them about the human sacrifices!*

Nothos stuck doggedly to the subject of the barbarian king. "The Memory Keepers say we're losing ships to Atistaeus at an unprecedented and dangerous rate. And nations that rely on us to keep the sea secure are bellowing like gored bulls. They want us to declare war and invade Pylos." He raised his hand as if to ward off her protest. "Of course, the Law forbids invasion. Certainly. Nevertheless, if there is a connection between Atistaeus and Oenopion, we need to know it."

"As I say," Kishar repeated, "I have no proof of such claims. This Poseidonist heresy is my concern. It is a growing, brutal thing, and if not stopped, I believe it will rip the very fabric of Keftian society."

Damkina rearranged the shoulder of her sari and smoothed it with one hand. "I hear you. I assure you I will consider your words."

"I ask that you cease to consider, Most Reverend. I'm here to urge that you act. Close their temples. Forbid this worship. There is nothing in the Law that protects this growing spiritual sickness, and it is very dangerous."

Listen to Kishar!

"I am following the correct course, Kishar."

Damkina's delicate lips were set. Our efforts this day would bear no fruit. I clenched my teeth to keep from calling her a fool.

Again Nothos spoke. "Direct your concerns and prayer to our men at sea, Wise One. This Pylian king is a butcher."

Kishar shifted in her seat. "But, vizier, he doesn't do his butchery in the heart of Knossos."

The Badger hung onto his point. "Kishar, we've lost twenty-some vessels—and their crews. And with them, as you know Wise One, the Lady's priestesses who served those crews."

My shock tumbled out in words. "The Poseidonists kill the Lady's sea priestesses?"

The surprised gazes of all three shifted to me. Nothos gave me a sad smile. "Just so, Danae's daughter."

I scarcely listened to the brief ending to this barren audience. A conflagration errupted in my mind. The Red King—a death-loving Poseidonist with no peer—was killing my sisters at sea. For years I'd hoped to serve on a passenger or merchant vessel, but with the jarring irrevocable force of an earthquake, my goal shifted. Alektrion had told me of the priestess on his first vessel, how he admired her courage, her physical strength, her compassion. I saw myself on a warship. If I were allowed any say at all, that's where I would serve. The Lady's navy was the People's bulwark against unbelievers—against the likes of Atistaeus of Pylos.

Later, Galatea and I were bathing together. I told her nothing of the audience but did say I'd decided to serve on a war vessel.

"I'm not surprised. I know how you felt about your warrior. For your sake, you really should forget him." Almost without taking a breath, she put this grim subject away. "I'm still praying the Goddess will let me serve in Knossos. You know, I'm good with people. I even think someday I may serve very close to Damkina."

What was wrong with her? "Galli, didn't you understand what I've said? We're losing ships to the Red King. Many ships."

"Then you're very brave to consider serving on a warship. I'm not that brave. I want to stay right here."

That night bad thoughts accompanied me to sleep. Damkina was foolishly blind to the Poseidonist threat—and in her way, so was Galatea. Perhaps Galatea would someday serve close to Damkina. Perhaps Damkina tolerated around her only those who shared her blindness.

If so … My poor Keftiu.

27

Through bloodshot, burning eyes, Alektrion squinted as he stared north over the tiny quay of Gournia toward Kalliste. He sat on a grassy bluff in the late afternoon, alone. Nearly a year he'd spent in Kato Zakro, the same at Sitia, and six moon cycles at Mochlos. He downed another swig from the narrow mouth of the wineskin. Almost two and a half years had slid by since he'd left Knossos, and within a week of leaving he'd started drinking again. Mercifully, his nightmares had not returned.

For over a day now, he and Anchices and Talos had been stuck in this provincial backwater because Anchices needed new sandals, but they should make it to Mallia within the week. He sat on ground soggy from unrelenting spring rains. Dampness had soaked through his tunic. He should care, but he didn't.

Some scholars blamed this year's strange weather and frequent downpours on the great quantities of ash spewed into the air by Kalliste over the last half a year. The volcano had awakened. Most of the ash fell and all of the lava flowed to the east of Alyris, so the city was in no immediate danger. He worried about home, especially about his parents. But not much.

He didn't worry too much about anything. Not really.

Maybe his trouble was that he needed to go back to sea. He wasn't a politician. Sarpedon could wage his campaign against Atistaeus without Alektrion of Kalliste.

Despite drinking himself to numbness every evening—from the day they'd left Knossos, he'd insisted on his own sleeping room so he could do so in private—he had performed well. No one could fault him. His recruiting for Sarpedon's secret army had been impressive. So much so that regular communications from the Admiral repeatedly held praise. Talos had once tried mentioning the drinking.

"By Kokor," Alektrion had yelled back in drunken anger, fists clenched, "criticize again what I do when I'm alone and it'll be the last time you ever speak to me!"

His friend with the destroyed face had shrugged and turned away. So long as Alektrion managed to function, neither Talos nor Anchices would complain again.

He took another drink. A drop of rain hit his arm.

"Demon's breath." He should probably find shelter.

More wine sluiced down easily. *Better that I'd died with Laius. What's the point of dragging on?*

He stood and teetered to the edge of the bluff. Just one step more.

Down went some more wine. He slumped to the ground. Up went the wineskin. His aim was off. Wine ran over his chin onto the front of his cloak.

"You're no good," was the last thing he remembered before he passed out.

∿ ∿ ∿ ∿

A raucous call punished him into consciousness. Others followed, equally painful. Alektrion jerked upright. The air was fresh, the smell of still wet ground pungent. No rain. It was morning—no, mid-morning. Not ten feet from him, arrayed in a half-circle, stood six hooded carrion crows, staring sharp-eyed with disapproval.

"Away!"

Their frantic take off fanned air over his face. He ran his hand over stubble on his jaw and cheeks. Two days without a shave. He was cold and wet and chilled to the core. "Any man who goes on like this is worse than a fool."

He rose. His back screamed disapproval. Three heavy steps, and he balanced at the edge of a four-story bluff. Great boulders lay in a jumble immediately below. The beach was white sand. Offshore a merchant vessel under full sail glided on the pale blue sea like a floating pelican; headed east, perhaps to Rhodos or on to Kyprus. He shivered from the onshore breeze blowing on his soggy clothes.

Maybe he should step off the bluff.

The ship swept onward, forward into its future. What about his future?

He stared at the sand and boulders, and slowly resolve grew. He would return to Leesa. Laius wouldn't have bet even a quarter of a pistata on the chance that after two and half years she'd talk to him, let alone accept him. And doubtless he would be told she'd taken another lover. Maybe many. But still he would go back.

He rubbed his arms and took a careful step back from the bluff. He had to be prepared to learn the worst. But either he returned to see Leesandra or stepped off the bluff, or his life would drag on through what most often felt like pointless days. One way or the other, he must put his feet on another path because he was running headlong to a meeting with the Ancient at the end of this one.

He turned toward the inn. Striding toward him were Talos and Anchices. Seeing his condition, Talos frowned. Anchices said, grinning, "You are a right pretty mess."

"That I am."

They turned and walked toward the inn. Anchices continued. "We relay a message from Sarpedon. He commands that you return to Knossos at once."

"Perfect. I have it in my own mind to do just that."

"My sandals aren't ready."

"You and Talos stay here until they are. I leave as soon as I can throw what I have into a pack."

ᖚ ᖚ ᖚ ᖚ

Just past dawn Alektrion arrived at the inn. The only people about in Knossos were the fresh fruit and vegetable vendors. The innkeeper, an unhappy looking woman with ugly facial moles, but with a heart as sweet as date juice, gave him a hearty embrace. "My handsome Scorpion! Come, come. I have only a small room empty, but in two days you may have your old one."

He said he intended to go out again as soon as he bathed, and though she was surprised, she hurried her youngest son to bring hot water. Alektrion did morning prayers, broke fast with hot porridge and fruit, and was standing at the door to Sarpedon's townhouse well before mid-morning.

"That fool is no longer associated with this family," Sarpedon's wife snapped. "I threw him out months ago. He's a troublemaker who won't listen to reason."

"Where is he?"

"His youngest sister's taken him back." She slammed the door.

At the sister's townhome, Alektrion found himself warmly welcomed and ushered upstairs. Sarpedon rose from behind a desk, pleasure in his eyes, his embrace as tight as a wrestler's hug. "My dear Alek. You've traveled nearly as fast as your messenger. I'm pleased to see you. I need you."

They took chairs, and Sarpedon gestured toward a pitcher on the table between them. "A mixture of pomegranate, fig, and pear."

"Not for me."

Sarpedon paced, a frown deeply dug into his brow. "Much has happened since you left. Twice the ground in Knossos quaked to the point of triggering panic. The second time, sea waves following the shaking disrupted boat-building at Krylissos, and sadly, we've lost several vessels in battle with Atistaeus. Not all have been replaced. They must be. Swiftly."

He moved back to sit opposite Alektrion. "Kalliste suffered much worse. The Poseidonist priest, Oenopion, is telling the People these are signs that his god is angry. They've taken to calling their god 'Earth Shaker.' Claim he and he alone has the power to bring this quaking in the Mother's body." Sarpedon shook his head and pursed his lips. "It's frightening how many people believe these lies. On Kalliste, now that the mountain is almost constantly active, the Poseidonists are extremely successful."

"What is it Oenopion wants?"

"He's obvious about what he *says* he wants. He comes perilously close to demanding they be allowed to make public blood sacrifices. We've had tremendous street fights. Shocking behavior, Alek. But Oenopion's clever. Were his statements even the slightest bit stronger, Damkina or the Council or both would silence him. And only the Goddess knows what even more outlandish heresy he spews in private. But whatever he claims to want, I have proof he receives support from and gives comfort to our harshest critics. He says to make war on Atistaeus would offend both Poseidon and the Lady. He's even agitated that I, Sarpedon, be banned."

"By the demon!"

"Ah, but that's not the most astonishing news." Sarpedon paused, his gaze seemed to bore into Alektrion's skin. "Minyas has openly embraced Poseidon. For me there's no longer any doubt. Minyas is in league with Atistaeus. I believe it's he who secretly provides Oenopion with money. I have it on good authority he actually attended one of their rituals and during the ceremony drew a dagger and slew a goat."

Traitor!

"My problem is, I have no proof to take to the Council or Damkina."

"What about the Council? Has the woman who warned us about Minyas ... what was her name?"

"Semlena."

"Has she made any headway?"

"Three of the thirteen now openly favor an invasion. Two others are sympathetic. Four—those from Phaestos and Kato Zakro—are adamantly opposed. The feelings of the others remain well disguised."

The reasons Alektrion had returned had had nothing to do with Atistaeus or Sarpedon or intrigue, but once again he felt his anger rise. "Talos, Anchices, and I can report the loyal sympathy of four thousand men from the eastern cities. But they're restless and uncertain. There's little to offer them but ominous shadows."

"We're about to change that."

"Yes?"

"I have from the south and west several times that number of names. Now what's needed is to organize. Those willing to follow must know who their immediate commander will be. For those positions, we'll use retired marines. And our recruits must make or acquire weapons. All in secret. I've raised adequate resources for a good beginning. And we must train those who aren't already fighting men. This training is what I want from you. And I feel the pressure of time. Atistaeus's forces in the Great Sea are pressing us hard, as far to the east now as Naxos."

His hatred for Atistaeus had rekindled—as strong as ever. It was good news that Sarpedon had need of him for something important. He nodded.

The Admiral smiled. "Good. Let's talk then of how this can best be done."

Alektrion spent several more hours in the study, so absorbed he was surprised when he emerged that it was already late afternoon. He had told Sarpedon he intended to try to see Leesandra. He knew how Sarpedon felt about "scheming priestesses," but there was no way he could, or would, conceal his intentions from this man who had given him so much. Sarpedon had frowned, then said, "What will you do if she's taken another lover? Or if she won't see you?"

His reply. "Then that will be the end of it."

He had planned to go to the Temple this day. Now he thought of waiting. Perhaps he should get settled in. "What a ridiculous excuse for not finding out bad news." He turned toward the Temple and marched forward. With every step his heart beat faster. To a porter attending the southwestern entry he said, "I must see Leesandra of Phaestos, daughter of Danae." The porter he'd singled out was somewhat old for the job; Alektrion hoped age indicated understanding.

The thought suddenly occurred that Leesandra might have been sent away. "Do you know, does she still reside here?"

"Danae's daughter is well known. She oversees the storehouse."

"You do speak of Leesandra of Phaestos?" Could his Leesandra could have risen so high in so few years?

"As you say."

"Will you take a message to her?"

"That's not my duty." The porter glanced at Alektrion's naval dress. "Keftians may enter at the eastern portal. You'll have access there to any number of people who can tell you where to send word to her."

Alektrion felt sudden warmth under his tunic. "I'm not initiated. I'm not Keftian and cannot set foot in any areas except those for foreigners." From his sidebag, he fished out ten pistatas. "Will you take a message from me, search out someone who can tell you where she is, and deliver the message to her?"

The porter's gaze wandered to the honors embroidered on Alektrion's sleeve. "My brother was at Impios, marine. Keep your pistatas. What is your so urgent message?"

"Tell her that Alektrion of Kalliste waits for her here."

The porter smiled. "I shouldn't be long."

He found a bench in the shade, let a kindly breeze cool him, tried to prepare himself for an answer he didn't want to hear.

In less than a quarter of an hour, the porter returned. "The priestess says you should meet her in the hetaira garden."

It took all of Alektrion's will power not to run the whole way. With a heart driving his blood so hard his head throbbed, he waited for her under the Koumaria tree.

She appeared at the head of a path lined with full blooming white and lavender crown poppies and walked to him with extraordinary grace. His vision swam. A flounced kilt of dazzling colors lay over her skirt and both swayed at her ankles. Her tight linen blouse hinted at pleasures of warm breasts beneath the fabric.

She flew into his arms, her body shaking, her arms wound tightly around him. *This is my heart's home.* Her head was lowered, her cheek against his shoulder, and nestled in a swirl of dark curls was his sea eagle hairpin.

He managed to force out of a throat constricted by emotion, "You wear my pin."

"I am never without it, Alek."

She looked up at him. Tears streaked her cheeks. She took his hand and pulled him toward the bright red door.

28

In spring of my twenty-third year, Alektrion returned to me. I'd thought I was fulfilled and happy, thought I knew the meaning of joy, but the moment I saw him I learned the depth to which a woman can deceive herself. Had he not returned, I would have lived my entire life unsuspecting of what I lacked, existing as only half a being. I learned to know full joy, a sweet glow in the center of my being, only after Alektrion's return.

Sadly, in the years since his leaving, my life had journeyed on without him. Had he remained in Knossos, my time and duties would have shaped themselves to have a consistent place for him. That routine wasn't possible now. My responsibilities had grown too weighty, and he was often away from Knossos for weeks at a time for his admiral. I didn't know how he spent his days or exactly what he did for Sarpedon. He didn't want to speak of it and, fearing what he might tell me, I didn't ask. We saw each other no more than once each moon cycle—but our moments together gave me immeasurable joy.

Perhaps in part to make up for my unreasonable—and, to the Temple, unsuitable—love for him, I gave more than full effort in my duties. I also took a vital step toward serving as a warship priestess by requesting training in the healing arts. As often as I could, in places where I thought it might matter, I discreetly mentioned my goal.

A little over a year passed, and I was appointed Damkina's chamberlain. Sarpedon's agitations provoked heated discussions between Damkina and her advisors. Alektrion's admiral continued to insist Knossos make war, and rumors regularly reached Damkina that key people involved in the Poseidon heresy were in league with Atistaeus. I came to agree. I was astounded when Damkina didn't.

Then Keftiu suffered two devastating quakings. Several hundred people were killed. A fourth of the city's homes were damaged. Oenopion pounced on the opportunity. He spread the rumor that the "Earth Shaker" was warning that we must declare him a god equal with the Lady. I felt a kind of stunned anguish. Why would the Lady allow this devastation during such troubled times? The Poseidonists' increasing strength was shockingly demonstrated when Minyas openly embraced Poseidon. I shuddered to the core.

Never would he have done so unless he felt certain of substantial public support.

Galatea sensed my revulsion. We never spoke of this outrage, but another prickly branch had sprouted on the thorny barrier between us. She visited Kishar's less often. She spent time with sisters I didn't know. I wondered what they talked about.

When I chanced to meet Lynceus, we spoke mostly about his poetry. He had even written a poem especially for me about a sea priestess—thrilling, beautiful, even funny. But when he spoke of his half-sister, he grew sad. "She's taken a lover, a young prince from the mainland. A Poseidonist, if you can believe that. Galatea must have completely lost her senses because, from the Temple's perspective, her choice is wildly unsuitable for one of the Mother's priestesses." He sighed. "At least it used to be."

I wondered, feeling a surge of guilt, if Lynceus knew my own lover wasn't Keftian. And what he might think.

One day Zuliya and I met in a garden near the Temple. "What do you think Damkina feels about the Poseidonists?" he asked.

"They alarm her, of course. But frankly, I don't think she has any idea how vile they are."

He crumbled bread into the garden pool for its silvery white fish. "The Lady's Voice might be wise to declare that the religion is false and to raze their temple and shrines."

I said, trying to speak in a calm voice, "That would solve nothing. The Poseidonists would take up clubs and sticks. Any weapon they could find. Kishar says if we do what you suggest, we'd have fighting and death in the streets."

"But I've heard talk among military men that the priest, Oenopion, should be banished to Lissimos."

"Zuliya! Surely you don't agree. Banishment is a death sentence. That's not the Mother's way. Banishment is for only the most heinous crimes."

He shot me an inquiring look. "Perhaps such a move is necessary. Perhaps that is what is required now. Damkina appears dangerously close to losing control."

My blood thrummed in my ears. "Burning a temple, any temple, is against the Law."

He took my arm and we resumed our stroll. "The idea you seem to favor, to simply close their temple and shrines and forbid worship is scarcely less futile than Damkina's doing nothing. I fear someone who can command had better wake up soon or—"

I stopped, glaring at him. "Are you saying I'm asleep? That I don't know exactly how contemptible this false religion is."

"I didn't say that. But I recommend you consider what I've said." He took my arm again, and changed the topic to my father and news of home.

Within the month, Galatea and I were chosen for the Council of Fifty. If one includes the hetaira and the laborers giving their voluntary year of service, over ten thousand of the People lived and worked in the Temple environs; and the Council of Fifty, chosen from senior priestesses and priests, advised the High Priestess on all aspects of Temple activity. The appointment distressed me: this wasn't a usual path for a sea priestess. But it was a position of notable influence, so I resolved to use that influence as forcefully as possible.

That summer's uncommonly long heat wave left the city baked and dusty, the animals thin, the People tense. The drought was so extraordinary that the Memory Keepers added it to their chant. The summer passed, autumn arrived. Heebe had made a boon friend, a woman whose family had rebuilt their quake-damaged country home. Heebe asked me to make the dedication. I agreed, thrilled to spend a day under the sky.

We took the Phaestos road walking together in the early morning. Not far beyond the turn-off for Kishar's house, traffic dwindled to nothing. Except on market day when the road was filled with carts and people on foot, this far out of Knossos, one usually met only Temple messengers or large caravans. At a traveler's way-station we turned onto a dirt road and hurried onward half-an-hour's walk. The limbs in the olive orchards on both sides of us drooped with unpicked fruit. The air was crisp. The pleasantly acrid scent of burning wood from the farmstead's ovens reached us just as I caught sight of the single-story manor.

The dedication was suitably solemn, and afterward the manor's mistress served us celebratory sweet bread, honey, and salepi tea. At midday we started back. We had just stopped beside the stone well of the traveler's way-station to drink when I heard a low grumbling sound. The ground lifted me as though I were a child's doll.

Heebe and I shrieked. From below us, demons seemed to ram the earth. Suddenly I was thrown away from the well and landed on my back. A stone the size of a bucket barely missed my forehead. Boards and bricks flew in all directions. My chest was gripped with such terror I couldn't breathe. Sweet Mother. I'd never experienced shaking this strong. I grabbed at the dirt with both hands as if to stop the horrific rolling.

I turned to speak to Heebe as an even greater jolt rocked the ground. The stone wall of the well twisted and then collapsed; the pressure split the wooden beam supporting the rope and bucket. As thick as a man's thigh, the beam split with a squealing crack into three long shafts that flew apart. One of them, the size of my arm, pierced Heebe in the belly like a warrior's spear, rammed her down flat on her back, and buried its jagged tip into the heaving earth.

Heebe's shrieks turned into a warbling scream. The sound filled every corner of my mind. Her legs and arms writhed. Icy waves of horror raced under my skin from my chest to the tips of finger and toes. *I'm not here. This isn't happening. Sweet Mother, let this not be real!*

The shaking stopped. Heebe's screams continued. My legs wouldn't carry me. I crawled to her.

She clutched at my blouse.

I saw no blood. The stake simply went in one side and through her body; its other end disappeared into the ground.

I pushed myself to my feet. Hands shaking, I grasped the end of the wood thinking to pull it out.

Tears streamed down her face. "Help me. For mercy's sake." A spot of red touched the corner of her mouth. She gasped for air. Her every labored breath burned in my chest.

I pulled at the stake. It didn't budge. Perhaps it was driven in too deeply. Perhaps terror had weakened me.

Tears pouring down my cheeks, I ran to the building that had been the wayfarer's station, looking for the woman or her husband. It sat in dismaying ruin. Nothing moved but the dust in the air that was settling over rubble that had been a home.

"Little bird. Don't leave me."

I rushed back to her and knelt. "I can't move it."

She clutched wildly at my hand and then my skirt.

"I'll go. I'll get help."

But from where? The manor lay far behind us. We'd met no one coming along the road. No workers in the orchards. I rose to run to the Phaestos road.

She cried, a pitiful wail. "No, no. Don't leave me. For pity's sake, kill me."

I knelt again and took her hand. Merciful Goddess, she squeezed mine so fiercely. Tears blinded me. I scrubbed them away.

She grabbed a fistful of my blouse. Her grip was easily as strong as Alektrion's. "You can't save me. The moment the thing's removed I'll die." Her voice trembled but her words were sure. "Find something. A knife from the house. I can't bear this pain."

Violently, I shook my head.

"Would you ..." She gasped for another breath. "Leave me. Like this?"

"Dearest, dearest Heebe. I won't leave you. But I can't kill you."
Merciful Mother! Help her. "I'll pray the Ancient comes quickly."

Only the Ancient can end life. That's the Law. That's the Law.
Still my arms ached to bundle my skirt and press it to her face to
release her quickly.   Instead, I scooted on the ground and lay her
head in my lap. She began again to wail. Shuddering, I stroked her
hair.

The wrenching sound ripped into my heart. She'll die any moment, I thought. I prayed. *Please. Let her die now. Please.*

But she didn't.

"You must take her, Great Mother," I sobbed.

But she did not die. She grew ever weaker, her moaning fainter,
but the Ancient didn't come.

"Leesandra." Her voice was a whisper now. "End this pain. I beg
you."

"You are my dear nanny," I said, words choked because a great
hand was strangling me. "I love you, dearest Heebe."

"Yes. I know."

The sun moved, the shadow formed by the stake in her belly shifted
over the ground.

She squeezed my hand, clutched it tightly, but her grip was wan-
ing pitifully. "My dearest Little Bird," she whispered, her last words.

I knew the moment her spirit left. She drew a breath, did not let it
go, and drew no other.

I bent over her, spirit sick. I kissed her cheek, inhaled deeply of the
smell of her skin. Soon that smell, which had filled my baby days and
comforted me through childhood, would be forever gone. A chilling
void, dark, empty, lonely, and silent spread around me. A great primal wailing welled up from my spirit's center and between snatches
of breath spilled out in an unstoppable torrent. No one, not even my
mother, would love me more steadfastly than Heebe.

The sun was long past midday when I suddenly realized she'd
grown cold. I laid her head on the ground and slid away.

I don't know how long I waited on the rubble that had been the
wall of the well, but a loud, excited voice finally drew me back to this
world. I looked up to see a disheveled donkey caravan hurrying into
the yard. The three men and two women spoke gently to me. The
men freed Heebe from the stake, then set to work to find the bodies of
the station mistress and her family. We wrapped each of the family
members in the birth position in some good linen one of the women
found in the rubble and we buried them.

I explained that I wanted to take Heebe back with me. The men
put her linen-wrapped body across one of their animals. Nothing

seemed amiss along the first part of the road. I was alone with my thoughts. Dark, dark thoughts. What had Heebe ever done to deserve such horror? How could the Lady—the Lady whom Heebe had loved with such unfailing devotion—have permitted it?

And I, too, had permitted it, hadn't I? Heebe had begged me to free her. I remembered Alek and what he'd said when he killed the wounded swallow. "Sometimes we have to do things, terrible things, to accomplish a good end." I'd been satisfied to recite the Law while my whole body had been screaming for me to wrap my skirts around her face and press them there until she fell asleep.

Was I a coward? Was I heartless, even to the pleas of my dear Heebe? "Listen to your heart," Zuliya always said. "Your heart is a good one." Why had I not stiffened my backbone and done what my heart counseled?

I looked back to where her body lay across the sturdy donkey. Tears overwhelmed me. I quickly shifted my gaze forward and pressed the back of my hand to my lips against my sobbing.

By late afternoon, as we drew closer to town, I was sure of one thing: I'd hardened my heart to Heebe's cries and every moment of pain she'd suffered thereafter was an everlasting debit against my spirit. I had done a great wrong.

We encountered more traffic. Frightened shouts and stares from people we passed assaulted me.

"Disaster."

"I hear the Temple's caught on fire."

"Boats were shoved right up onto the shore."

"Hundreds, maybe thousands dead."

The Bull Ring had collapsed. Within the day messengers brought astonishing word of ruin as far south as Gortis. The Temple churned in chaos.

The day following Heebe's death, I forced myself to rise. To pray. To preside at the ceremony to bury her. Life, I repeatedly chanted, must continue to flow.

We weren't alone at the burial ground. Families and friends of the many dead kept us grim company. I tried to feel nothing. I wanted desperately to behave with the dignity and even the joyful spirit such a moment called for. Heebe was, after all, returning to the Mother, to rest and refresh until the Lady would again send her to this world. But, the pain of Heebe's dying—how could the Mother allow it? And Knossos was reeling under the burden of so many dead. Years ago I hadn't understood how the Goddess could have allowed the sacrificial death of a single slave boy. Beneath my grief and guilt, anger stirred again.

Heebe had made many friends, so altogether some one hundred people gathered despite the surrounding devastation. Galatea brought her new lover, Hylas, a royal youth who was studying at the international academy. He was a Poseidonist from Korinthos. Galatea had brought a Poseidonist with her to a funeral for Heebe!

A small meal awaited our party in an area of the burial garden set aside for after-funeral feasting. Everything had gone smoothly enough when Alektrion said to Zuliya, "You have studied with many teachers. What do you think causes this shaking of the earth?"

Zuliya hesitated a moment, fingering an earring in thought, when Hylas burst in, "Everyone knows the God does it when He's angry."

To this point, Hylas had been noticeably quiet, I imagined because of being with so many strangers. A tense stillness immediately charged the air. Galatea put her hand on Hylas's arm and said diplomatically, "But surely, He acts only with permission of the Goddess."

Alektrion's face reddened, but he and Zuliya remained silent. The woman who owned Heebe's boarding house asked Hylas, her eyes full of surprise, "Are you a Poseidonist?"

"I worship the God." He held his jaw firm. "And by these shakings the God is warning that He's angry His authority isn't recognized on Keftiu."

The look in the woman's eyes could have lit fires. "The followers of this foreign religion are destroying the Lady's harmony."

Again Galatea interrupted. "I think we should all remember that we seek harmony. And the only way we can have harmony is if all people worship as they wish."

I simply couldn't keep still. "You're wrong. I know what the Poseidonists do, and it mustn't be allowed on Keftiu. Not ever."

Galatea's lips drew into a tight line and she linked an arm with Hylas's. "What is the reason for your implacable dislike? If Damkina would simply agree to let those who believe in the Achean god worship as they like, all this strife would end."

No one moved. Alektrion balled one hand into a fist.

"The hour grows late," Zuliya said. "My leg begins to pain me. I must go back."

"I'll accompany you," Alektrion said.

"Yes. It's late," I added. "We have wished Heebe good journey. The damage around us is great. We have work to do and Heebe would be the first to tell us to put our hands to it."

The guests dispersed, the afterfeast wasn't eaten.

From that time, whenever Galatea and I passed in the halls or courts of the Temple we nodded, but always feigned hurry, as if we had pressing business, and so couldn't stop just now to chat. The one time

I tried to smooth things, she said I was unreasonable, turned her back, and walked away.

On the fourth day after the quaking, news arrived from Kalliste by fastship. The messenger was brought before Damkina. "Most Revered One, the mountain of fire on Kalliste has fully awakened!"

A terrifying coldness gripped me. My parents! My friends!

There had been no warning, just a sudden jolt and a deafening cataclysmic noise from the mountain. Rocks were thrown from the volcano's mouth, boulders so large they could be seen from Alyris. The stench of rotten breath from the mountain saturated the air, debris billowed into the sky.

"Kalliste is being smothered with a killing ash. And the mountain shows no signs of relenting. I bring word that every ship, large or small, that remained serviceable follows close behind me. They carry fleeing people. Virtually everyone."

Murmurs rippled among the assembled council members and staff.

What of my parents? Our house servants? Meidra and her family? My work immediately doubled so I couldn't leave the Temple, but Zuliya waited each day at the harbor, watching as overflowing ships arrived from Kalliste and empty ones raced to return. Refugees flooded all of Keftiu's northern ports.

The twelfth day after this disaster, a ship arrived carrying my father's chief aide. On the day of the eruption, my mother and father had gone to the dedication of a workshop in a town northwest of Alyris. They did not return—and would not.

I broke away from Zuliya, went to my tiny room, and threw myself onto my knees beside my bed and cried. I remained there for two days, until Alektrion sent a message. He had returned and was concerned for me. So selfish was I! So consumed with the grief of those around me. I had not thought of his possible losses.

I learned from Zuliya that Alektrion's parents were alive and had fled to Sitia. I never learned Meidra's fate. The days, weeks, and months that followed blended into a maelstrom of woes. I never saw Alektrion. The work necessary to transfer all Kallistan naval functions to Keftiu consumed him.

Four months after the great quaking, in the dead of winter at the end of the festival of Gavrinos, the despicable heretic Minyas gave an impassioned speech before a special assembly of the Council. He asserted that the Goddess had allowed these grievous ills to strike Kalliste and Keftiu because She wanted to take Poseidon as Her co-equal consort and that the People weren't listening to Her.

For two days Damkina closeted herself with Nothos and four of the Wise Women. Council members and others whose hands took the pulse of the People flowed in a constant stream into and out of her antechambers. From one of her maids, I learned she spent each night in her sanctuary behind the Mother's Womb. I was sure Damkina was seeking wisdom by taking the poppy.

On the fourth day, she assembled the hundreds of Temple priestesses and priests in the Central Court. Dressed in the full attire of her authority with a living charis wound round each arm, she sat on the balcony overlooking the Central Court in her Chair of Speaking. She would speak with the voice of the Goddess.

"The worship of Poseidon is contradictory to the Lady's Way. The temple of Poseidon will be closed. Further public worship of Poseidon is forbidden. Soldiers will enforce this decree."

Yes! At last. Knowing Alektrion's heart, I listened for what she would say about Atistaeus.

"We will stand firm against all who challenge the Lady's Way or the People. Our navy, our impenetrable defense, will remain strong. But we do not make war. War is the greatest cause of disharmony and imbalance. Further talk of an invasion of the mainland will cease."

Alektrion and his admiral would not celebrate this night.

"The Temple must be cleansed. Some among you, the Lady's chosen, have been seduced by barbarian ideas. You believe it's possible to serve the Goddess and at the same time accept the worship of Poseidon. I say this divided loyalty is heresy. It is not acceptable. Those who hold this view destroy Temple harmony. They must leave.

"Examine your hearts. If you will stay and rededicate yourselves to the Goddess alone, move to the court's northern end. If not, move to the southern end. Those who cannot give absolute obedience will reside henceforth at the complex in the olive groves west of Knossos until this heresy ceases."

I searched for Galatea. When I saw her moving to the opposite end of the court, one among several score of priestesses and priests, I couldn't hold back tears. She was my first friend on Keftiu. Together we had survived Hopthea. And loved Thunder. And taken our first steps onto these very grounds. When I'd met her, Galatea had wanted nothing in her life but to serve the Goddess. Her family had produced High Priestesses. Sometimes I'd wondered if she didn't aspire to that position herself. Now she'd cast her lot with those who defied the Lady's Voice. The thorny barrier between us was now as sharp as that between the living and the dead.

Sadness shifted to alarm. Perhaps a fourth of the Mother's servants were moving with Galatea. The Mistress of Weavers grabbed my arm and said, "I've been so afraid of this happening. Can you believe so many of the Mother's own servants are willing to compromise with this foul religion? Damkina should have acted long ago. My heart is broken, Leesandra. What is happening to the People?"

"We must pray it's not too late."

"I have heard there are even some among the Wise Ones who say these disturbances of the earth show that the Mother does wish to take Poseidon, not Velchanos, as consort."

"No Wise One would ever support such a defilement of the Sacred Marriage." Of this I was confident, but still, the number of brothers and sisters joining Galatea was frightening.

"Tragedy," Zuliya said later of Damkina's pronouncements. "Closing the Poseidonist temple won't stop Atistaeus. But she's stirring a hornet's nest, sure enough. She's going to have to start watching her back."

"What do you mean?"

He shrugged. "Just an old traveler's worry. Oenopion is dangerous. He won't let this move go unanswered."

A month passed. My thoughts were absorbed in preparations for the festival celebrating Velchanos's return from the underworld. Not surprisingly, the festival had the largest attendance any Memories could recall. Knossos bulged with refugees; there were no rooms to be had, two and three families occupied spaces designed for couples, and many people lived in makeshift encampments on the city's edges. Sea season began and Sarpedon was determined to see for himself the damage on Kalliste. He also wanted to check naval facilities on other islands. He took Alektrion with him.

Shortly after the festival, I received an urgent message from Alek. *Meet me at once in the hetaira garden. It concerns Damkina.*

He looked tired, disheveled, and was extremely distracted. He'd obviously not taken time to rest or bathe. "I must speak to the vizier at once. Can you arrange it?"

"Of course." I'd never seen him so agitated.

I started to take him to Nothos's offices by the most direct route when I remembered his uninitiated status. I stopped. I felt myself flush and hated that there was any reason I should be embarrassed. This man had dedicated his life to serving the Goddess, yet he could not set foot on dedicated ground. It was wrong! He had never once complained, but once told me about a Temple on Samos. There he had been welcomed.

I said, "I'm sorry." We retraced our path to go the longer way, the one used by foreigners.

The Badger's reception room was full, his door closed, but seeing me, his warden smiled and opened the door for us himself. Nothos had been writing. After an exchange of greetings, he gestured to chairs in front of his desk and we sat. "And what word, then, does Sarpedon send to Nothos that is so urgent?"

Alektrion leaned forward, his hand gripping the edge of the desk, and said, "One of Sarpedon's spies, a despicable little weasel who's usually right, claims he's heard of a plot against Damkina."

"Why does this not surprise me?" the Badger said with an archly lifted eyebrow.

"I don't mean a political plot against her authority. I mean a plot to kill her."

His face remained like stone, but Nothos blinked several times. "Preposterous. This is no barbarian land. No one would raise a hand to the Lady's Voice."

"I tell you, take this threat seriously. This informant has never been wrong."

"Then be more specific. Who exactly imagines they can do such a thing?"

"I can't be more clear, other than to add that the little weasel suggested I get myself here as fast as my feet would carry me."

Nothos leaned back, pressed the tips of his fingers together in a little pyramid and gazed at the ceiling. "Not to offer any disrespect to Sarpedon," he looked back at Alektrion, "but my Head of the Guards has reported no whisper of any such connivance. I find the idea unbelievable."

Alektrion's voice remained calm, but the muscle at the corner of his jaw clenched. "With all due respect to the Temple's Head of the Guards, this news is urgent. It must be taken immediately to Damkina."

The office door swung open. Glaucon, the Head of the Guards, stepped in. He was even taller than Alektrion, and though the Memories said he'd been slim when he'd begun Temple service, the years had thickened his waist, chest, and hips. His hair was still dark, no trace of gray. He entered slowly, as if with studied care because of his great size. For some reason, from the day I'd met him, he reminded me of my bull, Thunder. I respected him. In a deep voice that matched his commanding body, he said, "Please excuse my interruption, Nothos, but I bring important news."

I half rose, thinking we would be dismissed, but Nothos gestured for us to remain. "I believe you've met Alektrion, Sarpedon's chief aide," Nothos said to Glaucon.

The Head of the Guards nodded.

"Alektrion, too, has brought news you should hear. But first, what have you?"

Glaucon stepped to Nothos's desk and placed on it a large gold shoulder pin, then took one of the chairs. I stared at the pin, breathless with surprise. I recognized it. He spoke. "Lynceus, the son of Minyas, has been killed. He was murdered sometime yesterday, Nothos."

Lynceus? My dear poet? Murdered? I clutched Alektrion's arm and held on tightly.

"How? Where?" Nothos demanded.

"In his aunt's townhome. As you know, Minyas retreated some time ago to their county estate, but his son remained in the city. He was stabbed. This pin was in his hand."

Murder! Brilliant, gentle Lynceus. *The world is spinning too wildly for me to hang on.* "I knew Lynceus." My voice was so soft I scarcely heard myself. "He was my friend."

"The pin most certainly belongs to his murderer," Glaucon added.

Again I spoke, softly. "Surely not. I know the pin's owner."

The three men stared at me.

"The pin belongs to an Achean youth from Korinthos, named Hylas. He's in his last year at the international academy."

Nothos frowned. "How can you know this?"

"I know Hylas. The pin is his family's crest." I looked to Alektrion. "You've seen the pin. I'm sure Hylas wore it to Heebe's funeral."

Alektrion looked at Nothos and nodded. "Yes. I do recognize it. He bragged to me that it's his family's crest. His father is their king."

What could have possessed Hylas? How could he do such a dreadful thing to Galatea? Kill her brother! Why?

Glaucon strode to the office door, opened it, signaled the warden. "Have my aide in here at once."

Nothos strained forward and addressed Alektrion. "Tell Glaucon what your little spy claims."

Alektrion complied.

"The Mother's Sweet Opening," Glaucon spat, so agitated he'd forgotten my presence. I heard the door, and Glaucon's aide stood in the doorway. "See to the arrest of a Korinthian youth at the international academy," Glaucon directed. "Hylas by name. He is accused of the murder of Lynceus. And send word to Damkina I'll come to her shortly—and she's not to leave her quarters under any circumstances."

The aide touched his hand to his heart then turned to go when the most awful, shrill keening penetrated Nothos's office. I gasped. Nothos, Alektrion, and I rose from our chairs. The bizarre sound continued, grew in volume. Someone in Nothos's office took up the cry. The old priestess, I thought. She'd been there when we came in. I looked from Glaucon to Nothos seeking an explanation.

Nothos had gone as white as milk. "This ... must not be," he whispered.

29

The direful wailing made Alektrion's skin shrink against his flesh. Leesandra asked, "What does it mean?"

Nothos seemed unable to speak. Glaucon answered. "It's the death keening, Danae's daughter. It means the Voice of the Goddess is dead." The soldier bolted from the office.

Too late, Alektrion thought. *I've come too late.*

Nothos snapped out of his paralysis. He rose, ran around his desk and out into his antechamber. Leesandra followed Nothos. Alektrion followed her. They hadn't proceeded far, though, when she rushed past two door wardens and onto dedicated ground. Alektrion stopped.

She quickly realized he couldn't follow and ran back. She took his hand, squeezed hard. "I'll come to you this afternoon if I can. Just before dinner." She spun around and, with her skirt whipping at her ankles, rushed after the vizier.

Perhaps he should inform Sarpedon. But Sarpedon would know within the quarter hour from his personal Temple messenger. At the massive cedar doors to the south portico, dignitaries from a dozen lands waited, expecting an audience with Damkina. They milled about, asking each other what the wailing meant and why half the guards had rushed away. What, by the Goddess's evil children, was happening? Knossos had suffered enormous disruption, to say nothing of what had been unleashed on Kalliste. And now Damkina! The world was upside down, as if Kokor had slain the Mother and She was no longer present to protect Her People.

And what about two deaths in peaceful Knossos, in such close succession? Lynceus and Damkina. And Minyas a figure in the lives of both. It was no coincidence that Lynceus was Minyas's son. In his bones Alektrion had no doubts of a connection. And how did that hot-headed fool Hylas get involved?

By the Goddess! He stopped in place, astonished. He remembered something else the weasel had said. "If I'm right, and I'm always right, look to the mainland."

Alektrion had assumed that the weasel referred to Atistaeus and to Pylos. Hylas was a Korinthian. And Korinth was allied with Atistaeus. A political link between Korinth and Pylos certainly didn't prove the deaths were joined, but an especially rotten smell tainted the air. A Pylian smell.

Lynceus was the son of Keftiu's most wealthy man and, perhaps more important, the young poet had been well liked. Honored. Hylas would be desperate to escape. All of Keftiu could not hide a Korinthian prince accused of killing Lynceus. And escape meant a boat.

Alektrion changed direction and walked just short of breaking into a run. Down the Phaestos road, down a little side street known for its taverns, down another, even more narrow, to the boarding house of Talos and Anchices. Talos sat at the front of the building whittling while he listened to old men discussing the wrestling match held the previous day between the champions of the Seven Cities. At Alektrion's gesture, Talos rose and followed Alektrion to the public square. "Where is Anchices?" Alektrion asked. "He knows the shipping news at both harbors."

"In Amnissos. Probably aboard the *Shark*."

"The Lady's Voice is dead. And Lynceus, the son of that traitor Minyas, has been killed. I think the killer will try to escape on a Korinthian vessel, and I need you both. We're going to catch the slimy piece of Achean seal dung before he gets away."

Talos gave Alektrion a wicked grin. One-eyed Talos loved a fight.

They went to Talos's room and armed themselves with knives—carrying weapons was forbidden on Keftiu, but they could at least conceal knives. Talos brought a blade for Anchices. They found him on the wharf just leaving Sarpedon's flagship. Alektrion explained his suspicions.

Anchices nodded. Unlike Talos, Anchices took the news grim faced. "Three Korinthian vessels are here now. One, a small ship bearing amber and exotic furs, arrived yesterday. I can't imagine it leaving soon, not before its cargo is offloaded. Two other ships are big vessels." He paused, thinking, then, "The *Golden Stag* wasn't due to depart for a week, but she could be readied in hours if her captain wanted to leave badly enough."

Alektrion nodded. Anchices turned and led as they wove their way down the wharf dodging people and goods. The *Golden Stag* lay on the harbor's far side. And she had been brought to the wharf for loading. Anchices asked, "What do you intend, Alek?"

"We'll board and search her."

"Without permission?"

Alektrion didn't bother to answer. He darted up the loading ramp. Four seamen were passing beehive-sized amphorae from a stack on the deck to men in the hold. They stopped working. Glaring, one asked, "What are you doing here?"

"I'm on official business of the port controller. We're ordered to search this vessel. It's been reported you carry unregistered, illegal amounts of Temple wine."

The seaman's look hardened still more. "Where's your papers?" All four men squared their stance. Again the seaman spoke. "You're not searching anything. Not until our captain is here. Not without permission."

"You heard my friend," Talos broke in with his fearsome, guttural whisper. "Just keep out of our way. Or get off the ship if you don't like it."

The four men rushed them. Alektrion took a blow to the jaw. He returned it, grabbed the man's arm, twisted it behind the man's back, ran him to the side of the ship and shoved him over. The sound of his yell and the splash split the air. An audience would soon gather.

He heard scuffling. Something hit him on the back of the head. Momentarily blinded, he grabbed the railing, ducked in case another blow was coming, spun around and charged into his attacker's midriff. They crashed onto the deck. Alektrion landed a solid blow to the man's jaw. His assailant went limp. Alektrion leapt up and turned to find Talos and Anchices grinning over two more motionless bodies.

Celebration was brief. Four more men clambered onto the deck from the hold. More scuffling and slugging. Alektrion took a hit to the right eye, but the four seamen rapidly found themselves on their bellies on the deck with Talos and Anchices binding their wrists. Alektrion's eye was giving off flashing lights, throbbing, and starting to swell shut.

From the wharf someone yelled, "What's happening there?"

Alektrion strode to the railing. A handful of men stared back, all plain seamen or laborers. "We're on business of the Keftian admiral, Sarpedon. It's best for your health if you tend to your own affairs." He didn't wait for argument or reply. His threat wouldn't likely stop them from reporting what they'd seen. If the Korinthian murderer was here, and if he was to find and question him personally, there wasn't much time. "Anchices. Search the bow. Talos the stern. I'll look mid-ship."

By ladder he entered the mid-ship hold. In a few seconds his good eye adjusted to the dimness. The dank air smelled of oil and salt, wet clay and musty straw. He drew his knife. His swelling eye made judging distances difficult. Twenty some odd baskets occupied the far right corner. Maybe behind them ... Or behind the pile of stacked amphorae in the left corner ... He glanced over his shoulder. Two rows of giant oil pithoi on beds of straw stood laced into their holding cradles.

Keeping one eye on the pithoi, he strode toward the baskets. Straw rustled from behind the pithoi. A male figure dashed toward the ladder. Alektrion tackled him waist high. The struggling man screeched loud enough to be heard in Phaestos. Alektrion brought him to his knees, then to his belly, and then used one hand to slam his forehead against the deck—hard enough to frighten, but not to kill.

The body beneath him was slender. He didn't even have to see the face to know it was Hylas. Aware that he didn't have much time, he took his weight off the young prince's back, flipped him over, put a knee in the center of Hylas's chest and twisted one arm above Hylas's head. The Korinthian's hand held a long-bladed knife. Alektrion easily twisted the weapon free and threw it into a corner. He placed his knife to Hylas's throat just as Talos and Anchices slid, one behind the other, down the ladder into the hold.

"Why did you kill Lynceus?" Alektrion demanded.

"You Keftian pig. Get off me."

Alektrion pressed the knife firmly against the flesh. He spoke very softly. "You don't understand, little boy. Tell me what I want to know, now, or I'm going to kill you."

He felt Hylas's muscles tense and, even in the dim light, could tell the Korinthian lost color. "I repeat, but only once. Why Lynceus? And how is Minyas involved in the death of the Lady's Voice?"

Hylas still remained silent.

Alektrion sliced a shallow curve along the Korinthian's throat. Hylas howled. Blood rose in the wound, trickled down pale skin and dropped into the straw. "Your life, young prince, means nothing to me. Don't think of escape. I will know why you killed Lynceus before we leave this ship or you won't leave it alive." Using his knife hand, Alektrion grabbed Hylas's hair and again banged his head against the deck.

Hylas stuttered, then blurted out, "You spineless Keftians will never stop the Red King. He's going to have Keftiu, one way or the other."

Alektrion heard footsteps running over the deck above him. "By Kokor, tell me!" he shouted. The knife hand at Hylas's throat, tensed for a final cut. "Why Lynceus?"

Talos put a fist around Alektrion's wrist. "Don't do it, Alek. You've caught him. Leave him to the Temple. Glaucon will deal with him. Sarpedon needs you. He won't want you involved in a killing now."

A deep voice said from the deck, "What's going on here?" A handful of Temple guards clambered down the ladder.

Hylas screamed, "He's going to kill me!"

Alektrion couldn't let go. Talos's fingers tightened on Alektrion's wrist like wet, shrinking hide. "Don't, Alek."

Shaking with the effort, Alektrion pulled his blade from the youth's throat. He stood, backed away from the Poseidonist scum, and turned to find Temple guards staring at him and the insignia on his arm. "This man is wanted for the killing of Lynceus, the son of Minyas," he said. "Don't let him get away, or Glaucon will have your skin."

Walking back to town with Talos and Anchices, he tried to put the best light he could on capturing Hylas. He hadn't gotten the answers he wanted. But Hylas had mentioned Atistaeus. Alektrion was certain now of a link between the deaths of Lynceus and Damkina. Certain, too, that Minyas was the key and that Minyas and Atistaeus were in league. But why kill Damkina? For the most part she had been totally ineffective. Had Damkina remained in place, Atistaeus wouldn't have needed to fear an invasion of Pylos. And Knossos was in turmoil—divided and unsure in its religious loyalties, growing ever weaker from within. Why kill her?

Ten days after Damkina's death Alektrion finally received word from Leesandra that she would see him. Several times he'd tried to reach her, but she would send a note saying the Temple was in chaos, she couldn't spare a moment. They met under the koumaria tree. She looked worn and thin. He embraced her, kissed one cheek. The flesh under his fingers definitely felt diminished.

"I'm so very tired," she said.

"I see that, my heart."

"I didn't ask for a room. I can't stay that long. I know you captured Hylas."

"I wish I'd had more time alone with him. I learned only enough to make me certain he's in league with the Red King. What about Damkina? The official rumors say she fell ill from something she ate. I don't believe it."

"She was poisoned."

"Who—?"

"Glaucon doesn't know. Everyone who had anything to do with placing food before her that day was detained. No one confessed."

"Somehow Minyas is involved in both deaths. It's no coincidence his son was also killed so close in time."

"I am so terribly angry at Galatea. And yet I grieve for her. Her brother is dead, and her lover will be banished to Lissimos as soon as a new Voice is chosen."

"When will the Wise Women decide? Until they do, Knossos is rudderless."

Since Damkina's death, Sarpedon had been fueling speculations, some about the Hylas-Minyas-Lynceus-Damkina connection, but mostly about the possible identity of the new High Priestess. "If the new Voice is capable of rational thought," he had said, "we have time before the end of the sea season to launch an attack."

The new Voice would be young, that was certain. Between twenty and twenty-five. A younger woman, it was said, wouldn't have enough life experience nor have been sufficiently tried, and an older woman would be more inclined to listen to her own voice, not that of the Goddess. Damkina had been chosen at the age of twenty-one.

"In other times," he said, "a delay in making the choice might not matter, but it does now. We still have time to—" He stopped, halted by Leesandra's views on invasion.

"We still have time to what?"

"It's not important. I just wonder about Damkina's replacement."

"The councils of the seven cities vote tomorrow. Each will send two names. Within the week we'll know the fourteen candidates."

Alektrion checked at the Temple portal daily. Finally the list of nominees was posted. Halfway down he read:

Leesandra of Kalliste, daughter of Danae.

He read her name again, clenched suddenly sticky palms. *Sweet Mother, No! She's mine.*

Sweat broke out on his forehead. What were the chances Leesandra would be picked? On the face of it, only one in fourteen. He tried to calm himself, but his body wouldn't listen. He had to snatch her away. Come by night and take her some place else. To Samos. To Canaan. To Agyptos if necessary.

If Leesandra were chosen High Priestess, they would have much less time together. Time! *Fool!* Time wasn't the problem. The Lady's Voice never—*ever*—set foot off dedicated ground. She couldn't even enter the hetaira quarter. He would never lie with her again. No anticipated stolen moments. Not twice a year, or even once. Never!

A man strode up to read the list, and Alektrion prayed that his raging feelings weren't pasted all over his face.

If Leesandra were chosen High Priestess, he might as well be sent with Hylas to Lissimos. Every year at the Sacred Marriage she would take a new lover, always a young and virile youth.

"She's mine!" he whispered. *Mine alone. I'll not share her.* The man beside him left.

Moments passed. Finally, he forced himself to finish the list. He found Galatea's name. His mind went racing off again, spinning now for entirely different reasons. Galatea was a compromiser. That her name was even on the list meant there were compromisers in very high places, indeed. And should Galatea be chosen, any chance of stopping Atistaeus on his ground instead of at Knossos's door would evaporate.

For two more days he had to wait to meet Leesandra.

"I know what you're thinking," she said the moment she saw him. "It will never happen."

"But it could."

"It won't."

"How can you be so sure?"

"I've never sought to serve in the Temple. I've always had my eyes set on sea service and my intention is well known."

"Then why is your name on the list?"

"Those nominated are never told the reasons, the whys."

"Do we have a room?"

She shook her head.

"You don't have time?"

"I didn't think it would be wise."

He looked around. They were alone in the garden. He thought of her patron, Kishar. How many other candidates had so powerful an advocate among the Wise Women? He knew for a certainty that Leesandra was Kishar's favorite.

With surprising force, shame swamped him. For days his every thought had been centered on how to keep Leesa for himself. What of her? What about the People?

He laid the palm of her hand along his cheek and looked into her eyes. "Would you want this if you are chosen? Could you accept, knowing I could never again lay eyes on you, except from behind a silk partition in the Audience Chamber."

She pressed her cheek to his chest and hugged him tightly. "When I'm with you, as I am now, I want to say no."

"Will you say no?"

She put a finger to his lips. "It won't happen, Alek."

"But what if they do pick you?"

She turned from him. "When I'm in the Temple, Alek, and I see the confusion, and I think of what I've given up to follow the Lady's call. I think if She were, however unlikely, to pick me, I would have to serve. Can you understand?" She looked at him again. Her eyes took on a fiery look. "Certainly Galatea mustn't be chosen."

He started to kiss her. To his surprise, she pulled away.

Whatever happened, he must believe always that her love was his alone. "I tell you right now, a part of me will die if I cannot have you." He swallowed hard. "But the Mother will choose as She wills. Whatever you want, I'll do."

He waited, hoping to hear her say she would reject the call. No matter what he'd just said, that's what he wanted.

She leaned close and kissed his cheek. He pulled her to him, concentrated on her warmth along his body, smelled the light rose perfume in her hair. *I will remember every move, smell, sound, and touch.* He felt sick, shaky—terrified.

Again she pulled away, stepped from him. "I have to go."

"Leesa—"

"Help me, Alek. I can only be strong if you help me."

She turned and left. He stood staring at the door through which she had passed from the garden.

Weeks passed, then a full moon cycle. He tried to be faithful to the spirit of his words, but every time he thought of being physically cut off from her, a vast emptiness engulfed him. He discussed all of the candidates with Sarpedon, and from Sarpedon's perspective, as from Leesandra's, the worst possible choice would be Galatea. Sarpedon prayed Leesandra would be chosen. "You are close to her. You'll be able to persuade her to invade," he said with hopeful enthusiasm.

At last the Temple received word: in ten days, in the Northwest Court, the Wise Women would select the servant whom the Lady had designated as Her Voice.

Sarpedon wasn't in Knossos when the day arrived, but Talos and Anchices were. Alektrion stood with them in the crowd of assembled notables. The fourteen candidates appeared at the portal and filed into the court. Galatea was there. Radiant as ever, she held her back very straight and stared over the heads of the crowd with firmly set lips.

She had stated publicly within a day of the list's posting that were she chosen high priestess, she would take a permanent consort of her choosing. She would make the worship of Poseidon open and co-equal with that of the Lady. Should the Wise Women pick Galatea, they would effectively sanction the Poseidonist heresy. Alektrion couldn't believe this calamity would happen, but then, the world had already become nearly incomprehensible. Anything seemed possible. If Galatea was chosen, Sarpedon would be exiled from Knossos. Alektrion would likely be forced to go with him.

Leesandra looked as beautiful as he'd ever seen her. She caught his eye but didn't in any way acknowledge him before she sat on one of the portable seats. The muscles of his jaws and neck and back tightened, then his guts did the same. It was as if he awaited a possible death sentence.

Five Wise Women appeared. They glided onto the same elevated area and sat. In moments, the oldest—bent from her extraordinary eighty-two years—rose and walked slowly toward the fourteen candidates. She stopped in front of Leesandra.

30

Nonia offered me her wrinkled hand. I told myself, Don't look at Alektrion. The pain of losing him would break my composure.

I am Leesandra. Daughter of Danae. Granddaughter of Ninkasi.

Nonia led me away and, though my heart beat wildly, a strange calm took charge of my spirit. The People were in great pain, and the Mother of All had chosen me.

Through the northern portal, down the long corridor past the wall relief of the Lady's Bull, out into the Central Court. I stole a look behind. The other four Wise Women and the most senior of the Temple priests and priestesses were following including those who'd been candidates with me. Except for Galatea. What a great relief to know that Galatea would be taken back to her place of semi-confinement.

At the entry to the Mother's Womb, we halted, and all remained behind, except Nonia and her sisters. These Wise Ones, including Kishar, accompanied me within. We passed into the interior shrine. No one but the Wise Women and the Lady's Voice ever entered here. This place would be mine alone. Here I would pray. Here I would take the poppy. Here for the rest of my life I would listen for the Goddess to speak.

I felt surprised that the room had cold and unadorned stone floor and walls. The feeling was that of a cave. Then I realized the effect was intended. Keftiu's most sacred sites were the Mother's caves.

Flickering candles stood on either side of a small table of offerings. On the floor opposite the sacrificial table, a deep-woven, brown and black rug provided the room's only bit of comfort. A storage cabinet, darkened with great age, stood against another wall. Nonia shuffled to the table of offerings. From the cabinet Kishar and one of her sisters fetched bread, olives, and dried pomegranate and placed them on the table.

"Danae's daughter, you come here to submit yourself into the Mother's care," Nonia said, "to submerge yourself into Her spirit so you can speak for the People to Her and She can speak to Her People through you. Embrace the Mother, Leesandra."

She pointed to the bare floor below the table of offerings. I did as she commanded: I lay on my belly with my forehead and breasts and the palms of my hands pressed against the floor.

I let you go now, Alek. My tears dropped onto the cold, hard stone.

Nonia chanted, ancient words that married me to the Mother and to the People, never to be parted. The ritual was long. My mind wandered. I couldn't stop it. So much in the world was amiss. And someone had killed Damkina. I shivered. I would have to be very careful.

Finally she stopped. "Your life is no longer yours. You serve the Mother, and we serve you." She and Kishar helped me rise. Each embraced me and kissed my forehead. "Come." She shuffled to the cabinet and opened small doors to reveal a cupboard holding three statuettes.

"These represent the Lady in her three beings—Maiden, Mother, Ancient," Nonia explained. "You may look upon their faces and draw strength as often as you wish. I entrust them into your care as they've been held in trust by the Voices before you. Let nothing happen to them. Should ill befall them, the People will suffer."

I leaned closer to see better. The Maiden's arms were upraised. In each hand she clasped a writhing charis. She wore a checkered apron and, perched on her head, was the mammon, the small animal that symbolizes Her power over all land creatures. The Matron, too, wore flounced skirt and bare-breasted bodice, with three charises wound about Her symbolizing Wisdom, Strength, Compassion. I would need all three. The Ancient wore the white sari of the Wise Women and stood with arms extended forward in the position from which She calls life out of the body.

"You are to remain in communion with the Lady for the next five days," Nonia continued. "All your needs will be cared for. We will bring food and drink. In the cupboard you'll find writing materials. And poppy. Take the poppy as often as you wish, being mindful of what you've been taught about its proper use. In five days, we'll take you before the People."

They turned to go and for a brief moment I was afraid. Afraid of the burden I'd accepted. Afraid ... oh yes, afraid that somehow their choice was a mistake.

And then I was alone.

A tightly covered jar in the cabinet contained fresh poppy cakes. I took three out, sat cross-legged on the rug, and ate them. I relaxed, closed my eyes. The dark embraced me.

I am on Kalliste lying in my special place under the plane tree. The earth is cool. I look up into the canopy of the great tree and as the wind moves the leaves, I watch sunlight wink in and out, flicker and flutter.

The sun shifts in the sky. Time is flowing.

A raven calls, "Come!" I drift up toward the branches.

"Come!" the raven calls again.

A current of wind, sharp with the scent of sage, catches us. We spread our wings. "To the sky," the raven urges. Though it croaks in a raven voice, the sound is my Zuliya.

Down Kalliste's flank, side by side, we rush. Below us, an endless field of nodding asphodel. Purest pink. A thousand sunrises. Far beyond the meadow, the sea. Light green, dark green, crystal blue, dark troubled blue.

"You belong to me," the rumbling surf voice of the Great Ocean says.

A stronger wind ruffles my feathers and my raven companion soars right. I follow, turn into a sky swiftly being eaten by blackness. My raven heart hammers and I think, *I don't want to see what's ahead.* But the wind has talons in us both and won't let go. Directly ahead, Kalliste. Spewing lava and boulders and flames and smoke.

"The world ends," the raven croaks.

Terrified now. I thrash and pound against the heavy air to free myself.

The determined wind hurries me toward the volcano.

We cross into the plume of ash and smoke. Scalding. Eyes and nostrils clogged. Demon screams come shrieking from the volcano's mouth.

"Get out now," I yell to myself and the raven.

But we are sucked into the volcano's hot, red craw.

"Follow your heart," he croaks.

I think *Yes, I will*, and a blast of sulfuric breath from Kalliste explodes beneath us. We are catapulted free.

I tremble with relief. I'm safe. But we have been blown down the mountain into a city, and my guide is leading me to a black stone temple.

"I will never go there," I say, but the raven enters a window and I follow. Worshippers fill a room. I tell myself, I'll not look at the altar, but I do. Spread over the stone is a huge, blood-soaked cloak.

A priest with red sash is standing, back to me. He begins to turn.

He faces me, and—

It's my father. My father who loves foreign ways too much.

I screech to Zuliya, "Make the dream stop."

My father runs his thumb along the white scar on his chin. Ropy, pulsing. An ugly flaw.

"A reminder that life is hard," the raven croaks. "He bears it proudly."

"But to be proud of a scar is un-Keftian."

The priest's face blurs as if turning to water. I am looking instead at Galatea. She pierces me with an angry look. "They are remarkable," she says. "They should worship as they choose."

"You're wrong!" But I'm sure she doesn't hear me because now Alektrion looks at me with his gold-touched brown eyes. "Their soldiers are the best." I am so grieved.

Suddenly I'm in school and seven years old. My teacher doesn't know I'm standing on the other side of a partition. To a woman, my teacher says how shocked she is that foreigners sleep in the Keftian ambassador's home.

It isn't good to stand out! Love of things un-Keftian will bring down on us the wrath of the Goddess.

"No," my airborne companion says and flashes his wings to catch my attention. "Your father seeks wisdom, as a wise man should."

But I'm not listening. I'm back in the temple. With wrenching effort, I labor through the room, my beating wings throbbing in my ears like a gigantic bedsheet being snapped heavily and with astonishing slowness in the air. I burst from the window into the dark sky.

Escape, escape. Before it's too late.

All the people of Alyris are in the streets, running, rushing toward the sea. But ahead of them I see that the god Poseidon hides in the sea and his mouth is open. Huge, with long teeth and blood-red tongue. And as the people plunge into the water, he eats.

I awake, trembling, on the rug in the Mother's Womb. I would need to understand every bit of my first dream here. I shivered, and recalled a blue wool cloak in the cabinet. I wrapped myself in it and then went back to the rug. Before I could forget, I fetched papyrus and stylus. I wrote the images. My strongest certainty was that the Poseidonists were a terrible danger to the People. Their desire to control, rather than to simply be, was incompatible with harmony. What I didn't know, but must discover, was how to stop this growing evil.

I took the poppy four times in the next four days. Each time the Mother spoke again—not as the real voice I'd heard in the rain so many years ago, but bubbling up in silent whispers out of dreams and from the back of my mind. I asked Her what She expected of me. I asked Her what the People should do to bring the world into harmony again.

Once, when I meditated again over my first dream, I remembered the raven had said my father was a wise man. This utterance made no sense, and it seemed wrong. The unwillingness to conform that my father stood for frightened me. But the thought was so peculiar, so surprising, I wrote it down and told myself not to forget it.

By the fifth day, I was the Lady's Voice.

I saw Alektrion again when Nonia presented me to the People. The Wise Women had dressed me, girdled me, rouged my nipples, painted my feet red, and placed on my head the conical hat last worn by Damkina. Because he could never attend ceremonies and festivals, Alektrion had never seen me in ceremonial dress with my breasts exposed. Would they remind him, as symbolically they were supposed to do, of the joys of coupling? Of the harmony coupling brings? But not just the joy of physical uniting of any pair. Would they remind him of our love? Did he hurt as deeply inside as I did?

He stood between his friends, Talos and Anchices. He was so close. The mid-summer sun struck his eyes at that angle that showed their gold, and my heart trembled. Tears brimmed. I breathed deeply to stop them. I had kept myself strong thus far.

I am very happy, my beloved. I prayed he could hear me. *We make a terrible sacrifice, you and I, but this road is my destiny.*

Kishar intoned the ancient words of consecration, and then wound a living charis around each of my extended forearms. The snakes' strong bodies were cool, but immediately began to take on my heat. Their coils were tight, bands of power coming up to me from the earth, their home, the Mother's body.

I closed my eyes. *Great Mother of All Life, give me wisdom.*

The harmony of the world was unraveled at many edges. It was my task to reweave it.

∾ ∾ ∾ ∾

The evening after my presentation, I gathered my senior staff in the room of the swimming Dolphins: Nothos, my vizier; Glaucon, the head of my Guards; Lalilia, my chamberlain, (always a woman from the Snake clan); Kishar and her sister, Sorona, the two Wise Women, one of whom would be at all times within the sound of my voice; Ninsuna, my scribe; and Blauthophon, one of my several Memories.

I already missed the freedom to leave sacred ground to consult with Zuliya. As with Alektrion, the only way I might see Zuliya now was in the Grand Audience Chamber where we would be separated by a silk partition that shielded the Lady's Voice from the direct gaze of foreigners.

"We begin together in grievous times," I said. "But with your help, we will recover from the disaster at Kalliste. Keftiu will have harmony again." After a few words to each about their duties, I dismissed all but Nothos and Glaucon. "Your first task is to bring me proof of whose hand was behind Damkina's death." I asked what each thought was needed to accomplish this end and, after listening, I ordered a tripling of the number of spies and a doubling of the price offered for information.

"Now, to our other major concern. What is your assessment of the view that the Red King will be satisfied with nothing less than invasion of Keftiu?"

Glaucon spoke quickly. "That is exactly his goal."

The Badger shook his head and set his shoulders square. "To attempt to invade the Mother's Heart would be madness."

I countered with my immediate worry. "Whatever each of you feels, it's essential I have complete loyalty among the military. What has been done to assess the minds of our officers and men?"

It swiftly became clear that Damkina had assumed no one among the military would question her word. One of Zuliya's sayings—a favorite of his Mitanni general—leapt to mind: "A leader who assumes will suffer a short journey."

"I want spies inserted in the ranks, from the lowest recruits to the officers. I must know if there's any sympathy among the Guards for the Poseidonist heresy. And this religious dissent will cease. We will suppress it—by peaceful means—but decisively. Hear my word. All must be done in accordance with the Law. Close the temples. Forbid entry. But the Guards can use force only if they are attacked and only in defense.

"Second, I'll renew the proclamation that there will be no further talk, openly or in private, of invasion of Pylos. The penalty for merely discussing it will be a five-year shunning." I thought of Alektrion and Sarpedon. Both would be furious, but they must submit. *Dear Mother, make Alek understand.* "This talk of invasion ends now. If we don't follow the Law in a matter this grave, we can only expect even further disasters."

A deep frown creased Glaucon's brow. My Head of the Guards had already made clear he agreed with Alektrion and Sarpedon. Still, he nodded and emphasized his acquiescence by tapping his fist to his heart. I dismissed the two men.

Mestra—a sister I'd personally chosen as my attendant—helped me into my new bed. I knew her from the Bull Academy and could trust her completely. She would test my food and would watch during my sleep.

Blushing slightly, she kissed my hand. I instantly thought of Zuliya. "May the Sweet Mother guide your every step, Most Honored."

The next morning the astonishing news came that Galatea had helped Hylas escape. Glaucon assured me they would be found. Nothos said they would not. Galatea had left me a message:

"Dearest Leesandra, friend of my youth. Our paths have grown so far apart. I wish you the Lady's wisdom as you serve as Her Voice. I cannot accept the death by banishment of my Hylas, so I have chosen to flee our beautiful island. Hylas has told me what happened to Lynceus was an accident. I believe him. I cannot do otherwise. You will understand."

Poor Galatea, I thought. Everything lost—for a man.

A shaft of guilt struck me. I'd never told Galatea about the human sacrifice. Perhaps …

No. I had told her. I'd just never argued with her. I'd done as I'd been taught and avoided conflict, and the result had been to allow a terrible evil to take root. Had I risked her displeasure and some temporary unhappiness, I could have forced her to face the ugly reality and maybe she wouldn't have taken up with Hylas. Surely she would never have taken this disastrous path away from the People.

Three days later Nothos urgently requested a private audience. I met him with a racing pulse, fearing something dire. The Badger crossed his arms over his chest. Wearing a frown, as if he disapproved, he said, "I have news I believe will please you, most Honored."

I was standing beside a table and gestured to ask if he also was thirsty. He shook his head. "Continue," I said as I poured myself watered wine.

"Arrangements have been made so you may see your tutor in more private surroundings than the Grand Audience Hall. The Wise Ones devised a solution."

I had met once with Zuliya and it had proved extremely awkward. I didn't sit on my usual chair of authority, but had a regular chair placed near the Sacred Partition. Zuliya sat close on the other side, so at least we didn't have to raise our voices. The Coan silk stretched upon the partition's lattice, which stands wall to wall and rises from the floor to three times a man's height, is so thinly spun one can see through it, but people appear blurred. I didn't like seeing Zuliya's face unclearly. Even more cumbersome, the room was usually full of attendants, Temple staff, and foreign dignitaries. While we talked, all had to be kept waiting outside. Seeing Zuliya would never be easy or comfortable again, but I had told Kishar it must be arranged. Zuliya had wisdom and experience I would not do without.

"I understand," she'd said.

Now I asked Nothos, "What solution?"

"You know the small house at the edge of the southeast quarter?"

I nodded.

"At its edge, it stands on sacred ground. We are enlarging the rooms to spill onto non-dedicated consecrated land. Your tutor may enter by a new door on that land. You will enter from sacred ground. A small partition will be made that will separate sacred from non-sacred land. You can move freely on your side, he on his."

"Are the rooms ready then?"

"No, Most Honored. It will be three, perhaps four days."

I had another thought. I was almost afraid to ask. "Is this room to be used by me only with Zuliya, or may I use it with whomever I choose?"

Nothos shook his head. "I am to tell you, for I inquired about exactly that eventuality, that the Wise Women say the small southeast house is yours to use as you see fit. They expect only that you honor your vow to never step beyond sacred ground nor defile the Temple by allowing any non-initiate to step onto it. "He hesitated, then added quickly, "Which I am certain you would never permit."

His words sank in. I sat down my cup and took the nearest chair.

If I chose to, I could see Alektrion. Nothos apparently expected me to be pleased. Instead, I felt a great weight settle onto my chest. I had let Alektrion go from my heart. But what, then, did this new situation mean for us?

I rose and crossed to my gruff Badger and laid my hand on his arm. "I thank you, Nothos. I thank the Wise Ones. Please go at once and tell Zuliya I wish to see him the first morning after this room is dedicated, immediately after prayers."

31

The knock on Alektrion's door sounded like thunder. Demon's breath, the sound was so loud it hurt. It came again, even louder. Whoever the miserable son of Kokor was, he was going to break down the miserable door.

He lifted his head off the table. The room spun. He clenched his fist and yelled, "Go away!" The door opened letting in light from the hallway, even its modest strength enough to stab like a lightning bolt through his still-reeling mind. "I said go away," he growled, and let his head fall back onto his crossed arms.

The door closed. Footsteps approached. Then silence.

"I'm not having visitors." He chuckled. The effort brought on a surge of dizziness. He raised his head and reached for the half-full cup of ale. A deeply tanned hand beat him to it, snatched the cup off the table.

Alektrion looked up, glaring. Sarpedon stood staring down at him.

"Oh, seal dung," Alektrion muttered, and let his head fall again onto his crossed arms. It was too much effort to hold it up and besides, doing so made him dizzy.

"This room stinks, Alek. So do you."

"Right."

"Anchices has told me you drink every night. Is it true?"

"Sure is."

"It's a wonder you manage to function so well."

A reply would require too much effort.

"It's been five days now since your priestess became the Lady's Voice. I have needed you. Expected you. I gather this stupor is how you've spent all five days."

It sank into his mind that the figure standing before him, tormenting him, was his admiral! His superior officer. He was sorry Sarpedon had come. Too bad the man would see him this way. He raised his chin, tried to straighten up, sucked in a steadying breath, grabbed the edges of the table to keep things level. He focused on Sarpedon's lips, not his eyes. Too embarrassing to look into his eyes. "Sorry I was rude. You know you're welcome."

Sarpedon walked to the window and opened it halfway. More light. Alektrion felt another stab to his brain, and a lick of heat added to his misery. The man brought a chair to the table and sat. Still wincing at the light, Alektrion watched Sarpedon's gaze search his body and then his face. "Do you intend to remain this way?"

"No. Well, maybe yes."

"I've never cared for priestesses. Always thought you were wasting valuable time with her. But sometimes men do get attached to a woman in a way that's beyond reason. Clearly this is how you feel for this one. So is this how you're going to respond to this great thing that has happened to her?"

"I can never be with her again."

"Perfectly true. But do you think this dissipation is how she expects you to act? Does this honor the woman you seem to think so much of?"

"And I could never have had her because I was born a half-breed." He surprised himself at how much bitterness came through in that sentence. He definitely needed a drink, but Sarpedon had set the cup on a chest, halfway across the room.

"Why do you drink at night, Alek? I'm greatly saddened to hear it. A man who drinks as you do has something eating at him. What's eating you?"

Alektrion was silent.

"How long have you been this way?"

"A while. Since maybe sixteen. But it's not something you need concern yourself about. I'm sorry I've been away the last few days. Give me a few hours. I'll bathe. Eat something. I'll report this afternoon." If he could get Sarpedon out of the room, he could have a drink.

"Does Leesandra know that you drink like this at night?"

Heat of embarrassment crawled up his neck. How could she? Except for that once, in the hut on Sarpedon's property, she had never been with him at night. She must never know. She would never understand.

"You are one of my most valuable men, Alek. Perhaps my most valuable. What you do does concern me. Look at me."

He focused on Sarpedon's eyes, but could take the earnest, hurt look for only a moment. He looked back down at the table top. Sarpedon rose, went to the door, disappeared. Alektrion heard him talking with the housewoman, heard the words food and bath.

His admiral returned. Alektrion said, "I'm fine now. I thank you for coming." He struggled to rise, but the room spun and turned upside down, and spun some more. He sank back onto the seat.

The housewoman hurried in, followed by two boys carrying a tub. While Alektrion wished fervently Sarpedon would leave, he found himself being undressed, hauled to the tub, and after the boys filled it, plunked into the hot water. The heat sank into his skin and sent a wave of heat straight to his head.

With Sarpedon giving directions, the boys washed Alektrion, dried him, got him into a clean tunic. The housewoman arrived with a bowl of something. The thought of food was horrific, but Sarpedon sat him in his chair, put warm egg soup in front of him, and watched him eat it.

By the end of the soup, the dizziness was gone, but he had a rare headache. He guessed that the amount of ale he could consume in four or five days as opposed to only a night might well account for the headache.

Sarpedon leaned forward, as if preparing to rise, and looked straight into his eyes. "I expect you this afternoon at my home. We'll not mention this again. You're a man grown, and you've never, except in this one instance, let the drinking interfere with anything I've asked of you. But I care for you. You have a demon. I pray you find it and get rid of it. Since you say you've been drinking this way long before you met Leesandra, then what's happened to her now isn't the root. You speak with such bitterness of being non-Keftian. Well, I've never cared whether your mother was Keftian or not, and who you are as a man is what has earned you my respect, not your race. But a man who drinks every night in private, or every day for that matter, is a man not fully in control of himself."

Sarpedon rose, came around the table, and put his hand on Alektrion's shoulder. His grip was gentle but firm. "Find your demon, Alek. And kill it." He squeezed Alektrion's shoulder, let go, turned, and left Alektrion alone with his thoughts.

He went to the window and looked down into the street, watched Sarpedon emerge, a man with a small body, but a brilliant mind and lion's heart. A man who was very disappointed in his chief aide. The admiral turned, walked briskly away, and disappeared into the crowd.

The open window let in the infernal heat. This summer was proving uncommonly warm. People rushed by. The lane was crowded, as all streets were now, so many refugees mixed with Knossons. Was it only his imagination or could he see anxiety on every face? He saw not one cheerful, optimistic expression. In Knossos, that used to be practically all you did see.

Sarpedon was right that Leesandra would expect better of him. There were things that needed doing, and many were things no one else could do better than he could—no matter where or to whom he had been born.

In the faint hope of keeping the room cool, he closed the window. The half-full cup of ale stood on the table where Sarpedon had set it. He walked to the cup, picked it up, went back to the window, re-opened it, and dumped out the rest of the drink. To the three startled women who looked up at him when they heard its splash, he mustered a smile.

He turned back and was stopped by another knock. "Enter."

The housewoman stepped inside, a parchment in her hand. He thanked her for delivering the message, then ripped open the seal and read:

> Alektrion of Kalliste. It has been arranged that you
> may have private audience with Leesandra, the Voice
> of the Goddess, three days hence. Ask at the southern
> portal and you will be given directions to the meeting's
> location.
>
>   Nothos, Vizier to the Lady's Voice

The message made no sense. There was no possible way he could see Leesandra in private. He inspected the seal. It seemed authentic.

∾ ∾ ∾ ∾

Alektrion approached the small house built into the southeast section of the Temple and stopped to examine it. He smelled freshly sawn wood. From what he could see of the front, the house had the undamaged look of newness. A porter at the southern gate had said it had been specifically constructed and dedicated to allow The Lady's Voice access to her Nubian counselor. Evidently, whatever rules applied to Zuliya would apply to any other non-Keftian.

His heart suddenly buoyed with anticipation of what only days before had seemed the impossible, he strode to the door and knocked. A young boy opened it, which, for some reason surprised Alektrion. He quickly realized that he had imagined he would be greeted by Temple staff. Someone notable. Or perhaps by Leesandra's handmaiden.

"Alektrion of Kalliste. To see the Lady's Voice."

The boy asked him to enter, showed him a table with wine and pear nectar and fruits, and said, "The Most Honored will be here shortly." He turned and hurried from the reception room into what Alektrion imagined would be another, larger room.

The urge to pour wine made his hand tremble. He pressed it hard against his thigh and turned away. He didn't want to get anywhere near the wine. He wouldn't even pour nectar, which was all he had been drinking for the last three days.

He followed after the boy into a room the size of one in a merchants's comfortable home. Two smaller rooms were attached, one on either side. The woody smell of construction was even stronger here. All the rooms were furnished like a home, at least as far as Alektrion could see, but a fourth of the way from the room's other end stood a striking partition made of silk and dark wood. The partition's outer wooden frame ran from wall to wall and from ceiling to floor. Thinner crossed beams formed window-like rectangles within the larger frame. The wood was richly carved with images of the sacred horns and the butterfly of regeneration. Stretched inside each of the smaller window-like frames was the finest silk he'd ever seen. Its color, when you squinted at it, was white; it had no decorative pattern except an occasional hint of dragonfly wings and was so finely spun it seemed almost not to be there. He walked closer and saw that the silk in the "windows" was stretched across the center so that a wooden ledge the width of a man's palm extended out from the silk on either side. He wondered how a person could get past this barrier, and a quick glance revealed that, off to one side, a small door of identical wood and silk had been built so it blended with the rest of the design.

He was tempted to touch it, but hesitated—touching it might not be acceptable. Behind the screen, the other side of the room held what appeared to be an audience chair, several other stools, a brazier, a table, and an ordinary chair.

A door in the center of the wall beyond the partition opened and Leesandra stepped in. She wore a sari of light green linen bound at her waist with a charis fashioned from gold. Her hair was piled high on her head. She had fully made up her face with kohl at her eyes and something on her lips that made their red color glisten. In her hair, she wore his pin.

She walked directly to the partition, stood opposite him no more than two steps away and smiled.

He said, "I had believed I would never see you again."

"As did I."

"Then how has this happened?"

She stepped to the partition, put her hand against the silk, looked at him with what he was certain was longing. He stepped forward, raised his hand and pressed it against hers.

Her body smelled of attar of roses, an Anatolian scent only the wealthiest could afford. Through the silk, his hand felt her heat. His heart was pounding furiously and he felt throbbing in his fingertips and palms, wondered if it were his heartbeat or hers. Perhaps it was theirs, beating as one.

She said softly, "I love you, Alek."

"And I love you. Forever."

Again they let silence bind them together. He looked at their hands, pressed so close. So this was what he would have of her. This simple touching of hands would have to fill the horrendous dark void. Somehow, he would have to make it enough.

She said, her voice strangely tense, "We can't stand like this forever."

He smiled back. "No."

"I'm going to go get a chair so I can sit next to you here."

"Agreed." He didn't take his hand away, and neither did she.

She said, "I'm going to take my hand back now."

Together they pulled their hands away from the silk.

They fetched chairs. She placed hers where one of the wooden ledges was at comfortable elbow level. She laid her arm along the ledge, twisted her wrist so her fingers again pressed against the silk. On his side, he did likewise and again their hands touched—almost.

She explained that she had insisted to Kishar that she would meet regularly with Zuliya and that Kishar had convinced the other Wise Ones that this arrangement was more suitable than using the Grand Audience Hall. "The partition lies at the end of sacred land, Alek. My side of this room is old. It's dedicated. Yours is new."

For a moment they were quiet. Then she said, "I can't stay long. I must meet with Nothos and Glaucon. But I made time for us in order to explain."

She was so solemn.

"You would eventually learn that I meet here with Zuliya. And you would wonder why I wasn't meeting with you. I am now The Voice of the Goddess, Alex. My destiny is very clear to me and I have accepted it. My duty is to the Goddess and to the People, and—"

"I understand that. You know I do."

"What I'm trying to say is that what was between us is over."

He felt a strange, sudden silence, was acutely aware of the warmth of her hand coming through the silk, warming his palm. "Nothing is over. Was what you just said a lie? You don't love me?"

"It was no lie. I do. But my heart has changed. My attention, my energy will go too often and too much to you when it should be elsewhere. We can't be together. And this arrangement—" She lifted her hand from his and gestured to the screen, then sought his hand again. "This arrangement is utterly unfair to you. We must sever now, Alex. Without me, you will find a woman with whom you can share the future."

Did he see, through the translucent silk, the glint of tears in her eyes? He was sure of it. She wasn't thinking clearly. "I want no other woman. You know that."

She said nothing.

"To be able to see you, to talk to you—"

"It cannot be, Alek."

She stood, leaving his hand pressed to the silk. He pulled it away and stood.

"I asked you to come here because I love you. I ask you to leave now because you love me. I ask you to leave and make yourself a life. That will please me. It will comfort me as I do the work the Goddess has given me."

He stood rooted to the floor wishing he had somehow misunderstood her, but her intent was unequivocally clear.

"Go." Her voice was choked, soft, but very firm. She took a step back and waited for him to obey.

He clenched the hand that still felt her warmth into a fist, turned, and walked on leaden feet to the door into the entry chamber. He turned. She was already gone.

He stumbled out into the blazing furnace of the day.

His throat was dry. He needed a glass of ale. He set his course toward the alehouse closest to the temple. He thought again and turned left heading for the city's largest gymnasium. He would exercise there, bathe again, have a massage, and drink peach nectar until his piss went pink. He would stay there until they threw him out, and then he'd go to his room and fall into bed, exhausted. He had spent every evening the last three days doing the same and, so far, it had worked to keep him from drink.

32

Meeting with Alektrion after my elevation was unspeakably painful. To see his face, even if through the blur of silk, quickened my heart with such pleasure. But to know I would never again rest in the comfort of his arms made me feel ill. I closed the door to the little house behind me after leaving him and stopped, swallowed hard several times and took several deep breaths. To separate was necessary.

Nothos had sent a messenger saying he and Glaucon must see me on a matter of greatest urgency. I returned to the patio adjacent to my sleeping quarters and, in the shade of a canopy, waited for them. Summer was in late prime, and Keftiu suffered drought. The growing season had been abundant, but in mid-summer an extraordinary heat wave had developed and persisted. To keep cool, I wore only a thin sari.

Glaucon arrived wearing a long face. He took the position of reverence with his spine so stiff I thought he might topple backward. I gestured to a cushioned bench.

"I'd rather stand, Most Honored."

"I take it you bring unpleasant news."

"I wish I weren't here."

In spite of air that felt like the inside of an oven, I felt a sudden chill as though I had just fallen into the Great Sea in a winter storm. Mestra, who'd been working on an embroidery, rose to leave. I signaled her to remain.

"Speak then."

"First. It's looking less and less as though we'll capture Hylas and the priestess Galatea. I fear they've escaped us. But we've learned why Hylas killed Lynceus."

Lynceus's name conjured his grotesque but dear image and a flood of sadness. "Go on."

"The Korinthian was, as we have suspected, one of the plotters against Damkina. We've found and broken the Temple cook who supplied the poison. He implicated two other Temple servants. And he implicated Hylas. It's his understanding the plotters were at the merchant Minyas's home. Lynceus overheard them talking. He was discovered, and Hylas killed him on the spot."

"I know Minyas is behind this treachery." I wished I could strike the traitorous merchant dead. It seemed that my chances of success or failure depended ultimately on my ability to contain Minyas. "To heretic, we can probably add the evil of murder."

"Yes, Most Honored. But the cook can't tell us that. He swears—and I assure you it's the truth—the only person outside the Temple who contacted him was Hylas."

Glaucon sat, but stiffly. "Their hope, Most Honored, was that the Priestess Galatea would be chosen as the Lady's Voice."

Ah! At last the reason. Had Galatea been chosen, she would have been positioned to bend the Law as she saw fit. And no doubt she would have done just that. She might have gone so far as to make Hylas her consort.

Just how far had Galatea been corrupted? Had she known about the plan to kill Damkina? If Glaucon was correct, Galatea had successfully escaped with Hylas, and I'd never know the answer to that painful question. My stomach turned as if I were rolling on the waves of that cold winter sea. "We can take some satisfaction in knowing Minyas must be frustrated nearly to splitting."

Glaucon gave an annoyed grunt. "I find no such satisfaction, Most Honored. The viper is still holed up in his country villa. He's surrounded himself with a large body of mercenaries. Do you wish me to bring him here to question?"

"I need proof, Glaucon." Frustrated, I balled my fist and stuck my knee. "Have you no proof that Minyas was behind the plot?"

"None."

"Then I'm forced to move carefully. He has a large following. Without proof—"

"Regretfully, Most Honored, I fear this matter isn't the bad news I bear." Glaucon broke in, his customarily impassive face gone strangely pale. The creases across his forehead and beside his mouth deepened further.

"Speak, then. You know you've nothing to fear from me."

Suddenly, his robes rustling, Nothos swept into the patio. He tapped his chest over his heart but did not sit. "I came as quickly as I could. I was halfway to Amnissos when I heard," he said, his voice breathless.

"What is happening?" I demanded. "What is all this agitation?"

My vizier looked at the head of my guards. "You've not told her?" Something in Nothos's tone made me feel as if a monster were grabbing at my feet, trying to pull me under the cold winter sea. Glaucon shook his head and stared at the patio's stone floor.

"Told me what!?"

They looked at each other, obviously hoping the other would shoulder the responsibility to speak.

"Most Honored ..." My vizier paused—Nothos, the Badger, the unflappable, seemed at a loss for words. "It's Atistaeus. He's delivered us a disastrous defeat. Over four hundred of our ships are lost, with most of their men. Other ships are unserviceable without extensive repairs. We've lost three admirals, Chrylsis among them."

Mestra's hands stopped over her embroidery.

Mother of All. Chrylsis, my Head of Navy, lost. And over four hundred ships. Such a catastrophe shouldn't be possible. So many of Keftiu's ships at once. "How? Where?"

"Taken completely by surprise. In a bay off of Tenos."

"Why would there ever be four hundred of our ships in the same place during sea-season?"

"A trap. Rapaciously clever. Atistaeus must have planned this ambush for years. Chrylsis was fed false information through a spy who had always been utterly reliable. The information led him to believe that the bulk of the Pylian fleet might be divided and each half penned separately within two bays, to be disabled at leisure. But he estimated he would need over four hundred ships."

More details of the debacle followed. Now, it seemed, the cold winter sea was about to swallow the Temple.

"Atistaeus has a new kind of ship, Most Honored. He's found a way to double a warship's number of rowers. There was no way for Chrylsis to anticipate the speed with which the Pylians moved."

My mind raced fearfully ahead. A little over two moon cycles remained of sea season. Not much time, but enough that if it was his plan, Atistaeus could attack Knossos. I started to ask how many ships we had to throw into Atistaeus's path, but realized the absurdity of my asking such a question. My ignorance of naval strategy made knowing that kind of information useless. I asked, instead, which other admirals had been lost. Hearing that one was Metron of Sitia, the man I would have chosen to elevate to Chief Admiral, I bolted to my feet. Truly, truly disastrous! I had a sudden shocking vision of the Red King sailing into Amnissos.

It took only moments to know what I had to do. Because it would take Alektrion away from Knossos, a large part of me didn't want to do it.

"Bring me the little admiral," I said. "Bring me Sarpedon."

Glaucon's eyebrows lifted slowly. The Badger crossed his arms and narrowed his lips.

I continued, "Whatever I or you or anyone else thinks of Sarpedon's views, he is unquestionably our most brilliant strategist. Sarpedon is what Knossos needs now. I will send him to take charge of the fleet."

I dismissed Nothos and Glaucon, then sat, watching Mestra's hands continue the never-ending task of embroidery. With her every movement, she was creating beauty for the eye. I envied her straightforward purpose. My task was to create beauty, too. To return harmony to Keftiu's life. But the means needed to accomplish that end were far removed from anything beautiful.

My head spun with plans, but my heart thought of Alektrion. Unless I intervened, when Sarpedon left, he would take all of his aides with him. Into danger. Unless I intervened.

33

The day following his meeting with Leesandra, Alektrion once again knocked on the door to the little southeast house mentally rehearsing what he would say. The place where his beating heart should be felt as though it held a lifeless lump of metal. The previous afternoon, Sarpedon's messenger had located him in the gymnasium, and he had at once obeyed the call to come to the Admiral's home. Over four hundred Keftian ships had been lost, their crews with them, an otherwise inconceivable disaster, except that Chrylsis was an egotistical near-incompetent who should have been put aside as Admiral-in-Chief years ago. Chrylsis had wormed his way into high position principally because of an ingratiating temperament. No matter what the issue, Chrylsis found a position that offended no one.

Repeatedly Sarpedon had warned Damkina that her Chief Admiral's judgment wasn't up to competition with the Red King. She'd ignored him. Sarpedon's wisdom was now proven, but Damkina was no longer here to appreciate her mistake. Twelve thousand good men had paid for her foolishness with their lives.

An hour ago, he had composed a note to Leesandra insisting that he must meet with her. The door opened and before him stood Zuliya. The Nubian said, "I am speaking with Leesandra. And given what she has told me, I am most surprised to see you here."

"I must see her."

"Did she not make it clear that she has decided she should not see you again?"

"Zuliya, I must talk to her about what has occurred to our forces. About Atistaeus. She must be persuaded to invade Pylos."

Zuliya folded his arms, did not move, and did not invite Alektrion inside.

"May I enter?"

"I do not believe she wants to see you, Alek. When she makes up her mind, she is stubborn. She waits inside for me, and if I let you in, you will go to her to talk. She will be extremely displeased."

"Please. Ask her for me, then, if she will see me."

"Wait."

Zuliya closed the door. Alektrion paced. The door opened again. "It is as I said. She will not see you, Alek."

"Zuliya, she must be made to listen! Sarpedon is beside himself with worry. I left him stomping around his library."

"She has told me something I am at liberty to tell you. She will elevate Sarpedon to Admiral-in-Chief."

"This is wise. But it isn't enough. Will Sarpedon be able to deal with Atistaeus as he sees fit?"

"What do you mean?"

"Will he be able to invade Pylos—and the sooner the better?"

"I don't know the answer to your question."

The urge to simply shove his way inside was so strong Alektrion dug his toes into his sandals to keep from charging inside. "You say she won't see me. Will you take my words to her then?"

"I will."

"Tell her she must listen to sense and to the voices of people who have had actual contact with Atistaeus and his forces. The Red King is a spreading deathweed, and he cannot be stopped unless she roots him up at his base. Tell her, Knossos must invade!"

Zuliya gave him a wan smile. "I will convey your words." Once again, Zuliya closed the door.

Again Alektrion paced. An eternity passed. He wondered if Zuliya had assumed that all he was to do was to convey Alektrion's message. Was Zuliya even aware that Alektrion was waiting outside for some response? He raised his fist to knock, but the door opened.

"She listened. Her answer is, 'I will strengthen Keftiu's defenses to ensure that Knossos is inviolable. But there will be no invasion. The Lady's People do not make war. I will elevate Sarpedon because he is the shrewdest military mind the Goddess has given Knossos. But only on the condition that he agrees, and will take oath, that he will abide by the Law.'"

"By the Goddess, Zuliya. The woman is wrong!"

"She does not believe so, young Alek. With her whole heart she believes that your willingness to invade, that any talk of invasion, is somehow a part of a sickness that has caused the Great Mother to bring on this testing of the People."

"I must talk to her."

"No. It will do no good. Besides, I assure you she would only rise and leave the room should you force your way inside, as I am sure you most sincerely wish to do."

"Zuliya, do you agree with me? With Sarpedon? Can you influence her? It seems she doesn't want to see the truth. It's as though she doesn't want to act. Doing what is necessary seems to frighten her. She uses the Law as an excuse to avoid pain and responsibility."

"I have been with her for many years, since she was a child. In those days I gave her my opinions freely. She is a woman now. Now I speak to her when I believe she will hear me, but on this subject, I assure you, her mind is firmly set. Only the passage of events will reveal who is right and who wrong."

Alektrion had tried. He had failed. He felt tired, as if he'd been wrestling with Talos. "Thank you for speaking for me."

"I need no thanks."

∾ ∾ ∾ ∾

Two days later, he left Knossos with Sarpedon. The *Shark* was accompanied by seventy warships and twenty fastships with the whole lot followed by the much slower repair and supply vessels.

At Stokanis, Anchices and Talos and four others were each given command of their own vessel plus a pod of ten warships each. During the commissioning, Alektrion sat rigid. He had so far succeeded in staying away from drink, but doing so left him nervous. And though he was pleased for both friends, having his face freshly rubbed in his non-officer status galled. Finally the ceremony appeared to be ending. Sarpedon gestured for Alektrion to join him in front of the assembled crowd of rowers, enlisted and paid marines, and officers. "Alektrion of Kalliste is my right hand," he declared in an uncompromising tone. "When he speaks, he speaks for me, and you'll give him the respect and obedience you'd give to me."

The men burst into wild cheering. Alektrion was stunned. He'd had no sense of this reservoir of affection. The men began to disperse. Alektrion went to Sarpedon and touched his heart, bowed his head. He said, "I am grateful for the confidence you've shown in me this day. I've been wondering, ever since—"

Sarpedon clasped his shoulder. "We said we would never speak of it. You've never let me down. To my knowledge, you've never failed the men who serve me. I did today only what is intelligent, and I expect not to be disappointed."

Again Alektrion bowed. Talos and Anchices approached and saluted Sarpedon. Anchices said, "May we take him to celebrate?"

Sarpedon smiled, dismissed them, and returned to the *Shark*. In the company of Talos and Anchices and a handful of other officers, Alektrion soon found himself in the best alehouse in Stokanis. The smell set his mouth watering. He began to sweat. Under the table he clenched his thighs. The serving girl stopped next to him. "Ales for us all," one of the officers said. "And bring us hot food that will put strength in a man's limbs. All of them."

The allusion evoked laughter. The girl turned to go, but Alektrion caught her arm. "Bring me peach nectar," he said as softly as he thought he could and still be heard.

She leaned closer. "What?"

"Peach nectar," he repeated, no louder than before.

She nodded and left.

A boy arrived with the food. Talos reached across Alektrion for the bread. As he did, in his whispery voice he said, "It's a good choice of drink, Scorpion." He broke bread and handed a piece to Alektrion who sat to his left, broke off another piece and handed it to Anchices on his right. Anchices asked a question. The drinks arrived. Alektrion was certain all of the officers had heard his order, but not one man remarked on his choice. Not one made a joke. He sipped on the nectar, satisfied. Grateful.

Later in the evening Talos said, "You know why the men cheered so loudly for you, don't you?"

"It took me by surprise."

"During the years you've spent recruiting, you've spent far more time in their billets and around their campfires than Sarpedon ever will. The men talk to Anchices and me. The Keftians like the Scorpion as a man as much as they respect your reputation as a fighter—Keftian or not. And the mixed lot of mercenaries feel a special kinship with you. They take pride that you've risen so high."

Yes, Alektrion thought, as a navy man his being half-breed served him well in some ways. One could always find a positive side to anything, if one chose to look for it.

The fleet couldn't proceed directly north because the facilities at Kalliste had been destroyed and the islands of Anafi and Ios had towns too small to handle the resupply of so many ships. So they rowed along the coast, west-northwest, to Khania. Years dropped from his shoulders. He felt twenty again. Eager for action. And he had a plan. Before moving on Atistaeus, Sarpedon would send out a scouting pod of ten fastships. Sarpedon must be convinced that he, Alektrion, should take charge of this scouting group.

The wind was strongly against them, and the trip to Khania took five days. Sarpedon learned that Atistaeus had moved, not to Milos, which would have been his most direct route were he headed for Keftiu, but toward Khithera.

"I don't understand him," the little admiral huffed. "In his place, I'd press my advantage. Why spin such an elaborate ambush if one isn't prepared to follow it up? It looks as though he's taking his victorious fleet home."

Within days, twenty more warships from the south-central sector joined them. Having his well-rehearsed argument firmly in mind, Alektrion approached the door of the *Shark's* deckhouse. The admiral waved his hand eagerly. "Come in, come in." He remained standing but nodded toward one of the folded campstools.

"I'd like to talk about the scouting party."

"Not just now, Alek. Late yesterday, I received an urgent message from the Lady's Voice. What she suggests is brilliant, Alek. Brilliant."

Alektrion opened, then squatted on the short stool, eager to know of his Leesa's brilliance.

"Everything depends on whether Atistaeus plans to continue south to invade. If he does, we'll have to block him as best we can. But if he makes the mistake of going home, with all or even part of his fleet, we're going to pen him in at Pylos."

"Pen him in?"

"Let me read the relevant part." The scroll crackled as Sarpedon unrolled it partway. "Here." His eyes glittered.

> *Assuming Atistaeus doesn't continue south to invade this late in the season, allow the Pylian king to return home. Make arrangements, however, for Keftiu's fleet to over-winter somewhere near Pylos.*
>
> *As over-wintering in Alyris is no longer possible, both Council and Temple have agreed on shifting to Naxos. Atistaeus will expect the same. Instead, you will move much further west. As soon as Atistaeus is in winter harbor, I order that you move in great force to whatever place you decide is best. To Khithera or possibly somewhere along the southern coast of the Peloponnesis itself, if you can find a suitable place where the inhabitants won't create difficulties. Next spring, before Atistaeus can get one ship out of his harbor, we will arrive on his doorstep in mass. We must prevent any of his ships— warships or traders—from going to sea. Not so much as a fishing dory shall leave Pylos.*

Sarpedon let his hand drop. "We'll pen Atistaeus in, Alek. No ships into Pylos. No ships out. It's not invasion. We stop short of breaking the Law. But—"

Alektrion shook his head. "I can think of ten reasons very quickly why the plan won't work. For one thing, how long can we sustain sufficient strength at Pylos without being seriously weakened elsewhere? Atistaeus is not the sea's only brigand."

"I've thought of that reason, and twenty more, Alek. But for every problem, I believe there is a solution. Perhaps most importantly, though Atistaeus has a number of allies on the Peloponnesis, he's not loved elsewhere. He's been raiding everyone. The Keftian hegemony remains intact. No matter how bitterly outlanders carp and complain, no one wants a pirate like Atistaeus in charge of the Great Sea. The key will be finding the right replacement port for Alyris."

They spent another hour debating. Much later, after dinner, Sarpedon outlined for his three commodores, each responsible for thirty warships, the planned blockade.

Alektrion listened to the arguments, and a conviction grew in him that, though complex and subject to many intangibles, Leesandra's idea could work. Diplomacy would be needed to reassure countries not strongly allied with Keftiu that the same tactic wouldn't be used against them. Otherwise, they might unite with Atistaeus out of fear of what might happen if Keftiu pursued a blockade policy elsewhere.

Sarpedon rose, a bundle of snapping-eyed energy. He waved his hand, emphasized key words with a poke of his finger. "Pylos can be resupplied indefinitely with minimal essentials from mainland allies, but who cares? The donkey's asshole will be cut off from all trade. His glorious dreams of expansion will be ended. We simply let him sit there in his little barbarian castle till his balls rot."

Before he left, Alektrion mentioned the scouting party again, but Sarpedon put him off with a curt, "I'll think about that later." Two days later, Alektrion again received a summons. "Come swim with me," Sarpedon said as Alektrion entered the cabin. "This heat is enough to drive a man mad."

Sarpedon was already naked. Though firm of arm and back and thigh because he'd used the gymnasium regularly during his years in Knossos, Sarpedon's middle was growing soft with creeping age. Alektrion freed his belt, dropped his kilt, and stepped out of his strap. Side-by-side they dived into the sea. They swam to a small offshore islet in Khania's harbor in a race that wasn't really a race. Alektrion, as courtesy required, let Sarpedon arrive first. The islet was too steep to climb out, but a ledge on the lee side made a platform where two or three men could rest side by side, half submerged. Alektrion lay back and found a niche for his head.

All day the sky had shown the bruised look that promised rain. They lay quietly, contemplating the ominous white column that had appeared three days ago on the northeast horizon. The milky shaft had begun small, but had quickly grown. Easily visible from all points along Keftiu's northern coast, the plume jabbed the sky like an eerie white finger of the demon Shilat. Yesterday, a fastship had delivered word that its source was Kalliste.

"What do you think it means?" Alektrion asked.

"I don't seek for meanings. I leave that to priestesses and seers. But I understand the fear it sparks among the People."

"I can't bear to think of Kalliste anymore. I see the island as I knew it as a child. A gem of a place. Now everything's covered with ash and lava. The Temple, the baths, the hanging gardens. I hear there's not a living plant or animal to be found. And to think of the Building of the Speakers entombed..." Alektrion sighed. "The fresco on its north wall was the most beautiful thing made by the hand of woman or man I'd ever seen."

Sarpedon stretched alongside Alektrion. "The water close to the island boils in places. Dead fish float belly up around the coast. The place stinks of death."

The sea in which he soaked was warm, still Alektrion shivered. Maybe Sarpedon didn't seek for meanings, but he felt sure Leesandra would be chilled to the marrow by this sign from Kalliste. Keftiu's seers would be searching the faces of their bowls of water; the priestesses and priests would be making earnest sacrifices.

Leesandra would say the Mother was warning Her unfaithful children to turn from the worship of the false god. Maybe. But maybe the white finger in the sky was a warning that if the Poseidon lover Atistaeus wasn't stopped, by attacking him on his own grounds if necessary, the People would face even more death.

Sarpedon looked away from the plume, toward Khania's harbor. "I received confirmation that Atistaeus does not move south," he said, his tone dismissing the subject of dead Kalliste. "He's definitely withdrawing back to Pylos. So we can proceed at top speed. I sent Anchices forward yesterday to scout Khithera. I'll know soon if he thinks we should site the new port there."

Alektrion clenched his jaw, biting back protest, then said, "I had wanted to talk with you about the scouting."

"I knew what you were thinking. You know it wasn't possible. Besides, what I need you to do is take a fastship and return to Knossos. Because we have to move quickly now, I've prepared dispatches directing the fleet's redeployment. I want to use Temple pigeons. Fastships from here will be too slow and, given the weather, maybe unreliable." Sarpedon chuckled. "I need a new supply of Temple-born homing pigeons, so I can use them to keep the Lady's Voice apprised of every development. As soon as possible after we return to the *Shark*, you'll leave for Knossos."

A fastship to Knossos, Alektrion thought bitterly. He would oversee the transport of pigeons. Anchices had been sent forward to Khithera, and not because Anchices was a better warrior, but because he was Keftian.

Let go of it, he told himself. It only sucks away your spirit.

"This blockade has to work, Alek." Sarpedon's tone grew uncharacteristically reflective. "You know, I'm a military man. I care about things practical. How to fight and how to win. But now and then, usually when I've overdone the wine and I'm alone, but in this case right now with you, I try to imagine the world if the Red King prevails. I find myself thinking what the world will be like if we fail to stop him"

"The Temple tells us that can't happen."

Sarpedon began to sift the water, scooping it with his hand and letting it dribble through his fingers. "We sit at the center of the world, Alek. We're the envy of the world. You know why? Not really for what seem the obvious reasons. Not because of the high quality of the goods we use and sell. Or because of the unparalleled refinement of Keftian life. Not even because those who love and respect power see our power everywhere. We're envied most because we live in peace. And it's peace that brings the other good things to the People.

"The others, those who envy us, don't. They fight, and they want to spread their sickness. Intelligent outlanders envy the Lady's just Laws. They want to live like us, but their people are unwilling to submit to the Goddess, and their leaders lust for glory. Without submission to the Laws, they fight like cats over everything.

"The irony, of course, is that here I sit, the man who's argued for years that if we don't take the offensive and invade, Knossos is doomed. The unthinkable will happen, I say. But the Law strictly forbids invasion. Defense, yes. Aggression, no.

"So I've been asking myself, who's right? Maybe the Wise Ones and your little priestess, who has now become the Mother's own Voice, have been correct all along." Sarpedon curled one hand around the balled fist of the other. "Maybe the loss of Alyris has opened eyes that should have seen this option earlier. Maybe this blockade can wear Atistaeus down."

Sarpedon sat up and water ran off his shoulders. He cupped some in his hands and, after washing his face, stroked his thin fingers through shiny hair. "I pray fervently to the Lady that this plan will stop him. Because if it doesn't, the light at the center of the world will go out. I know what I'm saying. If Atistaeus prevails, we will all live in a very, very dark place."

Sarpedon slipped into the water. "Let's race again." He started stroking toward the *Shark*. "And this time, Alek, make a genuine try to beat me!"

∾ ∾ ∾ ∾

Two days later a frustrated Alektrion sat cross-legged under a canvas on the elevated stern of the fastship *Kestrel*. They'd made good time yesterday, but in the late afternoon the weather changed dramatically. The oppressive, windless heat had given way to rain and a fierce western squall. Sarpedon wanted haste. Instead, at mid-morning they were anchored in the lee of a small offshore islet, their sail furled. The rowers had rigged a canvas to keep off the worst of the rain. The thirty men sat huddled under it—at the moment, passing out freshly brewed salepi tea.

Alektrion stared, able to see just over the whipping canvas toward the northern horizon and the white plume. He still fumed because Anchices had been the one sent north to scout. His thoughts were so absorbed that at first he didn't see the change in the plume. Then awareness hit. The white plume had gone black from its base to a third of the way up the column.

He stared as a pillar, as black and dense as the darkest night, thrust upwards obliterating the white column. It continued its rapid climb into the sky, its base now tinged an angry red.

The hairs stood on his arms, legs and back of his neck.

The top of the black column put out branches as if a tree composed of the very bowels of the earth were growing in the air. Terror grew in his chest in consort with the fearsome cloud. He found his voice. "Look!" he shouted.

Then a change in the squall-whipped, foam-topped waves drew his attention. A band of darkened water rushed away from the rising black pillar toward *Kestrel*, a swath perhaps half a stadia wide. Rippling like the foot of the abalone, the band reached the ship, passed under her, lifted her slightly. Alektrion turned to watch it racing shoreward, but, as if he'd been hit by the fist of a giant hand, he was slammed face down onto the deck and deafened by a stupefying roar.

He lay panting, his cheek stinging, his head ringing. He fought to breathe, his mind unable to grasp a single straw of thought. After a few stunned moments, he rolled onto his back and pushed upright to look again at the black pillar. It continued its heavenward climb. The crown had spread wider, an evil black mushroom growing at an astounding rate.

The men babbled. Some held hands over their ears. Some shook their heads. Some mouthed prayers. Many stared dumbly at the black rent rising from the horizon high into the sky. Alektrion touched his cheek and his hand came away sticky with blood.

In less than an hour, hot pebbles began to pelt them, mingling with the cold, driving rain of the squall. The pebbles were gray, featureless. Within another hour the hot pebble rain turned to a warm rain of small stones. He thought of Leesandra, formless thoughts of her eyes, of the smell of roses in her hair, of the sweet curve of her neck. Fear fueled a primal longing to be with her.

"What should we do?" men shouted.

"Shouldn't we put in to shore?" clamored several.

"No, no. We have to go further out," others insisted.

He reminded them that, given the westerly squall, which if anything was blowing stronger, going farther out to sea was impossible.

The bowman shouted back. "We must put out to sea, Scorpion. There will be a great quake. A wall of water will follow. It could sweep us onto the land."

What the bowman wanted was impossible. "The sea would swallow us," Alektrion shouted. "Nothing can be done. We must stay anchored."

Now octopus-like, the crown of the pillar put out black tentacles, reaching out from Kalliste, spreading over the entire Great Sea. The rain of hot pebbles and cold water continued, thickened.

Alektrion pulled some canvas close over his body to protect his skin from the heated missiles. The men argued about the sail. "We have to pull it down. We need more cover," some said. "No! We have to save it in case we have to flee," said others.

"Use it for cover!" Alektrion shouted.

The sail came down.

By late afternoon, pumice chunks pelted the sea's choppy surface and occasionally made a hit on *Kestrel*. The rain became a dark-gray heated slurry. If the fall of slurry continued, it would capsize *Kestrel* from its sheer weight. He ordered the men to scrape it up with their cups and dump it over the sides. His terror, at first so sharp it had cut his mind off from thought, was now a ferret-like thing that rushed from keen to dull and back again. The dreadful column, the deafening explosion, the hot rain of earth was touching everyone living in or around the Great Sea. He thought the sound alone might well have been heard at Samos. Maybe even Kyprus.

Why was this happening? "What do You want from us?" he whispered.

By the time the sun moved to two hours above the horizon, the shaft from the heart of the earth had stopped growing taller. Lightning streaked in angry forks within the pillar's head. The base glowed a demonic red.

The declining sun was a huge, bloody ball in a bloody-red western sky. In the rest of the heaven, the combination of rain from the squall and the debris in the air produced a darkness like night. Again he prayed, What do You want from us?

Then something changed in the column. It seemed to collapse slightly. *It's beginning to shrink.* From the crown, a ring of the column appeared to slide downward like a tiara slipping down on a woman's forehead. The ring separated from the column, plummeted three-quarters of the way down the column's flank, and in less than a heartbeat it exploded outward.

The ring separated from the central core and rushed away from Kalliste in all directions. Toward Keftiu. Toward the *Kestrel.*

"Up anchor," he bellowed. "Up anchor. Fast. Fast."

He must move them behind the islet, even if into the murderous squall. He must put something between them and the black cloud. He looked at it again, rushing toward them at unbelievable speed.

Ever closer. Now so close the balls of red fire and jagged forks of lightning pulsed brightly at its dark heart. He felt heated air. The breath of the demon.

"Up anchor," he bellowed again. "Kokor himself comes for us."

As if blasted from sleep, the two bowmen stood, hauled in line, the muscles of their backs raised under their skin like tree branches with their effort. But too late.

Alektrion drew the rain canvas over his head and threw himself on the deck, doubled over like a child in the womb. The black cloud struck.

A sudden pressure change blocked his ears, still he heard a thunderous cracking sound. The mast. Shattering, searing pain lanced through his legs. It lasted a moment, but then all he could feel was that his back was burning.

No air. Impossible to breathe.

He choked. His chest heaved. He needed to whip the canvas off his head. He needed air so badly. But his muscles couldn't move.

Time stopped, frozen in a fiery now. He was burning alive. He would die.

But he didn't.

The suffocating heat decreased. His lungs heaved, sucked in air. He heard screams. Trembling head to toe, he peeled the canvas back and curled around to see. Men alive but stripped of their skin shrieked. Others lay dead and blackened. *Kestrel* steamed in places and burned in others as the squall put out fires that had, in a few seconds, blackened every bit of wooden surface. Were it not for the squall, Alektrion realized, they would all be dead and *Kestrel* would be burning brightly in the semi-twilight that was rapidly growing darker.

Great Mother, he thought, what is it we've done that so enraged You?

He lay a moment, collecting his strength. When he thought he could stand, he made the attempt. A hot iron of pain rammed up both legs to his chest and sent bolts of white light to his head. He lay, gasping. His head cleared and he looked at his legs, now growing less visible in the fading light. He hadn't thought about his legs since the mast hit them. They were bruised and swelling below the knees.

He touched one. Again came searing pain.

He stared in anger at his legs. He was alive. Unlike some, he'd not been incinerated at once. The canvas had apparently protected most of his skin. He didn't even feel any pain on his back. But both his legs were broken. Hand over hand, he dragged himself across the short deck, grasped *Kestrel's* side railing and pulled himself into a sitting position. He was contemplating the mess of his legs when he felt the ship begin to sink.

He stretched over the side and looked forward at the anchor line, then watched in fascination as more and more of it came out of the water. The water seemed to be dropping away from the line.

He looked to the shore. Watched, stupefied. The Great Sea pulled itself back from Keftiu exposing more and more mud along the shoreline, like lips pulling back to expose the gums of the Mother's teeth. The sight was so sickeningly unnatural that hot acid rushed up the back of his throat. Swallowing hard, he forced it down. The sea continued to recede. Back and back.

Where was it going? Was the black hole at Kalliste swallowing it?

Only when screams of the men stopped abruptly did he turn to look back toward his home, and he stared, at last, into the face of his death. A wall of water, ten times taller than the Temple of Keftiu, utterly black against the crimson dark sky, moved with gargantuan grace toward them.

Ah, Leesa, he thought. The Mother's rage is boundless.

34

I thought I'd listened well. In a poppy vision, The Lady gave me what I felt was the perfect plan to defeat the Pylian king. And surely, I thought, if the Lady has provided so perfect a plan to defeat Atistaeus, She'll grant me a plan to quell this religious rebellion. How then, can I explain the events that began to unfold only three days later? None of my Memories have ever recorded such things, so I wouldn't wonder that those who read this record may be tempted to believe they can't have happened. But I've sworn to record only the truth.

Five days after Sarpedon—and my beloved Alektrion—left Knossos, a white plume appeared on the northern horizon, and Knossos suffered a mild earth shaking. From the highest roof of the Temple, I could see the plume rising up like a pillar of white smoke; it lay in the direction of Kalliste. Fastships soon confirmed that Kalliste was its origin. Steam from the volcano was erupting with enormous force, and the water surrounding the island was so hot it boiled.

Two days later, I was in the Grand Audience Hall receiving foreign dignitaries when I felt, at first, an almost gentle rolling. The ambassador from Byblos stopped speaking in mid-sentence, and we all waited for the shaking to stop.

It didn't.

The massive bronze hanging lamp closest to me plummeted to the floor, crushing the ambassador. One of his eyes, pressed from his crushed skull, rolled forward, was stopped from ending at my very feet only by the sacred partition.

The shaking grew fiercer. Floor candelabra fell, clattered against the room's paving stones. Wooden pillars and doors creaked. Dust rose in the air. With an astonishing jolt, like being hit from behind by a bull, I was thrown from my audience chair and at the same moment heard a sound like a clap of thunder so loud it seemed the world had split open above my head.

I crouched on my knees quivering before my chair. Screams filled the chamber. Some people ran—most were slammed onto the carpets or flagstones. Others curled into balls and covered their heads. I smelled spilled lamp oil. Panicked thoughts of flames made my flesh shrink to my bones. Then I remembered it wasn't night. The torches and braziers weren't lit. Perhaps we'd be spared a fire.

Unbelievably, the shaking continued. The two pillars supporting the cedar doors leading to the reception court toppled. My fear shattered into terror. What if the Temple fell? The massive stone blocks would crush me.

I thought, Get up! Flee! The thought was futile. I lay fear-frozen like a terrified hare until at last the earth stopped moving.

I thought, It's over.

How wrong I was.

My councilors gathered around me, Kishar the first to my side. "You must retreat to the Mother's Womb." They cared for my safety, but I needed to retreat to gather my wits. Trailing attendants, I rushed down the grand staircase and into the Central Court where we all stopped as one and stared at the impossible. The Tree of Life lay on the stones. The pillar upon which were engraved every one of the Laws had broken at the base, had toppled, and had split lengthwise in half. Priestesses and priests stood around it, tears streaming down their faces.

Cold waves skittered over my arms.

"H ... help them," I stuttered to Nothos.

My attendants gave me little time to stand gawking. They rushed me through the Womb's antechamber. Inside the ceremonial chamber, I paced. And I prayed, with fervor, that the Temple, that the People, would survive this day.

Soon news of the quaking's enormity filtered to me. The Temple hadn't collapsed, but portions of the southwestern portal had, as had many surrounding outbuildings—religious and governmental. The cloud rising from Kalliste was now as black as night.

Within the hour I received word of the filthy rain. At first, stones and pebbles. In not too many hours came a fine, sticky, smothering layer of gray flour-like obscenity. The ash mantled everything, poisoning the water in the fountains and gutters.

"The sky grows dark, as if night approaches," I was told.

"The People are terrified."

I retreated once more to my inner sanctuary, but unable to offer any thought to the Ancient save the one word, Why? I forced myself to repeat ritual prayers of humility. I asked for wisdom. I returned to the ceremonial chamber where Kishar and Sarona waited, and I said, "I have to go to my own rooms. I can't stay here where only women can come. I must talk to Nothos and Glaucon. I must be accessible."

With great reluctance, my two Wise Women followed me.

In the Central Court, I paused a moment wondering at a late afternoon sky so deeply sunken into gloom that night seemed near. Not long before the time of sunset, Mestra had drawn me a bath. I sat huddled in the water deep in the eastern quarter, worrying that as of an hour ago not one runner from the seven cities had reported. It was then that the killing cloud struck. I didn't see it and so I cannot speak first-hand of its nature, but I know well the result.

Observers said it crossed the Great Sea with ferocious speed, a monstrous black thing writhing with fireballs and lightning. It swept the land in a twisting, churning, irregular wave, toppling boulders and walls, burning to a cinder everything that wasn't covered. Trees and vines caught fire, but almost at once the fires were smothered by lack of the air they need, leaving only smoking remains. Hair sizzled and curled. Exposed flesh melted, then scorched. Many people escaped burning only to be suffocated. The death cloud leaped and jumped so that it left islands of life in its wake untouched on the ground, but all the birds in the sky fell to earth, blackened.

The killing cloud spread outward from Kalliste for several hundred stadia. The eastern half of Keftiu felt the worst of its fiery fist. Phaestos, my home, was incinerated. The Temple at Kato Zakro burned to the ground and all the People there perished. Even parts of the island of Rhodos were touched.

I experienced this horror as a sudden vibration of the walls of my bathing chamber and an enormous increase in heat. I sank into the water, grew short of breath. Just as I thought I'd surely die, breathable air returned.

Mestra helped me into a robe and we searched for Kishar and Sarona. They had been sitting on my terrace. Mestra and I found them, burned beyond recognition.

My beloved Kishar cradled in my arms, I'd scarcely begun a plunge into a black pit of grief when a great hissing and roaring filled the air. The sound came from the wall of water that followed the killing cloud. Mestra and I peered into the unnatural gloom. Below us, what seemed the whole ocean swept up the gorge of the Kairatos.

The death wave, too, was capricious. It lifted all the ships in the harbor, regardless of size, and carried them inland, but some small ones were dropped within the first stadia or two while others, much larger, were later found as far as twenty stadia from the sea.

All structures within four stadia of the shore—homes, docks, wharves, shops—were destroyed utterly, many leaving behind not the slightest trace. By the time the hissing, foaming wall reached the Temple, thirty stadia from the ocean, it had lost power. Only smaller buildings or those built poorly were toppled, but water rushed into all buildings lying in low land. Darkness devoid of all light fell long before the liquid wall reached its deepest inland thrust, but by morning the water receded, leaving below me a muck-filled, scoured valley.

The horrors of the next days are beyond description. My most vivid memory is of the stench: dead bodies, burned flesh, dead fish, ocean muck. And the seemingly unending night. Ash fell for ten days, and for ten days, we never saw more than a hint of gray sun disk against the blackness. And the inconsolable grief: Nothos's entire family was lost without a trace and hourly I received more messages of death.

Had Alektrion burned in an instant or did he at that very moment suffer? I longed to cry, but tears wouldn't come. My mother and father were long since dead, victims of Kalliste's first eruptions. Then Heebe. I prayed for Zuliya, that he at least might be alive and might return to me. He'd not been in the tablet house, but had taken five of his students to the home of a tin importer who collected rare Sumerian writings. "They went to read the story of Utanapishtim," one of Zuliya's fellow scribes told me. "There is a great irony in the story, and perhaps also hope, Most Honored. It is about a virtuous man—the ancestor of Gilgamesh of Uruk—who survived a flood that covered the entire world. We are living such a story. Perhaps we, too, will survive."

On the second day, I went to my inner sanctuary to pray. The statuette of the Ancient had fallen from the cupboard and shattered, and I shook like a terrified child. "Let nothing happen to them," Nonia had warned.

Thinking I had to do whatever I could to hear the Goddess most vividly, I took the poppy. My visions were indescribable, the worst nightmares of dismembered bodies, of screaming demons, of myself torn apart, and then of my chest exploding.

I allowed Mestra to come as far as the ceremonial chamber of the Mother's Womb for I had no Wise Women to attend me and there was no specific prohibition against her presence there. But I forbade her to enter my sanctuary. My screams so terrified her, though, that she broke the Law, rushed into sanctuary, and tended me until I came out of the trance.

The People were in despair. Those strong or bold enough to fight their way through the rubble and choking rain came in panic to the Temple. Again and again they asked, "Is the world ending?"

Desperate, I tried again, on the fifth day, to use poppy. My prayers reached no further than the nearest stone walls. This time, I fell into a sleep that left me with no memories. I tried again on the sixth day, but once again I was opened to a demon.

The Lady had ceased to speak to me.

Late on the tenth day the choking, filthy rain thinned and stiff winds, still blowing from the northwest, began to clean the air. Four of the seven-member Council had survived. Their most pressing problem: disposal of the dead, both human and animal. They begged me for help. In a few brief hours, less than a day and a night, the Temple guard had been reduced by half. I assigned half of those remaining to organize burial crews.

People slowly emerged to create order as best they could, cleaning, sorting, scouring the countryside for anything useable.

On the eleventh day, I received word that Zuliya waited in the little southeast house. Only Zuliya remained alive now of those whom I had loved. I was certain Alektrion was dead. I ran the whole way, heedless of the startled gazes around me.

I rushed to the lattice and placed both hands against the silk. He raised his palms to mine. "To see you again," he said, his voice trembling. I felt his hands shaking. "How very fortunate I am."

I was crying like a child, tears of loss so grievous when I tried to speak, words twisted in my throat and refused to come out. I thought, over and over, only Zuliya remains. I finally regained composure. I resolved I wouldn't cry again. Never would I let anything, or anyone, reach so deeply inside I could hurt that much.

We pulled chairs close to the lattice and talked. From the moment I'd found Kishar's body, a part of me wanted nothing more than to go into a dark place, lie down, and never rise, but I reminded myself often that I was the Lady's Voice. And whether She spoke to me or not, whether or not I understood the reasons for the devastation of the world, the People were suffering. I asked my venerable teacher how the Temple should best proceed to reduce the People's pain.

I listened for a while, and then, unable to stop myself, I asked the question that never left my mind from the moment I awakened to the moment I escaped into sleep. "Why, Zuliya? Could She be this angry with all of us because some are weak? Why Kishar, who loved the Great Mother of All more than life itself?"

He shook his head. "I am not the one who can answer your question. I don't see the world as you do. You know that."

"Then what answer do you give yourself?"

"I don't ask why."

"I don't believe you. You can't simply accept this horror, without thought. It wouldn't be natural not to ask why."

He scratched at his short beard and even smiled, only the smallest curving of his lips. "Yes, yes. You've caught me there. I confess that almost the first thing I thought when I watched the beginning of the black rain was, 'Why is this happening?' But the answer I seek is not in the wrath, or even the whim, of some god or goddess. I want to know how the world works. I don't seek answers beyond that. I don't think there are any, no matter how desperately we may crave them. Does believing that this suffering is the result of the Lady's wish to punish the People or of Poseidon's wrath at not being recognized bring comfort? It may satisfy the need for explanation. But it's a false, hollow comfort. To me, such an idea is no comfort at all. It is repellent."

"I need to believe there is a reason. If I cannot find a reason, I don't think I'll be strong enough to lead through this darkness."

"I'm sure there is a reason. But it is not that some deity is angry with Kishar or the People or you."

"My dear friend." I put my hand to the silk again and he raised his to meet mine. "Your world is too ... impersonal. It would frighten me to believe the Goddess doesn't care for us. But my heart is profoundly grateful you're alive and here at my side."

He wiggled his fingers and grinned, then thumped his wooden leg. "Then have your servants help me get out of this thing. I'm tired and it's rubbing."

I called for the boy and girl attendants. "You'll stay here, right in this room," I told Zuliya. "I'll have a bed and tub brought in. Five days ago I sent someone to try to find you, and the house where you lived is gone."

"And my landlady?"

"Disappeared."

Gone. Disappeared. Words I heard again and again. I reestablished communication between Keftiu's major cities, but two moon cycles passed before we'd heard from all. Most of the roads were gone. The flow of goods stopped completely.

Nor would it have served any useful purpose if the roads were intact. The crops in the fertile fields on Keftiu's eastern half were destroyed. The depth of the powder, in many places up to a handspan, layered everything. Soon I learned that the Temple stores of essentials—oil and grain and wine—would, if rationed carefully, barely see those still alive in Knossos through the winter. The other cities, and to a great extent all families on Keftiu, were left to fend as best they could. Long lines of people were soon at the portals seeking supplies.

Glaucon estimated, from the numbers of burials, that at least twenty thousand had died in Knossos, a fourth of the population. By winter's end, he expected another ten or fifteen thousand to join them as casualties of starvation or illness. Numbers so vast I could scarcely comprehend them. But the day Nothos told me that all but three of the Wise Ones were dead, perfect comprehension sent a cold, clammy slickness over my skin.

"Who remains?" I asked.

"Blauthea, Philomea, and Sestrae. Blauthea and Sestrae were at the sacred cave at Psychro. Philomea was at the cave in the Idha mountains."

Utterly incomprehensible! I had no idea how Philomea felt about Galatea's nomination to be the Lady's Voice, but Kishar had said that Blauthea and Sestrae supported Galatea. At least two of the three remaining Wise Women had hearts willing to compromise with a bloodthirsty, barbarian god. Once again I asked myself, why?

Another two cycles of the moon turned and shortly before the season when travel by sea became hazardous, I received the first communications from fleet officers, and within a few more days, any hope of mounting a successful blockade of Pylos evaporated. The Lady's navy survived only as scattered remnants, most vessels in desperate need of repair. One report came from Sarpedon, the first remotely good news. The death wave had reached Khania, but he'd anticipated it and put his ships out to sea. And most significantly, a strong westerly gale blowing there had weakened the killing cloud—Sarpedon reported no deaths by burning and suffocation—and he reported only light ashfall. He asked if he should winter his ships in Khania or return to Knossos. I dispatched one of the few undamaged fastships to tell him nothing was left at Amnissos but the bay. He was better off to shelter around Khania, and I would decide come spring how to proceed.

In a private communication, he said Alektrion had been on his way back to Knossos in a fastship when the disaster occurred. That he had heard nothing from Alektrion since then, although parts of the wreck of his fastship, the *Kestrel*, had been recovered. "I am sorry," he ended the note, "but were Alektrion of Kalliste alive, he would have gotten word to me by now."

I sat with the bit of papyrus in my hand and Alektrion's eyes in my mind, and hot tears flowed again. Waves of grief, one upon another, swallowed me. I'd foolishly thought my heart had grown incapable of feeling any more shock or grief or pain. The craving to retreat to my chambers and to darkness struck again. I was going to learn there is no limit to the pain the heart can suffer. The thought of never seeing him again. Unbearable. To never hear his voice. Never touch his hand. Not because separation was a necessity and I could still imagine him alive, laughing, a presence still in the world, but because he was dead. Never—a cruel, cruel word.

Silvanos festival became another kind of disaster. We were to celebrate the beginning of the Maiden's journey to bring Velchanos back to us, to bring us renewal in spring. But there would be no renewal next spring, and everyone knew it. Nothing was going to grow. All in the Temple performed the rituals as they should, but hearts were not properly prepared, including mine. Few of the People attended. I couldn't blame them. There was no hope in the world, only a dark spiritual night.

Days and weeks streamed past. I found myself plagued anew with the Poseidonist heresy. The miserable priest Oenopion had survived, as had Minyas. Minyas had retreated to his country estate many months before the disaster. There he remained. Again my troubled spirit asked, why?

The winter was shockingly, bitterly cold. Some scholars thought the coldness was related to the explosion of Kalliste. What had been a beautiful island, Kalliste was now only a ring of blasted land encircling a vast bay. Most of the time, I sat before a weakly glowing brazier in the sitting room of my chambers wrapped in a fur cloak. Glaucon reported daily. He would take a chair opposite me, and Mestra would bring heated but very watered wine—the need to conserve precious essentials weighed heavily in all minds.

In late winter, Glaucon brought especially grave news. "Minyas is building a large private army, Most Honored. By Kokor's own luck, most of his property sits even higher than the Temple. A goodly amount was untouched by the flood and because it sits behind a row of foothills that parallel the shore, it was also sheltered from the killing cloud."

"Does he have enough men to threaten the Temple?"

"No. Certainly not." Glaucon's shoulders stiffened as if to emphasize our relative strength. "But the idea of any private army, let alone one dedicated to a foreign god, is unacceptable. Let me crush him."

"Does the Temple have enough armed men to stop him? We can't draw men from the seven cities. Can we stop him cleanly? Because we can't have a civil war, Glaucon. Not now."

The stiffness melted from Glaucon's shoulders.

My thoughts ran toward the future. "The People will need every last drop of energy to simply survive this winter. And I shudder to think what spring may bring if it's true the Peloponnesis was scarcely touched."

We sat in silence staring at the glowing coals. At about the same time, I received the communication from Sarpedon about Alektrion's death, a fastship from the northwest reported that the rain of ash hadn't penetrated much further west than Melos. The mainland was apparently largely unaffected. And before the disaster, Atistaeus had pulled back to the sheltered side of one of the Peloponnesian fingers. At such a location, the killing wave probably would not have reached him. Our enemy was very likely unscathed.

In mid-winter, Oenopion scorned my decree that the temple of Poseidon remain closed. Supported by a mob of over five hundred, he drove off the Temple guards and rushed inside. For days the place was occupied by fifty armed Poseidonists, and on the temple's portico for all to see, Oenopion performed blood sacrifices.

Once such an act would have caused me to weep, but that Leesandra was no more. Stony of heart, I ordered the temple closed and shed no tears when Nothos told me the price of closing it had been the lives of twenty-one men.

I went to see Zuliya and told him what I'd done and how I felt.

"Don't grow cold," he said.

"I'm not cold. I do what is necessary."

I prayed that the Poseidonists' animal sacrifices were their worst evil. I feared much worse. I had irrefutable proof that immediately following Kalliste's explosion, at the height of the terror, human sacrifices had been performed—most by Poseidonists, but the great blasphemy was that at least two were performed at shrines to the Mother. If such practices continued, I was certain the Goddess would abandon the People altogether, nothing would ever grow again on Keftiu, the People would utterly perish. I decreed that anyone participating in human sacrifice would be banished to Lissimos, and I would speak the death banishment without the slightest qualm.

The time for winter to give way to spring arrived, but winter storms persisted. The Sacred Marriage loomed ahead. If Silvanos had been difficult—full of dread and empty of hope—what would I feel during Belamnos? How could I possibly put my spirit right so that when the young God and I joined, harmony between the male and female forces would be restored to perfection? With Alektrion's death and the unfathomable rupture of the world, harmony had deserted me.

I thought perhaps the Lady would want me to cancel Belamnos or alter it in some way to reflect Her desires for the People. But no matter how often I asked Her, I heard nothing.

The three remaining Wise Ones chose the young man who would be the Lady's consort, the greatest honor of his life. I pitied him. The Poseidonists were saying their god had proved he was greater than Velchanos. In a hundred ways, Oenopion spoke the same message: "Velchanos is weak. The Lady must take as her consort a man who can speak for Poseidon, and that man is Minyas. Poseidon has chosen Minyas to be High Priest of Poseidon for Keftiu."

Exactly one cycle of the moon before the start of Belamnos, Minyas arrived at the Temple accompanied by two thousand armed men. He demanded audience. Glaucon pleaded with me to take him prisoner, no matter what the cost in blood.

"He says he comes to talk, not fight," I countered. "He must come into the Temple as any one of the Mother's servants, barefoot and without weapons or guards, but we will listen."

"I fear for you, Most Honored."

"No, Glaucon. Take precautions, but don't fear. My life is in the hands of the Goddess."

∾ ∾ ∾ ∾

I mounted the three steps and sat in my audience chair thinking that, whatever Minyas wanted, in the end I'd talk with him in private. I indulged a flicker of hope that his coming was a sign that perhaps he had repented.

The cedar doors to the audience hall had been repaired. They swung open. Those Temple functionaries attending the audience, including two of my Memories and Nothos and Glaucon, watched as Minyas strode boldly toward me. He was still slender and carried himself with assurance. Those large, dark eyes still dominated his face. So much like Galatea's. He stopped at the required distance from the sacred partition, but though he took the position of reverence, he didn't wait for me to acknowledge him before dropping his fist. Instead, he relaxed into a polite but confident pose and began to speak, again without permission.

I heard the sucking in of many breaths.

"Most Honored. The People have served the Great Mother since the beginning of time. But the extraordinary events we've suffered make clear we've not been listening to Her as we should. The Goddess has grown tired of Velchanos."

My heart raced. My friend's father, my enemy, the enemy of my Lady stood before me, hideously swollen with pride.

"The Lady seeks as Her consort a God of power," Minyas continued. "And the People have not listened to Her wishes. God and Goddess have spoken, Most Honored. I am sure—"

"Silence!" My voice sliced into every corner of the room. "You dare to speak to the Lady's Voice with such disrespect. You dare to tell me what the Goddess wants!"

His eyes narrowed and his lips thinned. "I have the committed support of the King of Pylos, Most Honored. His purposes and mine are in agreement. If, at Belamnos, I am made your permanent consort and am appointed High Priest of Poseidon, I will bring Atistaeus into alliance with Knossos. An invasion can be avoided. The Goddess will keep Her place of honor, with Poseidon at Her side as She wishes."

He paused, expecting me to speak. Holding my breath, I remained silent. In memory I heard one of Zuliya's sayings: "Let a fool speak his piece, the better to have his head."

Minyas continued, his tone ever so reasonable. "Even before these brutal disasters, the world was changing. Atistaeus isn't the only outlander who looks on Keftiu with desire. I've known for a long time that the People must ally themselves with an outsider who can strengthen us. Only by uniting with the mainland—on our terms—can we prevent our ultimate eclipse. Without their strength, Most Revered, Keftiu will fall to others. Let us talk. I know you want what is best for the People. Allow me the opportunity to convince you."

I was shaking so violently my hands trembled. I clasped them together. "Do speak on, Minyas of Knossos," I said in sweet accent.

His tone hardened. "If you refuse this offer, you will doom the People to conquest. Atistaeus prepares at this very moment for a spring invasion. He will come, and surely you must realize Knossos can't stand against him. If you refuse my offer now, when the battle is over in spring I will elevate Poseidon. Unavoidably, if this is done by force, the Lady will suffer a decline in status throughout the world." He stopped speaking.

"Have you finished?"

"Yes."

I rose, my pulse pounding in my throat. "Your words are blasphemy. Your heart twisted. Your mind fooled. I agreed to this audience, and you will therefore be allowed to return to your country lands. But you are forbidden, on pain of death, to return to Knossos. Dare put so much as a toe in the city, Minyas, and I'll banish you to Lissimos. Should you ignore this warning and come again with men under arms, blood will flow."

I descended the steps to the floor, turned my back on him, and strode out of the audience room.

Glaucon was at my side. "Let me take him now, Most Honored."

"No, Glaucon." I put a restraining hand on his arm. "He has two thousand men with him."

I spent that afternoon and evening pacing in my quarters. Take Minyas as consort? Recognize the blood-loving barbarian god? I knelt at my shrine and took an oath. "Poseidon will never be worshipped here."

But Atistaeus wasn't going to be dismissed by defiant words. There had to be a way out.

Early the next morning, Nothos arrived with even worse news, as if that were possible. He waited, trudging a rut in my sitting-room rug, until I'd thrown on a robe. Saying nothing, he handed me a scroll. From its seal I knew it came as a pronouncement of the Wise Ones.

I read no more than the first two lines when my knees turned to water and I had to sit.

> *Do not defy the Goddess as Damkina did. The Lady has chosen Poseidon. Velchanos must make way.*
> *Restore the harmony of the world. At the Sacred Marriage, take Minyas as permanent consort.*

Prominent at the bottom were all three names: Philomea, Blauthea, Sestrae.

Nothos knelt beside me. To Mestra he called, "Bring Leesandra wine. Not watered." To me he said, "What do they say?"

I handed him the scroll. He sat opposite me and read the message. Mestra brought the wine.

"No," I said, brushing it away.

Nothos studied my face, far too keen a politician to speak his thoughts before he was sure of mine. Finally, he said, "Your burden grows heavier. What will you do?"

"I can't talk of this yet." I turned to Mestra. "Get my cloak. I go to my sanctuary."

I told Nothos to reveal the pronouncement of the Wise Women to those members of the Council, the Naval academy, and the Temple staff with whom I'd need to confer after praying. "What I decide will not be done in secret. All must know the stakes and the conditions. Also tell my teacher, Zuliya. I'll want to talk to him."

Desperate, I took the poppy again. I found myself with Alektrion. His arms encircled me, his lips found mine, and my body blended into his. I longed to stay there, secure in his heart, but the spirit of Zuliya found me and yanked me away. "You must decide," Zuliya said, shaking a finger at me. My spirit traveled to the Kalliste of my childhood—perfect in its peace, its gardens full of flowers, its beaches secured by the sea. But the volcano began to rip apart and the visions became black and of death.

Finally, late in the night, the dream passed. I still had no answer. The Goddess no longer spoke to me. Whatever decision was made it would be, as for months all important decisions had been, mine alone.

I returned to my chambers and drew up a list of those with whom I wanted to speak the next day. I would see them in the small audience chamber so that Zuliya could be there. Then I called for Ninsuna, the best of my scribes, and began dictating this record which you now read.

~ ~ ~ ~

Ten days have passed. In that time I've listened to the counsel of many. I've found a deep peace, which surely only She can have given me. I said as I began this record that I no longer hear the Mother's voice and, sadly, the silence persists. I have recalled Sarpedon to Knossos, telling him he must come as early as possible, even before the sea is entirely safe. If in the spring we are to defeat Atistaeus, we must gamble, and the Goddess—or fortune—must be with us.

I've also sent word to the three cities from which we have any hope of aid asking that they send men. Glaucon is to recruit as many men as he can to add to the Temple guard. He also prepares plans to capture Minyas.

Nothos believes our cause is hopeless. "The elite of our warriors and nearly all of our experienced military leaders are dead," he said when I told him my decision to fight rather than submit. "Sarpedon is only one man, and he has at most eighty ships."

I countered. "Zerthon says we know Keftian water while Atistaeus doesn't. He says we'll have that as an advantage."

Nothos snorted disgust. "Zerthon is little more than a rusty academic." He caught my gaze, his face drew down in sadness. "Most Honored, I must speak of something most ... most painful. I fear you cannot possibly defeat the Pylian barbarian. And you cannot leave the Temple. They will force you to take Minyas as your consort. Or..."

"Or?"

He let out a long, soft sigh, and then his voice turned hard. "Surely you understand that you must deny Minyas any legitimacy. You must also remove any possibility that the Pylian King could become consort to the Great Goddess. In one stroke, the barbarian god would be given a place in the Temple itself."

I had already thought the battle through all the way to the end. I wasn't afraid. I felt only weariness. "There will be no Sacred Marriage. You needn't worry. I know my duty, Nothos. And if I must, I'll do it."

Nothos has promised that within the week he'll bring me what is necessary. He is a zealous guardian of the old ways. It's painless, he says, and fast. I won't have to wait long.

I immediately confided my decision to defy Minyas and Atistaeus to Zuliya. He, too, remains gloomy. We were in the small audience chamber, and I'd just dismissed the four members of the Council having listened to their final pleas that Minyas be repudiated. There were times, such as this one, when I wanted to tear the silk down with my own hands.

"You have, as you always have had, my total allegiance," Zuliya said. "We will see this matter through together. But I must tell you, as an old hand to a Mitanni general, if Atistaeus comes in full force, I don't believe Sarpedon can defeat him."

"Would you have me take Minyas as consort, then?"

He elevated his false leg onto the stool in front of his chair, sipped some salepi tea. Having his bright red shoe thrust before me, I remembered how very odd I thought Zuliya was the first time I saw him in my father's den. I smiled. He was now the last person alive who owned any piece of my heart.

He pursed his lips, looked at me out of the corner of his eye. "The Wise Women have counseled you to do just that. You could listen to them."

I couldn't suppress another tiny smile—and I'd ceased smiling some time ago. "It troubles me to defy them, but they're old and afraid and terribly wrong."

"I have always taught you to listen to your head and your heart alone. What does your heart tell you?"

"It tells me, my dear friend, that I would rather die than give the smallest bit of recognition to the bloodthirsty, war-loving, barbarian god. A god whose priest proudly claims that He has caused the suffering and pain the People have endured."

"Ah, well. Clearly then, we fight."

"Yes. We fight."

And if I am to live, we must also win.

35

Alektrion's legs felt desperately in need of rest, but he couldn't wait. He'd been on the journey to Knossos for over two moon cycles, and he was now so close nothing could stop him: not the pain in his legs, not that it was the middle of the night, not the knowledge that he was filthy and disheveled.

He trudged up the incline to the Temple's northwest portal. Five guards stood duty, three more than usual for this time of night. What else would he find changed?

He turned to walk south. "Wait!" a deep voice called out. A stocky youth with a sour expression approached. "What are you doing here at this hour? No lines are allowed to form until just before dawn."

"Lines? Lines for what?"

"You're not looking for grain or oil?"

"No."

"Then I repeat, what are you doing here?"

"I'm an aide to Sarpedon, fleet admiral. We've just returned from the west, and I'm—"

Raised eyebrows stopped Alektrion. He wasn't believed. And why should he be? He looked terrible. He changed his story. "I'm in bad need of a hetaira."

"At this time of night? No hetaira would take you this late." The guard sniffed at Alektrion with disgust. "And no hetaira of the Goddess will take you smelling like a pig three days dead."

Alektrion made a show of examining his tunic. "You're right." He smiled soothingly. "A man is sometimes in too much of a hurry."

The guard didn't smile back. "Come back tomorrow. Clean."

Giving the guard no chance to inquire further, Alektrion turned and left, heading south. He saw many signs of collapsed stone work and reconstructed walls. After skirting around the Temple's southern end, another guard waited in his path. This older man immediately recognized Sarpedon's aide. So surprised was the man that he forgot Alektrion's half-breed status and saluted, fist over heart. "By the Lady's daughters and sons! We've all believed you were dead."

"I came as near to the Ancient's cold embrace as I ever could and live to remember it. Tell me. I see signs of much damage. Does the small audience room still stand?"

"Yes, Scorpion. You'll find it quite sound."

Alektrion nodded, then hurried on. At the door he thumped several times before it swung open. The boy stood blinking, a flickering oil lamp in his hand.

Metal bands seemed bound around Alektrion's chest, making breathing hard. He could imagine how bizarre this midnight visit would seem to the boy. "I must see the High Priestess. Is it true that she lives and is well?"

Behind the child appeared a dark figure dressed in a short sleeping gown. "What's going on here?"

Alektrion recognized the voice. "It's me, Zuliya. Alektrion."

The Nubian stepped closer and thrust forward the lamp in his hand. A crutch supported his other side. This was the first time Alektrion had ever seen Zuliya without his false leg. Why was he here? And in a sleeping gown? "By all of gods of Egypt!" Zuliya hobbled backward. "Come in. Come in."

The boy also backed into the room and Alektrion entered. "I have heard that she lives, Zuliya. Is it true? And is she well?"

Zuliya turned to the boy. "Wake the serving girl. Tell her to find a room for me. Somewhere. Any room. A place in the hetaira quarter. Then you prepare a bath for the High Priestess's guest. He will take these rooms now. But first, bring me my leg."

Alektrion put his hand on Zuliya's arm. "Does she live?"

"Yes, yes. Of course. And I believe she will come at once. Things are not as they were before."

The pressure on Alektrion's chest eased, he sucked in a deep breath. He sniffed with disgust at the smell of sweat on his ragged cloak. "I know I'm a horror. Perhaps I shouldn't have come until tomorrow. But I need to see Leesandra."

"But of course you do." Zuliya lowered himself onto a couch. "You must wonder why I'm living here. She insisted. My own rooms were destroyed." The boy returned from the sleeping room. He handed over the wooden leg and dashed off like a hare to stir the girl.

Zuliya looked up at Alektrion, shook his head. "Young warrior, I cannot tell you how glad I am to see you alive. The Lady's Voice has suffered over this great tragedy. But I will tell you that my Leesandra's heart died within her when she finally felt certain you were dead. It will be a great joy for me to see her happiness."

Alektrion watched Zuliya strap on the artificial limb. The girl appeared, sleepy-eyed. She started for the door, but Zuliya stopped her. "Bring me papyrus and the writing box."

She left, returned with the materials. The sound of running water reached Alektrion from a room he assumed was now used for bathing. "Find a place for me," Zuliya said, shooing the girl toward the door. He began writing. "I only wish I could bring these words to Leesandra in person. I would give the venerable jewels of Isis to watch her face as she reads them."

The boy reappeared. "A bath is ready," he announced, staring wide-eyed at Alektrion.

"Here, boy." Zuliya rolled the tiny bit of papyrus tightly. "Straight to the High Priestess's rooms. Give it only to Mestra."

The boy rushed away. Zuliya said, "It should not take too long." An appraising look from him lingered on the scars on Alektrion's legs. "If I were you, I'd scrub quickly."

On aching feet Alektrion walked to the bathing chamber with Zuliya close behind. "I stink like a sweaty bull."

"Umm," hummed the teacher. "I see you have come back to us with a slight limp. How were the wounds caused?"

"The mast of my ship. Fell across my legs." Alektrion stripped off his kilt and strap, mounted the stairs and stepped into the tub. "I was more fortunate than you, good teacher. I kept both legs, but it took the skills of a remarkable healer, many months of confinement, and even more months of recovery."

He stiffly lowered himself through the cloud of steam and sank into the hot water. His aching body throbbed with relief.

"I would have sent word to Leesandra and my admiral, but my rescuers were simple, isolated folk. They have nothing for writing and besides would not spare anyone from work to bear a message such a long distance."

Using a sponge and starting with his face and its beard, he scrubbed hard. The beard would come off as soon as he could get his hands on a razor. Soon, if Zuliya spoke true, he would see her face.

"I will want to hear it all, later," Zuliya said. "Now I leave you alone. But before I do, you should know our Leesandra is cruelly pressed. The details should come from her, but to be short with it, she has been assured Atistaeus will soon invade and, rather than surrender, she has chosen to try to defeat him."

Zuliya poured water for him while Alektrion washed his hair. "I do not think Knossos can win," Zuliya continued. "Such a fight will be a case of the flea against the dragonfly, as the Mitanni say—but there are others who tell her it might be possible."

Alektrion squeezed his hair dry.

"And her other option is so painful for her to contemplate—well, I'm not sure she can view it with a dispassionate mind."

Alektrion started to ask "what other option?" but he heard the soft rustling of slippered feet. Mestra appeared in the door of the bathing chamber. "My lady is here."

Water flew in all directions as Alektrion jumped out of the tub. The boy had left a robe on a stool. Alektrion snatched it up, threw it on, rushed into the main room. Leesandra stood behind the silk and wooden barrier. She looked at him, her face so drained of color the thin white scar down her cheek had disappeared completely. She lifted an arm in front of her, as if seeking support. "So, it's true," she said, then crumpled slowly to the floor.

He rushed to the screen, his hands raised to batter their way through the wood and silk.

She looked up at him, raised her hand, her palm flat in a restraining gesture. "No, Alek! Don't! You mustn't. I'm fine. Truly."

He pressed his palms against the hated silk wall. Love for her stole his breath; he feasted on the vision that had kept him alive when others around him had given up and died. She was wrapped in a night robe of light green. Her hair fell to her waist, the golden hairpin of a sea eagle perched at her right temple. Her eyes seemed somehow larger. Mestra passed through the screen's small door and knelt beside her mistress.

"Help me to stand," Leesandra said to Mestra. She hadn't taken her gaze from Alektrion's face, not for a moment. She rose, took three steps, and pressed both hands against his. "Ah, beloved," she whispered. "The Mother, in Her infinite mercy, has given me back my heart."

The smell of roses came to him—the smell he had dreamed of, often in the midst of incredible pain. This scent was real. Not imagined. Not just desperately wished for in the darkness of agony-filled nights. He'd dreamed of this moment, and now he savored it. He stood, his heart thundering in his chest and her hands pressed against his so tightly as to make their souls melt together.

Zuliya grabbed the boy and pushed him toward the door leading into the Temple. "Come back in the morning. Not until then. Tell the girl, too." Zuliya disappeared through the opposite door. Mestra followed the boy and shut the door to the Temple behind her.

Tears streamed down Leesandra's face. "Whatever's wrong with me that I'm crying so?"

"You're as happy as I am."

"Oh Alek, Alek. How dear is the sound of your voice." Her lips quivered. She had begun to shake. The tears flowed faster. She snatched her hands from the silk and with both, one to each cheek, brushed at her tears. She drew in several deep breaths and gradually her shaking stopped. "Let's sit," she said.

They took chairs, and each pressed a palm to the screen. The need to make love to her made his body throb. He clenched the hand resting on his thigh, tried to concentrate on her face, on her words. To be with this stubborn, brave woman from his youth had the astonishing ability to make all the pain of the world outside melt away.

"I saw you limp. I want to know what has happened to you." Then, "Oh, Alek. I just want to drown in the sound of your voice."

He told her all. How the monstrous wave lifted his ship, carried it inland, and dumped it in a ravine. How he and two others had survived, but only he had had the strength to drag himself, his throbbing, broken legs useless behind him, to a shepherd's hut. By the time he could send the shepherd to look for his companions, they, too, were dead. "The shepherd's mother healed my legs. I had the great fortune that she was a woman with a lifetime of caring for injured cattle as well as wild creatures."

The telling took a long time. But finally he said, "Now I must know about you. Zuliya says your position with respect to Atistaeus is dire. I need to hear your troubles."

She sighed and her eyes clouded. "All vessels in any Keftian ports east of Knossos were destroyed. The killing wave obliterated not only the stores we might have used to make repairs, but killed the workers with the skills needed to do it. And what is terribly frightening, the disaster scarcely touched the Achean fleet, Alek.

"I'm still unsure about our vessels at sea. None have returned from the east. In fact, no traders have come from any of the eastern islands— Kyprus or Rhodos. Nothing from Byblos. Nothing from Agyptos. Perhaps only because it's winter. But it's possible all ships to the east were destroyed. Perhaps the devastation in the east reached to where the world ends. I simply don't know."

"What about Sarpedon?"

"Ah, Sarpedon. Now that's a different matter. Your admiral not only survived, Alek, he saved his ships."

Sarpedon. Alive! Pleasure struck a warm, solid blow in his chest. "All of them? With their tenders?"

"He lost only eight warships and a few supply vessels. I've instructed him to return, I pray in time for us to prepare to meet Atistaeus. If Sarpedon makes it at all, he should be here soon. No later than the next seven or eight days. Perhaps tomorrow."

Visions of the sea that he'd kept to his left while walking the last few weeks rose in Alektrion's mind. "The weather is still treacherous."

"Nevertheless, he has to come, Alek. He's our only hope."

"If he knows that, he will try. But then what if he can't make it? Perhaps ..."

He thought of her disgust for the Acheans, of his own hatred for Atistaeus, and hesitated, then decided he had to speak; they must consider all options. "Perhaps if you offer Atistaeus an alliance. Perhaps that would appease him."

"Are you saying you'd have me accept this barbarian into the Mother's Heart as her king? Atistaeus will take nothing less than our submission, Alek."

"Knossos is so weakened, our resources so devastated, why would he want to invade now?"

"We may be weakened, but you know as well as I that the People sit at the center of the world. To possess this location, if only to serve as a base for conquest, would satisfy the cost of an invasion." Her gaze was sharp with accusation. "He doesn't want cooperation."

He thought of Laius. "I despise Atistaeus of Pylos. So then, who from the naval academy is still alive and is capable of planning a defense?"

She shook her head, pressed the tips of her fingers against her eyes. "There is no one, Alek. No one but Sarpedon. And now you."

He shook his head. "I'm no strategist. I've no schooling."

"You have experience. You've learned the hard way, at sea and at Sarpedon's side."

"Leesa, if we have no more than eighty ships, and Atistaeus comes in force with his fleet of two hundred, it will require much more than naval genius to defeat him. Zuliya was right. We'd be a flea against a dragonfly. Zuliya mentioned another choice."

The frown line between her eyes deepened, a line she'd not had when he left her a scant eight moon cycles ago. She rose and went to a bulls-head rhyton that sat on a corner table. From it she poured a cup of what he supposed was wine, drank a bit, then returned. "Aren't you thirsty? I'm certain there is wine in the antechamber."

"I no longer take wine. Or ale. I prefer clear thoughts at all times. But you didn't answer my question. What did Zuliya mean by another choice?"

"There is no other choice." Her words held heat.

"Zuliya seemed to think there was."

"Atistaeus isn't our only problem, Alek." She rose again and paced, rubbing her arms. He couldn't remember ever seeing her this agitated, not since that first riot, the day he bought the hairpin she still wore. "It's Minyas. He has made a pact with the barbarian. Minyas demanded I take him ..." Her voice was sharpened with sarcasm.

"High Priest of Poseidon, Minyas calls himself now. He demands that at the Sacred Marriage that I take him as consort for life. The ceremony is only weeks away."

He surged to his feet. "Consort for life?"

"Exactly. In return, he's sworn Atistaeus won't invade. The Lady's Voice would merely have to acknowledge submission to Pylos. I've refused his 'generous' offer." She put her hands to the silk.

"I can't imagine Zuliya thinking such a thing possible." He could not refuse to meet her gesture. He put his palms against hers and inhaled scent of roses. The thought of her taking any other man to her bed sickened him.

"You have to understand how Zuliya thinks," she said quickly. "First of all, he knows I care for you, but I don't think he's fully aware of how repugnant the idea of lying with Minyas would be to me. He's only thinking of the logic of things. And there is something on his side."

Alektrion pulled his hands away. "Ha! Whatever could be on his side?"

She sat again, gestured for him to sit, too. "Only three of the Wise Ones still live. But all three sent word to me—Oh, it frightens me even to say this aloud."

"Tell me!"

"All three sent word that if the People are to put the world in balance, the Temple must recognize both male and female deities. They've given their voice to Oenopion's argument that this calamity has come upon us because The Lady is tired of Velchanos and seeks a stronger mate."

"Anyone with half a brain would know that's blasphemous nonsense! The Wise Ones utter this nonsense? Truly? I don't believe it! Kishar?"

She sighed. "Kishar's dead, Alek. The world is no longer as it was. No one can doubt that. No one can be surprised if things that were once considered unbelievable are now believed."

He rose again and paced. "Sarpedon must come, and soon."

She made no reply.

"I know virtually every man-in-arms in Knossos—and every old geezer who ever carried a spear or wanted to."

He stopped and looked at her. "Does Glaucon live?"

She nodded. He continued pacing. "Then I'll begin tomorrow, with Glaucon, even before Sarpedon returns. We must gather a land force." He continued to spin ideas. She assured him some were already being done.

As he talked, she grew more animated. "Yes," she said at last. "Oh, Alek. It's so good to have you here. My blood flows hot again. For the first time, I truly believe." She clasped her hands together.

He stopped and studied her. So slight. So beautiful. She was part of the trophy for which Minyas lusted. A trophy Atistaeus himself might try to claim if they didn't win this battle. *So the flea will have to consider the possibility of losing and make plans accordingly.* "You mustn't have false hope, Leesa. Nothing will save us if Sarpedon doesn't return soon. And even assuming he does, I'm not sure even his genius can make eighty ships best two hundred. If we lose, we'll have no option but to escape. You have to be prepared for that. We have to decide where we might go."

The sparkle in her eyes extinguished. Such a strange look it was that clouded her face. Puzzlement? Hesitation?

He pressed his point. "There's much less damage in the west, even on Keftiu. Or we might leave Keftiu. Go far to the west, to a place so far away no one has been there before."

"I ... I don't think you ... I can't ... umm ..."

"What?"

She wrapped her arms around herself as if she'd felt a chill. "You wouldn't understand."

"Of course I would. What is it?"

"Only that we must win. We must! And I feel in every bone and sinew Sarpedon will come soon. The Lady will show us what to do. I pray, and you must pray, that we're never faced with such a terrible, terrible choice. We must win."

"Well, you can be sure I'll be praying, more than once a day, to smear Atistaeus's blood on his own cloak."

∾ ∾ ∾ ∾

Three days later, Sarpedon sailed into Amnissos with only three warships. Panicked rumors flew to the Temple. Knossos had no fleet left at all!

Alektrion threw himself into clothes to go to the harbor, then a messenger arrived from Leesandra. Sarpedon had sent word—to be kept closely confidential—that the remainder of his ships, including supply vessels, were sheltered to the west where the damage from the ash and killing wave was less. Until he knew their ultimate plans, the men would find better forage there. Alektrion put a hand over his rapidly thudding heart and breathed with relief.

A day later he paced the small audience room in the southeast house, eager to see his admiral. His belongings had been moved into the now very crowded small chambers on each side of the main room. On a trestle table that commanded the center of the main room lay charts of the Great Sea and all of Keftiu's northern coast. The charts were a secret known only to the highest Temple and naval authorities. They were the foundation of Keftiu's mastery of the ocean. Here was gathered the knowledge of ages, gleaned by the scholars of Keftiu from the minds of generations of sailors. Nothing like them existed anywhere else.

In one corner, Zuliya lounged in his favorite chair, slowly stroking his beard, his feet propped on a stool as he read.

The door leading to the Temple opened. Nothos entered, followed by Glaucon, two female Memories, two female scribes Alektrion didn't recognize, and Zerthon, the only high naval officer in Knossos to survive the killing wave. Zerthon, who resembled a dried stick, was an academic whose opinion Alektrion had never much valued. The boy closed the door behind these notables.

Zuliya put his reading aside but remained seated.

Leesandra's retainers moved through the door in the partition into the main part of the room. Formal greetings were exchanged. Most had taken seats when a guard opened the outer door Alektrion and Zuliya used.

The guard announced, "Sarpedon of Mallia."

Talos entered first. His mangled face had never looked more beautiful. Anchices glided in behind Talos. Then in strode the little admiral. Another surge of joy warmed Alektrion. How fit and scrappy Sarpedon looked. The realization struck suddenly that the admiration—the affection—he felt for Sarpedon had grown to be like that Alektrion had felt for his father.

Sarpedon embraced Alektrion so firmly it squeezed his breath away. Sarpedon's voice was tight with emotion. "Kokor himself couldn't kill you, Scorpion."

Talos settled for slugging Alektrion on his arm and proclaiming in his whispery way, "Scorpions take a lot of killing."

Anchices embraced him fiercely, but said nothing.

The door to the Temple opened and, following close upon the heels of Mestra, Leesandra entered. She wore a crimson gown, her slim waist cinched by a golden girdle. Dark, upswept curls held a simple gold tiara of poppy pods. He remembered the single time he had seen her in ceremonial gown, her breasts exposed, on the day she had been presented to the people as the Lady's Voice. The memory stirred his loins. Sometimes, like now, the need to hold her again, to caress her breasts, to kiss her, to posses her, if even for a fleeting moment, left him breathless. Her cheeks were drawn, concern writ clear, the pale scar giving her face dramatic emphasis. All took the position of reverence. Zuliya, Alektrion noticed, had sprung at once to his feet.

Leesandra directed them to sit. She stood in front of the sacred partition, her audience chair several steps behind her. "The People have suffered the near destruction of the world," she said. "Our hearts are weighted with grief sometimes so heavy that rising in the morning is difficult. We ask ourselves, Why?

"There are many reasons—otherwise the Mother of All wouldn't have allowed this indescribable suffering—but perhaps the single greatest failure of the People was to tolerate, at least in some hearts, the barbarian god. This so-called Earth Shaker is a destroyer. A punisher, a jealous god, a god of vengeance. He thrives on the death of animals—sometimes he demands things even worse. His followers don't wish to live in harmony with all peoples as the Goddess commands, but to bring others in subjugation to them and their god of domination. If Atistaeus isn't stopped, the world may never be in balance again. Certainly not in our lifetimes or those of our children or our children's children for as far as the Goddess gives me to see into the future.

"We are here to learn from our admiral, Sarpedon." Leesandra gave Sarpedon a nod. "We want to learn the status of our fleet. And most importantly, we want to know what the People must do to repel an invasion. It's given to us in this room to prevent the final destruction of the world's harmony."

Leesandra seated herself in her audience chair. With characteristic quick ease, Sarpedon presented his case. His assessment was grim. Knossos had eighty-six warships, each carrying forty marines. Atistaeus would probably arrive with no less than two hundred warships. "Possibly more, assuming he spent the winter building while we were barely managing to keep our men from starvation. His warships carry up to fifty marines each."

Leesandra spoke. "You've been contemplating our situation for months. How might we prevail?"

Sarpedon bowed his head, then looked sharply at her with a hard gaze. "We are greatly disadvantaged in numbers of ships, numbers of men, numbers of weapons. The destruction of Kalliste has left Keftiu so weakened I cannot, in honesty, offer much hope."

"There must be hope," she said firmly, her eyes equally intent.

"What little hope I offer, Most Honored, lies in surprise." Sarpedon's gaze skimmed the pile of charts on the table. He deftly extracted the third from the top and gestured for the serving boy and girl to hold it so all, including Leesandra, could see it.

"Atistaeus knows all of the islands close to Kalliste are poisoned by ash and are now useless for forage or water. When he comes, he'll have to come from the west by way of Khania." With a forefinger, Sarpedon traced the route he expected Atistaeus to take along Keftiu's northern coast. "This means we can't be taken by surprise. And by the time he arrives at Kyttaion"—he pointed to a small fishing village on the promontory west of the bay of Knossos—"we'll know his exact strength.

"Our only hope is that Atistaeus doesn't know how many of our ships escaped the disaster. We've received no intelligence from the east, so neither has he. The survival of my ships at Khania has been kept a close secret. He can't yet know about them.

"Clearly if I bring the fleet into Amnissos, all of Knossos will know. So I propose to keep the fleet west of Kyttaion, as it is now, until the last moment. Then they will sail to Dia."

Again using his finger, Sarpedon traced a line northeast from Kyttaion to the far side of the large island lying some twelve stadia offshore of Amnissos.

"We can't mount a frontal attack or even stand defense against two hundred and some ships, so we'll hide behind Dia. We'll let Atistaeus think Knossos is undefended on the sea. If I'm right and he decides he's safe from the rear, in the rush to offload his marines he'll let his ships become too tightly clustered in the harbor. They'll be unable to maneuver. And he'll send his troops ashore in one body with the goal of fighting inland to take the Temple and capture the Lady's Voice."

This reminder of the danger to Leesandra made Alektrion's skin tighten.

Sarpedon lanced his finger from Dia to Amnissos. "We'll fall upon his tightly clustered ships from behind."

Alektrion did some quick calculating. With a stiff northern wind from behind, a warship under sail could run from Dia to Amnissos in three-quarters of an hour. With a wind to their backs, they could fall upon Atistaeus while his marines were ashore. With no wind but with rowers working at top capacity, they could row the distance in perhaps an hour and a half. But if the wind blew against them, several hours would be needed. In this worst case, Atistaeus could easily recall his men to their ships and meet Leesandra's forces head on. Fortunately, this was early spring. A wind against them was unlikely.

Glaucon spoke up. "What if he finds out your ships weren't destroyed?"

Sarpedon shook his head. "We may have Poseidon-lovers in Knossos, but you'll find none in Khania or in any of the northern shore villages. The rural people worship the Goddess as they always have. At these villages, I left behind instructions that if barbarians appear, they're to be told that, since the disaster, the People have seen no ships at all on the Great Sea. Your only worry, Glaucon, is here in Knossos. This secret must be kept or our only hope is lost. Betrayal is our greatest danger."

Nothos leaned heavily onto the table toward Sarpedon, his expression agitated. "I can't believe you intend to simply let Atistaeus come ashore unopposed. He'll rush straight here and capture the Lady's Voice. A forced marriage with Minyas must not happen. The Lady's Voice must be protected."

Sarpedon waved a forefinger in denial. "No, Nothos. We can't let him get that far inland. Our limited resources must be directed to where we may have some chance to stop him."

Sarpedon took a step back from the table. Nothos cast a worried look toward Leesandra. Alektrion's heart agreed with Nothos; he wanted maximum security for Leesandra. But, tactically, Sarpedon was correct. They couldn't do both.

Sarpedon continued. "We must mount the strongest protective land force we can." His hands lifted, palms directed forward as if anticipating protests, Sarpedon looked at Alektrion and then Glaucon. "I know, I know. Atistaeus will have some ten- to twelve-thousand battle-hardened warriors and Knossos now has something under eight-thousand armed men." He offered a crooked smile. "And not all of them battle-wise. My guess is the Acheans will arrive within the month. I expect you, Glaucon, and you, Alektrion, to at least double our numbers before then. Find people willing to put their bodies between Atistaeus and the Lady's Voice if you have to use grandmothers, shaved-headed boys, never-yet-married girls, and toothless old men."

"What about Minyas?" Leesandra asked. "He has some two thousand mercenaries. They could come at our defenders from the rear. Should we deal with him before the Acheans arrive?"

"No. He knows you've chosen to fight. And he no doubt thinks you've absolutely no chance to succeed. As we speak he's probably gloating that I returned with only three ships. Trust me. Minyas will sit happily waiting for his collaborator to arrive. We'll plan a special surprise for him, but we'll not stir up that hornet's nest prematurely."

The room fell silent.

Leesandra rose. All followed her example. She thanked Sarpedon and told him she expected similar briefings daily. For Alektrion, the following days were a blur of non-stop activity. He envied Talos working as Sarpedon's right hand in planning the sea engagement. Even

Anchices would be with the ships. But he understood the logic. The very first day the admiral drew him aside. "Glaucon is a good man, but he's spent his years concerned with the security of a Temple that's never faced a serious threat. You've ten times his battle experience. He needs you more than I do."

Fifteen days after Sarpedon's first report to Leesandra, Belamnos should have begun. Instead, the festival and the day of the Sacred Marriage came and went—for the first time in the world's existence—uncelebrated and unattended.

The unparalleled cancellation made Alektrion so uneasy he felt a tight fist yank at his guts every time he thought about it, but he was also secretly relieved. For at least another year, Leesandra would not bed another man.

Twenty-four days after Belamnos, a runner arrived from the west. The invasion force had been sighted. Sarpedon sent his ships to Dia. Three days later, another runner arrived. Alektrion was in a make-shift conference room with Sarpedon, Glaucon, and the three commodores, including Talos, who'd been elevated to that rank. With the naval academy buildings in ruin, Sarpedon had commandeered a villa adjacent to the Temple. The space housed tables and benches for charts, writing tables for the three fleet commodores, and a place for Sarpedon and ten others to sleep. The runner reported Acheans encamped just west of Kyttaion.

The admiral's gaze searched the messenger with the intensity of a hungry ferret sizing up a plump mouse. "How many ships do they have?"

"Two-hundred and twenty ships, admiral, carrying fifty marines each. But…"

"Yes?"

"In addition to supply ships, they've brought huge modified trad-ers that carry only men. Approximately two hundred men in each. And they have thirty such ships."

A chilly hand squeezed Alektrion's heart. He and Glaucon, by tak-ing anyone over the age of eleven who was breathing and willing, had cobbled together a rag-tag force of some twenty thousand. Of these, only ten thousand had any serious military training. Even if Sarpedon and his eighty-six ships and thirty-five hundred men could wound Atistaeus from the rear, by their sheer numbers and superior skill the Acheans would surely—

Jaw clenched, he cut off this dispiriting line of thought, but felt renewed vindication for having planned an escape for the Lady's Voice.

36

As soon as the meeting ended, Alektrion drew Talos aside. "The numbers aren't good."

"Agreed," Talos said. "But if anyone can stop the barbarians, it's Sarpedon. I myself plan to slice 'em up in large numbers." His raspy voice seemed eager. "But we were right to figure a way to take the Voice of the Goddess to safety."

Alektrion nodded. "I hope Atistaeus comes soon. I want to end this nightmare." He understood Talos's sentiment. His own body ached with the need for finality. "A windless day would be most ideal for the butcher. My guess is, the very first day this wind from the northwest dies, he'll come."

Alektrion searched Talos's eyes. Wordlessly they embraced— Alektrion didn't want to let go. He gave Talos a final resounding thump. "The Goddess protect your path," he said with choked effort.

"And yours," Talos whispered.

In the evening Alektrion went to Leesandra. They shared a simple meal, as all meals were now—thin barley soup, bread, dried figs—he on his side of the partition and she on hers. When they finished and the girl had removed the remains and left them alone, he put his hand to the screen. "You know we're badly outnumbered."

"Yes."

"I believe it's possible for us to prevail. But if we don't—"

"We'll win. We have to. The world was created by the Mother for us to live in beauty and harmony. If the People lose this battle, harmony will cease. You must have faith. I fear it's the People's loss of faith in Her that has brought all of this on us."

He inhaled her gentle flowery scent. "You have to hear me, Leesa. And don't think I speak out of lack of faith. I'm simply a practical man. I'm not so sure as you are what the Goddess intends for us in every given moment. I never have been. I can think, for example, it's possible we just might lose this one battle, but still be able to fight Atistaeus again. Maybe fight him in some other way. And I think it's my duty to keep you safe if we lose."

She shook her head. "We must win, Alek. There is no other way to keep me safe."

"Yes there is. Talos and I have made arrangements. His wife's family are fisherfolk. They live in a small village that is less than a two day ride to the west."

"Alek, an escape is futile."

"Hear me out. Tomorrow I go to my troops. I'll not see you again until the battle is over. However it goes, if I am alive I'll send a message. If we've won, I'll simply tell you I love you. If we've lost, be prepared to leave with me. In disguise. Bring only what you can carry yourself. If I'm able, I'll come here just before dawn to fetch you." He moved his hand against the silk, tracing the feel of her fingers, aching to stand and tear down the screen and take her into his arms. "If for some reason, I'm not here by dawn or you fear for your safety sooner, you must go yourself, with Mestra and Zuliya, to the Lady's Chair. Take the tunnel you've told me about. You remember Talos's youngest girl, Aliya, don't you?"

"Yes."

"The girl's been told to meet us. If I can't return to you here, go with Aliya. She'll take you to where Talos and I have hidden donkeys. She'll take you to Talos's family. I'll find you there, then all of us will leave on one of their fishing boats."

He paused. She said nothing but she took her hand away from the silk. He felt a twinge of alarm. "Will you promise me you'll do what I say?"

"You are my heart," she whispered.

The faint sound of the conchs announcing sunset reached into the room's silence. His heart seemed to be beating like the heart of a man facing execution: fast, heavy, expectant. It was time to leave.

He stood. "I have to go."

"Yes," she whispered.

"Can you imagine that I am holding you?

"Yes."

"Can you imagine that I kiss your eyelids, then your hands, and then your lips."

She nodded.

"Do you know I love you better than my own life?"

Tears appeared in her eyes. She put both palms against the silk.

He placed his hands against hers. Still, he felt her slipping away from him. "I'm going now. But I will return. I promise."

"And I will be here, Alek."

He stepped back, paused to memorize his vision of her, turned and walked away. She called after him, "The Goddess guard you, my Alektrion. You are the joy of my life. Remember that. No matter what happens."

∾ ∾ ∾ ∾

Two days later, at dawn, Atistaeus moved. Alektrion's guts were so knotted he had difficulty breathing. He stood on the roof of a four-story townhouse a stadia-and-a-half inland from the beach and could easily see the Achean fleet. Brisus, a boy of thirteen who was his aide, stood beside him.

The Pylian warships hadn't rowed much more than a quarter of the way into the bay when a good breeze from the north-northwest began to huff at them from behind. This wind, favorable to Knossos, fanned the hope he needed, that his men desperately needed, to fight with passion.

Strung out below him in three lines parallel to the shore were the Temple's defenders. The first line, under Glaucon's command, was placed at half a stadia from the beach prepared to defend every street and alley leading inland. They were a mixed lot: a few seasoned warriors leading the squads, some temple guards, and some reasonably able-bodied men and women with the few limited skills ten or twenty days of training could provide. *At least they're all properly battle armed and battle dressed.*

The second line, roughly a quarter stadia behind the first and similarly composed, had a similar function: to slow the advance. The third line, positioned immediately below Alektrion, was under his command.

Ah, yes. His lips turned down in a bitter grin. At last we're so desperate that though I'm no higher in rank than a lowly squad leader, I have this command.

The third line was the hard line, only soldiers. The third line—which he had trained and drilled and sweated over, and loved—the third line had to hold. If it didn't, all would be lost.

He found himself pacing and stopped. "Come on, come on," he muttered. The boy looked at him. He shook his head. "Not you, son."

The Achean ships, at least two hundred strong, drew in close. Alektrion spotted the flagship, the third vessel to enter the bay. The Temple had learned, shortly after first sighting the invading fleet, that the Red King himself was leading. Alektrion thought of Laius, gritted his teeth, wished for the thousandth time he was on the water with Sarpedon and Talos and Anchices. He imagined that nothing could keep him from boarding the flagship and slicing a gut wound in Atistaeus's belly.

Just as Sarpedon predicted, the Achean ships crowded together. Only the vessels at the edges of the mass would be able to turn when Sarpedon attacked. Alektrion's spirits lifted still more. Let it be!

The first Keftian sails emerged from behind Dia. He felt a hot flash of euphoria. More sails followed. Knowing that from Atistaeus's low position on the water he couldn't yet see the Keftian ships, Alektrion watched the surface of the water like a hungry osprey tracking prey as Keftian sails streamed toward Amnissos.

Each moment was an hour. Why didn't the invading scum make their move?

Finally, like pirates—brigands and thieves, not the warriors of honor he'd so admired in his youth—the Achean horde took to shore boats, hit the broad beach and, unopposed, began the drive inland. Brisus snorted a boy's snort and said, "Looks like they're taking the bait."

Buildings blocked Alektrion's view of the front line. It was the angry shouting, the clang of metal against metal, he followed listening as if to see with his eyes the Achean advance. With distressing speed, the shouts moved closer, grew louder, the ring of metal sharper. *Not surprising, given their enormous advantage in numbers.*

"They'll be here shortly," he said to the boy.

In one hand Brisus held the conch by which Alektrion could signal his men. Two short honks, repeated over and over, signaled advance. One long, one short, one long signaled retreat. Two long signaled surrender. It was the boy's task to stick by Alektrion's side at all times.

The second line held longer than he expected. Sarpedon's ships dropped sail. They were already torching the rearmost of the anchored Achean vessels.

The sound of running feet drew his gaze to the square below the townhouse. Enemy warriors streamed up the alley behind the city's largest public bath. At the sight of the hated gold and blue plumes, the boar-tusk helmets, and the bi-circular shields, he snatched sword and shield, turned, and with Brisus on his heels, galloped down the stairs to join his men.

The Achean wave flooded the square. He threw himself at an outlander. Bellowing, he bashed his shield against the other man's. The soldier stumbled, fell. Alektrion drove his sword into the man's exposed throat. A clean, fast kill. The mark of the Scorpion. A good omen.

The second man Alektrion engaged lost a hand.

The third he left lying on the flagstone street, his life flowing out from his belly. Alektrion thought of Laius.

Jabbing, slashing, parrying, dodging, hacking, maiming and killing.

The smell of dust mingled with sweat and gore, the grunts, shouts and screams, and the sound of blood rushing through his own ears blocked out thought. The familiar haze of red spread over the scene. He gave himself to the killing.

Time lost relevance.

Then he sensed something wrong. Half or more of the Acheans around him withdrew. But not all of them! The Achean retreat in panic to save their vessels that Sarpedon was counting on didn't appear to be happening. Without that panicked retreat into a tighter space, the Keftians could never prevail. *Sweet Mother, they must all retreat!*

Alektrion fought on, but he was backed down one street. Down another. Only twenty men left to him. That all of the Acheans didn't retreat to the bay very probably meant they were holding onto their ships against Sarpedon.

"The square of the Two Swans," he shouted. "Retreat! Regroup!"

The Keftian line broke and ran. They'd been pushed a quarter of a stadia inland. Had the line broken elsewhere? No way to know. He suffered a wave of panic, drove it deep inside. His comrades must feel it, too. He prayed all would stand with him.

Muscles burning, chest heaving, he rushed into the square. He and the men with him turned, and an avalanche of Acheans fell on them.

Slaughter.

He looked for the boy, saw him shaking in a nearby doorway, wide-eyed but faithful. For a moment Alektrion thought of surrender. Save some lives.

From behind, his legs were knocked from under him. He toppled backwards. A boot slammed into his side. Fire exploded in his chest and his breath whooshed out. A different boot stepped on his sword arm. Another crushed onto his shield arm, pinned it to the flagstones. Men stood over him. Another loomed with upraised sword. Alektrion looked into a fierce face. High cheekbones, strong jaw, light skin, light hair. The warrior was Achean, a man with whom Alektrion shared his half-breed blood.

The sword hand hesitated. A conch's penetrating honk jabbed the overheated, stifling air. The sword hand raised a bit, its owner readying his final thrust. Two conch blasts followed the first. The sword hand paused.

"Go ahead, Achean," Alektrion said in the warrior's own tongue, anger and defiance and fear all mixed in his mind. "Finish it."

The Achean lowered his sword. "You're spared, Keftian. That's the call to accept surrender."

∾ ∾ ∾ ∾

Alektrion sat on the exercise field in front of Knossos's largest public bath tied shoulder to shoulder with other captives, his hands bound, a rope looped around his neck connecting him with generous slack to

Brisus on one side and a stranger on the other. For over four hours, he'd sat in the blazing afternoon sun watching as other captives were brought to the field and added to the pack, now numbering well over a thousand.

The sun bored into his skull. Sweat dripped down his cheeks and sides. He regretted once again, with grim wryness, that he'd never been elevated above squad leader. All Keftians whose tunics bore the insignias of officers were taken inside the cool bath.

His thoughts shifted again to Leesandra; he couldn't keep them from her. Rumor had spread down the lines of prisoners that Atistaeus had surrounded the Temple and had given Leesandra until morning to surrender. Alektrion prayed that the minute it was dark she would take the tunnel to the Lady's Chair.

The men around him stirred, a murmuring swept across the field, there was movement at the front of the bath. Squads of Achean marines herded a line of fifty or so Keftian high-ranking officers with hands bound in front of them out the bath's wide door, between the center columns of the portico, and into the middle of the field. Alektrion spotted Sarpedon at the head of the line, and his chest swelled with relief.

He scanned the line of bound men and found Talos. The men, he decided, must be the high-ranking officers who'd survived. He looked again, carefully. No Glaucon. No Anchices. He clenched his jaw as fury grew. Another friend stolen from him. Another victim of the Red King's insatiable hunger.

The line halted the length of four warships from Alektrion. He watched Sarpedon. The little admiral stood erect, shoulders back, but his spirit had to be enduring a thousand cuts.

Half an hour passed. Nothing changed. The Keftian officers, their captors behind them, stood in the middle of the field while the unrelenting, late afternoon sun continued to punish. Alektrion dripped sweat. He longed for water. Suddenly, ten high-ranking Acheans emerged from the bath door, marched down the field, and took up places in front of the line of Keftians. Four slaves carrying a gilded chair followed and two other slaves carried a rolled rug.

The slaves spread the rug and arranged the gilt chair in the middle of it so whoever sat there could see both the line of captive officers and the mass of bound Keftian prisoners. Sun rays burnished the chair a rosy gold. The beautiful chair is for bloody Atistaeus, Alektrion thought. Very shortly, he would see his enemy's face.

From the door of the bath, two lines of drummers emerged. They marched onto the field to a slow, ominous cadence that was more funeral march than a march of triumph. A whirlpool of alarm began a slow spiral in Alektrion's chest.

At last the Achean king appeared. Atistaeus had removed his battle-dress and was wearing a robe of purple trimmed in gold. His shoulders were massive. He strode like a rutting bull across the portico and down the field. Straight dark hair was cropped close to his head. His face was rugged, powerful, with thick dark brows and lips twisted into a defiant grin that looked more like a snarl. Alektrion imagined that a bloody crimson aura—the spiritual essence of countless lives—enveloped the Achean monster.

To Atistaeus's left and slightly behind him struted Minyas. Alektrion ached to squeeze every hint of breath from the traitor's throat. The priest, Oenopion, clad in black and crimson-sashed, walked on Atistaeus's right. Two more officers and four retainers trotted dutifully behind.

Last came a brute of a man, his bulging muscles like those of an ox, a boar-tusk helmet huge on his huge head—the helmet's enamel teeth rosy-white in the afternoon sun's glow. Alektrion recognized him at once. He was the very giant of his first battle, the Pylian who had killed Prion. In one hand the giant carried a peculiar curved, short sword. On his opposite forearm rode the smallest man Alektrion had ever seen, a stunted creature the size of a three- or four-year-old boy. In his tiny hands, the little man carried a large bundle.

The alarm in Alektrion's chest spread into his throat. For a long moment he stopped breathing.

Atistaeus strode to the throne and sat. Minyas and Oenopion stood like display dogs to the right of the seated king. The giant sat his tiny companion on the ground. The moment the giant sat him down, the tiny man unfolded his burden and spread it in front of him. Murmurs filled the air. A shudder shook Alektrion. The object was a once-white sheepskin cape, now darkened with stains. The rank smell of it reached even Alektrion.

The Red King sat. He lifted his hand, clenched his fist, then struck it like a mallet onto the arm of his golden seat.

Without a word, two men guarding the line of officers strode to Sarpedon. Grabbing an arm each, they yanked him out of line and marched him up to the giant. They thrust him onto his knees.

No! Alektrion silently roared.

One man grabbed a fistful of Sarpedon's hair and pulled his head down and forward.

No! Alektrion's mind roared again.

The giant raised the sword and with one clean stroke severed Sarpedon's head.

Blood gushed from the neck. A great red fountain. For a moment the torso remained upright. Then it fell slowly forward and the body writhed as the arms and legs twitched. The man holding Sarpedon's head tossed it behind him.

A roar exploded from the seated and bound captives. Alektrion surged to his feet. A guard struck him a blow across the shoulders that dropped him back to the ground.

The next Keftian officer was forced to his knees before the executioner while the tiny man ran to Sarpedon's body, daubed at the pool of blood beneath it with a cloth, then ran back to the cape to smear the new blood on it. Alektrion's stomach recoiled. His fists clenched and unclenched, his palms itching with the urge to kill.

Sarpedon had said, "If we don't prevail against Atistaeus, we'll all live in a very very dark place." The darkness had arrived.

One after the other, down the line, the officers of Keftiu were butchered. Some walked, others were dragged to the giant. Some cried for mercy. Around him, Alektrion's fellow captives whimpered, groaned, sobbed. The Acheans cheered as each Keftian died, their shouts exploding with each fall of the blade.

Tears streaked down Alektrion's cheeks. A great flood of human blood spilled in punishment and revenge. Never before on Keftian soil. Never before.

Two men grabbed Talos. Alektrion shut his eyes, pinched his eyelids tight. His guts screamed a final scream and went coldly, icily numb. He squeezed his eyelids for a long time, long enough for him to be sure he wouldn't recognize his friend's body in the growing pile of corpses.

And behind his closed lids he imagined his own head coming off. When would Leesandra learn his fate? Would she flee in time? Savagely, with desperate effort to grab and hold his sanity, he shoved the thoughts away.

Only four officers remained when he opened his eyes again. The giant dispatched them with ease. His tiny companion was covered with blood, and the ground was soaked in blood as the two of them squished back and forth on it.

Both Brisus and the stranger on Alektrion's other side were quaking visibly. *They're also wondering—when will it be me?*

Atistaeus stood. He faced the prisoners. In a voice that boomed over the crowd, he said in horrid Keftian, "Because of your leader's defiance of the will of Poseidon, Keftiu has suffered great punishments. The Temple is surrounded and lies under my control. Tomorrow when I go there, I will take with me Minyas, a wise Keftian who is to be the High Priest of Poseidon. Within the week, Minyas will join with the Lady's Voice in the Sacred Marriage." He paused, the smirk quivering on his lips visible even to Alektrion. "Under the guidance of Pylos and submission to Poseidon, true balance will be brought to Keftiu."

I'll kill him, Alektrion thought, aware even as he had the thought how ridiculous it was. He would soon be dead, his blood mingled in the stinking pool under the giant's feet, his head on the ghastly pile.

Achean marines walked down the line yanking the Keftian prisoners to their feet. The king had seated himself again on the golden chair. Alektrion rose stiffly, his mind full of anguished thoughts of Leesandra. Knowing full well she would never leave before their agreed meeting time, still he prayed, Go now, Leesa!

A soldier signaled for Alektrion and the men with whom he was linked to start walking. The Pylian king sat smirking while the captives were marched past him. They weren't slaughtered. Instead, every fifth man was made to halt before the throne, kneel, and touch his head to the ground in front of the king's gold-sandaled foot.

The excruciating tension in Alektrion's muscles eased. Apparently he wasn't going to be killed, at least not at once. His breathing deepened. Perhaps there was hope. If he could get free within the next two days. Otherwise he'd be too late to meet her in the country. The agreement was to wait only four days before leaving by boat to go west. And he'd have Kokor's own time ever finding Leesandra once she'd left Talos's village for they would leave in secret and he would have no idea of their destination.

Beside the king stood the giant, his bloodied sword arm raised. "Keep your eyes on the ground," his tiny, filth-covered companion yelled over and over to the Keftians.

Once again the line of prisoners halted, but the Keftian warrior facing Atistaeus not only didn't keep his eyes to the ground, he didn't kneel. Without so much as a grunt of warning, the giant thrust his sword into the man's chest. Even as the Keftian fell to his knees, two other Acheans cut the ropes binding him to the men on either side of him. They grabbed an arm each, pulled him out of the line, let him drop to the ground, hauled him away.

With Brisus walking in front of him, Alektrion's group approached the throne. He took his eyes off the ground long enough to count up the line and determine that he would be subjected to the humiliation of kneeling. In what seemed only moments, he was but a few long paces from Atistaeus. His heart was pounding so hard he felt light headed. He would not kneel!

But then he thought, And you'll die at once. Will others take Leesandra to safety? Are you certain she'll go with them?

Once more the line halted. It moved again. Brisus shuffled past the giant.

It was Alektrion's turn. He stepped before the Red King. He couldn't leave Leesa. He dropped to both knees, but didn't touch his head to the ground; he stared straight into the cruelly handsome face, which now wore only a look of boredom. The expression turned quickly to surprise. Atistaeus of Pylos looked hard into Alektrion's eyes, and in the quiet of his mind Alektrion spoke. *I will kill you Atistaeus, you bloody bastard! Some way, some how, I'll see a Demon Child rip your guts to pieces!*

The giant took a step toward Alektrion, his sword arm prepared for a death thrust, but then he hesitated, apparently confused that Alektrion at least was kneeling.

The tiny man yelled, "Keep your eyes on the ground, pig!"

The giant changed his mind and the blow to Alektrion's head from the sword's hilt produced the required result; Alektrion fell forward, his vision a pool of blackness aglitter with splotches of red and purple. For seconds he was too stunned to move. He felt arms on either side lift him and the tug of the rope around his neck as the line started to move again. His vision cleared.

He staggered forward, toward the bathhouse, resolve keeping him upright. He would find Leesandra. He would take her to safety. And when that was assured, he would keep his promise to the Red King.

Inside, the bath was growing dark. Alektrion's mouth felt like he had eaten a mountain of hot sand. The guards ordered the prisoners to sit, and several older men carrying water buckets passed down the rows stopping to ladle a cup of water to each prisoner.

The face of the old man serving the row of prisoners in front of him caught his attention. He knew that face. But from where? "Brisus," Alektrion whispered, "do you know him? The old man serving the row in front of us?" The boy shook his head. But Alektrion was sure he'd seen that face. Not here in the bath. Elsewhere.

Yes. He remembered. At the Temple. His daughter, Mestra, was Leesa's first serving woman. He must be very worried for her safety. And he was likely very devout. Perhaps enough to take a risk.

Alektrion checked the location of the nearest Achean guard. Far enough away and at least not looking directly toward him. With his toe, he poked a young warrior in the row in front of him. The youth turned. There was not only fear in his face, but recognition that he'd been poked by the Scorpion. Alektrion whispered. "When the old man gets to you, tell him to step across the line and come to me. I have to talk to him."

The boy swallowed hard. He didn't nod. Didn't shake his head either. No one wanted to draw attention. Alektrion prayed the boy's heart would hold true.

The old man stopped in front of the youth. Brief whispers were exchanged. The old man looked at Alektrion, and then checked to see where the guard stood. He looked at Alektrion again. His eyes, too, were white-rimmed with fear. Alektrion held his breath and prayed that the old man would remember, would be willing to take the risk.

After one more check of the guard, the man stepped over the rope, bringing his water bucket with him. He hurried to Alektrion and squatted.

"You know me," Alektrion said.

"Yes. "

"You're Mestra's father aren't you?"

"Yes."

"Lean close."

Mestra's father put his ear close to Alektrion's mouth.

"You know I belong to the Lady's Voice," Alektrion whispered. "I must get free. Why are you here?"

The man whispered back. "I've worked at the bath for years."

"Do you know the drains?"

The old man nodded.

"Tonight. When all is quiet. Come free me."

The man glanced again at the guard, who began to walk toward them.

"Will you?" Alektrion urged.

The old man's hand trembled so violently the surface of the water in his bucket was all ripples. He stood just as the guard arrived.

"No talking!" the guard said, and struck Mestra's father in the stomach. "Get on with the water."

The old man moved to Brisus. The boy drank greedily.

37

Hours in the dim, torch-lit chamber crept by as if time were, itself, gravely wounded. Hemmed in by the restless jostlings of a thousand bound men lying in rows across the tiled limestone, Alektrion feigned sleep. The stench of urine and unwashed bodies soon fouled every breath he took.

What felt like the heart of the night arrived and departed. Despair settled like a chilled hand on his heart. Mestra's father wasn't going to come. His last chance to meet Leesandra was slipping beyond possibility.

Rustlings and murmurings erupted at the bath's far end. Torch-light shadows of men struggling writhed on the distant walls. Shouts rang out. Their echoes shook the room, and all guards save the one nearest him ran toward the shouting. Three dark figures immediately sprang, as if conjured, from the shadows. Two rushed the remaining guard. A tangle of men crashed to the floor, disappeared out of Alektrion's view, and another dark figure, bent low, swept down Alektrion's line. Mestra's father wore only a black kilt and, like his three companions, he'd darkened his skin with charcoal.

He slashed Alektrion's bonds, then pulled another knife from his waistband and shoved its hilt into Alektrion's hand.

"Free the men tied with me," Alektrion whispered. "Then do the same for others." Alektrion slashed Brisus's bonds, then to the men being freed whispered, "Follow me. Keep quiet and to the shadows."

His urgings were wasted. Others, awakened by the shouting, realized what was happening and called, "Free us, too!"

From Alektrion's left, a guard yelled, "Here! They're getting loose."

A score of guards rushed toward him. Pain-filled yelps, grunting and scuffling sounds bounced off the ceiling and walls. He freed the last man on the line, then grabbed Mestra's father by the shoulder. "To the opening of the nearest main drain. Quick." To the men he shouted, "Keep close."

The old man turned and ran in the general direction of the way he'd come. Alektrion glanced behind. The man's three companions continued to free Keftian captives and the scene was looking like a brawl he'd once seen in Byblos, but ten times the size and a hundred times louder. He forced down the urge to leap to his fellow warriors' aid. He had a plan, and for it to succeed, he must act quickly. Perhaps twenty freed Keftians were close on his heels. He ran past a torch, snatched it up, and yelled to the man behind him to bring the next one.

He caught up with Mestra's father and grabbed his arm, halted him. "Do you know where Atistaeus sleeps? I have to know."

"In the Speaker's townhouse."

Alektrion turned to the men following. "I need ten willing to help. We may still be able to cut off the barbarian's head." And if this night he could find and kill Minyas as well as Atistaeus, perhaps the Keftian cause was not yet lost.

Every arm shot high. "We're with you, Scorpion!"

The tunic insignia of the bald warrior who spoke indicated the rank of squad leader, and Alektrion remembered the man. Stos, was his name. "Not so many," Alektrion said." He indicated the first ten, including Stos. "The rest of you scatter!"

Mestra's father shook his head. "You can't reach The Red King, if that's what you're thinking."

"The outlanders don't know about drains. They don't have them. Won't be thinking to watch them."

Alektrion started for the drain cover that lay out of sight behind a fountain. Brisus stuck close. "You get away, too, boy!"

Brisus shook his head. "I'm staying with you."

A ladder led down. The Goddess blessed them: the water came no higher than their knees. He smelled wet tile, algae, and rotting things he preferred not to identify. Only he, the tallest, had to stoop slightly to run. Their own sounds of labored breathing and sloshing water raced ahead of them. He was gambling, he knew, that he could estimate correctly where the drain into the speaker's inner courtyard would come up.

They reached the location of the ladder of his first guess. "Wait!" he said. He climbed up and pushed open the cover. Wrong—but not badly so. They were in the street three houses from his goal. He repositioned the cover, scrambled down. "This way."

His next guess was correct. The eleven of them came up at the back of the Speaker's mansion, behind the wash house. The courtyard was empty. He gestured and two men quietly tipped a water barrel upside down under a trellis. Alektrion stepped onto the barrel, climbed onto the trellis. It led to an open window on the second floor. The others followed. The room was a library and was empty.

He entered a hallway and immediately heard the clanking sounds and laughter of eating and celebration coming from the front of the residence. He had hoped to catch Atistaeus in bed, but the butcher was still entertaining. Maybe, with extremely good fortune, Minyas, too, would be here. His pulse beat in his ears. How best to take advantage of that possibility?

Two armed warriors entered the hallway from a side room, perhaps the water closet. They saw Alektrion and the other Keftians and, yelling, they dashed toward the stairs. Stealth was no longer an option. Alektrion charged after them, caught one, drew his knife blade across the man's throat. Warm blood rushed over Alektrion's hands. He dropped the suddenly sagging body. Stos had hold of the other around the neck. Another Keftian hit him with a small stone statue. He went down with a loud thud.

Alektrion snatched up the sword of the man he had attacked and handed over the knife Mestra's father had given him to another Keftian. Stos took the sword and knife from the body at his feet, kept the sword and handed the knife to one of the other men. The sound of running feet came up the stairwell from below.

"I'm after the Red King," Alektrion shouted. "If the traitor Minyas is here, kill him as well. We may still be able to prevent complete disaster."

He rushed down the stairs and into a long hallway. Halfway to them were four armed men. Alektrion charged, yelling, "The Goddess," followed by the ten other Keftians. He shoved past one Achean, ducked another, then burst into an elegant room. Behind him he heard yells and blows. Perhaps ten diners stood at their tables. Some were Achean officers and were armed. Alektrion spotted Atistaeus at one end of a table and Minyas at the other. The eyes in the handsome face of the Red King gazed at him, wide with surprise.

"Get Minyas," Alektrion shouted to Stos, who had dashed up beside him. Alektrion started for Atistaeus. Alektrion was halfway to the butcher when the giant entered the room, his sword ready in his massive vice of a hand. Alektrian saw the Achean giant, as clearly as if it were yesterday, as the man who had jumped onto *Sea Eagle*, ran Prian through and then turned to cut the throats of *Sea Eagle's* unarmed rowers. The giant rushed Alektrion, bellowed, and brought his weapon down against Alektrion's. Driven to the floor, Alektrion felt spikes of pain from his arm to his shoulder and from his knees to his belly. The giant raised his sword to make another blow. Brisus streaked past Alektrion, dived for the giant's leg, grabbed it, and bit down hard into the thick muscle of the calf.

The giant howled, lifted his leg with Brisus clinging to it with his teeth sunk into the flesh like a fighting dog. Alektrion leaped up, thrust forward and drove his sword deep into the giant's belly. Another gigantic howl. Alektrion pulled his sword, drove it in again. The giant wavered, toppled backward. Brisus let go of the leg and fell away; the giant hit the floor like a fallen oak.

Atistaeus stood in front of Alektrion, sword in hand now, the surprised look replaced by rage.

"Kill him, Scorpion!" Brisus yelled.

"You!" Atistaeus said. "We looked for you!"

"You've found me!" Alektrion struck first. The Red King deflected the blow and made the second strike. The man was strong, well trained. Not only a lover of war, but well practiced in it. Alektrion backed into a chair, stumbled. They exchanged blows, the sounds of panting, scuffling, and shouting filling the room. Several blows more from Atistaeus and Alektrion backed several steps more. But he was getting a feel for the barbarian. He shifted to strike harder from the left.

Atistaeus backed up. He shifted approach and surprised Alektrion with a low-swinging, parallel strike. Alektrion leapt backward. Brisus tried to reach Atistaeus as he had done with the giant, but Atistaeus anticipated. With one quick thrust, he ran his blade into the boy's chest. Brisus fell.

The red haze flooded Alektrion's vision and the sound of a roaring ocean filled his ears. He charged Atistaeus and rammed him with a shoulder into the gut. Atistaeus went down onto his knees, sideways to Alektrion. Two hands on its hilt, Alektrion swung his sword with all his power, and Atistaeus's head, severed neatly at the shoulders, rolled forward onto the floor. Blood fountained up and out. The red haze in Alektrion's vision lessened as a swelling sense of pleasure raced like fire under his skin. The head stopped rolling, surprised eyes staring straight at Alektrion. Close enough to what Atistaeus had done to Sarpedon! And Laius! Just too quick.

"We've got to get out!" Stos grabbed Alektrion's arm and pulled him back the way they had come.

Alektrion resisted, surveyed the scene. "Minyas?"

Stos pulled harder. "Sorry, Scorpion. He got away. And Achean reinforcements are coming. We have to get away."

For a moment, frustration and disappointment gripped him, then he turned, knelt, picked up Brisus and slung the boy over his shoulder and headed toward the rear of the mansion. "Back into the drain," he shouted to the handful of men retreating with him.

At the open drain-hole behind the washhouse, he laid Brisus down, then felt for a lifesign at his throat. There was none.

"We have to leave him," Stos said.

Alektrion placed Brisus's hand in the position of reverence on the youth's forehead. Strangely, he thought of Serena, the priestess on *Sea*

Eagle. Thought how he wished she were here to place honey of farewell on Brisus's lips. He stood then turned and shimmied down the ladder and waited for the men. When they were all down, they took off splashing through the knee-deep water toward the Temple.

Within moments he heard angry shouts from behind. His legs burned from effort. They had failed to kill Minyas, who was now alerted. The only hope left was to reach Leesandra before Minyas did. His sweet, beautiful Leesandra.

They passed many ladders leading to the street, but when they emerged he wanted to be as far from the Speaker's mansion and as near the Temple as possible without going the wrong direction. The drain reached a fork. He headed in what he prayed was the right direction. At the next fork he was no longer certain he could guess orientation from below ground. At the next ladder, he grabbed a rung and pulled himself up. The men followed. On the street, they looked to him.

"You," he said, and swept a finger at two of them. "I have something urgent to do for the Lady's Voice. Stay here. Make certain no Acheans emerge."

Nods and rapid assurances were immediate.

Alektrion turned to Stos and two other soldiers. "Follow me!" He took off running and didn't stop until they passed well out of sight of the drain. His chest burned inside with each breath he took. He drew into the shadows of a narrow alley. "I must reach the Lady's Voice but I'll need help."

Stos said, "Why reach the High Priestess, Scorpion?"

"I've arranged to take her away before dawn. Before Minyas can reach her."

The warrior shook his head. "She'll not go with you."

The conviction in the man's voice yanked Alektrion to a full mental halt. His throat tightened.

"She will."

"The Lady's Voice never leaves the Temple. She'll die first. By her own hand if necessary."

38

A shudder swept across Alektrion's shoulders with such force it stole his breath. The warrior spoke with the absolute conviction of the devout. And with sickening clarity, Alektrion remembered Leesandra's evasions whenever he'd spoken of fleeing. "I know what I'm saying," he said with forced assurance. "She'll come. She's waiting for me."

Would Nothos kill her rather than permit defilement of the Sacred Marriage? Or could she take her own life? Would she?

No! Never. Leesandra was all he had left. She would never leave him to face this devastation alone. Surely she must know she was everything to him now. "Will you help?"

"I served with you at Impios, Scorpion," Stos said. "And I'll help. But you're wasting your time. She'll never leave."

The two other soldiers quickly insisted they, too, would help. Alektrion, fighting a mind-numbing panic, raced toward the Temple, running, hiding, using side streets and roof gardens.

An hour later he waited, perched well hidden in the crotch of an olive tree in the informal garden that fronted the Temple's southeastern corner. His insides were writhing, his mind in a fierce struggle to convince himself that Leesa was still alive and would come with him. Three Acheans stood sentry. He felt the knife in his belt. From one of the soldiers, he had traded the too-conspicuous sword for it. He felt reassured that it was secure in the event he might have to run. The olive tree lay as close as he could get without attracting the guards' attention. Part of him wanted to ignore caution and rush to the door at once. She was so near. But a more primitive part dreaded to find out what waited inside. What if the bald soldier was right?

He beat the thought down, focused hard on the guards. Soon the soldiers would create a diversion. A few moments of having the guards' attention turned elsewhere and he would be with her.

At least he could be thankful the Acheans had no reason to suspect the inconspicuous little building was anything special. The guards weren't particularly close to the door. And though dawn was approaching, darkness still favored him: the night sky was moonless and overcast.

The Temple itself was barely illuminated. When he'd first seen the Lady's Temple at Knossos by night, he'd stood in awe for a long time. So many torches! Thousands. A man had the sensation he could see as well as if it were day. Now, only perhaps a hundred flickered against the night. The glory that was Knossos was dead.

Bad word. He forced the thought of "dead" Knossos away. There was still Leesandra. She was waiting. She had to be.

Once he was inside, he would insist she take him to her quarters. Their only chance of escape was the secret tunnel from her rooms. He looked at his hands, shocked to find them trembling. *Kind Mother, let my Leesandra be alive! Surely not everything good and beautiful must die.* He clenched his fists and set his jaw.

From across the garden came the sound of muffled laughter. Stos and the two soldiers. The three guards turned. Two of them walked toward the sound.

Alektrion scrambled down, streaked low across a bed of flowers, over a knee-high wall, and up to the small building's door. He grabbed the latch, squeezed, pushed, and smacked up against the solidly closed entry.

Kokor's ass!

He listened, dreading to make further noise, but he had no choice. He tapped.

A boy's voice, frightened, came at once. "Who's there?"

"Alektrion," he whispered.

A scraping sound. Something was pushed aside. The door opened slightly. Alektrion squeezed in and eased the door closed.

"The Mother be praised," the boy said, grabbing Alektrion's arm. In his other hand the boy held a small lamp, the room's only light. "The honorable Zuliya was certain you'd come. Hurry. The teacher says you must add your voice to his."

The boy turned to go, but Alektrion grasped his shoulder. "Why isn't your mistress here?"

"She's already sent away those willing to go. Blauthophon. Others. And with them a journal she says must be saved. But she won't leave the Temple."

"Where is she?"

"In her chambers. With the honorable Nothos and Zuliya and the Wise One, Sestrae. The teacher fears for her and urges you to hurry. Our vizier insists she take poison. She may already have done so!"

He nudged the boy. "Run!"

As Alektrion passed through the door in the partition and stepped onto sacred ground, the weight of his transgression fell on him like a great stone. For an instant he could not move. Quickly he straightened, shook himself and ran after the boy. They sprinted through dimly lit, silent—strangely silent—stone halls. Down a narrow corridor, up wide stairs, across a terrace, into yet another narrow corridor. Before a door brightly lit by torches stood two of Leesandra's personal guards, fully armed. The boy rushed past them. Alektrion followed.

Inside, a large antechamber furnished as a sitting room led to several doors. Having fulfilled his duty, the boy turned and ran back out, most likely to go find his family.

Nothos paced the center of the room, pawing his beard. Zuliya sat hunched on a couch holding his head. He looked so grieved Alektrion's heart skipped several beats and his guts turned again. "Where is she?" he demanded.

Nothos halted, clasped and unclasped his hands, pressed them to his temples. "She won't speak to me."

So she was alive!

"Just as well," Zuliya snapped. He lifted his head and spoke to Alektrion. "At last! Isis *is* merciful." He nodded toward a door. "Make her see reason. She is deaf to everything I say."

Nothos whirled to face Zuliya. "You should not be here!" Then he turned blazing eyes on Alektrion. "Or you!"

Alektrion entered the indicated room and found Leesandra sitting at a dressing table, her back to him. Mestra stood nearby, weeping. Seated on a couch in a corner, dressed in white, as always, was the Wise Woman, Sestrae. Her eyes were closed and her lips moved in prayer.

The sea eagle pin gleamed against Leesandra's curls. To see her alive felt like being spared his own execution. For a moment, the trembling in his legs spread to his chest and arms. She wore a violet chamber gown—as though she hadn't yet decided whether to dress in robes suitable for death or for flight.

"Why aren't you ready to travel?" He sounded angry, though that was the last feeling in his heart.

She turned to him. The skin of her face stretched brutally over her cheekbones, her nose and lips were pinched.

Again he spoke. "I said I'd be here before morning. We must leave at once." He sensed that Nothos and Zuliya had followed him into the room.

She stood and rushed into his arms. Warm, slender, fragile, wrapped in the exquisitely alive smell of her rose perfume. He clutched her fiercely, his heart racing, then held her back. "We have to go, Leesa."

"You shouldn't be here," she said and pushed away. She returned to her stool, and sat. With eyes steady, but deeply sunken and rimmed with dark circles, she stared back at him. "And I can't leave."

368

Judith Hand

"It's nearly dawn! We have to go!

"I can't leave, Alek."

He thrust his arm toward the vizier. "Is it some nonsense Nothos babbles about poison?"

"It's not nonsense, Alek. The Law says I am not to leave the Temple. If I leave, it would be desertion. To leave is to betray the Law. The People."

Zuliya snorted. "I tell you again, think! You certainly cannot stay here. You cannot be taken by Minyas and Atistaeus. On that we all agree. But what purpose would be served by your death? If you take the drink," he nodded toward a small gold cup on the dressing table, "you will die and all hope for the People will die with you."

Alektrion silently appealed to her, *Listen to him, my dear heart, listen to him.*

"If I leave—"

Zuliya interrupted. "How often have I told you—begged you even—to think for yourself?"

"Zuliya, my head feels like it's going to burst apart from thinking. If I leave, the People will feel abandoned. The Lady's Voice never leaves this place. That's the Law."

There it was again. Her unbending, unreasoning devotion to the Law. The stubbornness that blinded her vision and, in the end, had doomed them.

In three quick strides, Zuliya closed the distance between himself and Leesandra. "The Law! The Law!" To Alektrion's astonishment, the Nubian reached down and grabbed her by both arms and shook her. "Stop this childish nonsense. There is too much in the balance here."

Nothos surged toward Zuliya and Leesandra. "Most Honored, this man is a foreigner. Neither of these men should be here. You *must* do what is right!"

Alektrion took a step toward her.

She stood, wrenched herself from Zuliya's bruising grip, her face ashen and her scar gone white. "Why call me a child? I see my duty clearly. I'll do what is necessary."

Zuliya stepped back. In an exaggerated motion, as if slicking water from his body, he skimmed his palm from the place over his heart down his arm and then shook his hand. "Then I shed you from my heart. I have failed miserably. Take the poison. But I'll not watch this evil."

Zuliya turned and limped from her chamber. Sestrae, Alektrion noted, was no longer praying. She was attending to their every word.

"Leave me, Alek. Take Zuliya and Mestra and leave this place. And you, too, Nothos." Her voice was rigid. False bravado, he thought.

The sound made by someone facing certain death who is resolved to make light of it.

The vizier clenched a shaking palm to his chest.

"Now, Nothos!" She sat again at the table.

The vizier stood his ground.

Alektrion held his gaze on Leesandra steady, thinking that if she lifted her hand and made the slightest gesture toward the cup, he'd take her captive and carry her off.

Then, with staggering speed, it struck him—in a crystalline, prescient moment—he would never leave Leesandra's side again. He started to say that if she didn't leave, neither would he, but checked himself. It would be unfair to tell her, to make his well-being any part of her burden. He took a slow, deep breath, then said what he knew was right. "This decision is yours."

From behind, Alektrion heard a deep sob from Mestra.

Leesandra picked up the cup.

"Do it, then," he said coldly. Despite the resolve of only a heartbeat ago, his bitterness spilled out. "Destroy your life. Destroy mine." He felt himself shaking. "But you will remove all hope from the People. All because of enslavement to a Law that very soon will have no place left in the world. By your own hand you will have killed its embodiment."

She turned to him, her back rigid, her eyes wide. "Why speak with such venom? Why hurt me? This is my duty."

"Do you love me? If you ever loved me, for the sake of our love, I beg you to listen! You are the Lady's Voice, Leesandra. You! Your duty is to serve the People. That's why the Great Mother chose you. That's why she gave you a wise teacher in Zuliya. Don't you see? You have the power to change the Law. The old ways no longer work. The old way has destroyed us. I don't understand—I don't know why and I never have—but your mind is closed. Foolishly, disastrously closed."

"Of course I love you." Her hand clenched the stem of the cup so hard her knuckles went bone white. "But I'm not wrong." Her hand began to shake.

"Yes, you are. You can't see beyond the past. And you have no vision of the future. Because of your close-mindedness, we are all ruined."

"You can't be right." She lowered the cup to the table, bent over and clutched her head with both hands, her face hidden from him.

Nothos pushed himself between Alektrion and Leesandra. "Pay no attention to this half-breed!"

Alektrion grabbed the vizier and without taking his eyes from Leesandra shoved Nothos aside. "Didn't you hear one word Zuliya said, Leesa?" More accusing words hung on his lips, ready to spill. He wanted to shout at her, *You were given the chance to save Keftiu and out of sheer blind mistaken stubbornness you threw it away!* But for love's sake he choked the words into silence.

He did love her. No matter what she'd done. No matter what she yet might do. She might shame him. Or hurt him. By her failure to act in time against Atistaeus, she had already done enormous harm to so many. Yet still he loved her—the girl of his heart who laughed when she talked with a spider, cried over the death of a tiny swallow, and gave all of herself to him when they had lain together.

Her shoulders slumped. She seemed to withdraw.

"You are right." She was whispering to herself, not him.

The room's silence felt like a smothering hand.

She shook her head but still did not look up. "Because of me, the Red King wipes the blood of my People on his cloak. Dear Mother, what have I done?"

What should he say? What could he say?

Still whispering, she said, "I know I was wrong about Heebe. I should have released her from her pain. " Her fingers tightened in her dark curls. "Sweet Mother. It's true. I have been wrong. I should have destroyed Atistaeus when I still could."

Should he touch her? Embrace her? Try to comfort her? What comfort could he offer? He didn't understand what she meant about Heebe, but about Atistaeus she was most certainly correct. She had been disastrously wrong.

He remained quiet for a moment, then knelt beside her stool and put his hand on her knee. She refused to look at him. Tears streamed down her cheeks.

"Oh Dear Lady, Dear Lady, what have a I done? How could I have been so blind? Help me. Forgive me."

He chose words with care and spoke softly. "And taking your life would be wrong, too. Have the courage to face this dreadful reality and do what is right for the People. Someone must be left to lead them, to give them hope. To show them the way to survive this disaster."

Nothos grabbed Alektrion's shoulder. "This fool is babbling blasphemy!"

With one arm, Alektrion pushed him back again. He tightened his grip on her knee. "You must decide, my heart. If we are to leave, it must be now or it will be too late."

Leesandra straightened. She brushed at her tears. She glanced toward Sestrae, seated on the couch, then she looked back at him. "I think I understand, now. All of my life, in things spiritual, I've been afraid. I thought security depended on unquestioning obedience. But

I've been wrong. I've mistaken stubbornness for resolve. Fear blinded me. Horribly."

Her hand grasped the cup and he felt the blood leave his head.

She turned the cup upside down and a green liquid, smelling of burnt grass, pooled on the white marble top of the table. She rose. "Go tell Zuliya, Alek. I've decided. At last. Yes . . . decided. The world I knew has passed away. The Goddess requires that we respond accordingly. I will leave."

Not since the death of Heebe had he heard such sadness in Leesandra's voice. He, on the other hand, felt as if he'd been reprieved by the Ancient Herself.

She continued. "To know that the Lady's Voice is alive and will return to Knossos can give the People heart."

He embraced her, felt her shaking. He let her go and was halfway to the door when he felt the dagger being pulled from his belt. Mestra screamed. Alektrion spun around. Nothos, the dagger in his hand, rushed toward Leesandra.

"You cannot leave here!" he screamed.

Mestra lunged toward Nothos. A jumble of flailing arms and flying robes blocked Alektiron's vision of what was happening. He charged Nothos and slammed the vizier face-down onto the floor just as Mestra also crumpled.

"Mestra!" Leesandra screamed as she threw herself down beside her handmaiden.

Nothos wriggled forward, rolled onto his back, and kicked Alektrion in the face. He still held the knife in his hand, its blade now bloody, and as Alektrion scrambled toward him, Nothos raked the knife downward. Alektrion rolled to the side, caught the vizier's hand, wrenched Nothos's wrist and arm so the blade pointed at Nothos's throat, and shoved the blade home.

Nothos stiffened, gave a thrashing shudder, and went limp.

Zuliya reappeared at the doorway. "What is happening here?" he demanded.

"Mestra, Mestra! Stay with me." Leesandra was sobbing. Sestrae had risen from the couch. She too knelt beside Mestra and took hold of one of Mestra's hands.

Alektrion saw the blood on Mestra's gown, not far below her heart.

A guard burst through the door. "Minyas comes. He is in—"

A second guard rushed in, calling for his comrade. The two ran back through the door and disappeared. Sounds of booted feet rattled from beyond.

Time had run out. Alektrion knelt next to Leesandra. "We have to leave. At once!"

Sestrae said, "I believe the warrior is right. If you are to leave, and I believe you should, you must go now."

Leesandra turned a tear-streaked face to him and said forcefully, "You will carry her!"

Zuliya touched Alektrion's shoulder. "Alek, there is no time left."

Mestra gasped, then whispered softly, "Most Honored…"

Alektrion took Leesandra's hand. "She will not live, Leesa."

No sooner had he said it than the light of life faded from Mestra's eyes and her head fell aside. Leesandra grabbed her, began to rock her.

Alektrion grabbed Leesandra's shoulders and pulled her to her feet. "Only you know the way. Lead us."

He felt her shudder. Then she pulled away from him with surprising strength.

"Come!" She tugged him in the direction of a door leading into a narrow passage.

Thudding footsteps approached the outer door. She rushed into a narrow corridor snatching up a torch to light her way. Zuliya and Sestrae followed. Alektrion brought up the rear and closed the door behind them.

They turned two sharp corners, passed through an indoor garden, down a flight of stairs, and into what appeared to be a blind alley ending in a closet filled with gowns, stacked hats, and rows of shoes. She snatched hooded cloaks from a cabinet shelf and gave one to each of them. One slight touch from her hand somewhere on the wall behind the cabinet and the cabinet slid aside to reveal a passage. Two unlit torches sat in cressets on either side of the entry. Alektrion grabbed one torch, Zuliya the other. They used her torch to set them alight.

The tunnel was chilled and smelled musty with age and disuse. Leesandra touched a small wooden lever in a stone niche. The cabinet slid solidly back in front of the opening through which they had come, and Leesandra led them down a long twisting tunnel

They came out through a stone door concealed behind the Lady's Chair, to the twilight just before dawn. Talos's daughter was waiting.

Sestrae turned to him. "Go with her, Scorpion. You and her teacher. She's made her decision. It's the right one. If the Voice dies now the People will certainly have only more grief to feed on." She grasped his arm and squeezed tightly. "See that she fares well. Minyas may try to claim she has died. I stay. It will be my task to make sure the People know the Voice of the Goddess lives."

Alektrion wrapped his other hand over hers. "I die before anyone harms her."

Scattered fires dotted the city. Alektrion imagined the looting, the rape, the drunken celebration. To ward off his grief, he took Leesandra's hand, savored the warmth and smallness of it.

She squeezed back, hard, but whispered, as if to herself, "We will find a way to lead the People out of this darkness."

He signaled to the girl to lead. Together, the four of them began to walk.

Afterword

The final entry of Leesandra's autobiography.

The battle is over. The Lady's People have not prevailed. The Acheans and their Keftian minions tread on Temple grounds.

I dictate from a place of hiding in the west of Keftiu, and the day after tomorrow, I sail with Alektrion and thirty others. Although we grieve, we are also determined. The Mother's great power sustains us. And in Her mercy, the Goddess has spared my beloved Alektrion and returned him to me. To have him at my side is a great joy.

Unlike what we were taught to believe as children, the world does change. I struggle to find a way to live with the knowledge that I did not see a profound truth until it was too late: to cling to the past out of unthinking, unquestioning fear of change can only result in disharmony—and sometimes destruction.

I close this record with this final thought. According to my dear teacher, only on Keftiu was our Lady worshipped in purity. Thus I bear witness so another great truth will not be forgotten. Let these be my parting words: There was harmony in the Lady's ancient way. Until these calamities befell us, we lived in peace and grace.

May the Great Mother of All light your path to the end of your days.

A Final Word

You doubtless wonder, as I do, what happened to Leesandra and Alektrion and their companions. How could this refined and prominent culture be so utterly obliterated by those that followed that when Sir Arthur Evans rediscovered it, he amazed the world? Surely, one thinks, the Keftians must have left traces. Did glorious Keftiu linger in folk memory so that, as many believe, by the time of Plato hundreds of years later, it existed still as the ancient dream of a peaceful utopia he called Atlantis?

Perhaps we may never know. Only weeks ago, however, I received—from the same archeological team that discovered the manuscripts you have just read in translation—a newly recovered set of scrolls. At present these new materials are being cleaned and treated to preserve them before I begin the work of translation. But before I surrendered them, I could not resist translating the opening. As I completed it, my heart pounded with elation because the first line reads as follows:

> Among the proud warrior bands that will live forever in the memory of mankind, none were more courageous or feared than the Amazons, spiritual daughters of the last High Priestess of Knossos.

If this latter reference is to Leesandra—and I confess I passionately hope this is so—perhaps we *will* learn something of Leesandra and Alektrion's fate. In particular, the reference to Amazons, the warrior women of myth and mystery, has once again set my curiosity aflame. In what manner, by what possible route, might a connection exist between Leesandra of Phaestos and a sisterhood of women dedicated to battle?

JRE

Author's Commentary
by
Judith Hand

I chose to write about the Minoans—or the Keftians as the contemporary Egyptians called them and as I prefer as well—because
they're not imaginary people. Their elegant and peaceful culture was
neither mythology nor fantasy. They were real, their existence a fascinating historical fact. And their existence is, in my view, profoundly
significant—a source of great hope for humanity—because they were
a high culture that didn't leave behind any evidence of warfare. Nor
did they leave us mural images of violence or human subjugation.
Nor, for that matter, do we find evidence of disrespect for women.
Quite the contrary.

That it's possible to have a high culture of such a temperament
contradicts the often-expressed view that all advanced human cultures practice war and that humans cannot live in complex societies
without war. If by reading *Voice of the Goddess*—my attempt to portray, in fiction, some aspects of what we do know about them—more
people want more information about this alternative for human social organization, I will be extremely pleased.

So then, what is truth and what is fiction in *Voice of the Goddess*?

They had a written language (Linear A), but it remains
undeciphered. We do have numerous archaeological digs on Crete
that provide a rich trove of artifacts, buildings, and most wonderfully, captivating frescoes which speak volumes.

Beginning in 1900, Sir Arthur Evans labored for a quarter of a
century to restore the temple of Knossos. Although Sir Arthur thought
the vast structure he was unearthing was a palace, many scholars
now believe it was a massive religious complex.

Another major excavation of this same historical period, still in
progress, is located on the island of Santorini (Kalliste), which lies
roughly seventy miles north of Crete. Begun by Dr. Spyridon
Marinatos in 1967, the project is carried on now by Dr. Christos
Doumas. I'm indebted to Dr. Doumas for the interview he granted
me in Athens during which he explained his argument that the sea
power of Crete probably lay with the navigational and other skills of
the Cycladic islanders, not in Crete itself. I've also drawn heavily on
the written work of Dr. Nanno Marinatos, daughter of Spyridon
Marinatos, for my interpretation of what the Santorini and Crete frescoes tell us about the culture.

Given, then, the frescoes, the buildings, and the wealth of artifacts, from seal rings to statues to bathtubs, what can we say for certain?

1. The central figure in critical frescoes of festivals and processions is always female. She is either the principal goddess worshipped, whose name was Potnia (which, in a closely related language, Linear B, is translated as "The Lady"), or she is the presiding
High Priestess. It is unlikely, though possible, that the Keftians had a
queen. Perhaps, as in a number of Near Eastern cultures where the
king was also head of the religion, this central female figure was both
High Priestess and Queen.

One never finds a male figure in such a commanding position.
The one such male fresco, often called "The Prince," is, indeed, of a
lovely young man, but the impressive headdress with which the re-
storers crowned him was found in an entirely different section of the
building! The youth might just as easily have been a star athlete in
their famed Bull Leaping events.

2. The prominent display of exposed breasts, in frescoes and other
artworks, certainly invites speculation. First, one can ask whether
this form of dress was simply a matter of fashion. I suspect Keftian
society was so deeply religious that no aspect of their life was untouched by their beliefs. That being the case, assessment of frescoes
and other art pieces suggested to me they most likely depicted religious, not merely social events, that is, religious ceremonies, religious
festivals, religious processions and the like. I therefore portray the
open-breasted blouse as part of a ceremonial gown, one worn only
by priestesses. I have no deep conviction here—perhaps all women
of high fashion wore them—but the choice worked for the purposes
of my story. And because, in a number of cultures, the breasts of a
goddess are taken to be symbols of nurturing, this meaning is one I
attached to the exposed breasts.

But the extraordinary snake goddess figurines have a sensuality
about them, a blatant sexuality that suggests something more: a celebration of sex, an invitation to the act of sex.

With this possibility in mind, three factors led me to the conception that the prominently exposed breasts may have been symbolic
of a uniting social function of sex in Keftian life: 1) the later existence, or perhaps persistence, of Dionysian festivals where sexual in-
tercourse was an established, accepted part of religious celebration;
2) the existence of some contemporary cultures in which ritual sharing of sex was, until recently, used to foster group cohesion and har-

mony (Crocker & Crocker, 1994); and 3) the recently discovered knowledge that one of our closest primate relatives, the Bonobo, literally "makes love, not war": that is, Bonobos use sex to decrease intergroup tensions and to avoid conflicts (F.B.M. de Wall, 1997; T. Kano, 1992).

3. We don't know the meaning of the clearly important interactions with a bull, though we have many depictions on seals and drinking vessels of various related activities. It's clear, for example, that capturing a bull using net and noose has a basis in Keftian reality. And beyond any doubt, stylized bull horns were objects of high religious significance. A famous fresco depicts three figures in the act of what many call bull leaping and which I have interpreted as "bull dancing." Two of the figures are female and one is male, as indicated by the light-colored skin of the former and the darker skin of the latter. This tradition, of using skin color to indicate sex, was also used by Egyptian artists. I have drawn on the work of Dr. Marija Gimbutas, particularly *The Language of the Goddess*, when creating my interpretation of the possible religious significance of the bull.

4. Never in the Keftian (Minoan) period do we find large numbers of weapons of war so typical of war-practicing civilizations. No cities on Crete during the nearly one thousand years of the pre-Keftian and Keftian period were ever fortified. No Keftian frescoes celebrate the subjugation or killing of captives. Clearly the cities of Crete didn't make war on each other, and it's generally assumed their position in the Mediterranean provided protection from the war-making cultures on the mainland. Indeed, it seems likely that the reason Crete was the very last of the so-called "Goddess societies" of Europe to succumb to more warlike cultures was that it had protection by the sea, probably coupled with a strong navy.

5. In none of the excavated sites on Keftian Crete do we find the small cramped quarters typically found in slave-holding societies, strongly suggesting slavery wasn't practiced. And writing at a much later period, one in which slavery was so common as to be expected practice, Aristotle remarked on the enlightened rule in ancient Crete. He noted that they accorded their slaves the same institutions as themselves, denying them only the rights to practice gymnastics and bear arms. Because indenture, as well as slavery, was a practice in contemporaneous societies, I have chosen in *Voice of the Goddess* to depict a form of enlightened indenture on Keftiu, but not slavery.

6. The paintings I described during Leesandra's initiation—a blood-streaked altar and three young women, one covered by a veil—are

exactly those uncovered in Santorini on the walls of a room having an adyton, the small chamber in many Cretan temples that one reaches by walking down a short flight of stone steps. The possible significance of the pictures is, of course, the product of my imagination.

There is no clear indication whether or not the Keftians practiced blood sacrifices. A sarcophagus showing a trussed animal comes from a time period that is properly considered Mycenaean, and the Mycenaeans (the culture that supplanted the Keftians) certainly practiced the sacrifice of animals. A paper by J.T. Hooker discussing trussed animals found on seals also deals with the same "Late Palace Period." Keeping in mind that some cultures that do not practice internal war often do not use animal sacrifice (*e.g.*, the Hopi of North America), my interpretation of the blood on the fresco altar is based on the general sense among some earth-based or fertility-based cultures that the blood of menstruation or the blood of childbirth is sacred. In *Voice of the Goddess*, it is that sense in which, for the Keftians, "blood is life."

7. In his non-fiction account, *Unearthing Atlantis*, Dr. Charles Pellegrino presents convincing arguments that the island of Santorini exploded in the autumn of 1628 BC. I rely heavily on Dr. Pellegrino's book for descriptions about the likely nature of that explosion and its effects on Crete. In a few instances, I shortened time estimates for some events (*e.g.*, between the first eruptions and the final cataclysmic explosion) in order to maintain story tension. A possibly similar type of volcanic explosion of Vesuvius was responsible for the fate of Pompeii and Herculaneum (*see* "The Dead Do Tell Tales" in the bibliography).

8. The Keftians enjoyed a high quality of life. The construction of the mammoth temple at Knossos speaks for itself regarding their architectural know-how. We find paved and well-drained roads—the extant section of the road between Amnissos and Knossos is the oldest paved road in Europe—indoor flush toilets, and plumbing connected to an extensive system of underground sewage pipes. On Santorini, steam piped from volcanic vents might have heated their homes in the winter. Faience models of three-story townhomes have been found on Crete. The range of goods uncovered, from elephant tusks from Syria to pink granite from Upper Egypt to copper ingots from Cyprus, testify to a vast trade network. We have no evidence of their money. Certainly, no metal coins like the pistatas I fabricated have been found. They may have used some other portable medium, such as shells or quantities of unworked metal. Finally, we have no evidence on Crete or Santorini that the people slept with locked doors.

9. Social stratification was apparently not as extreme as in contemporaneous societies. For example, one does not find extravagantly rich burials for a king or queen. Their labor, natural resources, and architectural talents seem to have been spent on the population at large, on construction of warehouses, irrigation systems, country villas and fine-quality homes. The frescoes do not tout the achievements of the ruling class, in marked contrast to the art of Egypt and other contemporary high cultures.

10. They apparently did not practice the veneration of individuals. A noteworthy feature of Keftian (Minoan) art is that few, if any, works are signed. Nor do we find monuments dedicated to specific persons. The single individual of fame associated with any of ancient Crete's artifacts, Daedalus, is associated with the story of Minos—a king—so probably belongs more properly to the time of the Mycenaeans. These observations are the inspiration for my description of Keftians as being a people who valued "blending in."

When this unique civilization fell, it was rapidly eclipsed by the Mycenaeans. So profound was the fall and so dark the eclipse that this society was completely lost to human memory. Indeed, the name Sir Arthur gave to this rediscovered culture—Minoan—refers to Minos, a king of Crete mentioned by Homer. That Minos was a king strongly suggests that, if he existed at all, he was Mycenaean.

From the diligent scribes of Egypt, we have the name Keftiu for the island of Crete. I prefer the name Keftians because there is no evidence that, during the time of this distinctive culture, Minos or any other male figure ruled them. But, in truth, we still do not know what "the Lady's People" called themselves.

Judith Hand

For readers interested in more information about Keftians, visit:
http://www.jhand.com

To contact the author, write:
JHandMail@aol.com
or
Judith Hand
PMB 173
1835A South Center City Parkway,
Escondido, CA 92025-6504

Bibliography

Castleden, Rodney. 1990. *Minoans: Life in Bronze Age Crete*. NY: Routledge.

Chadwick, John. 1976. *The Mycenaean World*. NY: Cambridge Univ. Press.

Crocker, William H. & Jean Crocker. 1994. *The Canela: Bonding through Kinship, Ritual, and Sex*. Ft. Worth, TX: Harcourt Brace College Publication.

Doumas, Christos G. 1983. *Thera, Pompeii of the Ancient Aegean*. London: Thames & Hudson.

Durant, Will. 1966. *The Life of Greece*. NY: Simon and Schuster.

Eisler, Riane. 1987. *The Chalice and the Blade*. Cambridge, MA: Harper & Row.

Ereira, Alan. 1992. *The Elder Brothers*. NY: Knopf.

Evans, Sir Arthur. 1921-35. *The Palace of Minos: An Account of the Early Cretan Civilization as Illustrated by the Discoveries at Knossos*. London: Macmillan.

Gadon, Elinor. 1989. *The Once and Future Goddess*. NY: Harper & Row.

Gimbutas, Marija. 1974. *The Gods and Goddesses of Old Europe, 6500-3500 BC*. Berkeley: Univ. of California Press.

Gimbutas, Marija. 1989. *The Language of the Goddess*. San Francisco: Harper & Row.

Goodison, Lucy & Christine Morris, eds. 1998. *Ancient Goddesses: The Myths and the Evidence*. Madison: Univ. of Wisconsin Press.

Gore, Rick. 1984. The Dead Do Tell Tales at Vesuvius. *Natl. Geogr.* 165: 557.

Hawkes, Jacquetta. 1968. *Dawn of the Gods*. NY: Random House.

Hood, Sinclair. 1967. *The Home of the Heroes: The Aegean Before the Greeks*. London: Thames & Hudson.

Hood, Sinclair. 1971. *The Minoans*. NY: Praeger.

Horwitz, Sylvia L. 1981. *The Find of a Lifetime: Sir Arthur Evans and the Discovery of Knossos*. NY: Viking Press.

Kano, Takayoshi. 1992. *The Last Ape: Pygmy Chimpanzee Behavior and Ecology*. [Trans. E.O. Vineberg.] Stanford, CA: Stanford Univ. Press.

Marinatos, Nanno. 1984. *Art and Religion in Thera: Reconstructing a Bronze Age Society*. Athens: National Archaeological Museum.

Ormerod, Henry A. 1967. *Piracy in the Ancient World*. Chicago: Argonaut.

Pellegrino, Charles. 1991. *Unearthing Atlantis*. NY: Random House.

Stone, Merlin. 1976. *When God Was a Woman*. NY: Harcourt Brace Jovanovich.

Taylor, William. 1983. *The Mycenaeans*. London: Thames & Hudson.

Thubron, Colin. 1981. *The Ancient Mariners*. Alexandria [VA]: Time-Life Books.

Waal, Frans B.M. 1997. *Bonobo: the Forgotten Ape*. Berkeley: Univ. of California Press.

Waters, Frank. 1963. *Book of the Hopi*. NY: Penguin.

Willetts, Ronald F. 1977. *The Civilization of Ancient Crete*. Berkeley: Univ. of California Press.

13²/02

DEMCO